Karma

a novel

Trena Christie-MacEachern

Karma
© 2024 Trena Christie-MacEachern

All rights reserved. No part of this book may be reproduced or transmitted in any form or by any means, electronic or mechanical, including photocopying, or by any information storage or retrieval system, without permission in writing from the publisher.

The author expressly prohibits any entity from using this publication for purposes of training artificial intelligence (AI) technologies to generate text, including without limitation technologies that are capable of generating works in the same style or genre as this publication. The author reserves all rights to license uses of this work for generative AI training and development of machine learning language models.

Cover design: Rebekah Wetmore
Editor: Andrew Wetmore

ISBN: 978-1-998149-60-5
First edition November, 2024

Moose House Publications
2475 Perotte Road
Annapolis County, NS B0S 1A0
moosehousepress.com
info@moosehousepress.com

Moose House Publications recognizes the support of the Province of Nova Scotia. We are pleased to work in partnership with the Department of Communities, Culture and Heritage to develop and promote our cultural resources for all Nova Scotians.

We live and work in Mi'kma'ki, the ancestral and unceded territory of the Mi'kmaw people. This territory is covered by the "Treaties of Peace and Friendship" which Mi'kmaw and Wolastoqiyik (Maliseet) people first signed with the British Crown in 1725. The treaties did not deal with surrender of lands and resources but in fact recognized Mi'kmaq and Wolastoqiyik (Maliseet) title and established the rules for what was to be an ongoing relationship between nations. We are all Treaty people.

Also by Trena Christie-MacEachern

The Light of Day

Maggie struggles to find herself, and her place in her family, in 1950s Cape Breton. She has to travel a long way —not just to Toronto and Boston, but within herself— to come to an understanding of her life, her father, and her hopes.

Available from Moose House Publications.

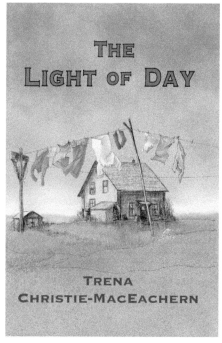

karma

kar·ma | 'kärmə | noun (in Hinduism and Buddhism) the sum of a person's actions in this and previous states of existence, viewed as deciding their fate in future existences.

From Sanskrit *karman* 'action, effect, fate'. Destiny.

Webster's Online Dictionary

For Glen

This is a work of fiction. The author has created the characters, conversations, interactions, and events; and any resemblance of any character to any real person is coincidental.

Karma

1 9
2 12
3 16
4 30
5 35
6 46
7 68
8 79
9 89
10 101
11 109
12 122
13 138
14 149
15 159
16 172
17 179
18 194
19 206
20 213
21 221
22 230
23 240
Epilogue 245
  Acknowledgements 251
  About the author 253

Trena Christie-MacEachern

1

Then

She's hung over. Again. How many times this week? Doesn't matter. Thought this place would be different. She said it would.

Peering in, I see mom's face. It's contorted, like she's in pain. Her face is smushed into the pillow. Her face looks greasy and her eyes are closed. Dad's side doesn't look slept in.

At least she managed to get her pyjamas on this time—she's wearing the pink polka-dot two-piece (V-neck shirt and pants) Dad and I got it for her last Christmas. Never wore it. Why now?

Her arm is hung at an odd angle. Her fingers are tucked under her chin and her room reeks of sour milk and sweat, or something else repugnant. I wanted to throw open the window to let in some fresh air, but I didn't. I didn't want to wake her because then she'd be in that 'stupid mood'.

I left the door as it was and tiptoed away. It'd squeak if I closed it.

I didn't bother packing a lunch, either. I grabbed some loose change from the jar on the counter and slipped out the front door.

Today I was heading to my new school. First day. Final year. Thank Christ! Last year living with my parents. If you can call living like this, living at all.

It was a warm September morning. Too warm to be wearing my blue sweatshirt and jeans. I didn't even care about school shopping this year.

I had on my newer shoes. Good enough.

And for my hair? I swept it around my right shoulder, tied an elastic around it.

I wasn't sure if I was going to fit in, but I walked with purpose to the bus stop like I was confident. Thank God I got the correct information on where the bus stop was. How else would I get to school today?

The secretary was able to provide that much. "It's just a block from your place. Corner of Elm and Waverly," she had said.

There were two girls already there, waiting. I studied them as I

Trena Christie-MacEachern

walked. They looked like grade nine students, maybe ten. I nodded my hello.

After a few minutes, I asked, "Is this the bus for St. Augusta High?" Of course it was, but I felt better for double-checking. I'd curse my self-doubt later.

They both nodded.

"You're new?" the redhead asked.

Their eyes were all over me and I felt oddly violated. They thoroughly checked out every inch of me: colour, brand, style. But I pretended I didn't care. I didn't.

"Yep, live up there." I pointed to the white bungalow with dark shutters. They didn't bother to look. It was the same house as everyone else's on this block.

"Senior or undergrad?" the dark-haired one asked, in her short skirt and pink cardigan. It looked like she'd been up for hours getting ready. Her book bag was slung low over her shoulder. Her hair was stylishly curled and sprayed, eyelashes mascaraed, lips glossed.

"Senior." I held my pen and my binders in my arms and clicked my pen. Perhaps too much.

"Most seniors drive," the reddish-haired girl said.

I shrugged. Sucks for me, then.

"Oh, there's a group of them now," one of them said.

We watched as a small car came to our four-way stop. A girl with big hair drove, a guy with dark hair was beside her, three crammed in the back. A boy with light eyes caught my gaze and then he looked at the two girls beside me. He lifted his hand to them and then turned away.

The girls giggled and knocked into each other, falling over themselves, like no one had ever indulged them with the least amount of attention. They beamed as the car drove off.

The red-haired girl, who I later learned was named Chloe, raised the back of her hand to her forehand and said, "Do you see that? He looked at me." And she cooed and giggled with the dark-haired girl.

"Who's that?" I asked distastefully, my face wincing, lips scrunched in a wrinkly pout. I felt like saying, *Jesus, get a grip!* How could anyone allow themselves to be so infatuated by someone you barely know? Whether he's a five-star celebrity or a senior at the local high school?

"Oh, that's Charlie David," they cooed. "A senior. And he's soooo cute."

And then I met him. And he called me Karma.

~

Karma

Now

His words run around in my mind over and over, doing loops 'til I feel both ill and exhausted. I sit back on the couch, tapping my fingers, feeling disgusted and lost like I should; like the sack of shit that I am.

I can't sit still. I jerk around in my chair, fidget, decide to call someone, but who? I can't tell anyone. I can't burden anyone with this!

I glide my thumb over my wedding band. It feels cold and smooth. I remember how embarrassed he was when he presented it to me.

It was our wedding day and it was all he could afford. A set of plain gold bands, the diamond so small, one wondered if it was there at all, just an indentation in the ring.

He joked. Thought he should have given me a magnifying lens to go with it.

He wanted me to have the one carat. He wanted me to have everything. On our tenth anniversary, he gave me a ring encircled with diamonds. "Never-ending love," he said.

I thought he sounded corny. I laughed.

When he placed the anniversary ring on my finger at the restaurant, he told me the three rings represented the past, the present, and our future. He held my hand and stared at me. I knew he meant it. Meant every word.

If there's one particular aspect I love most about my husband, more than anything else, it's how, despite all my faults and insecurities, he still loves me unconditionally. Fully. Completely. I feel his words in my bones, right down to my very core. Will it change? Did I finally push my limit?

I touch the three bands in unison, twirl them around my finger.

I feel sick.

Tears creep their way back but I blink them away. All I want to do is curl up on the couch and forget the whole thing. Maybe get a lobotomy. I squeeze my eyes tight.

How in the hell did I let this happen?

The tears come back to my eyes and I curse the day I met him. "Charlie fucking David. You son of a bitch."

2

Then

I should have known from the get-go this was a bad idea. A little voice inside my head told me to leave, get out, turn away. But when I was young and naive and wanting to fit in, in my new school, my senior year. There was little option.

I stood in line, shivering, wearing only a teeny jean skirt and bare legs, a skimpy shirt with spaghetti straps because Trudy said it would make them think I was older. I guessed they would be staring at my chest instead of my face, if that was any indication of proof of ID. I was pretty chesty, been wearing a bra since the sixth grade.

The only thing that I had on that I liked was Suzanne's yellow moccasins with beading. The real deal. Pretty and comfy, and made of soft leather.

I wrapped my arms around myself, sheltering from the cool autumn breeze and dipping temperatures.

Suzanne, of course, had been here before, been coming since tenth grade, she said. A regular. She winked at me. She was tall and willowy, with long, dark hair, dark eyes, and her skin: warm and earthy. She lived on the Reserve.

Trudy was the opposite of both Suzanne and me. She was a little thing, shorter than me, absolutely no chest to speak of, and her complexion, so pale, it was almost translucent.

"If I could turn my ass around," she'd say. And we'd laugh. She did have a big ass.

Suzanne and Trudy had been pals since Trudy moved here the end of ninth year. Except Suzanne had a steady then, and so they only hung out at school. Then, when Trudy's mom moved in with Suzanne's uncle, well then, they became related, so to speak, and then inseparable.

They were gabbing back and forth, impervious to the cold, exchanging a cigarette, offering me a puff, which I'd decline. I was nervous enough as

Karma

it was without the smoke to make my stomach sick.

"Don't be nervous," Suzanne said a little too loudly. I could smell beer on her breath. She had already had a few before Trudy picked me up.

I looked over my fake ID again, Trudy's cousin or something or other.

"Says I'm twenty-five," I said to them.

"They won't ask," Suzanne said matter-of-factly. "Put that away. Gawd!" And she shook her finger at me, like I was being scolded.

"Suzanne!" Trudy said, "be nice." She smiled at me, offering don't-worry-yourself assurance.

~

I knew I should have paid more attention to the school tour when I was with my mother, but I was more concerned with whether the principal realized she was half-lit. She was elongating her words, a dead give-away, and all I wanted to do was get the whole thing over with.

When Mr. Barron asked me about my final courses and walked quickly toward the cafeteria, I thought I must have looked crazier than my mom. I just turned around, shouted, "Yes, yes. Thank you. I'll figure it out. No problem," smiled, looped my arm inside hers so she wouldn't fall.

"Thank yoou, Missssterrr Barrronnn," Mom cooed, waving madly, like she was queen on a festival parade float.

I escorted her back to the car, the passenger's side, practically pushing her in, steam coming out of my ears. I never said a thing. In extreme cases of anger, I say nothing. I'm like my father that way.

And because I didn't pay attention to the principal, or get a proper tour of the school, I found myself lost on my first day of grade twelve, wandering into the auditorium instead of the girl's washroom.

When I finally found the washroom, it was more of a backstage change room at a modelling show. It was filled to capacity, and I watched as some were still getting it together for first class. I shook my head in disbelief. This wasn't anything like my old school.

They were fiddling with curling irons and hair-spray bottles. Some were taking necklaces and jewellery out of their bags, holding it up to their necks for their pals to either nod or grimace at.

One gal even stripped down to her skivvies right in front of everyone, pulling on a skin-tight dress and pumps. I wondered where the teachers were. Nerdy me.

My expression must have rubbed Suzanne the wrong way. "Hey! What's your problem? What you staring at?"

Trena Christie-MacEachern

Her tone was alarming and I cowered under her glare. I went to open my mouth. "Uh," was all that came out.

"Suzanne," said the little thing beside her. The girl with the big eyes and long, ash-coloured hair. "Be nice." She was staring at me from her reflection in the propped-up mirror, with a long curling rod wrapped with her hair.

"I am nice," Suzanne said sternly.

The small girl batted her eyes at Suzanne and focused on me.

"You new?"

I nodded. "I'm Karmalita," I said. "With a K."

"Trudy," she said looking at me, loosening her hair from the iron grip. "This is Suzanne." She gazed up in her friend's direction.

"Hi," I said.

"Bev, you look some nice," Suzanne said to the girl who had put on the skimpy dress.

She didn't respond to Suzanne right away. She was doing an assessment of herself, using the model's pout and serious eye, opening her mouth, closing it again, turning sideways, both left and right, fixing her hair.

"Thanks," she finally said flatly, as if she didn't give a rat's ass for the compliment. Or the fact that the compliment came from Suzanne.

That's when Suzanne fixed her dark eyes on me again. "That all you wearing today?"

"Huh?" I looked down at my apparel. "What's wrong with it?" I asked, confused.

I was wearing jeans and flats and a baby-blue sweatshirt. It was in this year and it was all the rage. Sweatshirts that is. Everyone was wearing them, in all the soft, pastel colours.

"Niners wear those," she said. "It's picture day, for frig's sake." She rolled her eyes at me.

"You mean grad pics?" I asked, puzzled.

"No! Course not," she huffed.

Trudy had to explain. "They always take a bunch of group shots on the first week of school and then we do it again before final exams in June. Kind of to see how much we changed in a year. It's a tradition."

"And you look like shit," Suzanne said as thoughtfully as she could.

"Well, I don't care—"

Suzanne lunged toward me, cupped my face with her long fingers, assessing me.

I wasn't sure what to do. Then out of the corner of my eye, I saw her

14

pull something from her pocket.

I squealed in short little outbursts. "Ah! Ah! Ah! Please don't—"

But Suzanne stepped back, stared at me like I was some weird, difficult thing. She showed me what was in her hand. It was a pencil, no, an eyeliner.

"Close," she demanded.

"What?" I squirmed. "I don't want that shit on my face."

"Well, you'll look better. Jeesh. Who dresses you? You got your hair in a ponytail and a sweatshirt on. If not for your tits, you'd look like a niner." Her voice and mannerisms were gruff.

"Wait, Suzanne," Trudy said. "It's okay, Karmalita. Here. Let me."

Suzanne handed her the pencil. In a serene, peaceful tone, Trudy asked me to close my eyes. I felt the cool of the pencil glide over my lid. It made me almost sleepy.

"Open."

I did everything she commanded without argument. Looked left, and then right.

And then Suzanne ripped the elastic out of my hair, taking several follicles along with it.

"Ow!" I yelped, raising my hand to my skull.

"Not so rough, Suzanne."

"Sorry! Holy F." She looked away and whispered under her breath, "Wimp!" Then stood silently as Trudy fluffed and styled my hair. She took a step back.

"There. You look nice."

"Yep. Better. You look senior now. With them big tits." Suzanne laughed like she had said the funniest joke, and Trudy laughed with her.

"We'll show you around," Trudy said. "You can hang with us. Because you're new. We were new once, too." She winked at me as we left the room. "And seniors stick together."

And it was because of Trudy and Suzanne that I met the love of my life, Charlie David.

Trena Christie-MacEachern

3

Then

The girls were right. The bouncer didn't look at my ID. He did take it, and then looked down at my chest and asked for the door cover. Five dollars. I handed it to him.

Trudy was waiting for me inside. Suzanne and her long legs were already at the back of the room.

The bar was divided into two sections. The main section, where we were, housed the dance floor. Sturdy wooden tables and chairs stood all around the perimeter of the checkered-tile surface. There was also a bar area with a long counter and stools. Fancy glasses hung upside down from the bulkhead with a large mirror behind reflecting decorative bottles and pitchers.

The place was quite packed for early on a Friday evening. Trudy had told us we should get here early or else they might turn us away. Especially if the Liquor Inspector showed up.

I looked around the room, checking if my mom was here. I didn't think she would be. This was not her thing, hanging out at bars. She preferred the privacy of her own home. I scanned the room anyway just to be sure, though.

The majority of the people looked middle-aged. An older woman in an outfit similar to mine was on the dance floor. A man with loose-fitting jeans and a baseball hat was dancing with her. She was laughing as he kept trying to slow dance with her and it was a fast song.

"Come on. Follow me," Trudy said, smiling. "We'll go to the back. That's where we hang out."

The back of the bar was a lot smaller than the front of the house. It was decorated with red brick and the ceiling was low. They had thick rectangular tables here, and round ones, too. Mismatched furniture, although no one seemed to notice.

The younger crowd hung out here. There was also a bar area to the

Karma

side, but just a table with a spout for draft beer. If we wanted the hard stuff, we had to go to the front.

I didn't want to stand out, so I grabbed the first available chair I saw. Suzanne was already walking back from the draft bar with a pitcher of beer and three glasses. She plunked them down in front of me and Trudy and looked over. Then she hollered to the bartender and, within minutes, he came with another pitcher and more glasses and said something into Suzanne's ear. She laughed out loud and made a face at me.

The bartender smiled broadly at her, the two of them already in on the joke. His name was Teddy, and he placed the pitcher at the other end where a group of guys sat and they said, "Salut!" to Suzanne.

"Enjoy, fellas," she said and they all raised their glasses.

~

So, these were the top dogs. Five guys and three girls. The ones who would shape and define the rest of my life, though I didn't know it yet.

The youngest girl, Loretta, or Lotty, was the girlfriend of Allan. Lotty was no bigger than a sprite, with a pretty face and a full head of hair that made up most of her body weight. Allan and Lotty had been inseparable since the fifth grade and already spoke of getting married when they got out of school.

He had his arm around her, and she sat on his lap like a little kitty-cat, albeit an intimidating one, smoking, drinking draft, watching everyone around her, yet not looking interested. She gave me a little nod.

Allan, the boyfriend, was a chimney smoker. He liked his hash, and funny cigarettes, as my grandfather used to call them. He was long and lanky. Lotty and Allan looked like a Jack and Jill incantation. He had scars on his lip and his cheek, a big, white gouge on his arm; a rough and tumble kind of bloke, as evidently, he had had a rough and tumble kind of upbringing. His glass of draft was already half empty and he slapped the table now and again when someone said something funny, while he kept adjusting his gal on his lap.

Eric, the best-looking of the gang, was a bit too smug for my liking. He seemed to speak only to Allan, who sat on his left, or to Clyde, on his right. He barely even acknowledged Suzanne for the drinks, sitting back in his chair as Lotty kept refilling his glass. He had the usual prince-like

17

look, blondish hair, slender body, tanned still from the summer, and significant cheek bones.

He'd look up when a 'breather' walked by. That means, according to Trudy, 'Tru', as Suzanne called her, a good-looking older chick. Someone of legal age. And you'd hear Eric mutter, "She's fine. That one's fine," and stare her down or holler for her to "c'mere." I wondered how he fit into this group at all.

Clyde was the big guy. The footballer, with dark, curly hair and square shoulders. His hands were the size of a catcher's mitt and it was often said that, although he had an easy-going disposition, you wouldn't want to piss him off or catch him in a foul mood. He was a sizer, looking more like twenty-six than a lad in his late teens, senior year. And when he smiled, his eyes disappeared, making his face resemble that of a happy Buddha.

Jimmy was standing behind Clyde, resting his hands on the back of his chair. He was looking around, not really partaking in the conversation. He seemed awkward and shy. Cute in an innocent way. Trudy said he didn't go out much, as he worked part-time and drinking was just not his thing. A smart fellow, hoping to make it into college, and more focused on studying hard and getting good grades. He stared at me for the longest time, then nodded at us as we took seats around the table.

I suddenly felt very self-conscious. Trudy smiled and acknowledged him with a small wave, then he turned around and was gone.

And, lo and behold, there he was. Charlie the charmer. He sat closest to me, and was considered the most personable of the group. Dreamy eyes, million-dollar smile. His sturdy build, with his muscles showing through his t-shirt, and the way he connected with everyone with genuine interest and ease, made me instantly fall for him. When he turned his attention to the three of us, I felt my stomach do loopty-loops.

"Who's your friend?" Charlie asked Trudy. Then, to me, "I wondered who you were."

I had run into him earlier in the week, actually bumped. I ran my hand over the spot on my shoulder where we had collided. From that moment we touched, it was as if he inoculated me with an invisible love potion.

"Are you okay?" he had asked with concern that day, touching my arm, and when I nodded I was, he smiled back. He had such a warm presence about him, and that devilish grin immediately made my cheeks glow hot.

And here he was, sitting no more than a foot from my chair, and seeing his face immediately made my belly flutter and my mouth dry. I swallowed, grabbed a sip of my beer.

Karma

"This is Karmalita. She's new."

"Hey," he said sweetly, and offered me his hand. He held mine for a moment while he studied me. "How are these gals treating you?" he asked.

I leaned into him, straining to hear his voice over the beat of the music. He smelled confident and manly and I wanted desperately to touch the fabric of his t-shirt. I nodded, mouthed the word 'good'. and then, silence.

Minutes crept by. I couldn't think of anything else to say.

He released my hand and, stupidly, I asked him, "Where did Jimmy go?" hoping to keep the conversation going.

Charlie looked over his shoulder, saw that Jimmy wasn't there and shrugged. "Dunno. Maybe to get more beer."

I took another sip, trying to find my courage for conversation. "I thought he didn't drink." I felt like running my tongue over a cheese grater. Could I think of something better to discuss? He'll think I'm interested in Jimmy! I smiled as sweetly as I could without looking too pathetic.

"Something must have come up, then," and he returned the smile with that mega-watt grin. God, he was cool.

I took a sip from my beer again, trying not to grimace. I hated this stuff. I would have preferred a cooler or a vodka with some soda, a mix of some kind, but Suzanne told me not to go strutting around here until the staff gets to know me. Otherwise, I could get thrown out. An embarrassment I didn't want to encounter.

"Hey! Karmalita!" Suzanne shouted.

I jumped and nearly knocked over my glass. I'm never prepared when she calls my name.

She extended her hand across the table, palm out. "Your turn, girl."

"Oh, right!" I fiddled inside my purse and pulled out a ten and passed it to her. She finished off her glass, stood up and strode back toward the bar.

"I've never seen a girl drink like Suzanne," Charlie said with a laugh. "She can drink any of us under the table. Except maybe Clyde, but it's awfully close."

He took a drink and then changed the subject. "So, how come you moved here in your senior year, of all years?"

Trudy watched my reaction. "Oh, long, dull story," I said and laughed.

"Maybe you'll tell me some time," he said, and knocked his shoulder into mine.

"How do you two know each other?" I asked, twirling my finger around in a circle on the table. They looked down at my spinning digit and I stopped, cringing internally. I always talk with my hands. "Sorry," I said, "design flaw."

Trudy smirked. She looked at Charlie for a minute, smiled. "Charlie and I go way back."

"She's the wheel girl," Charlie said with a wink.

"Yep." Trudy giggled.

"Trudy got us out of a few jams. But Suzanne got us into them." He laughed. "Remember that time at Barry's place near the Reserve?"

"God, yes."

Then, over the noise, Suzanne yelled and we saw her long arm waving. "Tru! Tru! Come here for a minute."

"Just a sec, guys. Coming!" she hollered back.

I turned around to see the bar filling up. I couldn't get over how many more bodies had crept in while my thoughts were focused on Charlie. There were a few I recognized from school, but most of them, I didn't have a clue.

By the time I looked back at Charlie, someone had already moved in. He was talking to a slender brunette with big eyes that looked like they were spaced too far apart. She was wearing hoop earrings and was chewing gum, holding a draft beer like the rest of us.

She wiggled her way between Charlie and me, chatting, then squatted down to his eye level, turned around and said, "Could you move back a little?"

"Sure," I said, only too happy to oblige. Not that I liked her dropping in beside me, or talking to Charlie, but when someone who is even a little bit threatening tells me to move aside, I do so without a second thought.

I waited for Trudy to come back, tapping my leg to the music, sipping my beer to make it last. By now, Suzanne's seat was gone as the room filled up with girls. A little auburn-haired gal was talking to Clyde. I thought she was in our math class, but I wasn't certain.

Suzanne was hanging out in the bar area, talking to Teddy. She was standing behind him while he was serving drinks. The two of them were laughing, nodding. She had a lit cigarette and blew smoke out the side of her mouth. She passed it to him and he took a drag. I felt like I was watching a tennis match with the cigarette.

Trudy finally appeared with a fresh pitcher. This time, she took a seat beside me. "How are you doing? she hollered over the noise. "You having fun?" She poured me some more beer.

Karma

I shrugged. "Yeah. It's good." Before I realized what I was doing, I looked toward Charlie and the brunette.

"You like him?" she asked and when I looked at her, she darted her eyes towards Charlie. My face got hot and I bowed my head, embarrassed. She laughed.

I looked up and took another swig, grimaced, hoping if I did this enough, the taste would grow on me.

"Add some salt," she said. She reached across the table, grabbed the salt shaker and shook it over my beer. The salt dispersed into the glass, descending like asteroids from the sky. The top of the beer bubbled up. "Helps," she said, and then shook a dash in hers.

She looked over at Charlie again. "He's the lady's man, eh?"

I nodded as I watched the way he interacted with the girl. He touched her arm when he spoke to her.

But he must have felt me staring because he looked over and caught my gaze.

Then the brunette stood up and blocked my view of him. She led him by the arm out to the front, to the dance floor.

Trudy turned her head to the side as if to say, *see?*

"Oh well." I took another slurp of my beer.

~

The Rolling Stones was blaring *Between a Rock and a Hard Place*. I had had my share of the beer, chugged a couple down already. I felt myself starting to get woozy and the room seemed like it was getting darker, smokier. I needed to get up 'cause my bladder was signalling it was time to go.

I nudged to Trudy where the washrooms were and she pointed to the hallway separating the front bar from the back. I stood up and the room felt like it was moving. It didn't help that the people standing around were swaying as well.

I laughed, thinking I looked foolish, wondering who was noticing that I was officially bombed. What would my mother say, or my father for that matter? *Like mother, like daughter?*

I grabbed hold of the chair in front of me. Thank God no one seemed to be paying attention. Trudy was talking to a guy, Suzanne was nowhere to be found, and the rest of the table was doing their thing.

Charlie was still chatting with the brunette. She was smiling at him and holding his arm, so I started walking.

Trena Christie-MacEachern

A woman banged into me. My head felt like I had a set of drums in it. Everything was so loud and congested...and hot. Sticky hot. My skin felt clammy.

I went to the bathroom and the line-up was at least six people, no telling how many were on the inside. The longer I stood, the more I smelled the stench of draft. I hiccoughed and tasted the acidic beverage at the back of my throat.

It felt like I was going to get sick so I turned and made my way back to the entrance. I needed to feel the cool air in my lungs and, maybe, that would stop the world from spinning.

The guy that took our money was still there, sitting sideways. One leg on the floor, the other dangling. He looked at me but we said nothing to each other. I pushed my way out, feeling suddenly claustrophobic.

Surprisingly, there was no one outside, except for a couple arguing beside their car. I tasted sour bile in my throat and put my hand to my mouth. I walked away from the entrance to the far end of the parking lot before the vomit forced itself out.

Thin, watery puke. Beer and salt made its way back up. I hadn't eaten since lunch.

I reached for my bag and realized I had left it on the chair inside the bar. *Oh, God, I don't want this. Christ! I just want to go home.*

I staggered behind a car to the thump of the music. I sidled up to the back of the building, realizing I still had to pee so God-damn bad. If I don't go now, I'll surely wet myself. I lifted my skirt, squatted, forced my underwear to one side and peed 'til the cows came home. I realized I probably went all over my shoes but at this point, I didn't give a rat's ass.

I hiked myself up, pressed down my skirt, and hobbled to Trudy's car. Thank God it was unlocked. I crawled into the back seat and left the door open a crack.

The air was cool, but I was so internally hot at the moment, I didn't care. I closed my eyes and waited. Breathe. *I'll just stay here 'til the spins subside a bit. Maybe then I'll go back inside and get some water.*

~

I must have passed out. In the background, I heard voices. I swear one was Suzanne's but I couldn't open my eyes.

My body shivered. I was curled in a ball in the backseat. The gang was hooting and laughing and I felt movement.

Someone slapped my ass.

Karma

"Yeah, the bitch is here," Suzanne said gruffly.

I heard male voices, too. The seat started to vibrate. There was movement and I drifted off again.

The next time I opened my eyes, I was spread out on my bed, still wearing my clothes from the night before. I glanced at the clock. It was past noon on Saturday.

My mouth was dry and I felt like crap. I had a splitting headache. I needed to quench my thirst, as my mouth was as arid as the Sahara Desert. Gross. Beer!

I tiptoed to the bathroom, hoping to avoid my folks, and turned on the faucet. I stuck my mouth under the running water and took deep gulps. The tepid water ran down my neck and soaked the outside of my shirt.

When my thirst was somewhat satisfied, I carefully opened the medicine cabinet and searched for aspirin. I found the bottle and took two, chased by a handful of water.

My reflection looked like crap. My mascara had smudged into my eye sockets so I resembled a druggie on a bender. My hair was wild, flat on one side, sticking up on the other, and my skin had a sheen to it. Not a pleasant glow from exercising but a sickly-looking, greasy film.

I dug under the cabinet for some skin cream and smothered my whole face with it, then rinsed a warm washcloth and wiped the makeup off. I tried to run a brush through my hair but, there was too much hair spray. I threw it in a ponytail instead.

I snuck back to my room, took off my clothes, put them in a ball, and tossed my housecoat on top of it. I found my pj's on the floor and threw them on, then curled up in my bed. I needed at least another hour to get rid of this ache in my brain. *Lord, how does my mother do it?*

Three hours later, I awoke. I dressed quickly in case Mom or Dad suspected anything. Yet I didn't hear any sounds coming from anywhere in the house. It was after three and, although I felt somewhat better, my body felt like it was run over by a truck.

I reminded myself to wash my clothes, as there was probably puke all over them. I immediately thought of my shoes, dug them out from under my bed and placed them on the back step to clean later.

The house was unnaturally quiet for a Saturday. I headed straight into the kitchen, banging around this time, trying to act normal when I saw Dad's note:

Doing some overtime. Be home soon, Dad

Trena Christie-MacEachern

I breathed a sigh of relief, then went in search of Mom. She wasn't in the living room, her usual resting place.

I tiptoed down to her bedroom and saw her lying on her side facing me, her mouth opened, and raspy noises were coming out of her throat and nose. She was totally out.

Into the kitchen I went and retrieved a tall, clear glass from the cupboard and filled it up with water. As I walked back to her room, I took a quick gulp of it, eyeballed it, then took another small sip. I grabbed a couple of old magazines and one of her favourite books, and tucked them under my arm. I placed the glass ever so gently on her nightstand and just as quietly, took her catalogues and placed them just so on Dad's side of the bed. I opened her book to a page and faced it down on the floor.

I walked out, leaving the door open in case Dad came home unexpectedly. I hoped he'd think she fell asleep reading and not start on her.

I went back to the kitchen and opened the fridge, wondering what to put on before Dad got home all bent out of shape. I kept the door opened, waiting for the something to spring forward. Some idea.

What did we eat yesterday? I thought back. Breakfast. Mom made breakfast for supper. A tell-tale clue she was drinking yesterday, too. Which was why I didn't eat. I told them I was going to get pizza with Trudy and Suzanne.

I moved stuff out of the way on the shelves. Cheese slices, bread, tomato sauce. Browning cauliflower, broccoli, some salad greens. Chicken breasts. My stomach started growling and I realized I was starving.

We could have a one-pot chicken dish of sorts with some veggies thrown in. Mom had made this concoction before.

I took out the big frying pan and threw in a bit of oil, then set it on the burner. I sliced the chicken into small pieces, threw some salt and pepper on it and fired it into the pan.

The pan made a whoosh when wet chicken met hot oil. I stared down the hallway to Mom's room. I didn't want this to wake her up just yet as she'd be in her stupid mood after boozing, and would start asking silly questions.

While the chicken was cooking, I nosed around the fridge for some veggies. I took out an onion, some carrots, broccoli, and the salad greens. *Why not?*

I made a sauce with soya and brown sugar, some hot pepper flakes, a bit of water and some cornstarch as a thickener. I dropped the cover on the frying pan and let it simmer.

Rooting through Mom's cooking cabinet, I found some sliced almonds.

24

Karma

I toasted those in the oven then set them aside for later, as a garnish.

The magazine fell off Mom's bed.

"Honey. That you? What time is it?"

Shit. She's awake. I froze, my arms stretched out in mid-air in front of me. I looked like a symphony conductor.

She groaned. "Honey?" she called again.

I didn't say anything. I waited to hear what she was going to do. When it sounded like she was getting up, I turned down the burner to minimum and snuck back to my room, closed the door, and hid there.

She padded by the door. I heard her take the lid off the meal I just made.

"Honey. This smells wonderful."

The plates rattled as she took them out of the cupboard and placed them on the table. "Want bread with this?"

I rolled my eyes, sighed, opened the door to assess, ready to face her. I sat at the table, arms resting on the wooden surface.

"Will you get the cutlery?" she asked. "This is going to be great. Where'd you learn this recipe?"

She tried to engage me in her conversation by asking questions or making statements because she probably thought I was mad at her for drinking again. So she babbled on. "Almonds are my favourite. They'll add a nice crunch."

She took a stray piece of hair that had fallen out of her bun and wrapped it around her ear. She caught me staring and smiled sheepishly.

She then took both of her hands and tried to smooth out her hair with her palms. Her hands jittered and twitched.

Her hands were once delicate and strong, able to do the most difficult of tasks, inputting IVs, stitching up wounds, inoculating. But no more.

She crisscrossed her hands and tucked them into her armpits. "I should freshen up. Before your father gets home."

~

Dad arrived at four-thirty, almost got a full work day in. It didn't even seem to bother him that today was Saturday. *Didn't they use to go out on Saturday afternoons? Grocery shop? See an afternoon matinee? Go for lunch?*

Mom had fixed herself up a bit, added a bit of blush and combed out her hair. She had two glasses of chocolate milk and had the coffee on the go when he arrived. She was trying, at least. I had to give her that much.

25

Trena Christie-MacEachern

They acknowledged each other quietly. I wondered if it was for my benefit. *Would they talk to each other at all if I wasn't here? Would either of them be here if it wasn't for me?*

Their distance with each other kept the focus off me and my recent activity, which I relished at the moment. I watched as they went through the rituals of 'how was your day?' and, 'what did you do?' Cringing, scared to hear what Mom's answer was.

"Oh, you know. A bit of cleaning and..." she trailed off.

Dad took a walk around the house, scanning as he already knew Mom was lying. I watched him pause in front of their bedroom door and see the books on her bed. It was almost as if I heard him sighing, like a relief had washed over him.

He relaxed. The mood of the house lightened like a door opened and fresh air came in. But it was the weekend, too, and the weather was nice, although I had missed most of it myself. But it appeared Mom was somewhat coping today; trying, at least. And Dad sensed that.

We sat and ate together and no one said boo about the meal. Not Dad for eating it, because, I had to admit, it was not one of my best concoctions. The chicken was tough and the sauce, bland. The only decent thing on the plate was the broccoli, a bit overcooked. The carrots were still hard, but the almonds were nice and even Dad said so.

He finished his plate, anyway, and gave Mom a soft squeeze, appreciating the meal. I didn't move or look at her, and she said nothing, either.

I did feel a bit crappy for using Mom's drinking to hide my own indiscretions, but I didn't need Dad having a stroke over two of his girls into the sauce. I needed to relish the peacefulness and harmony in the Smallwood house, even just for a little bit.

Neither had asked me about my new school, so I told them. I wanted to make small talk and feel like a normal family.

"So, school's good. I met some new friends," I said a bit too over-enthusiastically.

"Oh, yes, sweetie, tell us about it. I was waiting for you to tell us. Weren't we, Brian?"

My mouth hung open and I was amazed at her quick response. Dad stood at the counter, clearing off his plate and rinsing it before filling up the sink with soap. In good moods, Dad did the dishes when Mom cooked. Tit for tat, he used to say.

"Yeah, so I met two girls, Trudy and Suzanne. They're nice. Just kind of took me in."

"Well, that's nice. Isn't it, Brian?" Mom looked over at Dad for encour-

26

Karma

agement. She smiled. I thought she looked tired.

"Where they from?" Dad asked.

Of course, I don't know that much. I knew very little about them, or if, in fact, if we were real friends yet. "Gosh, Dad, I don't know exactly. Not far from the school. We didn't get into the nitty-gritty of housing."

"So, how'd you meet, sweetie? You in the same classes?"

Mom placed her elbows on the table and rested her chin on her fists. She looked at me intently, perhaps realizing she hadn't feigned the least bit of interest the last few weeks.

I laughed. "Well, I was heading to the bathroom, of all places. Didn't have a clue where that was."

Mom's eyes darted all across me. Was she really, finally, interested? I chuckled but kept talking. "Yeah, they were really nice, trying to help me fit in. They take pictures of all the seniors and wanted me to look my best so—" I had to divulge some info about the day, but not all of it.

"What's that on your arm?"

Mom's tone sounded strained. I took the napkin and wiped my mouth.

"And your face?"

She lifted her head and pointed to my eyes. "Is that makeup you're wearing? How exactly are they trying to make you fit in?"

Dad stopped what he was doing.

Shit, shit. I thought I got it all off. I totally forgot about the stamp.

"Oh?" I tried to make it sound like nothing. I laughed. "Oh, the girls thought I should try some on and I didn't like it, so I tried to take it off."

Then Mom went all ballistic. "Are these girls pressuring you to be someone you're not?"

"Mom! It's no big deal."

"Karmalita! You don't have permission to start acting like a young woman when, indeed, you are not!"

"Cathy! That's enough. Leave her. She said it was a mistake."

And that's when the pleasant Saturday turned into the start of the circus.

"No, Brian!" Mom sounded really pissed now. Dad had used the wrong word. "A mistake is what you made when you slept with that tramp."

I knew what was coming before she even said it. The start of every fight. I closed my eyes and bowed my head as I knew our semi-conscientious evening as a family was now over.

The two of them got into another raging, screaming match. The only consolation was I out of the discussion. I would no longer be the topic of discussion, which I never was anyway. It didn't matter if I went to Mars

Trena Christie-MacEachern

and back. The fight was always about Moms and Dad's shit.

I got up from the table and went to my room and closed the door.

Moments later, I heard Mom's bedroom door slam and Dad went out the front door and slammed that too. The lawnmower started up and I thought, *Everyone thinks we are this normal family. Dad is mowing the lawn on a lovely late-summer Saturday evening.*

~

The rest of the weekend, what was left of it, carried on at a snail's pace. Because the house was so small, there was no real place to go. There was the living room, our bedrooms, or the basement.

Dad was in the basement for most of Sunday, fiddling. Mom was like a caged rat. She kept walking around in circles, probably trying to find her stash, but because both Dad and I were home, she couldn't take the chance. Instead, she finished off every ounce of soda we had in the house, sucked on peppermints, and drank black coffee with tons of sugar. No wonder she was bouncing.

I played the good girl and did my homework and also most of the laundry. Mom had started it, but with Dad being in the basement, she wanted to avoid that room.

Dad was quiet, but he would always talk to me. I went down with a load of towels and there he was, taking stuff out of boxes that we hadn't had time to get to. He, like Mom and me, was just trying to stay busy.

He had found several framed photos of us, back when I was little. We all looked happy. There was a family picture of the three of us and our dog, Blackie. I remember the picture was taken in our old living room. I couldn't have been more than three. Mom and Dad were sitting on the floor. I was standing beside Mom holding onto her pinkie finger. Dad had his hand on Blackie's neck.

He was a black lab mix. They had him for ten years before I came along. He was their first baby and he died of old age when I was four.

Mom had a special memory wall in our old house. You faced when you first walked in.

At first, Mom hung a calendar on it just to fill the space. Then she decided to hang their wedding photo. She took down the calendar and kept building around the wedding photo. Whenever she saw a picture she liked, or Dad liked, she would have it framed and hung there.

She had a picture of me at Halloween, dressed in a nurse's uniform, and Mom standing beside me with her real nurse's uniform. There was a

28

picture of me and Mom and Grandma, the three generations; and of Dad and his buddy, Max, when they were young and handsome.

And all these framed photos were in this box that Dad was looking at. There were at least a dozen, in all different sizes.

"Are we going to put them up?" I asked. Some of them were faded and looking tired.

He didn't answer me, just kept unwrapping them and staring at them.

I took the one of the three of us with Blackie. "I like this one," I said. "I'm going to put it in my room."

He nodded at me and started putting the photos back, like I had interrupted his privacy and embarrassed him, or something.

"He was a good dog, that Blackie."

"I remember him a little," I said.

"He used to hide under your bed when it was thunder and lightning."

"Really?" I laughed. "He was a scaredy-cat, was he?"

"No, I think it was to keep you safe."

I smiled at the memory. I loved the idea that my furry, four-legged animal wanted to protect me. Maybe he sensed something more than fear? Maybe he sensed that I was lonely.

"Maybe we should get a dog?" I suggested, watching him wrap up the photos.

He chuckled. The lines around his eyes deepened when he smiled.

"Probably not a good idea," he said. "Your mother doesn't need that right now."

He tossed the last of the pictures back in the box, closed the lid and taped it back up.

"But maybe it will be good for her," I pleaded. Maybe an animal would make this family a family again.

"Look, honey, the only thing your mother needs right now is to dry out, or hit rock bottom. She can barely look after herself right now, let alone a dog."

As quiet as my father was, that was the most he ever said to me about my mother and her habit.

Trena Christie-MacEachern

4

Now

Mom wasn't always a boozer.

Long ago, when we lived in our old house, she was a regular working mother. She was a nurse, for God's sake. She used to take care of people. She used to take care of us, too, and she was good at it.

She used to keep her hair cut short and had streaks in it. I remember one of her friends telling her how becoming it was on her. A vee at the ears and a combo of light and dark hair hi-lights. I thought she looked kind of punk, kind of cool.

I was dead proud of my mom. She used to take care of herself. She went to the gym, she used to run, was into the community events: dinners, fundraisers, the after-school program. But that all changed.

It all changed the day she killed Daniel Timmons.

He was a high school graduate. Or was going to be. His graduation was to be that June. He was killed two weeks before he would have accepted his diploma. And he was everything a parent dreamed of.

They set up the memorial service in the gym to help his friends grieve his loss. I don't know why I was there. I shouldn't have been. But I was, and I watched and heard what a terrific athlete he was, how smart he was, his plans for that September, and what a thoughtful and kind boy he was.

People sobbed. How could this have happened? How could my mother just run him over as he biked alongside the road? There was ample room on the pavement. It wasn't even dark.

That accident on June 8th changed my life and my family forever.

Mom was no longer the good nurse. No, sirree. She was the most hated person on the planet. Everywhere she went, she received rude comments, mean stares, cruel whispers. Cashiers wouldn't serve her. She was asked to leave restaurants because she disturbed the customers. Better for one to leave than a whole party of five.

Eventually, Mom couldn't even go to work. She went on stress leave,

Karma

and that was ridiculed. Then compensation, and then she lost her job.

The family requested a police investigation. Thought she may have been drinking or, worse, drunk.

But I didn't recall Mom ever having a drink, really, like the way people spoke. She would have a drink at supper, or on the weekend, or a beer on a hot summer's day, but I never saw her dancing on top of a table, or stumbling home late at night.

But it didn't matter now.

She was sad, yes, I could attest to that. She blamed it on her body for failing her. But a drunk? Was she, in the beginning?

But if you're told often enough, you start to believe it.

And then Mom stopped getting up with me in the morning, and hid in the living room when I came home from school, with the curtains closed, the TV on low, her teacup beside her. It was tea in that cup, wasn't it?

Then dinner-time came and went. I'd be eating a pb and j when Dad would get home. At first, he would just shake his head and try and talk to Mom in his quiet demeanour. Then it was pleading. Then it was Grandma coming to stay.

Then after she left, the fighting started, and tears and crying and doors slamming and Dad staying away 'til late at night because he had to work more to make up for Mom's shortfall. Either that or he just couldn't stand to be around the house. It was just so dark and depressing.

Four long years of that misery.

Eventually, we moved. Dad thought it would be a good idea.

"Let's just get the hell away from here," he said. "Start over. Move on. God! Forget this place. Time is a healer," he said.

So, we did. Moved. Sold our two-story with attached garage and large property and travelled four hours away and purchased a modest bungalow with three bedrooms and an unfinished basement in a large subdivision where we could get lost in the crowd.

And, yes, I suppose I could have stayed for my senior year, but why would I want to? I could see the caption under my name in the class yearbook:

> Karmalita Judith Smallwood – only daughter of
> Brian and Cathy-the-Murderer.
> Future prospects: Hoping to gain employment,
> unlike her infamous mother.

I'd be booed off the stage when I accepted my diploma. The graduation

Trena Christie-MacEachern

committee probably wouldn't even allow my mother into the auditorium to watch.

I shook my head. I didn't want to be like my mother. I may have at one time, but not anymore. I would never find myself staring down the barrel of a gun, realizing I had no choice. Mom had a choice! And she must live with her consequences and get over it.

And, just like my mother, I have had to live with consequences and regrets for the rest of my life.

~

Then

She plunked down in the seat beside me in English class and handed me my bag. My desk was in the first row and I sat sideways so my back was against the stone wall. I was doodling on my scribbler to pass the time.

"Hey," she said.

I looked up and saw Trudy smiling at me, staring with those big eyes. "We didn't hear from you all weekend. Why didn't you call? Were you in trouble?" She placed her binder flat on the desk.

"Kind of. Not really. Hard to explain. You?"

Trudy shook her head. "My Mum doesn't care. She tells me I'm old enough to make up my own mind what I want to do. If I want to drink, I drink. If I want to have sex, I have sex."

I gasped and put my hand to my mouth. "What?"

Trudy giggled. "I know. Everyone responds that way. But it's true, right? We're leaving in a few months. We have to learn to make our own decisions."

Trudy sounded so grown-up. And actually, she was, pretty much. She wasn't disregarded like I was, she was making sensible and sound choices. She had bought her own car—not much of one, but it was hers. She worked part-time at a restaurant near the Reserve and her tips helped pay for her clothes, her gas, and her extra-curriculars. "I take boys home, too. Ma doesn't mind." She laughed. "She does tell me what she thinks of them, though."

I shook my head. I couldn't imagine. Well, I couldn't imagine *me* taking anyone home.

"Were you sick at all?" she said. "We didn't know where you went and you didn't tell us and then you didn't touch base all weekend after we dropped you off. Thought you were in deep shit."

Karma

"Was anybody home when you dropped me off? *God, I don't even re-member you taking me in.* "I'm so embarrassed."

"Actually, it was Jimmy who took you in. He drove us home. He usually does when we've had too much."

I raised my hand to my face. I felt myself getting hot.

"It's okay," Trudy said with a giggle. "Jimmy's alright. He's used to us. I usually drive, but not that night." She laughed again.

"Move!"

We saw Suzanne marching our way, her long hair flowing behind her. We actually heard her before we saw her. Her voice carried over the buzz of the classroom. "Mr. Watzup will kick me out if I'm not in here on time. And I need this credit."

She plunked herself down across from us. Everyone always left a chair for Suzanne opposite or beside Trudy. "What happened to you Saturday?" she asked briskly, hollering even though I could have heard her whisper it.

The class looked over in my direction. My face grew even more heated.

"Jeesh, Suzanne, not so loud."

"What's the big deal? You got drunk." She laughed out loud. "Not enough practice."

She banged her hand on the table. "I suppose you got sick too?" She looked at me. "In your bed? Or on the floor?" and she laughed again.

"Neither," I said, coldly.

"No big deal if you did. Well, that's good then. Good you got home and that you got in the right car. You imagine, Tru, if she got in the wrong car? You might be in Timbuktu now." She laughed so hard.

Honestly, this girl.

Just then, Mr. Watzup arrived. He was a little man with a white shirt and blue tie, glasses, looking a bit like Les Nesman from *WKRP*. He took out his agenda and went through the class list, checking off names.

"Mr. Gould not here?" he asked.

"Yeah, he's here. Just a little behind schedule," Suzanne stated.

"Who's that?" I asked.

Suzanne looked at me like I had two heads.

"Suzanne's cousin," Trudy whispered.

"I hear talking," Mr. Watzup bellowed.

Just then, Clyde walked in the door. Big and meandering. I couldn't get over the size of this boy. I wondered how he fit in his chair. The only thing he and Suzanne had in common, really, was their dark hair and

Trena Christie-MacEachern

eyes. He nodded at the teacher.

"You're late, Mr. Gould."

"Sorry, sir." He smiled and his eyes disappeared. The happy Buddha.

He nodded at Trudy and Suzanne, too, looked at me. I acknowledged him. He took a seat at the back.

Mr. Watzup began writing on the board.

"Shit," Suzanne whispered. Then she hollered, "Mr. Watzup. I need a pen. Forgot mine."

The teacher didn't look at Suzanne, instead spoke to her as he was writing on the board. "Ms. Stephens, you should be prepared to come to class with a pen. You know this. This is your senior year."

"I know, sir, but this one ran out and I've the other at home."

"Can anyone help Ms. Stephens?" Mr. Watzup asked the class in a flat tone.

"I have one for you, Suzanne," said the soft-spoken, pretty-faced kitten of a girl, Vicki. She stood up. She was wearing a mauve blouse, tight-fitting jeans, and flat shoes. Her hair was cut short but curled. I noticed her eyes were perfectly make-upped and almond shaped. Her lashes were long and her lips were shiny. Her cheeks blossomed with pink when she handed Suzanne her extra pen.

"Who's that?" I whispered to Trudy.

"Vicki Meagher."

"She's pretty."

"Yep," Trudy agreed, "and smart as hell."

And that she was. I learned she could get anything she wanted. All she needed to do was smile.

Karma

5

Now

It was stupid. This was stupid. This is something you'd see play out in the movies. Not in my stupid, pathetic life. God!

I'm horizontal on the couch with my palms covering my face, hiding my humiliation—my betrayal.

I'll have to find the money somewhere. I could sell my car? Stupid. I need my car. Maybe I could go to the bank, or to one of those lending companies that gives money to crackheads, gamblers, losers like me, at an outrageous interest rate. I could take the money out of the kids' bank accounts. Jimmy wouldn't notice that. Not at first, anyway. Then I could find a way to replace the money.

The phone interrupts my thoughts again. Its annoying ring makes me angry. This time it doesn't stop.

I reach for it. "Hello," I snap.

"Mom?"

"Oh," I soften. "Sorry. What's the matter, honey?" I look at my wrist. "Why aren't you home by now?"

"Mom! You're supposed to pick me up. I've been calling."

Jesus, I breath. "Oh, honey. I'm sorry. I totally forgot. I'll leave right now."

I grab my keys and purse and head out the door.

It was because Jimmy didn't want to go. I tell myself. He hates funerals. He opted to stay home, go to work, anything other than going to see his old pals one more time.

He did go to the wake—that was painful enough. It was like it was the first time he had seen these guys he grew up with. Yet, in that line-up, seeing everyone again, maybe it was just too painful or something? Something I couldn't explain, nor put my finger on. It was like he needed these guys when he was in high school, but after graduation, he had little to do with them. He cleaned house.

35

Trena Christie-MacEachern

But it was because of these guys that I met Jimmy. But it's also because of these guys that I'm in this position right now.

I adjust the rear-view mirror, turn the radio on low. Evidently, Mariah was in here earlier, left it turned on to blaring Crazy Rock FM. *The music these kids listen to.*

My mind drifts back to Lotty. I'm surprised she made it this long. She was a little waif of a thing. I remember seeing her for the first time up close, sitting on Allan's lap. Pretty, petite. God, how she aged. She looked more like a hard sixty-year-old than twenty-nine. I forgot she was younger than all of us.

Thought she would go somewhere in life. She was a whipper-snapper. Double-graded twice. But things changed when she met up with Allan and the crew. God, how they changed.

I shook my head. How much pot did she smoke? And drink? She always had a drink in her hand.

But Allan did everything to save her. He loved that girl.

He looked pretty rough, too. A sorry sight. Thin, couldn't have been more than a hundred and thirty pounds. Jimmy did a double-take. If he wasn't standing beside the casket, I doubt Jimmy would have recognized him.

His hair didn't change much: still long and straggly, albeit a bit thinner. His face was deeply etched with lines, covered by his thick whiskers. Looked like he didn't even shave. He still smelled like nicotine and strong aftershave and when he hugged me, he wept like a baby.

They said it was the first time he cried, and I stayed with him, holding up the line, while Jimmy stood awkwardly over in the corner, wanting to go home.

"How're you doing? And your mom?" he asked, when he finally let go of me. He was always thinking of others. The tears were in my eyes then, too, making it hard to talk. His voice rattled when he spoke and I suspect, in hindsight, he was probably sicker than he let on.

"Mom is fine, Allan. She'll be by to see you."

His smile stretched across his face. "You guys were damn good to her. I'll not forget that. And you. You're just like her."

He reached for me and took me into his arms again. "I'd do anything for you. I owe you. You know that, girl?"

I nodded against his shoulder. "I'm holding up the line, Allan. I'll keep going."

He held onto my hand. "It means a lot that you and Jimmy are here to see Lotty off. The whole gang, well, what's left of us. We're meeting to-

36

Karma

morrow at The Bullhorn. Why don't you guys come by? We can get caught up."

I knew Jimmy wouldn't hear of it. So I went on his behalf. And that's when the trouble began.

~

Then

I was hanging out at Suzanne's a lot. Anything was better than being at home. Trudy liked to come, too, as her mom worked most evenings.

It wasn't much of a house on the outside. One of the windows was broken, looked like duct tape was holding it together. The grass was barren, there was no front step, and the side stairs looked a little treacherous. And the inside was not much better. The dishes were piled high in the sink, some of the cabinets didn't have doors, the dog was always asleep on the couch, which was covered in black hair.

But her family was so wonderful and welcoming. They were some of nicest people I had ever met. The house was always warm, and it didn't matter who you were or where you came from. There was always food on the table and you were always asked to join them. Always.

The walls were covered with photos of their children and family members, grandparents, uncles; baptisms, weddings, family get-togethers.

Suzanne's older brother, Martin, who just got married, had stopped by for a visit. Suzanne and his mother kept on him, picking at him, egging him about news they were waiting eagerly for, when he would have babies.

I laughed to myself because there were already three younger children in the house. I wondered what it was like to have so many siblings. Her home life was just so different from mine.

The younger kids, despite their ages, were always included in whatever the older ones were doing, whether it was a game of cards or watching a scary movie. And at Suzanne's, you slept where you found a spot, whether it was with Blue on the couch, with Suzanne in her room, or on the floor.

"How come you called your dog, Blue?" I asked Suzanne's mom one day. "He's black."

"He was sad when we found him. Poor thing. All scrawny and hungry."

"He was a rescue dog?" I inquired again.

"Well, we rescued him. He belonged to the neighbour."

"He didn't let us pet him 'til close to a month. Eh, Mom? It was just so sad. So we named him Blue."

"Should change his name to spoiled," Suzanne's mother added.

Suzanne laughed and patted Blue's rump. "Ah, you're a good dog, aren't you?"

Blue responded by wagging his tail.

I never thought we were a burden to Suzanne's parents. Even though we were there all the time. They never said anything as far as we knew to Suzanne or Trudy. We just arrived, ate and slept. Mostly on weekends. Why stop a good thing?

But at one point, Suzanne barked, "What will we do this weekend?"

My immediate response was to suggest her place again. But before I could say anything, Trudy suggested mine.

"Your parents aren't home this weekend, right?"

I had totally forgot about it. Mom was going to see Grandma, which she was, but it was also code for trying to get her off the sauce again. Dad was going to go to help. They didn't need me around to see the likes of that, so I opted to stay behind. I said I had tests or something or another. A project.

So, the schedule was settled.

Party at my house.

~

I told Dad that Suzanne and Trudy would be staying with me for the night. He actually gave me twenty bucks, told me to get pizza.

I ended up buying chips and pretzels, and gave what was left to Suzanne to pick up the drinks.

It was just going to be our crowd, they said. The three of us, plus Clyde, Allan and Lotty; maybe Jimmy, Charlie, Prince Eric and his new woman, Bea.

I still didn't really care for the guy. Kind of a non-entity. Didn't really know what he had in common with the rest of the fellas, as everyone else was pretty friendly and relaxed, other than Jimmy, who was still kind of quiet. But Eric's dad owned The Bullhorn Tavern. Well, enough said.

This was probably another reason why he was attracted to the older ladies. The legals.

I couldn't see someone of age coming to a seniors' party. But one never knows. Although Suzanne said Teddy might drop by, too.

The evening started with Clyde and Trudy playing caps on the kitchen floor. I tried my hand at it with Suzanne. But I was getting drunk too

Karma

quickly and I couldn't hit Suzanne's cap off her beer and she was getting angry.

"For Christ sake, Karm. You suck. I ain't never getting a drink." Then she picked up her beer and guzzled half of it.

I gave up and let Lotty give it a try. The two of them were going tit for tat, Suzanne hooting and hollering over the tunes and the noise.

I sat at the kitchen table with Allan, who was smoking like a trooper, and drinking rum and coke. Mostly rum, and it was probably warm because I didn't have ice.

Then Charlie showed up.

He arrived with a very drunk and slobbering Prince Eric, who appeared dateless. Apparently, they had just broken up as Bea wouldn't come to our little soiree and so Eric told her to go fuck herself. He had been waiting for her at the bar all evening, and by the time she arrived, he was already two sheets to the wind. She wouldn't go anywhere with him then, drunk or otherwise.

Eric took it on the nose. He ordered her to be thrown out of his father's bar, only to have himself escorted out for causing a ruckus. Charlie had to go pick him up and then he took him here.

It appeared Prince Eric was not used to having things not go his way, and now, he was passed out on my living room couch with a bucket beside his head.

My stomach did cartwheels when Charlie arrived. When he smiled and looked at me, I melted like a chocolate bar that had been sitting out in the sun. I went all goo-goo and stupid and couldn't say anything. My words got all fumbled and I sounded like a tool.

To save myself the embarrassment, I just sat and nodded, yet he spoke so sweetly to me.

"Hey there," he breathed. He was all cool and gentleman-like. "Nice place, Karma." And although I usually hate that pronunciation of my name, it was all good when he said it.

"It's Karm. Just Karm. No 'ah' at the end," Suzanne snapped, coming to my defence. "She hates it when people call her that."

I wanted to crawl under the table.

But Charlie touched the top of my hand with his finger and said, "I like Karma better."

And I really did, too, after that.

He just had a way with people, all smooth and sweet. He made sure to say hello to everyone. Asked how they were doing. Gave them a pat on the back or clapped a high-five. Laughed. A lot.

39

Trena Christie-MacEachern

He and Allan were always laughing, and when Lotty came over and sat with her man for a minute and gave him a long, slow, seductive kiss while we just watched, in my case, awkwardly, Charlie would just start talking to me again.

It's like he knew I was lonely, because I felt it in him somehow too although I couldn't process it then. We filled a void in each other instead of focusing on other shit that was more pressing and distressing.

It wasn't long before I met him outside my bedroom door, the taste of beer on my breath, and his hands all over me, kissing me deeply. And I knew I was done for. I fell for him harder than any guy I'd ever met in my life.

He wasn't even extremely good-looking. He had nice eyes, dreamy eyes. Robin's-egg blue. But he had a great smile, and straight teeth. He wasn't tall either. I liked them tall and dark. Charlie was light, sandy-coloured hair and no more than five nine.

He was stocky, though. He had well-defined arms which I liked and he liked to hold hands. Every time I'd see him, he'd give me that wonderful grin of his and, again, I'd turn into a puddle.

I wasn't even sure exactly what it was that interested him in me. I wasn't a talker with him, more of a listener. And I wasn't one of those girls, the kind that has to sleep with their man in order to get him to stay.

I wasn't sure what I had, but I didn't care. I would hold his hand with my left and with my right, find his bicep and stroke his muscle, while he told me it felt nice because it tickled.

~

"Bad idea," Suzanne said, after she found out we had got together. She shook her head and wagged her finger at me.

"Why?" I asked, perplexed.

"Code."

"Huh? What code?"

"Geese, Karm. You stupid or something?"

"Suzanne," Trudy interjected, "don't say that. Be nice."

"Tru. You know the girls aren't to get with the guys in the group."

"Well, Lotty's with Allan and they've been together since forever," I stated.

"That's the whole point. They'll be together forever," Suzanne said, exasperated. "You won't be. Then, when you and Charlie break up, what's going to happen to the group? It will be weird and we'll be divided, and

40

then no group." She did a karate chop.

"It's not going to happen like that." I laughed. "Maybe Charlie and I will be together forever, like Lotty and Allan."

"Nah. Charlie's a wanderer." She said it so casually, so matter-of-factly, that it caused me to take a short intake of air.

"My Charlie?" I looked at Trudy for confirmation.

"I don't know, Suzanne." She looked at me thoughtfully. "Maybe Karm's right. Maybe they will be—"

"Read my lips, Tru. Not going to last."

Suzanne's words haunted me for a long time. I didn't want to believe it. Charlie was my very first official boyfriend, my first love, my true love. God, I adored him.

I let him have me. All of me. And he said I was his first, too.

Did I believe him? It didn't matter. It was just the two of us, in love, and in bed, he caressing my skin, my body, with his strong hands, my belly still doing cartwheels. I remember that first time with him and never wanting to let him go. I wanted to stay in that bed forever.

Even after Mom and Dad came home and found us, and chased Charlie out of the house.

~

Now

The Bullhorn looks pretty much the way it used to. I don't think they even changed the wall paper. Everything's the same, except maybe the chairs. They used to be wood, now they're black laminate with plastic-like material for seat cushions. Some were in rough shape, however, torn in spots down the back.

It felt odd to be sitting in front of the bar. Our spot was always at the back, hidden from the grown-ups.

I glance around and stare at our bartender. He's the same person that worked in the front all those years ago. Earl is his name. He's wearing the same signature white dress shirt, rolled up at the elbows, has shoulder-length, dirty-blond hair.

All the girls thought he was so cute. Heard he married twice.

"What'll you have?" he asks as he approaches our table.

Most opt for beer, I want white wine, Trudy asks for a Mojito—her new favourite drink after travelling to Cuba last spring.

We have all grown up, sort of, and moved on with our lives.

"I'll get these, guys." Eric stands up and nods to Earl. "You can put them on my tab."

"Salut," everyone says in unison.

"I think Trudy should be buying these drinks," Clyde interjects, as everyone knew she was doing just fine monetary-wise. "She can afford it," he ribs.

Everyone laughs.

"Next round," she states, smiling.

"How's the business?" I ask.

"Yeah, good. I'm travelling across the country now and Suzanne looks after home base. So, it's good. Busy, but good."

"The travelling salesman," Eric adds.

"Woman! Saleswoman. Don't you know your sexes, Eric?" Suzanne takes a gulp of her beer.

Allan remains quiet and sullen, taking in what everyone is saying, not really contributing much. Kind of a bad time to be getting together, to get caught up. After all, we're supposed to be comforting him.

I elbow Trudy and she taps Clyde on the wrist.

Clyde clears his throat. "Well, everyone." He stands up. "Ahem. We're here for Lotty, but most especially, Allan."

Allan looks down and smiles weakly. He looks exhausted enough to sleep at the table. The turn of events has taken a toll on everyone.

"Here, here," everyone says around the table.

"There isn't a more fitting place that we could meet, eh, Allan?" Clyde says. "Aside from the chapel. This is the place we hung out almost weekly."

Allan nods, turns his face, stares, drifts his thoughts to a faraway place. No doubt this place had special meaning for the two of them. I could still envision her propped on his lap.

"I'm not good at this," Clyde says with a laugh. His cheeks redden even darker than they already were. Clyde didn't change much over the years. A bit bigger, heavier, more fat than lean muscle. More McDonald's patron than football player.

He clears his throat again. "Lotty was a special girl. I remember when you two first met, Al. She was in fourth grade and you were in sixth? I think. It was before she double-graded. God, she was smart."

The whole table mumbles in agreement.

"We did a science project and the younger grades were invited to look at our projects. Yours wasn't finished." Everyone laughs. "Typical Allan, eh? And Lotty gave you some pointers on what to do because she had done one similar. Right?" He moistens his lips.

42

Karma

"What was it on, Al—you remember?" Trudy asks.

"Weather systems."

"Is that when you started dating?" I blurt.

Allan looks at me from across the table, takes a swig of his beer.

"Nah. When they held me back in sixth grade. I had to do the damn project over. And I went up to her and asked for the information again." He chuckles. "She gave it to me. All in this neat, little, blue folder. It was near Valentines."

He smiles again, looking away as if he's talking to her right then and there. "I made her one to say thank you. Just out of paper, you know? Kind of cheesy, but she loved it. Put it in her locker, like taped it to the inside of the door for everyone to see. And that made me feel good, you know?"

The boys nod in unison. Like they understand something a lot more than anyone is saying out loud.

"And we just started, like, hanging out. Innocent stuff, you know?" He laughs. "Like holding hands, and talking on the phone. I wouldn't go near her 'cause, you know, she was a lot younger than me. We were friends first. But she understood me, what was going on and shit. And when she double-graded again when I was in eighth grade, then we started high school together. We were full on then. She was my girl. Always and forever."

"Always and forever," everyone choruses.

"'Til the end of time." Allan bows his head and starts to weep. Tears drop from his face onto his lap.

Trudy reaches into her purse and brings out a tissue. We're all so sad for him.

"Everyone. To Lotty." Clyde extends his arm.

We all lift our glasses. "To Lotty." We down our drinks.

"Hey, hey, look who finally shows up." Eric looks over his shoulder.

"The clown."

I turn to see who they're talking about, and should have guessed.

Charlie.

~

I hadn't seen Charlie in about five years. He looks the same, but older. Still in shape although a bit more robust, hair still tousled but cut shorter, trimmed, tanned, wearing nice clothes.

He acknowledges everyone, nods to me, before he takes Allan in his arms and gives him the biggest bear hug.

"Hey, buddy, sorry I'm late."

"It's alright, man, you're here now. Have a seat, my friend."

Charlie waves to Earl and nods. "I'll have a Bud when you get a chance, man." He pauses. "Is that you, Earl?" he asks enthusiastically. "Hey, you haven't changed a bit. Man. You're still working here? Holy fuck. Eric's old man must have something on you to keep you working here this long?"

Earl laughs. "Second job, second wife, eh."

"Yeah, cool, cool." Immediately, Charlie's eyes focus on me.

I turn away to get Earl's attention. "Um, could I have another one, please?"

"I better get back to work," Earl says. "Coming right up, miss."

I laugh. He seems to remember everyone's name except mine.

"Where's Jimmy?" Charlie bellows.

Everyone glances in my direction. I squirm around in my seat. *God, how I wish he was here.*

"Ah, he couldn't come," I offer, feeling totally awkward at the moment. And even though no one else asked and was being polite, it was Charlie who stirred things up.

"He should be here," he scolds. "It's just like him—the ass."

I take a sip and consider sliding under the table.

"I'm sure he has his reasons," Trudy says in my defence.

"He doesn't like wakes," I say, a little bit more confident. "They make him uncomfortable."

"Well," Charlie says, looking around the room, outstretching his arms, "this ain't a wake."

"I'm sorry, Allan," I offer, feeling miserable.

Yes, Jimmy should have been here, but he wouldn't come, and I have no idea why he won't have anything to do with his old group. I look around. Maybe it's because Charlie and I were an item once? Maybe Lotty's death was harder on him than even I realized.

Allan slumps over his beer, puts his cigarette out, shakes his hand back and forth. "It's alright, Charlie. Leave it alone."

"Why you so aggressive, Charlie? Leave Jimmy alone. If he didn't come, he didn't come. That's that. For fuck's sake." Suzanne has her way for making people see the obvious.

We sit silently and awkwardly for a few minutes.

Trudy whispers something to Suzanne, then grabs her purse. "Well, guys, as nice as this is, we've a flight to catch in a few hours. I'm sorry we have to leave so soon, Allan, but we'll do it again, hey? All of us?"

Allan nods. The chair groans as Trudy pushes it back. She goes to Allan and gives him a hug while he remains sitting down. She whispers in his ear.

He nods. "Thank you," he says softly. "Thank you for coming."

She bends down and kisses him on the forehead.

Suzanne slaps Allan on the back. "You'll be okay, buddy. We'll be checking on you. Later, folks," she says briskly, and the two of them leave.

I feel a sudden void. As I stand to leave, Clyde reaches for me, "Karm, you need to stay, okay?" He looks at me with those sincere, dark, Buddha eyes.

"Ugh, I should go, I think. I should get home and check on Jimmy." As I look at who's left in our group around the table, I whisper, "I'll be the only female here."

"Nah, it's okay," Clyde reassures. "Allan's pretty broken up and he needs you. And both you and Jimmy were close to Lotty."

I sit back.

Now it was just me and the boys.

Trena Christie-MacEachern

6

Then

"I'm in deep shit with my folks," I told Trudy and Suzanne.

We were sitting on the grass outside the school. The first warm rays of spring sun shone upon us and we lay deliciously paralyzed. I picked at a yellow dandelion.

"What'd you do this time?" Suzanne barked, her long legs outstretched, hair gently blowing about her fine, strong face.

"They caught us again. He snuck in this time," I muttered, low and secretive.

Trudy gasped, raised her hand to her mouth. A smile spread across her face and she nudged my leg with her foot. "Really? Wow. You dirty dog."

"For fuck's sake, Tru. Ain't nothing special." Suzanne turned away, closed her eyes as if in disgust. Tilted her head to the sky.

Trudy wiggled closer to me, all eager and interested. "So? How was it? Getting better?"

My face felt warm, like I was getting a burn. I laughed a little. "Yeah." That was all I could think of.

"Does it still hurt?" She studied my face, looking intently at me.

"Nah, not really. Maybe a little." I fiddled with the dandelion, popped the flower off its stem, bounced it up and down on my palm.

"What your parents say? Are you grounded again?"

"Yep."

"For how long?"

Suzanne got up. "I don't need to hear this shit." She marched off.

"What's wrong with her?" I asked, confused. I watched Suzanne strutting fiercely to the other side of the yard.

"She just doesn't want to see you getting hurt."

I looked at her, dumbfounded. "Really? She has a funny way of showing it."

Karma

"Suzanne comes across all tough and mouthy, but really, she is soft on the inside. Just has a hard way of showing it."

I nodded. "Well, anyway. Not allowed to go out the next couple of weeks, and he is not allowed to call. I mean, for Pete's sake." I groaned, and rolled my eyes. "I just love him so much and want to be with him, you know? But I can't. Dad says Mom can't take any more issues." My fingers raised in the air, bending for the quotes.

"How she's doing?"

"Ah, I don't know. Trying maybe. Or failing." I laughed.

"Maybe you should invite Allan over?"

"Huh?"

"Allan. Has he met your mom yet?"

"No." I looked at her because I didn't understand what she meant.

"Allan is good with people. Charlie is, too, but not under these circumstances. Have Allan over for a visit. He's the fixer. See what happens."

"Allan would do that for me?"

"Allan 's a sweetheart. He's a good person to have on your side."

"Alright." I sighed. "I'll try just about anything once."

~

"Gimme a puff of that?" I asked nervously.

"You don't smoke." Allan passed me his almost entirely smoked butt. "Want me to light up a new one?"

"No."

I brought the butt to my mouth, quickly inhaled, felt the burn—the smoke was hot and gross in my mouth. "Fuck! Here. Take it back." I passed what was left of it.

"You sure today is a good day?"

I shrugged. "No day is a good day. But she's been sick, so maybe she'll be semi-sober, at least."

~

Mom stood at the door looking dishevelled and worn out. She had bags under her eyes, her hair was a mess and she was wearing jogging pants that were at least eight years old. They were her comfy pants. A baggy sweater made up her attire.

She had taken up smoking, too, and was breathing clouds out of the front door. She had been doing that for months, thinking we didn't know

47

Trena Christie-MacEachern

and couldn't smell it in the house.

"You skipping school?" she asked, holding the door open, a shawl wrapped around her back. She looked cross. Her mouth was turned downward and her eyebrows were furrowed. She was trying to see who was with me. She backed into the house.

Allan dropped his butt and stepped on it, twisting it with his foot. Exhaled. He looked up at the door. "Hi, Mrs. Smallwood. I'm Allan Rafferty."

He extended his hand. I looked back at him and then at Mom. No one was talking.

"Mom. This is Allan," I said a little louder. "My friend from school."

Mom remained frozen in the entrance, staring at Allan like she was in shock. Like she knew him from some place. She looked a little pale.

"Mom?" I said again, feeling my face getting warm, wondering what in the hell I was doing bringing Allan here. Mom's shit-faced, can't even communicate. "Mom?"

"Hello...Allan," she said warmly, gently. She offered her hand. "Please come in."

She held open the door for the two of us. "For God's sake, Karm. I'm not deaf, I can hear you."

~

His room.

I watched Dad with the roller. Whirrr whirrr. The sounds were soothing. I stood beside Mom. I was as tall as her belly. Her beachball belly. Biggest I had ever seen.

"Oh, I love it, honey. Do you?" She stood beside me, one hand on her stomach, softly caressing, the other on my back.

I nodded. How could I not? The rest of the house was creams and whites, but not here. The bluest blue, as bright as the sky, as tranquil as the ocean.

"When's he coming, Momma?"

"Soon, sweetheart. Soon." She smiled at me lovingly, kissing me with her happy eyes. Her hair was shorter then. Coiffed. "Come on pumpkin. Let's get out of here. The odour is getting to me."

~

"Grandma?"

She dried her hands on her apron. They smelled like bleach: harsh

Karma

and fumy. She walked toward me and gave me a stiff hug. She was washing sheets. Soaking them. Large, pink rings on the fabric. Momma's sheets.

"Where's she at? Did she have the baby?" I jumped up and down. "Can we see Josh today?"

But Grandma did not smile back. "No sweetie. Not today, Not ever, I'm afraid."

I ran upstairs, tears came down my face. It had happened again.

Grandma left me for a while so she could finish her work. She found me later, in Josh's room, sitting on the floor, smelling the sweet fragrance of his freshly-washed little sleepers. Josh, like the others, would get to the hospital, but never make it home.

~

"Where you from?" She eyed Allan skeptically. "You from here? You look familiar."

Allan was bending down taking off his shoes. "Yes ma'am."

"Rafferty," she said aloud, mimicking his words. Like by saying it, it would jar some memory for her.

He smiled awkwardly, ran his hands through his hair.

"Mom, dad, siblings?"

"God, Mom. Don't interrogate him." I laughed to break this form of questioning.

"It's okay, Karm. Yes, my mom's name is Barb. She's not well. My dad, Albert, died a number of years ago. I have a half-brother, Simon. He's older than me but he moved away. We don't see him either, so it's just me and Mom."

"What's wrong with your mother?" She brought the shawl closer around her shoulders, as if the thought of another sick woman had given her the chills, not the draft from the house itself.

Mom!" I shouted, mortified.

"Karm! Perhaps I can help, Allan. I'm a nurse."

Used to be.

Allan and I sat at the kitchen table. Mom already had the kettle on. She didn't bother to ask if you wanted anything, assumed everyone was having tea. Gave it to you whether you wanted it or not, whether you drank it or not. But better the tea than the wine.

"Ah, my mom. Not sure really." He glanced down at his lap, raised his hand to hold his head, thinking.

49

Trena Christie-MacEachern

"What are her symptoms? Throws up? Sleeps a lot? She on anything?"

The whistle of the kettle saved Allan for a minute. Its high-pitched screech broke the line of questioning.

Mom took out three tea bags, tossed them into the heavily-stained glass teapot, poured in the boiling water, turned the stove on medium. Then she took out three cups, filled each with a drop of milk and poured the steaming liquid into the cup. She made a perfect cup each time.

With two cups in her hands, she walked towards us. She placed one in front of Allan and the other in front of her, then she directed her atten-tion towards me.

"Put some eggs and toast on. And there might be some ham left in the fridge."

"What's this for? Since when do you need all this food?"

"It's not for me, it's for him." She pointed her face toward Allan, sitting opposite her at the table. "My God, boy, you're awfully thin. When did you last eat?"

~

Now

"C'mere. Sit beside me." Allan taps the empty seat beside him. I get up from my chair, move towards Allan and Clyde. Charlie is chatting with Eric. They're heavy into it. Without the girls or Jimmy here, the group doesn't seem like a group.

"How's your drink?" Allan asks, noticing his is already empty.

He lights up another cigarette. "Wanna puff?"

I take it from him, realizing it had been ages since I did. For old times, I inhale.

"Goes better with beer," I say, exhaling, my face wincing.

He smiles a sad smile.

"Gawd. How do you smoke so many of these?" I take a drink from my glass to wash away the taste. Cheap chardonnay.

I look over at Charlie. However does he do it? He still makes my heart race, although I fight it. After all, I'm happily married, and he and I were never a real couple.

Allan taps me on the hand. "Earth to Karm."

I focus back on Allan's sad, tormented face. "Sorry Al."

"He was never good for you, Karm. You know this."

"God, Al, yes. Why would you say that to me?" I stroke the stem of the glass, and then stop.

50

Karma

"The way you look at him. The way he looked at you when he arrived."

"There's nothing. I love Jimmy." I curl my hair behind my ear and sip my wine again. If I keep doing this, I'm going to get drunk. Fast. "Trudy and Suzanne doing some great eh?" Changing the subject.

Clyde folds himself onto the table beside us. "Yes, aren't they?"

"You into that line too?" I ask, knowing that he's a part of the team but forgetting how.

"Not pharmaceuticals like Trudy. Security."

"Ah," I say. "Of course."

"No one messes with the big man, eh, Clyde?" Allan interjects.

They clink beer bottles. Clyde's eyes disappear into his face.

I know if Mom were here right now, she'd end up saying something to Clyde about his weight. More importantly, what his weight was doing to his heart.

"You still at the power corp, Al?" Clyde asks.

"Yeah, but took some time off...with Lotty and all."

"Course, course." Clyde sits back, stretching out a leg.

I look over in Charlie's direction again. There's a young gal, probably not yet twenty-one, talking to him. You could tell she's interested by the way she's smiling at him. She's studying his face and eyes, her arms at her sides. She takes a finger and flicks an invisible spec off his shoulder.

Eric laughs. "Jesus, that Charlie."

Allan interrupts everyone's thoughts again. "How's your missus, Clyde?"

"No complaints here, Al, except for the kids. They never sleep. Think we're running on low battery all the time. If I get enough of these tonight," he holds up the beer, "I'll sleep like a baby."

"You mean pass out like one."

"Ha ha. All the same."

"Let's see a picture, Clyde."

Allan takes Clyde's wallet, looks at the family portrait of Clyde, his wife, and three kids. "They're some handsome. Baby looks just like you."

Clyde grins. "Oldest wants to play football. I've been tossing it to him, showing how it's done. Donna thinks I'm nuts. But no harm with starting early."

Allan stares thoughtfully for the longest time. He closes the wallet back up, hands it back to Clyde.

"You're a lucky man, Clyde. Three kids." He whistles. "Lotty and I wanted to have a whole bunch of them. But not in the cards. Not with her"—he pauses—"habit."

Trena Christie-MacEachern

He looks away. Stares at Charlie. His eyes grow heavy and dark.

~

Then

His hands were warm, sweaty almost, yet soft when I held them. Sometimes when we'd lie on the grass, I'd inhale his palms. Stick my nose right into the cup of his hands, lick his skin. He'd never wipe my spit off. He'd let it air dry in the sun.

He'd lay his head on my belly, too, and I'd caress him like a football, stroke his hair, draw lines on his face with my finger.

I knew when he was smiling, then I'd lean over and kiss him. Soft tongue, full lips, wet mouth. We'd kiss for hours.

The grass made imprints on our arms. The sun scorched our skin in the weirdest of angles: behind his ears, my left cheek, one hipbone, exposed ankle. We'd always laugh.

Once, I took some of Mom's suntan lotion to school and lathered myself and Charlie where there were bare spots: faces, necks, arms. We both smelled like coconut. I loved the smell of it—fragrant, tropical, reminded me of summer.

"I wish you could help me study," he said, running his fingers through my hair like a comb.

"Me too," I said. Although realizing I'd rather be kissing him than teaching him his math. We'd never get anything done. He'd flunk for sure.

"Think your folks will let me come over tonight?"

"Nope." Then I punched him in the arm. I wanted him to feel what I did, hurt, when they denied us our togetherness. "I have to study, anyway."

"We better go," he said. "Bell's going to ring soon."

He stood up first and pulled me by the hands so we were standing face to face. His breath was on me. I wanted to devour him. I loved the way he looked at me, studied me. Like he was having imaginary conversations with me, as I still wasn't much of a talker with him. We just had this crazy physical attraction. He wrapped his arm around me and we walked towards the school like that.

I told him to check out the bulletin board. I said there was a list on it for available tutors. "Maybe one of them can help you out."

"Yeah," he said sadly. "I better. Otherwise, I'll be in deep shit here. You'll be going off to college in the fall and I'll be left behind."

"Hey, don't say that."

My eyes furrowed. I couldn't imagine going anywhere without him. I stopped, turned to face him, put my hands over his cheeks and stood on my tippy toes, even though there wasn't much of a height difference. I gave him a soft peck on the nose. He leaned over and grabbed my book bag and slung it over his shoulder, and took my hand in his.

Our eyes adjusted from the bright, sunny, spring weather outside. Kids were streaming out of their classes on last bell, right before the day was out.

We sidled up to the cork board, looking for the list of do-gooders who would help those struggling on the final days of senior year.

"Hey! What about Jimmy? I bet you he'd do it. For nothing! Why don't you ask him?" Of course, Jimmy would.

"Nah, I don't think," he said goofily.

"Why? He'd be perfect."

"Jimmy is too, I don't know. I'd feel stupid with Jimmy trying to explain this to me. He's into calculus and stuff like that. Way too advanced for me."

I didn't understand his logic, but I dropped it.

"Here's one."

And there it was, all fancy looking, bordered, and on coloured paper:

Needing help with Finals?
Call the person who can help.
Any subjects. At any time.
Victoria @ 623-1057
after school and weekends.
Affordable Rates

"That was easy, Charlie. Rip a tag off with her number." At the bottom of her poster were pre-cut tags, about ten in a row, all with her home number on it.

"Do you know if she is any good, though?" I asked eagerly. "Do you know who she is?"

"Victoria Meagher. Yes, I know her. She was in one of your classes? English, maybe. She's dating one of Clyde's teammates."

"Oh!" I scanned my brain and remembered the pretty little helpful thing at the start of the year. "Yes. Oh, Charlie. I know who she is. She's as

Trena Christie-MacEachern

smart as a whip and pretty as—" I stopped myself and started to laugh. "Yeah, I heard she's good. You should call her. She'd be better than me too because we wouldn't get anything done." I giggled, nuzzling my nose into his neck along his collar bone.

"Mmmm, don't I know it."

"She'll take good care of you, Charlie."

~

They started off innocently enough. She had a boyfriend. Nice guy—a linebacker. Big as a tank. But, as usual, there was something about Charlie's personality that made him click with everyone.

They got together a few times a week for study. He felt instantly comfortable with her. She felt instantly attracted to him. And they were equally proportionate. She, a little petite thing, no taller than his shoulders, and he, five-eight, five-nine at best. She made him feel tall.

She'd laugh all the time when she saw him in the hallways, like they had some secret joke going on. And in the library, it looked they were having a tête-à-tête, a romantic liaison, more than studying math formulas.

But I put all that out of mind, the wondering thoughts, as I had my own studies to do. My grades hinged on going to college in the fall, and I wanted nothing more than to leave the constant chaos of my home and get out on my own. Even though there was a quell in Mom's habit, and she and Dad were at least being civil to each other, I still had had enough.

~

I thought I was going to have the summer of all summers. My senior year, heading for college.

I had a job with some spending money. Trudy got me on waitressing at the same place as she worked. Although the hours were pretty shitty and Trudy and I didn't always get to work together, I did make some cash.

My relationship with Charlie, however, was like summer itself, full of expectations and hope, of warm summer breezes, soured by August. It rained all the time. The air cooled, the water got choppy, and so, too, did our love. It drifted away like the buoy that broke from its anchor.

I felt all this before I knew it and Charlie's smile was just as cool, but his heart and mind were elsewhere. As I was preparing for my next jour-

Karma

ney, he found his own and someone he'd prefer to be with, better than me.

She was everything I was not. She was chatty and outgoing. She matched him so perfectly, it was as if the gods were aligned to this match-making, only that I was in the crossfire.

By mid-August, he said he wanted to meet me, and I felt the doom before I saw it. The day was darkening and the storm clouds were forming. Even the rain was spitting at me as it hurled from the sky. An omen for sure.

But I was hopeful. Even all the times he didn't show when the group of us got together at the dock, or met at The Bullhorn. And when we were at the beach, somehow, Victoria would be there, off to the side, clad her in aqua-marine, teeny bikini. I'd catch him looking her way, finding no more solace or interest in what Allan was saying, or me. No more deep kisses or hand-held walks.

And when I met him, half hour before the designated time, because I felt there was something he was not telling me but was going to, I saw them. He held her hand, like the way he held mine. He stared directly at her, she at him. I heard her laugh drift across the wind. It was like the weather didn't even affect them.

I had taken shelter behind the outdoor stage. We were to meet on our bench, the one dedicated to the volunteer who helped erect the outdoor park here. We'd lie on it for hours—our sanctuary. Cuddle, fondle, kiss.

And I watched them, like a Peeping Tom, feeling sick to my stomach, wanting to scream as loud as I could for him not to be touching her like that, because he was mine and we were supposed to be together forever. Why was this happening? I couldn't breathe.

And then they stopped. She looked down at her wrist, and they spoke silently to each other and he leaned down and kissed her, deeply and romantically, and held her face the way he had held mine.

But nothing came out of my lungs as I cursed myself for being the way I was with him. He always made me speechless because everything I could possibly say did not sound right coming out. I didn't want to bore him with my trivial talk, instead let my mouth and hands do and say what I thought was rich communication.

She walked off with her hands in her pockets, looking back, smiling at him, and disappeared down the path. He stood by our bench. The rain had started falling. He stood hunched over, as if trying to protect himself from the impending storm.

And there was no way out for me. I either had to stay on the band shelter until he left, or jump off for him to see me. I was shaking and cold and angry and sad.

He turned to see if I was coming from the other direction from the one Victoria had taken, and that's when I made my move.

He didn't see me at first. I moved as fast as my legs would take me.

It was our first fight.

Our only fight.

I called him all sorts of names. I even tried to slap him, but instead, in my silent rage, stormed off like the weather.

He didn't have to say he was breaking up with me. He already had.

As my legs grew tired from walking, the little rain drops turned into a fat, flooding torrent, drenching me to the bone, and washing away the tears that were pouring just as hard.

~

I ran into him unexpectedly. Saw him at a distance maybe a half dozen times. One time he saw me and waved, but obviously he was in a rush to get to class, too. I didn't need to see him anyway.

Jimmy probably said five words to me the whole school year. Seemed funny we ended up at the same college. Didn't even know where he was applying. Knew he received lots of scholarships to go anywhere. Everyone seemed to want him. Everyone, except me.

I relished my time away. New school, new students, new studies. I found myself doing everything I could to occupy myself. Partaking in aerobic and gym classes, writing workshops, chess club. Almost anything and everything.

I got into a rhythm and found other things to fill my Charlie-less void.

"Someone better will come along," my dorm mates said. "Or, wait 'til you're really in love."

And then, of course, the inevitable happened. Mom and Dad split up, heading to divorce court. Something not totally unexpected but shocking to me all the same.

It was good they waited until I left the nest. They stayed together just to keep me balanced, they said.

Dad moved out, found a little apartment. And Mom...said she's selling the house, might move into a new space of her own.

"Uh huh," I said, non-nonchalantly, when they called and told me at the same time. "Sounds good, Mum. It will be good for you. And how about you, Dad? You must be dating someone new by now."

Karma

I really wasn't paying attention that time.

~

There he was, standing at the entrance to the gymnasium. Alannah Myles was singing one of her signature tunes. The place was jammed.

My floor decided to all wear the same outfit so we wouldn't lose each other. We wore neon-green t-shirts with black marker written all over them: Black Velvet on the front, Lover of Mine with a question mark on the back. An ode to our favourite singer.

I was at the back of the line and he grabbed me by the sleeve. I tried shaking him off, not knowing it was him right away. Not his usual style of getting someone's attention. He was obviously drunk.

"Twins?" he said aloud, bending over to scream in my ear.

I rolled my eyes. Twins are two, there were at least ten of us.

"Yep," I said, trying to blow him off.

"I see you settled in?"

"Yep," I said, really wanting to leave.

The girls disappeared into the crowd, swallowed up like Jonah by Moby-Dick. He kept attempting to make conversation. Funny thing though, I didn't even really know his voice.

"Want to dance?" He smiled at me, bent down, stared me in the eyes.

"No. I better go. I have to find my friends."

"What?" He hadn't heard a word I said.

"I want a drink," I screamed.

"Oh," he said, nerdishly, hands moving up and down. "Here."

He passed me a plastic cup of what looked like water. "Vodka and Sprite."

He kept bee-bopping up and down. Like he was having the best time. "Down that, I'll give you another." The drink tasted surprisingly good. Sweet, cold, no real taste of alcohol. I chugged it back.

"Atta girl." He winked at me and smiled.

He looked nothing like Charlie. The total opposite. Long, lanky, total book nerd, studious, got good grades. He may have played basketball. Charlie was more into the weights.

"Here," he said, and passed me another.

"What are you doing?" I asked. "You part of the bar service or something?"

I placed the second full cup into the empty I just finished and felt the start of a slight satisfying buzz. The lights were flashing, Alannah was

Trena Christie-MacEachern

belting, the crowd was singing.

A couple of guys stood beside us and started talking to Jimmy. They eyed me and poked Jimmy with their elbow. I rolled my eyes.

"This is Karmalita," Jimmy introduced me to the guys. "She's from back home. Now, we're going to dance."

And he wheeled me in front of him, pushing his fingers into my back, edging me through the crowd to the congested dance floor, and away from prying eyes.

~

"Karm!"

I heard him call my name. I was sitting at the back of the cafeteria with two gals from my Psych class, Louise and Ann.

"Who's that?" they chimed, as their heads readjusted on their shoulders. "He's kind of cute."

"He's gangly," I said sarcastically.

"I like them tall," cooed Ann, scooping her long hair in her palm and letting it flow over her right shoulder.

I felt the heat hit my face. God, watching him strut my way, so straight and tall, holding his tray so tight, so nerd-like.

"Mind if I sit in." Telling rather than asking, I thought.

I held out my hand. "Be my guest, not my chair."

"How you all doing?" he asked, before hoeing into his cold-cut sub and carton of milk. He even had an apple and two chocolate chip cookies.

He placed his sub down and introduced himself. "I'm Jimmy." He smiled at Ann, loosely shook her hands.

"Aah, Jimmy from the other night? The dancer?"

Jimmy nodded up and down, still inhaling his sub. He put his hand to his mouth and then picked up the milk, sucked almost all of it down.

"Yeah," he said with a laugh. "You guys have fun?"

"I think Karm did. Didn't you, Karm?" Ann was being playful. Bad. She pushed my shoulder. I was sitting with my arms crossed, resting my back against the chair.

Jimmy looked directly at me. "You had fun. I know you did. We danced pretty well all night."

"Well, the dancing was fun." I teased.

And the night was too. Once I got buzzed and the rest of my girls met up with us on the dance floor. We were all group dancing. But obviously Jimmy had forgotten about that.

58

Karma

When he went to get more drinks, we found our way to the either side of the gym. That was the last I saw of Jimmy that night.

"Then you disappeared," he said, still looking at me.

"Places to go, people to see," I said.

He nodded again, finishing off his sub and assessing his cookies. This guy didn't mess around even with his eating. Looked like he made sure to have all the food groups covered. He was kind of sickening.

I got up from my chair, signalled to the other girls it was time to go. Jimmy started to get up, too.

"You stay," I told him. "I have class shortly."

"You want to do coffee later?" he asked.

"Huh?"

"Coffee. At the Perk House?"

"Ah. I don't think, Jimmy. I have a paper to do."

"Well, be a good time to take a break. What time is your class over?"

I felt myself getting frustrated, angry. I didn't want to be rude, but I wasn't interested in this guy either. He was getting to be a pest.

~

And a pest he was.

Even after I told him no for the coffee. He found my room, left messages on my chalkboard, sought me out in the library, sat with me in the cafeteria.

But the girls all thought he was sweet and charming, with his hazel eyes and slim build and his polite, easygoing way. But this chatty Jimmy wasn't something I was used to. He had barely said five words to me our whole senior year.

But between Ann and Louise, my floor mates, and this desperate act of pursuing by Jimmy, they managed to get me to meet him at the coffee house a couple of weeks later. I was really in no mood. I was on my period, cranky, and had a mid-term coming up I was really worried about. I didn't have time for this shit.

But here he was, going on and on about stupid stuff, wearing jeans and a buttoned-down, white, casual shirt tucked in, a pair of loafers, a nice watch, looking totally handsome, while I wore my old sweats, a wrinkled t-shirt, my hair in a ponytail, and he was bringing me over my coffee.

He sat down beside me, smiled, with those teeth that had been perfectly aligned with braces. Looked like he just had a haircut and he smelled like soap and mild aftershave. Even sitting, he was taller than me. He had a long torso and even longer legs. His fingers engulfed the paper cup like eagle talons.

"Thanks for meeting me," he said, smiling, looking grateful, and even a bit cute.

But I couldn't even admit it then. I acknowledged by nodding.

"How's your coffee? Need more sugar or cream or—?"

"No, Jimmy. It's fine," I said, coolly. I hadn't put the coffee to my lips at this point.

I caught my reflection in the window, saw my serious expression with him trying to talk to me. To me, we looked like a couple breaking up. I started to laugh.

"What?" he said, touching my hand. I squirmed and shook my head.

"Nothing. It's nothing." I took a sip of the hot beverage. It tasted good. I held it in my mouth for a moment before swallowing.

"So, what's this about, Jimmy?" I was direct. I was rude.

He smiled though, looked embarrassed. "Ah. um. This is hard for me."

"What is?" I sat up looking into his eyes.

"This." He pointed a finger back and forth between me and him. "Trying to make small talk. Would help if you at least tried talking to me."

I let out a deep sigh and stood up. I didn't need to be dissed, ridiculed, when I didn't want to come here in the first place.

"Karm! I'm sorry. Sit down. Please, just sit down."

But I couldn't be bothered. I just huffed and set off.

He caught up to me of course, with those long legs and grabbed me by the arm. "You're not making this easy, Karm. Jeesh." And he looked all sad with those puppy dog eyes.

"What do you want, Jimmy? Just tell me what it is that you want."

"You," he said breathlessly. "I like you. I always liked you. I liked you from the very first time I saw you at The Bullhorn. My God, you took my breath away then. Even now."

His cheeks were reddening but I couldn't say anything.

"You took away my voice. Every time I wanted to say something, my voice would disappear. Do you know how many times I punched the wall or cursed myself because I couldn't find the words? I wanted to so bad. I loved your confidence, your independence, your look. Everything about you was perfect. And then...and then you ended up with Charlie because I couldn't even say hello. Charlie got you. Dickwad Charlie." He said his name in disgust. "He always got the girl. But Charlie being Charlie, screwed up, and so, here we are."

He was still holding onto my arm.

"And I still like you, Karm. A lot. And if you give me a chance, I'll show you how a girl should be treated. How you should be treated. Not neglected and tossed aside or hurt. You should be treated like royalty, because that's what you are. And I can't believe I just said all that because nothing really comes out of my mouth when I'm around you because you are just too beautiful for words."

He trailed off into a whisper and I felt his warm grip around my arm.

And whatever came over me, his words or his gesture, or his touch? Or the fact that he kept trying to be with me, despite me being my bitchiest to him, I just stood open-mouthed, eyes wide, in awe, until he finished talking and then, suddenly, like I didn't know it was going to happen, I went to him, into his arms and kissed him, long and deep right there, outside the Perk House for all to see.

~

I considered my relationship with Jimmy, initially, like a special friendship of sorts. I didn't need to pretend with him. I didn't want to. He saw me in all my moods and he still liked me regardless. I was kind of in awe of that.

We started out slow. I had moved so fast with Charlie this had to be different.

Jimmy gave me my space when I asked for it, but was there when I needed him too. He was kind and sweet and thoughtful, all those things you want but sometimes take for granted. He helped me with my studies and with my wash. He even knew how to do that. I laughed out loud when he told me not to wash sweaters with towels because it makes them pilly. He was a walking brain.

Sometimes he would sneak over to my dorm room and simply wait for me, patiently. He'd rest his head against the doorframe, tapping ever so gently so as not to annoy me.

I'd open the door and see his sleepy grin smiling down at me. He'd stay the night. We'd just cuddle and sleep—we really were the innocent couple. He didn't force or push anything on me. He said he'd wait and we did.

And I found I liked him. I really did. He really was a nice guy, maybe too nice for the likes of me. I deserved to be with someone damaged, someone like Charlie. So unintentionally, I attempted to sabotage my budding relationship with Jimmy just to show him I was not worthy.

Trena Christie-MacEachern

He deserved better.

He would be busy with his homework and finals or going home on holidays or long weekends to spend with his family, because he came from one of them good, happy homes, and I would hook up with other guys. I was searching. For what? I wasn't sure.

I needed to be loved in some capacity. I knew it was wrong but it was never anything serious. It was just sex, wasn't it?

I did, however, fall for this one guy who made me smile when I thought of him, and he had all the magic I felt with Charlie.

But he turned out to be a dud, too. He had a steady, and cheated on her with me and maybe others. He had all the right moves and the right things to say and I stupidly bought into all of it. I was used and it was my own fault, although I cried when I found out. It felt like Charlie had left me all over again.

I hated that feeling and deep down I think I deserved it. I deserved to be unhappy and so I continually punished myself.

I kept thinking of Charlie. I thought about him more than I wanted. More than I should. He crept into my mind at night, and sometimes even during the day when I'd be in class, seeing someone that reminded me of him walk by, or a shirt that resembled his or a certain brand of cologne. It always made my heart race and then disappointment would reign once more and I wondered, when?

When was this feeling ever going to go away? How do I break up with him, so I can have the final say? Will that make his spirit stop haunting me?

~

Now

Eric is on the ball. He had ordered us some dinner at The Bullhorn. Fish and chips, a side order of coleslaw. Everyone cleans their plates. We were hungrier than we thought.

I am on my third glass of wine, with a fourth already in front of me, knowing, this has got to be it. I feel like my mother suddenly, trying to drink away my sorrows.

I chat at length with Allan. He's just so devastated over Lotty—his true love and soulmate. They had been together for most of his life, and although the last few years had been really hard with her, her habit, he said he would take her back in a second, without question.

My heart aches.

Karma

Clyde had left, he had to work the next day and a family to get home too. He's still such a lovable guy. He can't talk enough about his kids and maybe, he says, he'll start on a fourth, winking at the guys, forgetting that I am there.

I interject, "Not smelling like that." I hold up his empty bottle. "You'll be in the spare room by yourself."

Everyone laughs. Even Allan gives a chuckle.

It's the four of us left: Eric, Allan, Charlie, and me, and I have seen enough of the bar. The regular patrons are starting to file in, the ones who drop in for a quick drink before they have to go home, or the ones who just spend whatever they have in their pockets. The ones who feel their only friends were the bottle, or the ones, like us, who stop in for nostalgia's sake.

Being one of the few females in the bar, I had been asked to dance quite a bit, usually the slow waltzes, which I would, as graciously as possible, decline. Answering any of these men with a quick 'no' response would open me to a backlash of slurs and obscenities. It's another reason to make tracks.

"Alright, everyone. Let's get outta' here," Charlie is the first to remark. It's almost if he read my mind and The Bullhorn had lived out its purpose.

Allan would follow anybody at this point, being pretty full. His body sways like a slender birch branch when the autumn winds blow in.

"Yes, I have to get going. It's getting late." I stand up, put on my coat, look down at my watch. It's already past six.

"You, young lady"—Allan hiccoughs—"are not going anywhere." He wags a finger at me and then trips over the leg of the chair and empties the rest of his glass on the table.

"Who-ops," he slurs. His bottom lip puckers as he enunciates the word. He reaches for a cigarette.

I look at Charlie and Eric and mouth silently, "I really should go."

They both nod and Charlie turns to Allan, "Come on, mate. You had a full day. Let's get you off your feet."

"We go-ing?" he mutters, then laughs. His eyes roll around in his head. He blows out some smoke. "WA-ere, we go–ing?"

"My house," Charlie says thoughtfully. "You're staying at my house."

Allan is a sorry sight. Crying one minute, laughing the next. I'm glad he was going to stay with Charlie. It wouldn't be good for him to be alone, tonight of all nights.

Eric and Charlie help Allan into the back of the cab. But before Eric

Trena Christie-MacEachern

hops inside, his phone rings. He points his index finger in the air and starts talking into the phone, his shoulders hunched.

"Something's come up guys." He waves us off. He said he'd meet up later, but knowing Eric, he won't.

Charlie says he doesn't live that far away. I focus my thoughts on Allan as Charlie gabs with the taxi driver.

We pull up to his house, which is small. A bungalow-style but looks well maintained. Light brick on the outside, little concrete walkway, shrubs, shutters. Everything neat and tidy.

The cab driver ends up having to help us take in Allan. And although the lad doesn't weigh much more than I do, it's a skill trying to get him into the house. Like lifting concrete.

We manage to get him into the spare bedroom. I take off Allan's boots and open his jacket. I try getting that off, but to no avail. I was going to take off his pants, but think I'd better not—not my department—and pull the covers over him instead.

When I come out, the cab driver is gone, and Charlie has opened himself a beer and poured me a glass of wine. I stand by the wall, watching him, my arms crossed. He is shaking his foot to an imaginary beat.

He reaches for his drink, and then notices me. "Come sit. I took the liberty."

"I should go, Charlie. My intention was to leave with the driver. Jimmy will be wondering."

"Then he should have come," he says sharply. He taps the leather seat. "Come onnn. Sit down. I won't bite. Stay. Tell me all your news. It's been a while." He holds up my glass.

I blush, feeling silly. Why do I always feel this away around him?

I shake my head, drop my bag and reach for the glass.

"Good to see you," he says pleasantly, and clinks his bottle to my glass. "You look great."

Feeling hot all of a sudden, I open my coat. I'm not sure if it's the wine or the compliment.

His eyes look down at my chest.

"Eyes up here, Charlie."

"Sorry." He smiles. That devilish grin. "Been a long time since I had anyone here."

"Really?" I say, confused. "And why is that? You have a nice place." I look around the room, stone fireplace, nice leather chair, big TV, even a fig tree, all green and lush.

He shrugs. "Yeah. I guess so."

Karma

"You guess so?" I laugh. "Honestly, Charlie. You have the world at your feet and you'd never know it."

He stares at me long and hard. "I'm sorry," he finally says. "For screwing up. I mean, I know we were just kids and all, but, I liked you. A lot. If that means anything now."

I try to dismiss the conversation. I don't know how to respond. This is not how I envisioned things playing out in my scripted internal dialogue.

"It's okay, Charlie. That was a long time ago. You and I have both moved on." I down the rest of my glass.

Charlie puts his drink on the counter, gets up and pours me some more. "I had a lot of shit going on then. I didn't know if I was coming or going. Vicki just sort of...took over. And being the dog that I was, let her. But you were the one that really mattered to me. I remember your face the day that we broke up. All I wanted to do was to put my arms around you and hug you and tell you that I was wrong."

"So why didn't you?" I feel angry all of a sudden. All the things I wanted to say, and now would be my chance.

He shrugs again. Smiles, with those pearly whites. He reminds me of a puppy that had done his business in the corner. "I'm an asshole. What can I say? I knew it wouldn't last with Vicki. She was a world away from me. She was going places and I knew I couldn't keep up."

I laugh out loud. "And I wasn't?" I know he didn't mean for it to be an insult, but that's how it came out.

"Nnnooo nooo." He shakes his head. His fingertip lightly grazes my thigh. I feel the warmth come through my stockings and it sends me shivers. "I mean, I wasn't the man for her. I wasn't enough. I knew this even back then."

"Charlie. None of this makes sense. Why didn't you just end it then and move on?"

He looks at me with those sad, blue eyes, "Because I didn't want to look the fool," he whispers. "My ego was bruised. I let it happen because I was just too...I'm damaged, Karma. There are things you don't know."

He trails off and walks into the kitchen.

I follow him, grab him by the arm, his strong, muscular arm. "What do you mean?" I ask.

He spreads out his arms on the counter and speaks in the quietest of voices. "My father was an alcoholic. And abusive. I can't tell you how many times I got a broken bone from a punch or a push. My mom got the worst of it."

I remember a scar I used to trail my finger on down his arm. I thought

65

Trena Christie-MacEachern

it was from falling off his bike when he was younger.

"Did the guys know this?"

He nods. "But not the girls. I didn't want the girls to know because I didn't want the pity. Maybe that's why Mom stayed with my father, because she pitied him. He was all right when he was sober. I remember the two of them laughing, whispering together. Even nights when the two of them, would"—he looks at me, embarrassed—"you know? And that would confuse the hell out of me because she could be black and blue from being his punching bag to fucking his brains out the next night. I hated that man. God, how I hated that man."

"So? What happened?" I blurt.

Charlie closes his eyes. His face looks full of pain. His hands form fists and his veins pop in his neck. "Dad was on a bender for a couple of days. I wanted Mom to leave because I knew what was going to happen. I told the guys to come over so we could help get Ma out. But when I came home, she was already in a heap on the floor. God, there was blood everywhere. I didn't know if she was dead or not, and he screamed when he saw me, 'Come here you mother-fucker, you're next!' I remember my hair standing on the back of my neck and I ran into the living room. He was swinging his fists and got me on the back of the head."

He runs his hand over the spot where he had been hit. "That hurt like a son-of-a-bitch, but if I fell down, I knew I'd get it worse. I jumped over the table and ran to the basement. He caught me by the arm and that's when I saw my baseball bat on the corner of the stairs. I managed to get hold of it and when he came over to me, I swung it as fucking hard as I could. I heard the wind knock out of him and a crack, like something broke, and I moved. He fell like Jack and the Beanstalk's giant going down them stairs."

I stand open-mouthed and breathless. My eyes can't open any wider. I touch his arm and his fists release.

"Oh my God, Charlie," I gasp.

He shakes his head. "I ran out of there. Ran to Allan's as fast as I could."

"Did they show up? The guys?"

He shakes his head, looks solemn. "I thought I should go back, check on my Mom, make sure she was okay. But Allan told me not to. Said it would sort itself out."

"And, did it?"

He nods. "Kind of. Turned out, my Dad died that night. They called it a domestic dispute. Self-defence. Mom didn't know what happened. Didn't remember any of it."

"And you didn't tell her the difference?"

"Jesus. How could I?"

"Holy fuck."

"It was bad. Just a bad scene. But then, instead of getting better, the bitch, she gets on drugs 'to cope.'" He uses his fingers as quotation marks. "And I just thought, if I'm nice an' make everyone happy, then things will be okay. I'll be okay."

And I think of that first day that I laid eyes on this fella, the boy with the mega-watt smile and cool demeanour, but instead was hurting and trying to hide it. Charlie the charmer. "Oh, my God, Charlie. I'm so sorry."

"And then I met you. And I knew things were going to be good. And when I f-ed up, because that's what I do, I led Jimmy to your door. And those babies you have, should have been my babies that we made to-gether. I'm a fool, Karma. And Jimmy knows it."

"That's why you were angry at him? At me, when I showed up at the funeral?"

Charlie nods. "He took advantage of me when I was down. He knows that. But what can I do? It was my fault. I'm to blame. But Jimmy and I are at odds now, but don't worry about it. It's not about you. I mean it is, but you can't blame yourself. My stupid fault. So, I don't have anyone here, because, well..."

I gasp. He doesn't want anybody because I'm the body that he wants but can't have. And I think of all those times that I had pined for this man. Would have died for this man, and all the times I imagined being with this man. If only I had known his story. If he had told me...

"I—I don't know what to say, Charlie."

He opens his fridge, takes out a beer and the wine and starts to pour me another glass. He starts to cry. He bows his head and weeps.

I don't know what to do. I touch his arm.

After a bit he stops, wipes his face with his fingers. "Sorry," he says. He passes me my drink, then stares at me longingly.

We just look at each other for the longest time and then, simultan-eously, put our drinks down on the counter without saying anything. We go to each other, hard. Lips meet lips, entwined embrace, hands touching the familiar, remembering when this was the real thing. The real deal.

Oh, how I fought this feeling for so long. How I loathed this man. How I wanted to erase this man from my memory.

And as his tongue grazes my bottom lip, I know I'm done for.

7

Now

Motherfucker!

I bolt upright in sheer panic, like I had forgotten to breathe. And when I see my naked body, I let out a muffled scream.

What have I done?

I glance at the person beside me, and there Charlie lies, snuggled into his pillow, sleeping so peacefully, with the most serene expression on his face.

I want to kill him! I want to kill me!

What the hell happened here? I'm drawing a complete blank, but when I see my bra flung over the lampshade, it confirms the obvious.

I cover my face with my hands and cringe. Disgust is hard to swallow, but betrayal is unforgivable.

It glares four-eleven on the clock and it is still dark. I don't want to wake the man I just cheated with. I want to disappear.

I had slept with other men before Jimmy and I married, but that was different. I can't believe this has happened now. Now, of all times! Especially at Lotty's post funeral with...*oh my God! With Allan in the other room.*

If I had a rubber mallet, I'd hit myself in the head before crawling back into the hole that I must have just come out of. *Jesus.*

One nanosecond at a time, I edge out of the bed so as not to awaken my nemesis beside me. The mattress is so thick and high, I have to lengthen my leg and precariously stretch out my big toe to feel for the floor. I have to be precise. I have to slither away unnoticed, unheard. From start to finish, everything about this night is a circus. And to top it all off, Jimmy will be wondering what has happened to me.

Oh, Jimmy!

I squint my eyes and try not to think about him. Shaking my head, however, makes me realize the dull ache that is starting to pound at my

Karma

temples is going to get worse. My tongue is sticking to the roof of my mouth and I could cry for a glass of water and maybe hire The Amazing Kreskin to erase the day and have a do over.

But...maybe Charlie will have no idea what has happened either? Maybe if I can just get my things and get out before he wakes up—with all the drinking and the grief and the late night, and Allan...? If I could drag Allan into Charlie's bed somehow, it would surely confuse the hell out of him. I almost snigger at my pathetic thought.

Actually, I'd prefer to plead the fifth and call it insanity. What else can it be? *What the hell is wrong with me?*

I finally make it to standing on the carpet, albeit buck naked. I begin by carefully peeling my bra from the lamp shade and, with that in hand, I hunt for my other things: undergarments, dress, stockings, shoes, purse.

Did we stumble in here from the kitchen? Or was it a slow, seductive, sauntering move to the bed? Both thoughts give me the prickles and I feel a wave of nausea.

I tiptoe towards the end of the bed. My dress is in a heap on the floor. No stockings. I am on my hands and knees, fumbling, feeling like an idiot.

I slip my dress over my head and decide I'll have to go without my stockings or underwear, but then I catch a glimpse of what could be light fabric under Charlie's side of the bed, and reach out. I feel the familiar texture of soft cotton.

Immediately my body heats up and I want to curl into a ball. I want to turn inside out. I can't move. I can't breathe, but somehow, I find my strength and stand up.

A strong hand grabs my hip. I stiffen.

"Hey," he breathes softly. "What are you doing?"

His other hand holds my side and he shuffles me back to the bed.

This isn't happening. This isn't happening, I say to myself.

"What's wrong?" he asks, sitting up, reaching for the light.

"Shush," I say rudely. "I have to go."

He digs his nose into my side. I feel his warm fingers. My stomach is in my throat.

"Stay. Stay with me," he pleads.

He kisses me through the fabric of my dress, runs his hand up my leg. I'm clammy and hot.

He manages to turn the light on and I click it off just as quick. I don't want to see him. I don't want to imagine what we've done here. I can't look at him. *Christ's sake, I'm married!*

"What are you doing?" He laughs. "You look beautiful. You always look

Trena Christie-MacEachern

beautiful."

My back is against him. He is trying to fully sit up.

"I'm sorry, Charlie. Shit. This should have never happened."

"Don't say that. It was meant to. You know this."

I take his hands off me and step out of reaching distance, then see my stockings stretched out on the floor in front of me. I scoop them up. Roll them around my hand and wrist like a boxer getting ready to fight.

"Jesus, I have to go."

"All right," he says. "I'll drive you."

"No!" I say a bit too loud, then whisper, "No, Charlie. You won't. I'll—" I scan my brain. *How the hell can I get home at this hour?* "Do you live by any 7-Elevens?"

Charlie turns the light back on. I am temporarily blinded. "Karma, I'll drive you home."

"No. No, you won't! You're not driving me anywhere. Just answer my question." I feel tears coming into the corners of my eyes. I feel like I am losing my mind.

"All right, all right. Yes, a couple of blocks away."

"What direction?"

"What? God, Karma, relax."

And seeing him, all toned and tousled hair and sleepy eyes, I am torn between wanting to scratch his eyes out and wanting to throw myself on top of him again. I just have to get the hell out of here.

"Can you call me a cab? Just tell him to meet me there, at the 7-Eleven? Please, Charlie? Can you do this for me?"

I realize I am no longer whispering, but talking loud, forgetting Allan is among us.

I scan the room quickly for my bag and coat. My shoes must be out in the entrance.

Charlie follows me out in his boxers, putting a t-shirt on as he walks. I notice my wine glass still sitting on the island. The bottle of whatever it was that I was drinking looks empty, plus there are beer bottles scattered about the counter.

Charlie goes into the kitchen. I hear him pick up the phone and, a few moments later, gives an address.

I stuff my underthings into my bag, put on my coat, find a ponytail holder in my pocket and wrap the elastic around my hair.

I open the door without saying anything and Charlie grabs hold of me again, brings me back inside.

He hugs me close, kisses the top of my forehead, whispers, "When can

Karma

I see you again?"

I look at him for a second. "Never, Charlie. Never again."

Just then, Allan cries out, "Lotty? Is that you? Where are you? Come back to me."

Then a pause. Charlie looks toward Allan's room.

I slip off into the night, hearing our friend's anguish. "Oh, Lotty, oh, Lotty. Why'd you leave me?" His voice cracking with torment and pain.

~

Of course, no one would be the wiser at first. It was a funeral after all. A friend's funeral. Everyone was there. Everyone except Jimmy. Even Trudy managed to find time and flew in. Clyde, who had three kids, was there; Eric with the second wife.

Jimmy won't ask, I tell myself. Figured we did what we always did. Drank too much, stayed up too late, too drunk to drive home. He knows the routine. Like clockwork.

But waiting for the God-forsaken cab to turn up outside the 7-Eleven at that time of the morning with the cold stinging my legs, my bare legs, made me not think of Jimmy, but my Dad. My attention drifts off to him, wondering why I did such a thing.

Am I just like him? Was it because it happened to us as a family? His be-trayals? So many of them.

The memories come flooding back like I'm watching a video on re-wind.

I always thought my parents had a good relationship. We lived in a great house, a two-story with four bedrooms in a nice, rural community where everyone knew everyone. Small and quaint. We had vacations and family get-togethers and my parents' friends would often come over. I re-call going to other kids' birthdays and christenings.

There was always supposed to be more kids. But as it got harder and harder for Mom to have children, and the fertility drugs not doing what they were supposed to, the rift started.

All the times I was handed an ice cream and an extended movie be-cause 'the time is now'. The looks they exchanged as they closed the door behind them. "You all right, honey? We'll just be a minute." All the times I overheard, "Not now. I'm not in the mood. What's the point?" And had not understood.

The tears fall hard and fast.

After Josh, it was pretty much over. Having more children was just not in the cards for my mother despite wanting them and praying for them, and even going for the extra medical procedures didn't guarantee squat. Sometimes I would be hugged and caressed and bestowed with gifts. Other times, I was left totally alone and wondered if I was cared about at all. It was a confusing time.

And when Mom fell into her deep hole after Joshua, like a huge meteor had fallen out of the sky and created a rut so vast, I didn't think she would ever come back. I felt like a pinball machine that eventually no one wanted to play with.

"Come on, Cathy. Have a sip. It will make you feel better," Grandma encouraged. She held an amber-coloured liquid, the ice cubes clinked inside one of the crystal glasses we used at Christmas-time or on fancy occasions. Mom would be in a ball on the couch, looking like she had slept there for the umpteenth night.

"Run along, Karmalita. You go to your room, now. Mom's okay."

Grandma would smile that fake smile as she took a sip out of her drink, waiting for Mom to join her.

I wondered for the longest time if Mom's drinking or her depression was the reason for Dad's infidelity. Or if it was bound to happen anyway. Was that act of the marriage such a big part of the scene? Like brushing your teeth and not flossing? Would your teeth fall out if you didn't do both?

To prove my ridiculous theory I did just that, brushed and did not use floss. My teeth didn't fall out. The world didn't fall apart.

The cab finally arrives and I get in, tell him my address. He doesn't say anything as to why I'm out this late and I'm thankful, although it would have been good practice.

"My friend died," I blurt, holding my coat close to my neck even though it's my bare legs that are cold.

He nods. "Sorry for your loss."

I ask him to turn up the heat. He reaches for the dial and cranks it, as I am obviously shivering.

"What he die from?" the driver asks as he glances my way momentarily. "Cancer? Everyone dies of cancer."

"No," I say. "Drug overdose."

He looks at me again, this time glancing down at my legs. Suddenly, I'm uncomfortable. I should have said the cancer, but why lie? Although that's what I'll be doing when I get home.

I think about my Dad's affairs again.

I remember his sweet and bubbly co-worker from the office at the ra-

Karma

dio station when Mom was home drunk, or stewed, or sulking, or depressed. I had to go there for a school project: Tell us about your family. And everyone knew that Mom was a nurse but that gig was over after the accident.

"Karm, you remember Susie?" Dad sounded different. He sounded happy.

"Thought it was Susan," I said.

She smiled wide—a hint of lipstick on a front tooth. "No, just Susie." She flipped her hair back.

Susie the floozie. Tight shirt, tight pants, lipstick too bright for her face and that wide smile that made me feel sick, like eating too much candy floss and your stomach goes in knots. I think I knew right away. The way Dad whispered to her when she was leaving his office. The way he held her arm and escorted her to the door. The way they shared a private joke, or a wink before he closed the door, or he watched as she walked off.

Everyone knew.

He was beaming like a school boy, the way Tommy smiled when he got to put his hands down Big Barbara's top and got to feel her up. Everyone knew. Even though Big Barbara didn't know everyone knew.

And when Dad came home late or had to suddenly go back to the office because Susie needed help with something, he'd change his shirt and give Mom a peck on the top of the head, I suspected she knew then, too, but didn't care. She was too grief-stricken or too pickled to care. She couldn't even wash her own hair, for God's sake. What difference did it matter that her husband was off screwing someone else?

And I think Mom would have been okay even then with Dad doing what he was doing because he wasn't bothering her. But after she killed that boy and I started to get grief from it at school, their parental instincts kicked in. I'm still not sure exactly why they stayed together at that point. It would have made just as much sense to go their own ways.

I tell myself to shake it off, walk in like it's nobody's business and I have nothing to hide. Charlie won't say anything. He'll scamper off like a cockroach when the sun comes out. And Allan? Poor Allan—too drunk and comatose to know the difference.

And Jimmy? Well, Jimmy simply won't ask. He never does. About anything. The weather, my day, what's for supper, what are we doing this weekend? Nothing. He just is, goes with the flow, as easy and accommodating as a high-end hotel chain.

But there will be a cost. There is always a cost, whether you can afford

73

Trena Christie-MacEachern

it or not.

I push in the key, breathe, tiptoe inside my house. It's after five and Jimmy will be getting up in another hour and a half. Mariah and Paulie sometime after seven.

In the kitchen I grab the bottle of aspirin, pop two of those, followed by a large glass of tepid water. I drink it so fast I feel it's going to come back up.

I place my bag on the table, then take it off. Not knowing where to put anything—trying to seem as normal as possible.

The spare room: I'll, sleep there. He'll think I'm mad. Angry at him for not coming.

Perfect. A diversion. He'll never suspect. Then I can sleep it off. He won't bother me. When I wake, I'll shower. Clean myself up. Get the smell of him off me.

Shuddering, I sniff my sleeve. I can't tell if I smell like him or not.

I grab my balled-up underwear out of my bag, slip them on, pull off my earrings and watch, place them on the table, throw back the sapphire-blue comforter and slip under it. I don't bother getting changed, just wear my dress to bed.

I doze off into a deep, mindless slumber.

~

Then

"What's wrong?" he asked, studying me with those hazel eyes. I had been quieter than usual. Still trying to shake off the fact that I had been cheated on by another loser.

"Nothing," I said casually. "Just tired."

He was in tune with me, even though I didn't realize it then. He said you can tell a lot by just watching a person. Which was what he used to do with me. I'd be reading or doing a paper, and find him staring at me from across the room, or when he sat beside me on the couch.

He'd smile and tell me I was beautiful, then go back to what he was doing, but I'd catch him again later. I used to think it was odd at first, creepy. But it was just his thing.

I told him he'd make a good detective.

He'd laugh. "Not enough money in that," he'd say.

So, with his degree, and his love of drawings, Jimmy became a civil engineer and then eventually, a partner in the firm. He was that good. Level-headed, cool, focused, uninhibited by drama.

Karma

"You looked like you've been crying," he said, a little more forcefully, which was not like him. Often, he just ignored me when I showed any emotion.

"I haven't been," I lied. "It's allergies. The pollen gets me this time of year."

He nodded like he agreed, even though I knew he probably didn't. "So, you're okay with Charlie, then?"

"Huh?" I looked at him. *What does Charlie have to do with me?* I thought. Charlie hadn't crossed my mind in ages. "What are you talking about?"

I was starting to get angry. Then I pulled out a tissue from my pocket and blew my nose, just to show him that it was allergies.

"Charlie and Vicki are getting married."

I froze, and he watched me freeze. He watched every agonizing moment. It was like he socked me in the stomach.

"You didn't know? You really didn't know?"

"Of course, I didn't know, Jimmy. How would I know? I'm not involved in Charlie's life anymore. Why would you think otherwise? God!"

I stared at him, watching him watch me. "Do you get off on this kind of thing?"

And I was shocked and felt betrayed because a part of me still loved that son-of-a-bitch, and Jimmy telling me threw me. Just threw me.

So now I couldn't concentrate on Andrew, but Charlie, who just seemed to keep popping up in my life when I thought it was over.

I just slammed my book closed, got up and walked away. I couldn't stand any more of Jimmy's shit. And as I walked, my vision blurred and the hot wetness ran down my face. *Oh, for fuck's sake, stop it. Stop it, you ninny.*

Charlie was gone out of my life for longer than when he was in it. But he moved on so quickly. They weren't even together for very long.

And I sobbed 'til my face hurt and I didn't care at that point who was seeing me. College kids cried all the time over grades or heartbreak or stress.

And when I got back to my room, there was a note to call Trudy. Because of course Trudy knew and was looking out for me.

I called her when I was sort of composed, and I blew my nose when she answered the phone.

"I wish I was there. You doing okay?" she breathed, all calm and graceful.

"Tell her it's a good thing. Holy fuck," Suzanne barked in the background.

"Do you want us to come out? I can be there tomorrow after classes. I have a paper, but after that?"

"Yes, please come. I'd love to see you and have you here. Both of you."

And when they came, it was like Mardi Gras and Christmas all into one. It felt like the return of part of my soul that was missing.

God, I missed these two, and the first thing Suzanne wanted to do was to go out. So, we did.

First, to the campus bar, where I drank way too many beer and shooters. Followed by the Primrose downtown. A hot spot if you wanted to dance and hook up.

But it just seemed like I was filling a void, had been since forever. Since my Mom and Dad moved me to a new place, since they divorced, then Charlie and our break up, and coming here to college, and Jimmy, and trying to figure out what I wanted to do.

"How does anyone know what they want to do at this age?" I mouthed drunkenly to Suzanne and the bartender she was trying to scoop. *Why is she always with bartenders?* I laughed. "I'm doing a B.A. and then what? What!"

I screamed. "What is there after that? Maybe I'll be a drunk like my mother or a whore like my father."

I laughed, tipped my glass back, tripped and that's when I noticed Jimmy. He was standing there, steady as a stone, watching my every move. He reminded me of one of those mannequins at the department store.

He went to Trudy, bent down, whispered something to her.

I gave him the middle finger. "Get away," I slurred, "because you are as emotionless as..." I couldn't think of what was emotionless. "A fish," I finally yelled. "Like a goldfish. You just eat and shit. And study."

The whole time, Trudy was tugging on his shirt sleeve and talking to him while he was staring at me. Then I turned away and saw this cute, blond boy and started dancing with him.

The guy moved in on me and I let him. The two of us necked on the dance floor, then Jimmy turned around and left.

I woke up with such a hangover the next day I couldn't even breathe. Trudy was her usual self, giggly, watching TV, going to the store for Ginger Ale and popsicles for me.

Suzanne showed up later that afternoon, all relaxed and happy. "Holy fuck. When you gonna learn, girl?" she spouted at me, as she stuck her head in my room. "You can't drink, Karm. May as well stop trying."

Karma

And she was right. No matter how many times, I would get deathly sick. Sometimes for days. If it taught me one thing, I was never going to be like my mother.

It did tell me, however, that perhaps I was more like my father. I couldn't drink, but I could whore. I cringed. I'd rather drink.

But I knew in my heart that I would never become a mother. It just wasn't in the genes and I was totally convinced of that. Because even though I wasn't sure how many encounters my father had after he left my mother, or even while he was with her, he didn't come home with any other offspring. I never did have any half brothers or sisters. Therefore, my father was infertile just as much as my mother. And I left it at that.

Trudy and Suzanne left me with all the remedies for a hangover. Sodas and aspirin, pizza and popsicles, water and sleep. Eventually, I did get better.

And I did run into the blond guy who I made out with at The Primrose, but I didn't really remember him. He came up to me at study hall and smiled at me and I ignored him, only for him to come to me again at meal hall and start the whole thing all over again.

It was during dinner when Jimmy came up to him, tapped him on the shoulder and told him to beat it.

The blond guy gave Jimmy a hard time, said, "if she's your girlfriend, how come I practically had her shirt off and my tongue down her throat?"

I didn't see it coming. Certainly, the blond dude didn't either. Jimmy hauled off and smashed him in the face.

The guy whimpered like a baby goat, held his palm to his gushing nose. Jimmy strutted off with those long giraffe-like legs, and I did all I could to catch up with him, whether he wanted me to or not.

I was so confused. But I followed him, because Trudy told me, even Suzanne in her gruff way, that Jimmy was the guy who I should hold on to. He was the guy who idolized me but made them promise never to say a word.

I had to find out myself. That he would walk over hot coals for me while Charlie would make me take him piggyback. That he would wait until the end of time for me, and then some, because he knew that I was it for him.

And none of this made sense to me. I didn't know who I was, or what I was, or what I would become. I came from a broken home, an alcoholic mother who had killed a young man, and a father who couldn't hold a job but slept with anything that walked.

Trena Christie-MacEachern

How did Jimmy know that I was right for him? The only thing that I was sure of was that Jimmy was smart. He had a sixth sense for things. He was good at school, and books, could hold a job, could provide and support, would never see me stranded or alone, and, for some unknown reason, loved me.

By the time I caught up with him, he was just getting to his dorm room. He turned and stared at me like I was a bit of dust just floating in the air.

"Jimmy," I said breathlessly, "I'm sorry."

He didn't say a word, just opened the door and stood at the other side of the threshold.

"How do I tell you I'm sorry? Because I am. I really am. I've been such a fool."

My chest heaved in and out, mostly because I was winded from running. I was crying though, too, not sobbing, just salty tears streaming down my face and dotting my pink cotton shirt. "I don't know why I mess up. It's the only thing I'm good at. I don't deserve you, either."

He looked down at me with those wise eyes, not saying a word, which always left me uncomfortable because I didn't know what he was thinking.

I went to walk away and then he reached for my hand, pulled me inside his room and closed the door. His bent down to kiss me, his lips meeting mine, and he unbuttoned my shirt.

That night, while I attempted to make amends to the only boy who really truly cared for me, he took advantage in the only way a boy knows how. Nine months later, we became parents of a healthy seven-pound two-ounce girl we named Mariah.

8

Then

Allan helped me tell my folks.

Of course, Jimmy wanted to come. He felt it should be him doing the telling. He wanted to do everything the right way, but Allan, having such a good rapport with my mom, felt it was better if he broke it to her first. He was like the son she didn't have, and she treated him as such; and, ironically, it was Allan who helped save my mother.

There was just something about Allan that resonated with her, even after their first encounter. Whether it was something my mother saw, or felt, whether it was an ingrained sadness, or a lost soul searching that revitalized her zest for helping the sick or afflicted. And being a nurse, mom needed to fix things. And she needed to fix Allan.

None of us saw anything in Allan that needed fixing. He was a kind sap, friends with everyone and in love with Lotty.

But Mom knew cycles, how being alone without a father could lead you down a destructive path, and she wanted to get it licked before it started.

When Mom first saw Allan face to face, it looked like she had seen a ghost. I couldn't put my finger on it, and long after he left that day, she didn't go to the bottle like she usually did. Instead, I found her in the basement, looking for something. She was down there for hours and I didn't question her.

Every day thereafter, for weeks, I'd find her in the basement, going through our old things: pictures, albums, old toys, games, newspaper articles. There were so many stacks of old newspapers.

Yes, the woman even kept those, for some significant date or another. The day Elvis died, my first birthday, when the tornado touched down, when Mr. Ashley lost his barn and all the horses that were in it, the day Josh didn't come home—how she managed to find time for that—and of course, the day she ran over Daniel Timmons.

Trena Christie-MacEachern

It was like she was revisiting memory lane. Something jump-started her determination to face those tragic incidents.

And then, lo and behold, she found a graduation picture of the cyclist, albeit a bit blurry, sort of looking like our Allan. Not an exact match. Allan's eyes were smaller and his jaw too square and the hair a bit flat and lengthy, but it could pass as a possible brother or cousin of sorts.

And this explained to me my mother's demeanour. Did she think Daniel Timmons came back in another form? Her shot at redemption? A chance to fix all the doomed years and restart a part of her life?

And in a way it did, although it was too late for Dad at this point. The past was too hard, and too hurtful, the mourning and crying and heartache and affairs. He had moved on emotionally, physically, psychologically.

And I guess I couldn't blame him. Strangely, they seemed more at peace with each other after Dad moved out. They buried the hatchet, even though I was a reminder of their failed past.

Mom seemed to be calmer, too, when Allan was around, which was why he had to come with me in the first place. Their relationship seemed almost symbiotic, for her anyway. Helping him helped her.

Right after graduation, Mom set her sights on helping Allan get a decent job because his number one priority was to put Lotty through university as debt-free as possible. Mom was able to get Allan on at a transport dealership hauling furniture, cars, machinery, lumber.

He was such a likeable guy and a good worker, honest and loyal, it seemed everyone did what they could to keep him, even if there wasn't a whole lot of work to be had at the time. They'd find other things for him to do, whether it was janitorial duties, answering the phones, or driving the boss's kid and his team to their soccer games across town.

~

"She's knocked up."

That was the gentle way Allan told my mother of my situation.

With a sharp intake of air, I started hacking on my tea. I thought we would be discussing his job, or my school, or the weather first. Not simply blurt out what was my present condition.

"Allan! If I knew that was your lead-up, I wouldn't have invited you at all."

But that's how Allan was. To the point. No dancing around.

"Tissue," I pleaded, as my coughing induced tears.

Karma

"Who's the father?" Mom asked over her eye glasses. She was still standing by the stove, already putting on a second pot.

"It's Jimmy. You met him. Good guy. Really smart," Allan said, between inhales.

Mom's eyebrows raised again. "If he's so smart, shouldn't he know about a woman's fertile period."

I rolled my eyes.

"Maybe you should put that out, Allan." She looked in my direction. "For Karm and all."

"Course, course." Allan dubbed out his cigarette.

"Well, then," Mom said, sitting down beside me. "You're pregnant." She looked down at my stomach, even though I wasn't showing yet.

I reached for a napkin, blotted my face and then grabbed one of her cookies. I suddenly felt nervous, now that we had disclosed my life-altering event. Had I really thought this through? I nodded and then stuffed the cookie in my mouth.

"I think that boy has only been here twice since you started seeing him."

"Yeah, I know." Through munches, "he's so busy."

"You're keeping it." It was more of a statement than a question. Her small eyes assessed my face, while her long fingers cupped her mouth.

The way she studied me while she asked these pertinent questions made me wonder about her. How did she really feel about my situation? Was she excited or upset? I was too afraid to ask. This air between us—had it changed? The years of her wanting what I did simply by accident, did it make her angry? Or feel like a failure?

Would she resent me now after all those years she stayed with Dad for me?

These questions were not helping my psyche.

But since the introduction of Allan, Mom seemed more like her whole self, getting clean and taking on a new role of Substance Abuse Counsellor for those like her, feeling a connection on some deeper level with Allan than even I couldn't understand, but welcomed.

She waited for my response.

"Um, yeah. Jimmy's Catholic."

I paused, waiting to drop the next bomb.

"His folks know yet?"

"He wants all of us to tell them together."

Then Allan blurted, "They're gonna get married."

Trena Christie-MacEachern

~

Now

I jolt awake yet I'm worn out, confused. Where am I?

I hear the rat-a-tat-tat of gunfire, thinking I had left on an old war movie. *Wait! I don't watch war movies. Don't like them.*

I open an eye. I see Paulie sitting on the edge of the couch playing Mortal Combat on the X-Box. His Dad's. Paul is sitting cross-legged, his tongue is hanging out.

There is a half-empty bowl of Mini Wheats next to him. No milk. He is barefoot and wearing his old Spiderman pyjamas, which are too small for him but he likes how they feel against his skin.

He's going to be tall like his father. Zones out like him, too, especially when he is playing this mind-numbing game.

"Oh, Paulie, can you turn that down, please?"

There is a bomb blast which sounds like thunder. I hear the subtle tweak of fingers on the controller.

"Paul?"

Without even answering, he turns down the volume.

"Why are you home today? You not feeling good?"

My head is throbbing and I can't fully open my eyes. It feels like my lids are sealed shut—eye infection? Or a crying jag?

I wipe out the crusty buildup of gunk that collects in my lash lines. My lower torso feels funny and I realize my dress is wrapped around my body three times. It's so twisted, it's starting to cut off circulation.

"Hey, Mom," Paul manages to utter. His tongue is now protruding to the left side of his mouth as he concentrates on slaughtering the enemy with rifle power. Red fills the screen. "It's Saturday."

"Jesus, Paul. That's your father's. You're not supposed to be playing that."

"Mom! You said a bad word."

"Oh, sorry, Paulie."

I sit up. My feet are dangling, my dress is twisted and I feel as bad as I look. "Where's your dad?"

"Run"—*Boom!* Another grenade goes off—"ning."

It's time to hit the shower.

~

My hair is wet. Water drips down my back. I have my clean track pants on with a white Group Power t-shirt. I don't bother to put my hair in a ponytail. The force of having it pulled back from my forehead is a bit too much for me to take right now. I have taken two more Advil and not feeling a lick of it is working.

I sit at the kitchen table, having taken off my makeup from last night, but my eyes feel like two slits, swollen and sore. My neck muscles are out of whack, I have pains up and down my legs, an ache in my lower back, my head hurts, I'm trying to keep what little I have in my stomach down, and I have the shits.

It is exactly what I deserve.

I am nursing a tea with sugar when Jimmy gets in from his run.

"Whoa," he says, looking at me cautiously, assessing, twisting his face this way and that.

I can smell him, his sweat, mixed with his usual body odour and deodorant, the Tide I use to launder his jogging shirt. It is too much for me. I gag. I raise my hand to my mouth, try not to move.

"Jesus. How much did you drink?"

I can't answer him. If I shake my head, I know I'll vomit.

"Did you eat at all?"

"Yep," I whisper.

"You never learn, do you, Karm?" He chuckles, then gets serious. "Not good, Karm. Not good."

He takes off his runners then stands looking at me again. I can see the beads of sweat on his body, the glistening of his skin. He is trim and fit, making sure to exercise, run, swim, play tennis, or racquetball, basketball as often as he can. He leans in to kiss me on my damp forehead.

I extend an arm. "No," I practically bark.

He stops midpoint. "Sorry." He lifts his shirt to his nose, sniffs. "Yeah, I'd puke, too. I'll shower then make you breakfast. Maybe eggs or—?"

I run down the hallway, beating him to the bathroom. Poor Jimmy, thinking his stench is what setting off my stomach.

But sweetheart, it's not your smell, it's your rotten wife and what she did.

I puke into the toilet. My stomach is aching, my throat is raw. I should die this way. Let an artery rupture and be done with this agony. I don't deserve Jimmy and he certainly doesn't deserve me.

I cry pathetically into the porcelain bowl as he rubs my sweaty back. I don't even have the energy to ask him to leave.

Trena Christie-MacEachern

~

Then

We had a simple Catholic ceremony. My parents were there along with Dad's new woman, and Jimmy and his family.

Jimmy's brother, Tim, stood with him. I asked Trudy to stand with me.

They told me to dress conservatively. A skirt and jacket. It was cream-coloured. I wore pearls around my neck, my hair tied in a bun and I carried a small simple bouquet.

Jimmy wore the suit he had from his high school graduation. His boutonniere was a white carnation and I realized, as we said our vows, how I hated it. Such a cheap, plastic-looking flower. It didn't symbolize love.

Nothing about this union symbolized love. A rushed wedding to keep things hidden. I couldn't even wear a formal dress as I've ruined the show.

We moved into a small apartment. "Jimmy will finish his degree," his parents stated. Without question.

I hoped to as well. I'd continue as long as I could before the baby comes.

I got almost 'til Christmas of my second year. The rest, however, was a blur. Terrible labour, colicky baby, not enough milk, sleep deprivation, parental guinea pigs, diaper rashes, loneliness, late nights and endless feedings.

But then one day, out of the blue, our little sweet pea cooed when she woke in the morning. Gone were her sore bellies and squawks. She played in her crib and talked to herself and the two of us watched adoringly for what seemed like hours.

I was happy and content for us and what we created together. We were young, in love, bundled into a cramped, one-bedroom apartment while the snow crested outside on the window and I had what I always longed for, to be wanted and desired, loved, a family. My family.

~

In the mail slot, we received a pretty, rectangular envelope with what looked like soft, embossed cherry blossoms all around our names, written perfectly in calligraphed hand.

I went to open it and Jimmy snatched it from me. "You know what this is?"

"No," I said, scanning his eyes. "Is it an Honour's Dinner Banquet?" I

Karma

squealed. "I would love to go and get dressed up."

He shook his head. "It's Charlie's wedding invitation."

He waited for my reaction, studying my move.

"Oh?" I blew it off. "So?"

I grabbed it back from him. "We're invited, aren't we? So, we're going?"

I used my index finger and ripped open the thick envelope, pulled out another envelope. "Seems redundant, doesn't it?" I snapped sarcastically.

Jimmy turned to leave, went to the kitchen with his coffee. I opened the second envelope and pulled out the thick card and read the words they chose together, in gold script with tiny pink blossoms, and green ivy framing their invite:

Today I marry my best friend,

The one I laugh with, live for,

Love,

Please join us as we celebrate

our new life together as one...

I placed the invitation back in the envelope. My stomach turned and I blinked back tears. I didn't want Jimmy to see my reaction.

Of course, that's why he didn't want me to open it. Of course, that's why he left me alone to read this crap by myself. Of course, he knows me better than I know myself.

I tossed the invite back onto the table, went through the rest of the mail. The telephone bill, flyers for the grocery store sales, ad mail, but the invitation stared back at me, glowing amongst all the insignificant correspondence we received.

I realized the paper they chose had a sheen. It stood out to mock me. *Look at me!* It yelled in all its formal glory. *Look what you didn't have.*

I took the invite and threw it, chucked it like I was throwing a Frisbee, wanting it to land far away so I could forget about it. My heart was racing and I felt my face burn.

Jimmy walked back into the dining room, sat down beside me. I adjusted my expression, hoping he didn't notice my fat bottom lip jutting out, the hint of avocado on my face, Grinch-green.

I started chewing on the inside of my cheek while strumming my fingers on the table.

"You still wanna go?" he asked.

"Course," I snapped. "We got an invite to the dinner."

~

Their wedding was everything ours was not. Large, colourful, festive... planned.

We left the baby home. Mariah was six months old now. She was a sweet child, with glowing cheeks you wanted to squeeze and a pretty little mouth you wanted to kiss all the time.

Mom thought it a good idea to leave her home. "Have some fun, for God sake," she told me.

She thought I was way too serious now, which I wasn't. I was just a new mother.

Jimmy wasn't asked to stand in the wedding party which I was secretly happy about. Standing proudly beside Charlie, however, was Allan, his best man, with Clyde beside him. Clyde was starting to look a bit rotund.

There were two others I didn't know. Jimmy thought they must have been Vicki's brothers.

We were in a small United Church. The pews were full. There were bows and flowers on the end of four of them, for the family and the wedding party. I was taking it all in.

The music started: an organist played, followed by a soloist singing *Ave Maria*.

We stood in unison and I looked toward the door.

The ladies entered in their soft-pink off-the-shoulder dresses, carrying beautiful bouquets of pink miniature roses, Alstromeria and lilies.

Lotty walked in. She and Vicki attended university together, both taking sciences. She looked cute as a button, all dolled up. I'd never really seen her in anything other than jeans and a t-shirt.

Allan looked like the very proud boyfriend, and I looked forward to the day these two lovebirds would have their own wedding like this.

Trudy was also standing, which I found odd as I didn't know she and Vicki had become friends. I grimaced for a minute, feeling a sense of betrayal.

Suzanne belted from her seat, "Wow. You look some nice, Tru."

The tune changed to the traditional *Here comes the Bride* in instrumental and Vicki's father smiled broadly.

86

Karma

Vicki kept her eyes downcast, probably so she wouldn't trip, I thought. She then faced forward, towards the altar. Towards him. She looked radiant, too, I had to admit.

My heart skipped a beat and I reached for Jimmy's hand. He took mine, brought it to his lips and kissed my fingers softly before resting it back on the rail of the pew.

He stood closer to me, somehow knowing that I didn't have the dream wedding that every girl wanted deep down. A special day to have everyone looking at you in all our extravagant glory, as cheesy and as foolish as it sounded.

It's not supposed to be about the dress and the dinner and the flowers and the attendants. It's supposed to be about the two people who will spend the rest of their lives together.

Jimmy whispered into my ear just then, "I'll make it up to you, Karm. I promise with all my heart."

I looked up at him and smiled, feeling a sense of sadness, yet gratitude and love. Yes, love, in a strange, 'how did we get here?' way.

If not for Charlie and Vicki, I wouldn't be here with Jimmy. I wouldn't have had his baby, or be married. I'd be floating around still, like a dandelion seed.

I grabbed hold of his bicep, exactly how I used to hold Charlie's, and cupped his hand in mine, squeezed it tight. I leaned my head against his shoulder and breathed in his familiar scent for the rest of the ceremony.

The dinner was as festive as the ceremony, if not more so. Tables were decorated with candles and flowers, there were seating arrangements, cocktails and wine, a three-course meal. Who knew Vicki's family had so much money?

Jimmy and I had a nice time. We ate and drank, sat and talked with everyone, but mostly with Allan and Lotty. We laughed, carried on, and then realized we missed Mariah. All we wanted to do was get home to see her, even in her crib, lying asleep with her soother in her mouth.

We stayed 'til after the first dance and watched as the bridal party joined them. Lotty and Allan swayed to the music. Charlie waltzed with Vicki and he was all teeth and beaming. Clyde danced with his gal.

Jimmy asked me, but I was content just to sit close to his side, his hand entwined with mine on my lap.

It looked romantic though, with the lights overhead and the song *Love Lifts Us Up Where We Belong* playing. Jimmy nudged me again but I shook my head.

When the song was over, Allan and Lotty walked off the dance floor

87

Trena Christie-MacEachern

and sat with us. He lit up a cigarette and she flipped off her shoes and took her usual place on his lap, curled up, sipping on a beer.

We chatted for a while until we gave each other the secret nod, said our adieus and left.

Everything was how it should be.

I was strangely at peace heading home with my husband to see our child. It was a beautiful, summer night. The sky was bright and filled with twinkling stars and the Little Dipper was in view. The air was warm and sweet and we left behind a joyful noise of friends and family.

We would get most of the night in, entwined in each other's embrace, but as dawn approached, a frantic phone call came in, with Suzanne yelling and cussing, not making any sense 'til Jimmy told her to calm herself and slow down.

"Holy fuck, Jimmy! Allan drove home drunk and Lotty went through the windshield!"

Karma

9

Then

We couldn't get to the hospital fast enough. The traffic didn't seem to want to move. It was slow, sluggish, everyone out for a spin in the early morning with their families.

"Sunday drivers," Jimmy muttered.

I had my fingers in my mouth, chewing at the sides, ripping off the skin, peeling the polish. I had painted them only yesterday morning, Peony Pink.

The parking lot was full even at this hour. We drove around in circles, finally saw a spot that seemed like blocks away from the emergency wing.

I felt Jimmy's hand on my back as the two of us darted out of the car, walked at quick speed. I somehow kept up with him despite his long legs.

We entered the heart of the building, yet the dreary walls and sombre mood of the place told us otherwise. The smell of antiseptic and floor cleaner hit me first. The odour was metallic and washed out at the same time. A non-smell, yet distinct. The overhead lights were dull and dreary, just like the people that were waiting for their turn to get in to the see the doctor.

A little boy was huddled beside his overweight mother. His cheeks brilliant red and his eyes looked woozy, like he had been here for most of the night. An elderly couple sat to the left, looked up at me with worried eyes.

We were waiting for the nurse to answer our questions when we spotted Suzanne, still in her lemon-yellow dress, holding two paper cups of coffee.

"Thank Christ you're finally here." she said briskly.

We followed her without question. "Holy fuck. It doesn't look good. She's in bad shape," she said. She was shaking her head, taking a drink out of her cup. "Not good. It's not good." Her voice raised an octave even

89

though she was trying to whisper.

We followed her into a smaller room. There were metal chairs against the walls. There were a few people we didn't know sitting here.

"This her brother," she said pointing.

Lotty's little brother was curled up on a small sofa. It looked like he had simply passed out there. Whistles were coming out of his nose at odd intervals. The poor fellow was exhausted.

We saw Clyde then, stretched out, his eyes closed.

Suzanne placed her coffee down and slapped him on the leg, startling him. "Hey! Drink this. For God's sake, get it into you," she practically barked at Clyde then laughed nervously.

She sat beside him looking spent herself. She flipped off her shoes, opting to go barefoot. They landed upside down in the corner.

Clyde wiped his eyes, took the coffee without question, and sipped it. He took another big sip before he realized it was us with Suzanne. He stood up and extended a hand and a shoulder to Jimmy and to me, a big burly hug.

He was still wearing his partial wedding suit from last night. The jacket was gone, and his vest, but he still had the dress shirt with the pearl buttons, pinstriped, black pants and patent leather shoes. There were pink smears over the belly of his shirt. Blood. Dried blood.

My hand flew to my mouth.

I stared at Clyde, but Suzanne spoke for him. "Clyde and Katie found them. They were travelling right behind you. Right, Clyde?"

Clyde nodded. Took another sip. He stared off as he spoke. "They swerved first, thought maybe there was deer. The car just gunned for the ditch.

That's when I finally realized Allan wasn't here.

"Where's Allan?" Jimmy and I asked in unison.

Clyde's hand went back in forth rapidly in a perpendicular motion, like 'don't ask'.

Suzanne tries in her best way to whisper, "He's at Katie's place."

"What? Why?" I exclaimed. "Shouldn't he be here?"

"Shussssh, Karm. Holy frig," she said aloud, then, looking at Lotty's sleeping brother beside us, whispered, "If they catch him for drinking and driving, he'll get arrested."

None of this was making sense. I looked at Jimmy, who was standing, facing Clyde. He was quiet, taking everything in.

"He's right, Karm. It was an accident," he said.

"But how did it happen?" I asked Clyde. "Should Allan have been driving?"

"I'm not sure but you know how Lotty likes to sit next to him, Maybe, she grabbed the wheel? We turned around when we heard the crash but we didn't think it was that bad. We didn't think they were going fast. Luckily, I had a flashlight in my truck. When we got to the car, there was broken glass everywhere and Alan was cut to rat-shit. There was no sign of Lotty and no sign of the windshield. We had to go look for her. The neighbours heard the commotion and came to help. They didn't know anyone was still in the car. When we found her, they went to get blankets and then called the ambulance."

Clyde shook his head, his body shuddered. "God, it was awful."

"I just knew I had to get Allan out of there, or else once the police came, there'd be trouble."

He wiped his eye and sniffed. "This will kill Al." He paused for a few moments, processing what he just said, what he had witnessed, and took a sip of his bitter coffee. "I got Allan in my rig and took him to back to my place, then turned around and came straight here." He brought the coffee cup to his lips. "Jesus, I need something stronger than this."

"Thank God you and Katie were there," Suzanne said, shaking her head.

"Thank God,," I repeated.

"That's what friends do," Suzanne said and slapped Clyde on the knee.

Clyde closed his eyes.

"But what about Allan?" I asked. "What if he's hurt?"

"No. Not hurt. Cuts and stuff. Sore ribs. Maybe a concussion, right, Clyde? Katie knows first aid. Said he's okay. She'll bring him in later, once he sleeps it off and washes up. No sense having him around now, he'd be a mess."

I immediately thought of my mom and told Suzanne that she could check on him. Everyone agreed.

"Can we see her?" Jimmy asked.

Suzanne stood up without saying anything, led us down the corridor to Lotty's room.

"The nurses said we're only allowed two at a time," Suzanne said.

I couldn't bear to go first so I waited at the door. Jimmy entered with Suzanne.

Trudy was there in track pants and a t-shirt. She looked up, came over and hugged me. She looked worn out, too, like she didn't go to sleep yet either. I noticed her bridesmaid dress poking out of a duffel bag. Her hair was still in an up-do from yesterday. She must have been still partying with Suzanne and the rest of the crew when she got the call.

"How's she doing?" I asked softly.

Trudy held the door opened and I saw Lotty.

She looked like she was twelve. All eighty-five pounds of her, stretched out on the bed, hooked up to machines that beeped. She was breathing into an oxygen mask, tubes and ventilators were connected to her, she was bandaged and bruised.

"Very lucky," Trudy whispered. "Lots of injuries but she's alive."

She looked nothing like the Lotty I knew. Such a change from yesterday. Tears came to my eyes and I stifled a sob.

"Poor Allan," I said. I raised my hand to my mouth.

"I know." Trudy squeezed my arm. Her big, blueberry eyes were looking up at me. "He's heart-broken. He'll never forgive himself for this."

I looked around at everyone. Jimmy, Suzanne, Lotty's mother and father. Everyone was talking in whispers, nodding, hugging. The nurses didn't need to enforce the two-person rule. Not now anyway. We were quiet and respectful.

"Will she be okay?" I asked.

"Doctor said it's serious but she'll recover. She'll need physio, and time. But God, things could have turned out so different."

I nodded. "Maybe once she gets better, they'll finally get married," I said hopefully.

Trudy grinned wide. "That be nice, wouldn't it? Just what the doctor ordered."

~

Lotty had more damage than they originally thought. On top of the broken bones and fractures, a severe concussion and a shattered pelvis. Her delicate frame couldn't withstand the impact. She looked more like an extra in a made-for-TV hospital drama than our friend. None of it looked real.

We were all waiting for her to sit up and pull out all the plugs and cords and start laughing. Sadly, she didn't. She was doped up, too, as they tried to keep her pain at bay. Allan's crying all the time simply didn't help the situation.

Her parents didn't want him there. They felt it was negative air, and she needed to heal and get better. Her parents played classical music and shouted to Lotty in big, cheerful tones, like they thought Lotty's hearing was damaged, too. They held hands and prayed together, picked wild-

Karma

flowers and placed them in porcelain tea cups around the room and brought framed pictures of her and her siblings and friends.

When she finally came to, all tiny and soft-breathed, the first words out of her mouth were, "Allan?"

And all that frail, crying stuff that Allan had done, was gone. He was strong for Lotty. He held her hand and laid his arm around her like she was a fragile, glass bird. Like one sudden quick movement on his part would snap her in two.

He kissed her so delicately on the lips and smiled at her, brushing wisps of her hair out of her face. He whispered something so silently no one could hear, but she could, and she smiled as best she could back at him, and he leaned down and placed his forehead on hers.

It felt like we were watching something so special, so intimate, that we shouldn't have been there at all. That moment was made for the two of them, their bond, their relationship, and yet no one could turn away. No one could take their eyes off them, and strained to hear even the faintest whisper, a thought, to see an eye movement. This was true love.

But that little thing was in a lot of pain, and would be for a very long time. She would need weeks to heal, maybe months. She would need physiotherapy and pain medication. And time. She would need lots of time to take stock and regroup and put school off until she got better.

And, of course, Allan said he would be there. He'd work extra hours and overtime to make more money so she could get what she needed and when she needed it.

Charlie wanted to help somehow, too, and he did in the beginning, whether beneficially or not, intentionally or not. He introduced Lotty to a wonderful little pill that would help ease all her pain and suffering. "There's no charge," he had said, but there was a cost.

With Charlie, there was always a cost.

~

Now

"What's wrong?"

He leans against the wall, his arms crossed. He's staring down at me. I'm on the couch, flicking through the channels.

"What?" I look up at him, pretending there isn't. "Nothing, Jimmy."

"You're lying."

Fuck! Jimmy knows me so God-damn well. I couldn't keep a secret if I

Trena Christie-MacEachern

tried. Either he's that good, or I'm just that bad, wearing my heart on my sleeve.

My response: "You're paranoid."

He doesn't answer right away, just watches me surfing through the channels. *Christ, pick one! PICK ONE!*

I settle on an afternoon soap. Bad choice. I hate these shows and he knows that, too.

"Okay, then," he says with a sigh. "I'm taking the kids to the dog park. The MacLeans have a new puppy. Wanna come?"

I shake my head.

He sighs again, stares at me for a few moments longer. "Okay, enjoy your show."

I freeze. He knows damn well something's up.

He calls the kids, they run outside without having to be asked twice. The door clicks and the three of them are engaged in conversation about Sheltie, the new Chocolate Lab the neighbours got.

I turn off the TV. I don't want to be watching this type of trash. I get up and rush to the window to watch my family leaving without me. I see the three of them heading down the street. I could catch them if I tried. They would wait.

Jimmy really isn't walking fast, Paulie is on his bike, Mariah is swinging her arms. If I had a camera, it would be a pretty picture. God, I love them.

Then why did I—I bang my head on the window frame—*go and do a dastardly deed like sleep with Charlie? Why?*

I haven't even let Jimmy touch me since then. It's been a week since Lotty's funeral, a week since I let myself get drunk and taken advantage of. No, I wasn't taken advantage of. I was party to the charade.

I just wish I could recall all the details.

I remember the drinks and putting Allan to bed. I remember Charlie's story about his awful childhood. I shudder. I remember the kiss and some rolling around, waking up with nothing on, going home in the early morning...*fuck! I'm an asshole. How can I tell Jimmy? I'll break his heart. He'll hate me 'til the day I die. I'll hate me 'til the day I die.*

I peer out the window again. My family is gone. I can't see them anymore and I realize this is what's going to happen. I'm going to lose them. I'm just like my father.

I start to cry. Small tears at first, then an all-out bawl. I fold onto myself by the window in a crouching position, crying, howling, like my mother left me behind at a grocery store. Like I'm lost.

94

Karma

I'm blubbering uncontrollably when I notice Jimmy staring down at me and Mariah looking wide-eyed.

"Mom?"

I instantly stop, wipe my face with the back of my hand. Jimmy keeps his tone steady, looks at Mariah and hands her the dog treats they forgot. "Go outside with your brother. I'll be right there."

Mariah is stock-still. My eyes looking back at me. She is stiff as a board.

I stand up. "It's okay, honey. I'm just...sad. Sad about Lotty... and Allan. Okay, sweetheart?"

I see her face relaxing. She understands.

"I'm sorry, Mom, that you're sad." She rushes to me and wraps her arms around my waist, holds me for moment then looks up at me. "I love you."

She says it without hesitation, which does nothing for my current state of mind. I well up again and big drops hit her on her chin. I wipe them off with my palm and push away from her.

Jimmy tells her again to go outside and watch her brother.

I suddenly feel like I'm going to have a panic attack. My breathing is shallow and Jimmy's presence puts me in automatic defence mode even though he's my anchor. But right now I don't deserve to be saved.

He reaches for me, grabs me by the shoulder and takes me to him. He doesn't say anything, just holds me. He is warm and strong, smells like soap. Whenever he hugs me, I feel like I'm getting folded like a towel. His limbs are all around me.

I love this feeling, and him, and I hug him back tight, like this may be my last one. I sob again, my wet face saturates his t-shirt. I try to take a deep breath but shudder. *How many more warm hugs am I going to receive like this before he finds out, before I tell him?*

I have to tell him. The secrecy is killing me.

I release my grip on him and he kisses me gently on the top of my head.

"Jimmy, I—"

"Shh, It's okay. Don't say a word. I know. You haven't been yourself since Lotty's funeral. I know it's hard. Lotty was like our family. You two were close, but it's more than that, I feel it. Isn't it?"

I glance at the floor. He takes my hands in his, rests his butt against the table. He places his fingers under my chin and stares into my face.

"Whatever it is, we'll get through it, okay?" He brings me to him again and kisses my lips so softly, once, twice. "The kids are waiting. Will you be okay 'til we get back?"

I nod.

"Would you feel better coming with us? Getting some fresh air?"

I shake my head.

"Okay, we won't be long."

He kisses me again on the top of the forehead, stares at me longingly for a second, then is out the door again. I let out a long breath, not realizing I had been holding it since I said his name.

~

I make Sloppy Joes for supper, the kid's favourite, and a green salad to go with Jimmy's. I know he's not fussy about Sloppy Joes but he'll eat it. He's never said anything bad about my cooking, whether I attempt a gourmet roast beef or burn grilled cheese sandwiches. He is always appreciative.

God, I don't deserve him.

We eat in relative silence. Mariah's keeping an extra eye on me. Paulie is stuffing his face, asking for extra dill pickles. I love to see him eat.

Jimmy clears the plate and hands Mariah five dollars to take Paul to the corner store to get an ice cream. Paulie does a happy dance and asks Mariah what flavour she's going to get. She says the usual, which is chocolate.

He likes trying different kinds. "I think I'm gonna get a Buried Treasure."

"You've had that before."

"No, I didn't," he says.

"You did, Paulie. It has the stick in it with a picture of a parrot or a ship. That's the treasure."

"Ohhhh. I did. I like those."

The two of them leave and the door clicks behind them.

Jimmy pours us each a tea. I like regular black; he has something herbal going on. Jimmy is a health nut, except when I make Sloppy Joes.

He places the tea in front of me. I immediately take it between my hands and sit back in the chair in a balled position. He is too close and I just don't know what to say. How to say it. The guilt is eating me inside out. I start to tremble again.

He notices my shaky hands. "Dear God, Karm. What's going on?" He has his hand on my knee now, hazel eyes staring back.

I focus on his hair and notice little bits of grey going through it at the temples, making him look stately, like a politician in a good way. I take a

Karma

sip and look out the window, taking a deep breath.

"Jesus, you're killing me. You've no idea what's going on in my head here. Are you sick?"

I turn and look at him, his face is pale, he is hunched over. I can tell he is getting extremely worried. His mouth is set in a tight line.

"God, no," I say, hoping to appease his wondering mind.

He sits back, exhales, takes his hand off my knee. "Good. That's good. Now...spill." He gets back to the point.

"Why do you think there is something going on? Jesus, Jimmy. I'm just...emotional. I'm going through a sad period."

Jimmy starts to shake his foot out of irritation. He doesn't get mad *per se*, just gets extremely irritated and annoyed. I don't think he's ever raised his voice in all the years we've been together, not even with the kids.

"Is it Charlie? Did something happen between you and Charlie?"

The air goes out of the room. I sit completely motionless. My mind spins a million miles a second and even though he has just asked me that question only a millisecond ago, if I don't fess up right now or cause a diversion, my pause is going to spell catastrophe.

"Jesus, Jimmy! No!" I bark. I have to come up with something else. "It's..." I pause, maybe a bit too long.

"What? It's what?" His eyes are wild.

"It's Allan."

"Allan?" He's searching my face. His palms are on my knee. I can't believe I'm betraying my mother's trust, and even Allan's, but I have no other choice. I'm not ready to tell him the real reason why I'm behaving like a caged animal.

"Allan has cancer."

"What? How?" He stands up taking in the news. He didn't see this coming.

"I'm sorry, honey. I didn't want to tell you like this." *God, I'm a shitty human being.*

"How do you know it's true?" He is standing beside the counter, hand resting behind him, his eyes darting everywhere.

"Mom told me. And told me not to tell anyone yet. Even you. Allan has known. But with everything with Lotty, he wanted to make sure she was looked after first, before...shit, before she died. He was too busy with her, you know?"

And he was. After Lotty got addicted to pain killers, the sky was not the limit for her. Lotty turned into something out of a horror movie, try-

97

Trena Christie-MacEachern

ing to fill her addiction. After her accident and she was recovering, she seemed to be doing well for a while, but we hadn't been in contact a whole lot either. We were trying to give them their space, her time to heal. Get back on their feet.

And I was busy, too. The kids. Jimmy. We had our own life. We grew closer as a family after Lotty's accident because we realized how you never know what life has in store for you. Lotty was living proof.

That's when Paulie came along.

Allan was trying to keep Lotty on the straight and narrow, much to our ignorance. They sort of stopped going out, avoided the bar scene and all our favourite hot spots.

But it wasn't alcohol she was addicted to but the pain killers, and when she couldn't get any more of that, she went to pot, easy enough to find, and not really something to actually worry about. We've all tried it, no big deal, but the pot wasn't doing it for Lotty either so she started on more serious stuff, anything she could smoke, anything she could grind, snort. Everything she could get her hands on despite Allan's best efforts.

He'd go to work and then she'd go to work, that is, finding her stash. If she was out and she didn't have any money, she started selling stuff, her ring that Allan gave her, their stereo, clothing, leather bags, perfume. Then when that ran out, her body.

Allan didn't want us to know. He didn't want us to think of his lady in any unsavoury light.

By the time we finally went to see her, because I had enough of Allan giving us one hundred excuses, I was utterly astonished. What happened to my Lotty? She had lost a ton of weight, and had been no more than hundred pounds soaking wet to start with.

Her eyes got bigger, like they were drowning out her other features. She was shaky, and her voice raspy, like she had constant pneumonia or smoker's cough. Her facial features, once delicate and cute, were now heavily lined. Her face was a sickly shade of grey and she looked...old. Older than any of us, and she was younger than all of us.

That was the last time we saw her alive.

After the umpteenth 30-day rehab program, Allan took Lotty to Mom's for a celebratory dinner. We all hoped this was it. She didn't eat much that day, played with her food mostly. We obviously knew Lotty was struggling, but not truly realizing the severity of it. Allan remained tight-lipped.

And he was hacking then, said it was a cold. I remember he kept Lotty close to him all evening so she and I couldn't chat. She was like a doll be-

Karma

ing held by its owner. It was obvious, really, that she was loved so deeply despite the chaos and trail of destruction she was causing. She looked like a caged bird who would take flight anytime he took his hand off her.

And all the nights he was out looking for her, going crazy, not eating himself, smoking more, stressed, exhausted worried that she was going to end up dead somewhere, freeze to death, or worse, and this went on for months.

Allan nearly went completely out of his mind, yet didn't tell a soul except, finally, my mother. Because Mom had been there. She had experienced it herself.

She tried to help Lotty, but she couldn't be helped. Lotty fell into the abyss and Mom knew it was only a matter of time. She hoped she would hit rock bottom and find her way back up again, the way Mom had.

But instead, her last fix was her last breath.

When the cops landed on Allan's doorstep (she had been missing for close to a week by then) to come and possibly identify an unknown person, he knew it was her. He had that sick, sinking feeling. He knew then, too, what had been going on with himself, but his will to live was gone because Lotty was no longer there.

I remove my feet from the chair and place them on the floor.

Jimmy doesn't say anything at first. He bows his head, eyes remain downcast. I take another sip of tea, strum my fingers on the table, waiting. I look up at him. He wipes his eye with his knuckle. He's silent for a moment.

"Thank you," he says quietly, "for telling me this."

"I shouldn't have, though. You know you can't tell a lick of this to anyone."

He nods. "Come here," he says, and reaches out his hand.

I stand up, take his fingers in mine and he pulls me close. He hugs me with all his strength, with his warm, strong body.

"God, I don't know what I'd do if anything happened to you," he whispers in my ear and lays a soft peck there. "Allan. He's like my brother."

He releases me and starts rinsing the plates.

Just as the kids come back in, the phone rings. Jimmy picks it up while I check on the kids.

Paul's face is covered in ice cream. He ended up getting chocolate chip mint. It is around his mouth with a sticky dot on his nose. Mariah passes me a red licorice. One of my favourites.

"Thanks, honey."

"Get me anything?" Jimmy asks Mariah playfully.

99

Trena Christie-MacEachern

"You don't like any of this stuff, Dad," she says matter-of-factly. And then, "You can have one of Mom's licorices."

He sees it in my hand and pulls the end of it 'til it snaps. He puts it in his mouth.

"Who's that on the phone?" I ask, chewing my piece. "Mom?"

"Charlie," he says coldly.

I choke.

"What's he want?" I snap. "You hung up pretty quickly."

Jimmy goes back to the dishes. "He's looking for money."

10

Now

"Money? What does he want money for?" The licorice is half sticking out of my mouth.

Jimmy bends over to put the rinsed plate in the dishwasher. He shrugs. "In some kind of trouble."

"What kind of trouble?" I am practically Jimmy's shadow, greedy for information, and he is brushing me off like he knows something and won't tell me. *Does he know anything? Did Charlies say something?*

He notices my concern, stops with the dishes and focuses his attention on me. I swallow.

"I didn't exactly ask. Charlie is a douche at the best of times."

"But...what kind of trouble, Jimmy? Did he tell you—?"

Jimmy places his hands on both of my shoulders. "I hung up on him," he says coolly and goes back to the dishes.

"Wha? Why?" I am trying to look busy by helping with the cutlery, but Jimmy is taking mine out to rinse before it goes back in the basket.

"He said I owed him one, which I don't."

"Why would he say that?" My mind is wondering and my eyes narrow.

He has his back to me. I grab the arm of his his t-shirt and pull, making him turn in my direction.

"That's it, Karm. Discussion is over. Okay?" He says it a little bit more forcibly. "And if he calls back, you don't answer, or tell him no. Capeesh?"

I nod, but I'm not paying full attention. My mind is already adrift.

Jimmy bends down and looks into my eyes and says a little louder while holding my arm, "Okay, Karm?" Making his point completely clear.

"Yes, jeesh! Okay. Okay, Jimmy."

He continues the clean-up without saying anything else, but when he puts the milk in the fridge, he says, "Let's make Allan some burgers, or I'll pick up some steaks and we can cook him a meal tomorrow. See how's he doing."

Trena Christie-MacEachern

"Na-uh. Not yet, Jimmy. He doesn't know you know. He barely knows that I know. So, how 'bout, I go see him myself and then see what he'd rather? You know Allan, he doesn't want any pity, and if he doesn't feel up to it, well, we can just drop him off some food. Mom spends most of her time with him, anyhow, and she said Clyde was over, as well as some fellas he works with. We don't want to exhaust him."

"Mmm. Okay. But don't want him to think we forgot about him, either."

"He won't, Jimmy."

"Okay then. It's your call.".

"I'll touch base with him tomorrow while you're at work and the kids are in school."

"You feel up to that? With, you know, how you've been feeling?" He has genuine concern in his face.

"Yes. Being busy is good. It will be good to talk to Allan."

~

Today is my first day back in my routine and already I'm a bit rusty. Normally, I make the kids lunch the night before. Today I feel like I'm blindfolded and have my hands tied behind my back. Jimmy got up and went to work early, which caused me to oversleep, which caused Mariah's frantic scream.

"Mom! It's eight o'clock. I've a game today!"

We rush around the kitchen, getting Paulie dressed and ready, food to eat on the bus: banana and dry cereal, his favourite at least. He has to take a peanut butter and jam sandwich because it's quick, and Mariah has to buy. She says she doesn't mind and there happens to be a muffin and a granola bar left in the cupboard so she takes that as her snack before the game.

The lateness doesn't bother or faze Paulie at all. He's like his dad that way, his placid, everything's-okay-attitude. Mariah was once, too, but entering teenage-hood, and being a girl, and being late, especially on game day, makes things a little more hectic.

They get out with a minute to spare, with Mariah shouting, "don't forget to come get me at four-thirty."

I finally put the coffee on, still feeling a bit frazzled, and then the phone rings. Mom usually calls at this hour so I pick up and say good morning in my cheery tone.

"Hey," he says back in his cool, sexy voice. "That was a nice greeting. How'd you know it was me?"

Karma

My eyes widen. "Charlie?"

He laughs. "How are you doing? I'd like to see you again."

I can hear him breathing into the phone. I freeze. My mind is all over the place. I'm even looking out the windows for some reason.

"You there?"

I can tell he is smiling. He knows he has me frazzled.

"Ah, yeah, Charlie. Hectic morning, kids almost missed the bus."

"You want to meet up later?" He sounds killer sexy, his voice is raspy and cool, and I stop myself, bang my head on the cupboard door. I have my eyes closed. I'm utterly ashamed.

"Charlie, why are you calling here? Last week was a mistake. A big mistake. I was drunk a—"

"You and me, Karma—it was always you and me," he breathes into the phone.

"No. It may have been, Charlie. But that was years ago. We both moved on. You married Vicki and I'm with Jimmy. So..." I paused. "Stop this nonsense."

I try a different tactic. "Jimmy says you're in trouble."

"He told you, did he?" His tone changes. He isn't all come-hither now.

"Well, not really, just that you needed money."

That's when Jimmy's voice comes over my mental airwaves. *Don't answer the phone and tell him no.* "Shit!" I say aloud.

"What?" Charlies asks.

"Nothing, I—I forgot something." The coffee percolator is making its hissing sound announcing it's almost ready. "Charlie, I have to go. There's a strange—"

"Karma. Wait," Charlie practically yells. "I need ten thousand dollars. And I have pictures."

"What?" The phone is practically inside my ear canal now. "Ten thousand for what? Pictures of—" My mouth drops and my eyes widen and the tears are there and I know what he's going to say. Silently, I say back to him. "You have pictures of us? Together?"

"I'm sorry, Karma. I didn't want to go this way. I'm sorry. But I have people breathing down my neck and I need to pay them back and I already asked your hubby in a nice way but he hung up on me."

The air sucks out the room, out of my chest. I choke, "When, Charlie?" I say, in the most inaudible voice.

"As soon as you can, weekend at the latest. Call me back when you get it."

And then I remember him writing his number on a piece of paper and stuffing it into my purse when I was leaving his place that night.

"I better go," I say, beaten, feeling weak in the legs.

The phone goes dead, I don't remember if he said good-bye. The phone starts its beep-beep-beep, reminding me to place it back on the receiver.

Fuck, fuck, fuck, fuckers, shit-fuckers!

My eyes are wild, my legs are shaking, my heart is having palpitations. I feel sweaty and sick and I'm going to hyperventilate. And here it is, the shit-show, thanks to Karmalita Judith Smallwood.

I bang my fist on the counter and against the cupboard door. Where the hell am I going to get the fucking money?

~

I pawn the TV that was in the basement, and the stereo, get a whopping one hundred bucks. Then I go back and sell my jewellery. My watch that Dad and Mom gave me for my grade-twelve graduation, and my gold tennis bracelet. With my meagre savings, I'm able to come up with eighteen hundred but am still way short.

I'll have to sell the car! My God. What have I done?

I wonder if I can withdraw the Savings Bonds or the kids' school/savings accounts. Maybe Dad can loan me some money, or Mom, if I can spin a good story and they don't tell Jimmy.

God... Jimmy. He will be devastated. First, having to deal with me, and then all that money. *I can tell Jimmy that I thought the fake company Charlie mentioned was a good one? I can tell the gang about it?* Suzanne and Trudy. *Trudy's doing good now, maybe she can spot me? Then, I'll have to go back to work full-time and pay her back the rest.*

But no matter what way I think or how, I probably won't have it all by the weekend. *Then what? What can Charlie do to me then? If I tell him I'll get the rest of it, give him what I have to start, then maybe he'll see I'm trying here, and he could wait?*

The day goes by. I have done nothing. Haven't even put the dishes away. Haven't planned supper. I'm sitting on the couch, lethargic, after coming from the pawn shop. God, even that's a greasy move. Pawn shop.

I was probably only in that shit store once before! We were looking for an old guitar for Mariah when she took an interest in lessons. We thought we'd check it out, maybe get one dirt cheap, but the ones they had were too big for her and it turned out the music lady let her borrow her daughters 'til she saw if she wanted to really play.

Karma

And thank God we didn't buy one, because Mariah did lose interest. Turned out she didn't actually want to practice, she just thought she could take a lesson or two and then be able to play. She was doing a performance with a couple of her friends, a skit, and she thought it would be pretty cool to actually play a song or two. Expensive skit.

I'm between no energy and nervous energy. Biting my nails and shaking my legs while I am thinking, and sitting down on the sofa, sometimes lying down, trying to sleep.

The phone rings. I don't answer it. It's Charlie, looking for the money. I pick it up and drop it back on the receiver. It rings off the hook so finally I pick it up.

"What?" I scream. "What in the hell do you want?"

"Mom! Where are you? It's way past four thirty."

Jesus! The magazine flies off the coffee table and I yell for Paulie. "Hey, Paulie. We have to pick up your sister. I plum forgot."

"Maaa! I don't wanna. I just got home."

And I feel for the little guy, and normally, I would have called one of his friends to see if he could have gone there after school, but the day just got away from me.

"Sorry, big guy. We gotta roll. And no time either, she's waiting."

I could tell he's not impressed. But he comes, and I promise him a treat for being a good boy while he buckles himself up in the back.

Mariah is standing by the school curb, book bag in her hand. She is walking to the car, grim-faced. "I thought you would make the game."

I wave her in. "Mariah, I'm sorry. I got caught up."

"Everyone was wondering where you were." She throws the bag between her legs. She had changed into her gym pants and hoodie, hair tied back in a pony tail.

"How'd you do?" I ask, feeling sheepish.

She grimaces again. "We lost, but I got a goal." She buckles herself in. "Hey, Paulie."

Paul doesn't answer her.

"Can we get something to eat? I'm starving."

"We'll stop at the store for a treat, okay? I promised Paulie. Oh, and we're having Uncle Allan for supper tonight. I think."

Allan isn't their uncle but Mariah always calls him that. I close my eyes and grip the steering wheel tight. I was supposed to go see Allan today. *Shit.*

"Sorry. I take that back. I couldn't get a hold of him." I lie. Then I remember I haven't taken anything out for supper either. "How 'bout I take

Trena Christie-MacEachern

you guys for a burger since I missed your game? Hey, Mariah? And then I'll drop you off at Grandma's. You can eat there. There's something else I have to do."

The money is burning a hole in my pocket.

~

After I drop off the kids, I travel to the other side of town, another twenty minutes past the mall. *Why did he move out here?* It's not close to anything. Just rows of houses stuck in the middle of nowhere.

When the town was being built up in the sixties, they started building here to attract young homeowners. Busses and train systems were supposed to part of the plan, but that didn't happen either. It ended up just being seniors moving out here after they retired because they wanted space and quiet solitude, lawns to mow, trees to prune.

I don't remember it being this far out, though, when we drove here after Lotty's reception. I guess my mind was too busy thinking of other things.

Now I can't remember the name of the street Charlie lives on. I curse myself. I'm driving around and around, feeling like such a lunatic. A stalker. So many homes. And I can't believe I'm going to see Charlie. Alone! Something I know I should not do. Period. But I feel like I have no other choice.

I drive past the 7-Eleven.

The 7-Eleven. Thank God. It comes to me. It's a few blocks from here on Ester Avenue.

I reach for my purse and pat the money I have collected, making sure it is still there. I had put it in an envelope and, I have to admit, it looks like a lot.

What I could do with this money? New light for the bathroom, little jacket I had been keeping my eye on at the Leather Factory, waiting for it drop down in price. Jimmy needs new runners.

I take out the envelope and place it on my lap. My hands are sweating. I tuck the flap in and, for good measure, grab an elastic band and wind it over the envelope. I don't want to seal it. I want Charlie to see all the green, see it's real, and that I'm trying—really trying. My heart is beating a mile a minute and I'm breathing like I just ran a mile.

My driving, on the other hand, is the total opposite. The cars behind are honking their horns because I'm creeping along, concentrating, scared I will miss his place. Finally, I pull over to let them pass and keep

106

Karma

scanning. *Maybe it isn't Ester Avenue after all?*

I drive a little further, searching left to right. But what if I can't find it? What then? Drive back home and wait for him to call me?

But, lo and behold, there it is—the house. 192 Ester Avenue. The cute little bungalow with the manicured lot.

It feels too bold to pull into his driveway, too personal, so I park the next house over.

Thankfully, Charlie's car is there. I need to get this over with.

My hands are shaking. God, I'm so nervous. Nervous for so many things.

I want to see the pictures. No! I don't want to see the pictures. But I'd have to take them from him, make sure he doesn't keep them and use them on me again in the future.

Jesus, I hope he doesn't have copies.

My mouth is so dry it feels like I was on a bender for a week. My armpits and the small of my back are wet with sweat.

For a stupid reason, I check myself in the mirror. I haven't put on makeup this morning. I don't think I even brushed my hair, just threw it in a ponytail. *My God, he won't even recognize me.*

I slap myself on the cheek. *Smarten the hell up.* I shouldn't be worrying about what I look like let alone what I have on. Why is it even on the register?

What if he lures me in and the same thing happens? A shudder works its way down my spine.

The car clock reads five thirty-five. Jimmy will be home anytime. He'll be wondering where we are. I didn't even leave him a note. I won't even have time to get a few groceries. *Jesus Christ.*

I bang my head on the steering wheel and, for good measure, hit the horn by mistake and startle myself. I'm so mad I'm shaking, yet I'm nervous and scared, too. I check the envelope with the money for the umpteenth time, and stuff in it my purse.

My sweaty hands open the car door. I take a deep breath, two deep breaths, and step out. I walk toward the drive, then up the cement sidewalk. Breathe again, grab hold of the rail. Breathe, walk up the step, raise my hand, and knock on the door. I don't ring the doorbell. I'm too chicken-shit.

My rap is gentle, soft. I wait. I look down at my dirty sneakers. *Jesus. I'm dressed like a tramp.*

I peer at the window. The sheers move and I immediately freeze. *Fuck, fuck. Fuck.* I'm sure I must look like a deer in the headlights before it gets

107

Trena Christie-MacEachern

shot.

Then I hear footsteps and look up, see a face in the door. *What do I say first? Just hand him the money or ask to come inside? No, I don't want to go anywhere near there.*

The door opens and a small, dark-haired woman greets me. She looks like she is in her late fifties, early sixties.

"Hello?" she says meekly. "We are not interested in buying anything."

"Oh." I say, taken aback. I'm staring at her and she's looking at me. I scan the interior as much as I can see of it from where she is standing. "I'm not selling anything. I'm just, I'm looking for Charlie. Is he here?"

Her eyes furrow and she opens the door wider, turning her attention to someone else in the room. I see the couch where we sat, and the plant, and the end table with the statue.

"This is 132 Ester Avenue, correct? Not street?"

"Yes, that's right."

"This is Charlie's place, isn't it? Charlie David?"

The woman turns. *She's signalling for Charlie.*

Then, an older man walks to the door. He has a head full of grey hair and is wearing glasses and a long-sleeved cardigan sweater. He's holding today's paper.

I'm on the threshold now, peering in. I can see the island where I drank my wine, and the solid wooden stools, and the bedroom off the living room where we put Allan for the night.

"You must be mistaken, miss. This is our house. I think our son was getting a Charles something or other to fix our fence in the back yard. We were away for a few weeks. I can give him a ring and ask, or if you want to leave your number?"

My eyes widen, I take a step back. "I'm sorry," I mutter. "I must be mistaken. No, no thank you. Sorry to have bothered you."

I smile awkwardly, stupidly. I raise a hand to wave good-bye.

"No problem at all. See you now." They close their door.

I step back slowly, turn, grasp onto the rail and make my confused way back to the car.

11

Now

I drive in a daze. *What the hell is going on? Where the hell is Charlie? And what's he playing at?*

I'm chewing on my nails. Actually, my whole hand is practically in my mouth. I am two streets away from my place and realize I forgot the kids at Mom's. I curse myself and turn around.

A horn blares and scares the shit out of me. *I'm going to get myself in an accident if I don't start paying attention.*

I sit for a moment in the car as it is idling, wondering what my next step is. *Jesus, how can I be so stupid? What in the hell am I going to do?*

I have Charlie's number. I'll call him. Ask him what's up. Play dumb.

Second thought, I erase that out of my mind. My stomach grumbles and I realize I'm starving. No wonder I can't think straight.

I look at the clock again. *Shit! Jimmy is home. He'll be wondering what's up.*

"Frig!" I say aloud, bang my fist on the console. I'm now irritated and pissed off. My anger is revving up.

I barrel into Mom's driveway and rush inside. I don't realize my face looks like it could kill until my mother says something.

"Whoa. What's eating you?"

"Sorry," I spit. "Rotten day."

"Mmm hmm," she says, looking at me as she sits at the supper table with her tea.

I look at her plate, her empty plate. She sees me looking. "You eat? You didn't, did you? That's why you're so rancid."

She stands up and goes to the cupboard, grabs a plate. "Well, one of your reasons."

She looks at me over her glasses.

"Sit down, sit down. Lord, get a piece of bread into you. Mariah is doing her homework, Paulie's watching TV."

Trena Christie-MacEachern

"Shit, Ma, sorry. Didn't mean to just pawn them off on you."

She waves her hand back and forth, meaning it's no big deal.

"What did you make?" I ask, after slathering a piece of multi-grain with butter.

"It's zucchini lasagne. Meatless."

My face must express my utter disappointment.

"It's actually pretty good, and good for you. Low fat cheese, lots of spices, onions, mushrooms."

"Be better with a beer, or a bottle of red," I suggest.

"A bottle?" Mom doesn't look at me at all. She scoops the lasagne onto a plate, sprinkles pepper on top.

"Here, I'll get you a glass of milk. Or would you prefer water?"

"Milk is good." I take a bite. It's not bad and I'm starving, so anything is good at the moment.

"Betcha Jimmy would like it. He's pretty health conscious."

I nod. "He is."

"Shall I send a piece home with you? He called you know. Wondering where you all were."

I say nothing. Just keep eating. Can't even focus until the belly gets full.

"Where were you, by the way?"

I still don't reply until I finish my plate and take the bread and soak up all the tomato sauce with it. I tip back the glass and drink my milk 'til it's all gone.

"Thanks, Mom. That wasn't bad."

"I have wholewheat carrot muffins, if you want one of those with some tea."

"Jesus, Ma, where do you get time to bake all this stuff?"

Mom kind of smiles and puts her tea cup down. "Oh, I do it first thing in the morning, when it's quiet, before my AA meeting, or after I do some counselling. I make extra batches and take them with me. They like that. Fresh muffins."

"You have time to see Allan?"

Mom sighs heavily. "He looks dreadful. That poor man had his share of heartache. God, if I could take that pain away from him, I would. He doesn't deserve that."

"I was supposed to go over and see him, call him at least. Invite him for dinner."

"That be nice, Karmalita. Be good for him to get out of the house. Whether he will or not."

Mom takes my plate and places it on top of hers along with the cut-

Karma

lery. The stack rattles. She pushes them to the centre of the table. "He's not eating much either. And still smoking like a trooper, drinking beers. Moping, mostly."

"Well, that's to be expected."

"I'm worried for him. He's shutting down and refuses to get any help or want any treatment."

"You're a nurse. Can't you like, make him?"

Mom shakes her head. "I want him to get better but I can't make him do anything. Just like your father couldn't make me stop drinking. We have to want to do it on our own."

"But he's sick, Mom. He'll die if he doesn't get treatment."

Mom takes off her glasses and rubs her eyes. "Precisely."

"What?" I gasp. "He wants...to die?" My eyes nearly pop out of my head when that realization hits me.

Mom rests her chin on her palm and looks away. "When Lotty died, part of him did, too."

"Oh, God, Mom. This is terrible. I didn't know it was that bad."

"I talk to him every day and stop over when I can. I'm trying to get him to come here, you know, visit, like he used to. But he's in mourning, and sick on top of it. He has a lot going on in that brain of his. He was sick for a long time and didn't tell anyone. He was so focused on Lotty."

She reaches for my arm, "You're taking this hard, too. Jimmy was telling me you're not yourself."

I shake my head. "Jimmy's talking about me?"

"That's all he said, nothing more. And I asked, by the way."

"Oh." I nod.

"Go and see Allan. It will be good for you to see him. You guys share a bond of sorts. He's a good guy. He'll put things in perspective for you. Maybe you can help each other out."

I smile. "Yeah. Maybe you're right. Maybe he can. And yes, I will have a tea, and one of those muffins you made."

~

Mom calls Allan to tell him I'm coming over to see him, to give him a heads up. But when I arrive, it is like he didn't know I was coming.

The place is a catastrophe. It looks like it hadn't been cleaned since they moved in a couple of years ago.

I remember Mom telling me before I went to see him, "don't judge, Karmalita. You're going to see him, not his place."

Trena Christie-MacEachern

And to be honest, I could be messy and leave things like the wash and the mopping a day or so thanks to my procrastination; but here, I'm even scared to sit down.

Allan spent so much of his time trying to find Lotty when she went missing, housecleaning was the least of his worries. But the dishes are still mile high in the sink, the counters are littered, garbage is overflowing, ashtrays are filled to the brim, and of course, now, beer bottles are everywhere. Allan never was a bad boozer by any means, kept it to weekends and a drink after work on a hot day, but all that changed when they got in that car accident.

When Lotty was at her worst, well, he just didn't have it in the house at all. Period. This was an alcohol-free zone. I had actually forgotten he was not having a drink. But the reception we had at The Bullhorn, he was half in the bag before we even got there.

But, heck, that was completely understandable.

"Allaaannn?" I call out. "You here?"

"Hey Karm," his voice trails from his bedroom. "I'll be out in a minute. Take a seat."

It's weird to be here and know Lotty is not. I keep waiting for her to peek around the corner, ask what she can get me.

I shudder when I see the mess. *She would die. She was always so neat.*

I move the ashtray and papers off the sofa and go to stack them on the coffee table, but that is full also. I place them on the floor.

The Price Is Right is on and Bob Barker is smiling with that long, thin microphone to his mouth. I sit back, entranced, watching the contestants make their bids. I'm not good at guessing at the prices on the show.

Allan comes out wearing his dark denims and a long-sleeve, plaid shirt. He has the buttons done all the way to the top. The shirt hangs loosely over his slim frame. He is kind of hunched over, like his body is crumbling under the weight of his grief. He has a cigarette hanging out of his mouth and his eyes are squinting.

He runs his hand through his hair, and I notice he needs a cut. He is barefoot and besides his obvious weight loss, he looks old.

The corners of his eyes crinkle when he sees me. He takes the butt out of his mouth and exhales and sighs at the same time. "That was Lotty's favourite spot."

"Right here?" I ask, pointing. He nods, plops his cigarette in a beer bottle. It *sssssists* when the hot ash hits the remnants of liquid.

He sits beside me, his bony knees touching my leg and I thump him on the thigh with my fist. "How you doing, Al? Shit, don't answer that. Sorry,

112

stupid question."

He slumps so that his back is in the crook of the arm of the sofa. He places one of his feet on my lap. "Karm, I won't lie. It fucken sucks."

Then he raises a fist to his mouth and hacks and coughs 'til his eyes are wet and running. He sits up and coughs some more.

There is a bottle on the table with lukewarm beer, probably yesterday's, and he brings it to his lips and tilts his head.

I make a face.

He finishes it and places it back on the table. "It's alright. About the only thing that helps." He lets out a small belch.

"Really?"

"I tell myself that."

He remains silent and so I simply wait for him until he is ready to talk. He looks around, holds his hands together, leans forward, rests his arms on his knees. He doesn't look at me.

"I'm sick, Karm."

I nod.

"I s'pose your Mom told you."

I nod again.

"Did Lotty know, Al?" I ask quietly, almost in a whisper.

He shrugs and drops his head. "No way of knowing. Maybe? I dunno."

He smiles at me but his face is sad. It is the saddest smile I have ever seen. "This is not how I saw our life go, Karm." He sounds haunted now. "If I could have just done something."

"But you did, Al." I place my hand on his arm.

"I didn't do enough. She was just too, too far gone. I hoped that last bout would be her bottom."

"Her rock bottom?"

He nods. His eyes are wide, eyebrows disappear under his long bangs. "But she didn't wake up from it."

He bows his head and brushes his cheek with his palm, then touches his palm to his breast pocket, feeling for his cigarette package, opens it, takes one out and sticks it in his mouth.

"Maybe you shouldn't be doing that," I say, matter-of-fact, but he doesn't even blink.

He takes out his lighter, clicks it as he tilts his head sideways, and sucks in, the tip warming red. He exhales, holds the cigarette between stained fingers. "I just want it to be over with, you know? If I could just take a pill."

"Allan!" I snap. "Don't talk like that! Ever!" I start tossing the garbage

Trena Christie-MacEachern

and the ash into an empty brown paper bag that was lying at my feet.

"Don't, Karm. I don't want you do that." He reaches for my arm to stop me.

"Jesus, Al. No wonder you feel like you do. This place looks like a shit-hole. Lotty would be piss..." I trail off. "Fuck, Al. I'm sorry."

He eyes me, cigarette in his hand and then shakes his head. "It's okay. She would be."

"I can't imagine what you feel."

I want to change the subject, get on to something else positive, but he beats me to the punch. "Lotty would have liked her send-off."

I stare at him wide-eyed as I stack the coffee cups into each other.

"At The Bullhorn."

"Yes. Allan, I know this is corny, but I felt like she was there. That she was with us. Her spirit. Did you feel it?"

"We should check out Charlie's pictures. He has a bunch of candids."

I drop the cups. Two of them shatter as they ricochet off the table. The coffee splashes over my leg and pours onto the floor. I feel like I'm going to pass out. My legs wobble like Jell-O.

I start to cry. I'm sitting on the floor with my legs under me, on top of cheap, broken china, sobbing.

"It's okay. Here, here. Sit, sit. I'll get this. It's okay. It's just cups. They're just fucking cups, Karm."

I look up at him with my wet face. "Charlie has pictures of me." I'm nearly hyperventilating. I can't catch my breath. "Oh my God, Allan. I'm fucked! I fucked up. Jimmy's going to...I don't know what Jimmy's going to do."

I put my head down on my arm.

"What are you talking about, Karm? What's going on?" Allan's mouth is agape, eyes staring wide. No doubt I look like a psychotic lunatic.

And so I tell him.

I tell him about that night. About Jimmy not wanting to go and so I did. About going back to Charlie's place. And how we put him to bed, and drinking a lot. Then waking up very early and having slept with Charlie. "But I barely remember."

Allan doesn't interrupt when I tell him all of this.

"I just don't know how it happened," I say. "I should have known better. My relationship with Charlie is over. It was ages ago. Honestly, I don't know what happened. I must be just a fucking idiot."

"Grief makes us do stupid things," Allan says.

"And Jimmy, my God, Allan. This will kill him. This will end my mar-

Karma

riage."

I start crying again, realizing how true it could be when the words come out of my mouth.

Allan has his arm around me now, tapping my shoulder with his hand, doing the 'there-there' routine. I'm supposed to be the one comforting him and it's turning into the other way around.

"I'm sorry, Allan." I wipe my face, then stand up trying to regain some composure, release the sadness. "I'm supposed to be here helping you."

"You are and it's okay," he says softly.

This time I get the broom, sweep up the broken pieces of teacup. Allan sits and watches me.

I empty the shards into the bag.

After a few minutes I say, "You know? I think I may remember how it started with Charlie that night. He was telling me about his childhood."

I sit back down beside Allan, closer this time. I turn the TV off altogether to garner his full attention.

"What about it?"

"You know? The story about his abusive father, abused mother."

"Say what?" Allan turns to me.

"Yeah, that awful night where he accidentally killed his father but didn't tell anyone. Said you and Jimmy were supposed to show up and give him back-up but you didn't. Well, you did later."

Allan nods his head, his fingers slowing drumming on the coffee table.

"I see."

"You remember all of that?"

"I remember," he says coolly. He runs a hand through his hair, grabs another smoke.

"Maybe that's what happened to me? I just felt sorry for him." I wipe my eyes for the umpteenth time. "But isn't that awful, Allan? How do you live with yourself after something like that?"

I blow my nose as Allan mimicked my sentiments.

"Yeah, how does one live with themselves?" He sounds sarcastic.

I look at him. "What?"

"Nothing," he says, shaking his head.

"No seriously, what?"

"Just, that...was never supposed to be...told."

"Ever?"

"Ever."

I furrow my eyes. "So why did he tell me?"

"I'm sure he had his reasons," Allan offers.

115

Trena Christie-MacEachern

I sit back again, thinking, scanning my brain. "I went to his place."

"Something like a horse running back into a burning barn?" He smiles deviously.

I punch him on the arm. "No, Allan. Don't be a dick. To pay back some of the money. I collected almost eighteen hundred. I thought If I gave him some of it, he'd see that I was trying and leave me alone until..."

"I suppose he took it."

"This is the thing, Allan. It isn't his God-damn house."

Allan didn't seem surprised.

"Did you know it wasn't his place?"

He rubs his chin with his thumb and forefinger. "Nothing Charlie does or does not do surprises me anymore."

I look at him, confused. "Jesus Allan. We stayed at a place we thought was Charlie's, and it wasn't Charlie's. Do you remember any of it?"

"Not much."

"What happened the next morning? After I left?"

"He took me home, and he left. Thought he went back to his place. Wherever that is."

"And he's not with Vicki."

Allan shrugs. "Don't think. But"—he splays out his palms, facing up-ward—"who's to know?"

"Well, I just don't need him jerking me around, threatening me."

"He threatened you?" Allan's eyes got dark and serious.

"With the pictures! He says he has pictures. You said you heard your-self. Oh God, Allan. This is a nightmare. I can't even face Jimmy. He already thinks I'm losing it."

"I thought they were just group shots of us. Not sure. But that's what I thought."

"I don't even remember him with a camera."

Allan takes another coughing fit. His throat sounds raw and raspy.

I check the tables for more beer, then get up and check the fridge. There are a couple left. I grab one and open it, hand it to him.

He waves it away while hacking. He has one hand to his mouth, the other to his chest.

I put the beer down on the table and pat his back up and down and around in circles.

He subsides and then reaches for the bottle and takes a few sips. He takes deep heaving breaths. "If it's my last dying breath, I'll get to the bottom of this, Karm."

"Aw, Al. Thank you, but you need to take care of yourself first. Please?

Let a doctor look at you."

He shakes his head.

I sigh. "Well, I'm going to at least tidy up. And no arguing."

Allan, at least, agrees to that.

~

"How much he looking for?" It feels like her voice carries over a sound speaker. I tell her again.

There's a pause as she's thinking, then, "And what for exactly? Why does he want ten grand from you?"

"Pictures."

"What kind of pictures? Seems awfully expensive. Pictures." She laughs out loud. She responds to Trudy in the background. "I don't remember Vicki saying their wedding pictures were that expensive."

That's when I tell her. All of it. I tell her the whole enchilada. I bite my nails when I tell her. I know, somehow, she'll find out anyway, and I need to get it off my chest. I was actually making myself sick with the knowledge.

She doesn't say anything at first. There is dead silence on the other end of the phone.

"You still there, Suzanne?"

"HOLY FUCK, KARM! What's wrong with you?"

I cringe as Suzanne barks into the phone.

"Didn't I tell you all along that fellow ain't no good for you? Holy God, I can't believe what you just said."

She goes on and on as I sit in a ball on the couch, getting scolded, berated, but deserving all of it. I shrink further into myself, even though everything she says is true. She relays to Trudy every stinking word, although Trudy, no doubt, can hear everything the first time. Suzanne, when angry, repeats herself. Just to make the point more deliberate.

"And what about Jimmy? You tell him yet?"

She knows my answer without me saying it. "FUCK! Here, Tru, you take the phone. I'm done talking."

The receiver drops to the counter with a thud. There's something inaudible said, followed by more chatter and then I hear the receiver being picked up.

"Hey, Karm, It's me. How're you doing?" Suzanne and Trudy are like a good cop/bad cop routine and I don't think one could survive without the other.

Trena Christie-MacEachern

"Hey, Trudy." My voice sounds childlike and girly. Like I was back in high school, not a married mother of two knowing the difference.

There is a silence between us. She lets what Suzanne has said sink in. We know the enormity of it and nothing else has to be said on the subject. She is here to smooth over the rough spots.

"I can lend you some money, Karm. I have some put away already."

"No, Trudy. I can't let you do that." I can't believe she would offer her savings to a whore.

"If not me, Karm, then who? How will you get the money without Jimmy finding out? If he doesn't sense something's up already."

"You mean about the money or the sex?"

"Both. Allan said you're already all over the place. He said your mother knows somethings up, and Jimmy is even more in tune."

"Christ," I breathe. I place the receiver to my forehead.

What in the hell am I going to do? I'll just have to tell him. I'll have to tell Jimmy the whole f-ing story. Maybe I could make some of it up? Well, I don't remember most of it, so it's Charlie's word against mine. Christ.

"You still there, Karm?"

I bring the phone back to my ear. "Yeah."

"I'll see what we can find out."

Suzanne hollers in the background, "I'm sick of what Charlie is doing to everyone. First Al, well, Lotty, and now you."

"Wait, wha? What do you mean? What did he do to Al?"

I hear struggling. "Gimme that." Suzanne wrestles the phone out of Trudy's hands.

"I can't believe you don't know this. Jeesh, Karm. Charlie gave Lotty them drugs when she was first out of the hospital. Tru, what you call that drug?"

"Demerol."

"Yeah, Demerol. It's for pain. Lotty was still hurting when she got home so Charlie gave her some of his mother's pills. To help her. That's what he said. That's what he started doing. Getting his mother's prescriptions and selling them. Made a lot of money. But Lotty couldn't get enough. And the pain wouldn't go away. Whether it was real or all in her head, who knows? But she ended up an addict and she wasn't before."

"Charlie's responsible?"

"Yes, Charlie. He did anything for a buck because he wasn't working at nothing else. Easy money. Vicki was in school then. She was too busy studying and becoming something to notice. Looked like they had a perfect life, 'til the goons starting showing up."

118

Karma

I gasp. Cover my mouth with my hand. "I never knew."

"Jimmy knew."

I feel blind-sided. "Jimmy never told me anything."

"Course he wouldn't. Why tell you something your old, scumbag boy-friend was doing? Doing wrong!"

"But they're friends!"

"Were."

"And what about Vicki? Is that why they aren't together anymore?"

"Uh huh. She kicked him out. She had enough of it."

"How do you know all of this?"

"Vicki told Trudy."

I stare off, remembering that Trudy and Vicki were in the same classes both in high school and in college. Took the same degree starting out and Trudy stood in her wedding.

"I liked her," Trudy says. "Although we lost touch. She had to put up with a lot, with Charlie's indiscretions and all. She moved on, though. Last I heard she was dating a doctor."

"Yeah," Suzanne says, "And Charlie's pissed. He lost his golden egg. Maybe that's why he went after you. To get back at her."

"Suzanne!" Trudy snaps, her tone is loud and sharp.

I don't say anything or try to defend myself. What she's saying couldn't hurt me any more than I already hurt myself.

"Aaaa—sorry, Karm. I didn't mean it like that."

"No, it's okay, Suzanne."

I hear the muffled exchange of two friends chatting to each other and then Trudy's voice back on the other end, soft and gentle.

"Karm. We'll get to the bottom of this, okay? And the money is here. I'm not sure what Charlie's playing at but between the four of us, we'll get to the bottom of it."

"The four of us?"

"You, me, Suzanne and Allan."

Her words make me smile. "Thank you, Trudy. Just like old times."

I hang up the phone and look at the clock. I was on the phone for most of the afternoon and didn't do a lick of anything.

I decide I'd better start supper at least. I take the ground beef out of the fridge and make up eight patties. I'll call Allan to come over for a bar-becue. Just like old times.

~

What is Charlie is playing at? Is he using me to get at something? Or pissed

119

Trena Christie-MacEachern

at me? Or pissed at Jimmy?

My mind is spinning. I want so much to be at the other end of this mess.

I know I still need to get in touch with Charlie. I have his number somewhere. He gave it to me the night of Lotty's service. Probably thought I would call him instead of stopping by his place. *His place.* Wherever the hell that is.

And I can't possibly ask Jimmy where he thinks Charlie may be living. He'll wonder why I'm asking but he probably doesn't know anyway. As Allan doesn't. But Allan was too busy trying to look after and help Lotty to pay attention to what Charlie was doing or where he was living.

What about Clyde? Or Eric? Should I ask them? Maybe they'll know?

I quickly dismiss the idea. It's too ludicrous. They'll be wondering why I suddenly want to know where my old boyfriend lives and it will surely get back to Jimmy. I'll look even more suspicious.

I sit in my favourite chair, the comfy, old granny rocker with the quilted seat cushions, rocking back and forth, back and forth, finding some solace in the movement. Like I did when I was younger.

I used to sit in the rocking chair when Mom was drunk or when she and Dad had had a fight, or when Mom was crying for the umpteenth time and no one could comfort her. So I found a way to comfort myself.

My mind would drift off into a world that was not my own. I'd make up some place where the hills were made of candy and rivers were made of chocolate. I'd have a boat that would glide on top of that sweet molten sea, and I'd stick my fingers in knuckle deep and imagine what it tasted like.

Or I'd dream of being at the beach, the sand between my toes, the sun high in the sky, and the water a perfect shade of blue. I'd hum the tune to a song I knew. Usually, a nursery rhyme from when I was younger— Twinkle Twinkle, Three Blind Mice—and when I got older, I'd sing the lyrics of the bands I liked, like Blondie, Billy Joel, or Queen.

Sometimes Mom would hear me and sing along to the parts of the song she knew too. Maybe she knew deep down in her fractured heart that I was suffering.

Dad never sang, though. He didn't know the words to any of the songs, and sometimes I wondered if that what was secretly wrong with him. He didn't have music in his soul to help him heal his heart.

Today, I rock back and forth with no music. I sway, realizing the depth of the hole I'm in. Realizing I will have to tell Jimmy what happened between me and Charlie on the night of Lotty's funeral.

Karma

I cannot ask for forgiveness this time. I will not. I will have to take responsibility for any and all mistakes I have made.

I owe my husband that much.

Trena Christie-MacEachern

12

Now

"You all right?" my mother asks. Her dark brown eyes watch me with interest. She offers to tear and wash the lettuce. My hands are shaking.

It's time to tell Jimmy the truth. All of it.

I'm as nervous as a jack rabbit, so much so that it feels like I have sprouted whiskers and a cottontail. I can't stay focused on any task. I leave the ketchup bottle in the bathroom. I pour Mom her tea in one of Paulie's plastic cups.

She doesn't say anything. She looks at me odd when I offer it. She doesn't want to offend, embarrass.

When Jimmy gets home, I drop a plate with the tomatoes on it and I have to throw them out. I'm lost in thought, and stare out into the backyard, wondering, *Now? Do I tell him now? Where do I start? How do I begin?*

I feel a firm hand on my shoulder, and a soft peck on my cheek. I jump and whack him in the mouth with my head.

"Jeesh," he says, rubbing his jaw. "That hurt. I think you cut my tongue. What's wrong?"

He assesses the damage to his mouth, sticks his tongue out and tries to say, "Am I bleeding?"

He has changed from his work clothes into his casual ones. He's wearing his khaki's and a long-sleeve, button-down shirt. I love him in these clothes. He looks so handsome. Like he could be posing for *Gentleman's Quarterly.* He likes to be dressed even when he's home just kicking around, and because he knows I like this look on him.

"Sorry," I say, smiling awkwardly. Then I try to ask casually, "How was your day?" but quickly sputter, "you wanna beer? I'll get you one."

I as much as race out of his grip towards the fridge.

Mom is talking to Mariah at the supper table. She's helping her make homemade dressing, a vinaigrette of some kind. They have all the ingredients on the table and are measuring them into a mason jar.

I watch them talking, Mom is so interested in what Mariah has to say. I feel a pang of jealousy as my teenage years did not see this side of my mother. I craved it when I was young. The always-have-time-for-you mother, reading, and putting puzzles together, riding bikes, and holding hands.

I look around the house at what Jimmy and I built together, the pictures of us on the walls, the art work on the fridge, Mariah and Paulie's time at school, and suddenly I can't breathe.

How could I have done what I did and give all this up? I wish I could take it all away. I don't want to lose what I have because of one idiotic stupid indiscretion. One mistake!

And, it's as if my eyes have bored a hole into my mother's head. She turns and stares at me. Her eyebrows furrow even though she's in mid-sentence with her granddaughter.

My face is hot, yet I'm shaky and the lights seem too bright. All sensation and sounds are fading out like I'm underwater. I can't hear, I can't see. I can't talk.

I feel a fear like I have never known. Something big and dark and ugly, and then I'm falling.

~

I open my eyes. I'm looking up. Four heads encircle my view. Eyes wide, concern, speculation.

"Karmalita?" my mother says, bending over me. She is holding my hand.

"What happened, Grandma?"

"She fainted. Give her some room. She'll be alright. Happens to the best of us."

She looks at me, all-knowing. "Take a minute. Don't get up too soon. You might still be dizzy."

"My hand hurts," I say weakly.

"That all?" My mother sounds gruff.

"You whacked it on the table," Jimmy says. "Went down like a sack of potatoes."

"You pregnant?" my mother mouths.

I laugh out loud at the ludicrous idea. Then my eyes widen. *No! Oh Jesus.*

Tears form in my eyes. I start to cry. I'm lying on the floor, looking up

Trena Christie-MacEachern

at her, bawling uncontrollably.

"Jesus, Karm. What's wrong?" Jimmy gets down on one knee, looking at me.

Mom waves him off. "Jimmy, give us a minute. She'll be okay. Take the kids out."

"What? Where?" he says, his face contorts.

"To the store."

"For what?"

Mom takes a long breath, rolls her eyes. "For ice-cream."

Paulie shouts "yay" in the background.

"But we didn't have supper yet," Mariah interjects.

Mom takes a sharp intake of breath. "Just for a minute, Jimmy. Just go get ice-cream for dessert while this one gets back up."

I hear every word even though she is whispering. It is like they forgot that I'm here.

I sit up, I steady myself, my face is forward. The other hand is my shield so they can't see my anguish, my misery. I'm trying not to cry, but nevertheless, the tears and the sobs come fast and furious.

The door closes and Mom sits back. She sits on the chair behind me and passes me a tissue. There is a silence between us. She waits patiently for me to gather myself. She leans in and wipes my hair out of my eyes, wraps a strand behind my ear.

I blow my nose. Look up at her. I feel like a fool.

"Your reaction said a lot there, missy. Who is he?"

My eyes nearly bulge out of my head. "Mom!"

That's all I can get out before I start bawling into the tissue again.

She is down on the floor with me now. She takes my face and rests it against her chest and strokes my head, passes me another tissue.

"Oh, Karmalita. What are you going to do? I knew your face as soon as you looked me. It was the same as your father's. How far along are you? Does Jimmy know?" She is still stroking my hair as I take deep breaths and dab at my eyes, willing the emotions to stop.

"Mom. I am *not* pregnant." *At least I don't think I am.*

"Are you sure?"

We are still not looking at one another. I can't look her in the eyes so I talk into her chest. My eyes hurt, and my hand feels swollen. It's a wonder I didn't crack my head on the counter before I hit the floor.

"You feel up to sitting on a chair?" she asks.

I nod.

She helps me get up, grabs an arm and walks with me to the table with

124

Karma

all the oils and spices. She sits me down and gets me a glass of water. She places it on the table in front of me. I take it, sip, and place it down again.

"Spill," she says. She is serious. She wants to know what's going on or with whom I was with. I think she feels I owe her as Dad did it to her. To us. She'd rather know than be in the dark. She always wanted to know what she was dealing with.

"Charlie. I think."

Mom's head bows. "You think? Was there someone else?"

"No, Mom. I'm not like that. I just...don't remember. I don't! I don't even know if we did it...or not."

"And you're sure you're not pregnant?"

"Jesus, Mom. I hope not. I just started my period." I lie.

Mom looks up to the heavens. "Thank God," she says. Then she looks at me thoughtfully. "So you were going to tell him about the affair?"

I nod silently and the tears come again.

"With all of us here?"

"I wasn't thinking," I say breathlessly. "I just didn't think."

The hacking tells us Allan has arrived.

"So how much did you hear, Allan?" Mom asks.

After a fit of coughing for almost a minute he answers, "Pretty much all of it."

~

Allan doesn't really eat. He picks at his burger, smokes, and drinks beer mostly. It's nice though to have him and Mom here with us. It calms my nerves and the kids love the added company.

They are unusually quiet today, though, like they too miss Lotty and simply don't know what to say. Allan and Lotty were like Mariah and Paulie's surrogate uncle and aunt. I suppose my fainting spell didn't help the kids, either.

We used to have larger get-togethers with the gang. Lotty and Allan, Clyde and his wife, sometimes even Suzanne and Trudy and their latest boyfriends at the time, would join us. Often, we gathered here at the house with the kids running around. Mostly it was just Lotty and Allan, though.

Our gatherings didn't happen a whole lot, even less after Paulie came. And after Lotty got sick, hardly ever. I still remember Allan popping over and asking non-nonchalantly if we had seen her. If she came by. She used to pop in for coffee before the accident but after, never.

125

Trena Christie-MacEachern

We didn't have anything she wanted. That she needed.

He would sit on the sofa for a few minutes, poke at the kids, pretend everything was alright, then be on his way again. Searching.

How naive we were at the time, not really fully understanding what it was that Allan was experiencing, what he was feeling. We were oblivious really.

Paulie was younger then and he was a handful. Sometimes, I thought I looked just as ragged as Allan. Sleepless nights and busy days will do that to a person. And trying to keep up with dentist and doctor appointments, the meals prepared, the house cleaned, the kids fed, their homework accomplished and stories read. I often felt like I needed myself to be cloned. I wondered how large families did this routine.

Although we didn't know it, Allan had the same going on with Lotty. The long days and sleepless nights, and when he'd get home to a Lotty-less house, the searching would begin, often late into the night.

Once or twice she did get sober, or straight, or whatever the term was, for a while. Allan took her to Suzanne and Clyde's family for a spiritual cleanse, sweat lodge, smudging, healing circle. And it appeared to work in the beginning. That's when we'd see them again, together.

He discovered, unfortunately, he couldn't leave her alone. But Allan had no choice because he had to go to work to pay the bills.

Being alone made her anxious and her mind wandered. She couldn't control her fierce cravings. It was like the devil had her by the nose hairs and pulled her in his direction.

She fought it, Allan said. But the drugs that tried to make her better also created the beast.

I'll never forget that day when Allan called Mom, who then called and told us the police had found Lotty. Allan had been searching everywhere and he had reported her missing. Someone called it in.

We were all shell-shocked. A beautiful girl gone too soon.

Allan didn't even cry. I'm sure he did on his own, in the place they shared together. His eyes told me so. But he was brave and fierce when we went to see him. He hugged us, comforted us, because we needed it. Maybe more so.

I have never experienced exactly what Allan did, but Mom knew. She knew the ugliness of it herself. She had danced that line too close to the edge. Not that she did drugs. Alcohol was her solace but she said it was one and the same for people with addiction. She tried helping Lotty. She did all she could.

But Mom was there for Allan because she felt a connection with him

Karma

on some deeper level. She knew what he was going through because she had gone through it. Mom did it to us, to Dad and me. We knew she felt bad, but at the time she couldn't help herself.

She tried. Dad took her away to a detox centre, only to find her at it again.

But somehow in the end, she did kick it. She still struggles with it every day, I'm sure, and somehow, she found the courage and strength to find sobriety. Perhaps it was luck, or grace, or divine intervention or a combination of it all. We'll never truly know.

But why did she and not Lotty? I don't know what Mom's rock bottom was either. Maybe Dad's countless affairs, or the fact he finally said, "that's it," because he didn't need to put up with her shit anymore, and then I left for college?

She was finally alone to do what she liked. What she wanted. And when she found she had no one around, well, maybe something tweaked, her addiction faced her dead on. She found her way through the storm somehow.

I thank Allan for that. He did something for her. Something I'll never understand nor can explain. He's her angel of sorts. It's too bad that Lotty couldn't find her way through the darkness like Mom.

"It was delicious. Thank you, Karm."

I look at Allan. He pretty much dissected his food, pushed it around, took it apart, flipped it so it would look like he ate something.

I nod at him. He has lost so much weight. His cheek bones are bulging through his skin and he is starting to look like a starvation victim. His belt is notched pretty well to the end, so he tucks the loose part into his front pocket.

He grimaces when he stands up. "Think I'll go, if that's okay."

"It's only early, Allan. Why don't you stay?" Jimmy protests.

"Thanks man, but I'm beat." He does look haggard. His eyes are slowly sinking into his head. His hair has grown, the long strands are touching the back of his shoulders, receding a bit in the front. He looks older than his thirty-four years.

He brings his plate to the counter then comes to me, touches my arm, smiles. I notice the wrinkles under his eyes and how tired he really is.

Just as Mom gets up to see him off, he starts coughing. He bends over and hacks and spits. He can't catch his breath. He grabs a tissue from the counter, then holds onto the sink. Mom finally comes to his aid, starts rubbing his back, trying to soothe him.

"Mummy! He's bleeding!" Paulie's little eyes are wide and scared.

Trena Christie-MacEachern

We all look at the tissue darkened with red as Allan clings to the counter during his coughing fit. It's disturbing and upsetting and Jimmy and I look at each other.

Jimmy holds Paulie's hand until Allan finally catches his breath. He quickly stuffs the tissue into his jacket pocket. Mom keeps talking to him low as he lays bent at the sink, taking in air.

If anyone is going to talk Allan into getting help or going to the doctor, it will be Mom. If she can't get him to the hospital for the care he needs, she will find something else that will help him.

He nods. His face looks pale and sullen. He apologizes sheepishly while we all wave off his insecurities. Mom says she can go with him, follow him at least, 'til he gets home. He tries to decline but Mom insists. She follows him out the door.

~

"Crazy night," Jimmy says as he and I are left clearing up the dishes.

"Yeah."

"Poor Al. My God, what the man is going through. And you? What happened earlier? Are you okay?"

He looks at me intently while he scrapes the remnants of burger and bun into the garbage. "Are you, Karm? You gave me a scare. After everything with Lotty, I just couldn't bear if anything happened to you. To us."

He puts the plate in the dishwasher and comes over to me. He places his hands on the small of my back and holds me close. He lays his head on top of mine for a second and the two of just sort of sway back and forth. "I love you so much, Karm."

I say nothing. Fear and loathing flood my body. He pulls me away from him so he can look down at me. He's concerned. His hazel eyes stare at me, deciphering, analyzing, like they always do. "What's going on? Hmmm?" He twists his head sideways.

I turn to avoid his gaze, grab his fingers from around my waist and release them. I start clearing plates again, putting cups in the dishwasher.

He watches me cleaning. He's leaning on the counter, one foot crossed in front of the other, scanning. "Do you have something you need to tell me?"

There he goes again. Knows what's happening even before I do.

"No!" I snap defensively. Then more subtly, "No, Jimmy. You worry too much. Maybe you should check on Paulie."

128

Karma

"You're so edgy—fidgety."

I laugh just to make mockery. I turn on the tap to get the water running warm when the phone rings.

Neither Jimmy nor I make an effort to answer it. We don't seem to have the energy after the evening. The phone is usually for Mariah anyhow. She is getting to that age where her friends have to know her every move.

"Maaa," Mariah yells, "the phone's for you."

I look at Mariah when she comes into the kitchen and mouth, "Who is it?"

She shrugs.

"Take a message," I ask. I turn my attention back to Jimmy.

"It's nothing, Jimmy. Really. Just off. That's all. Not sleeping. Worried about Allan. He won't go to the doctor. He's grieving for Lotty and there's nothing we can do."

"Do you think your mom can convince him to get help?"

"She's trying."

I wring out the wash cloth, wipe down the counters with the aroma of fresh lemon, wipe the whole table in a circular motion. I grab the ketchup and mustard and put them in the fridge.

"I'm sorry, Jimmy. This must be hard on you. You've known Lotty and Allan since kindergarten. I must seem so selfish."

"No, it's all right. We are all doing what we can."

"It's on the fridge, Ma," Mariah bellows as she walks back to the TV room.

"What is?" I ask.

"Your message."

"Oh. Okay, thanks."

Jimmy and I wrap the leftovers with cling wrap. "You go up and take a shower, honey. You've had a long day. I'll finish up here."

"You sure?" He comes toward me again, tucks a strand of hair behind my ear. Stares at me. Bends down and gives me a kiss on the lips.

"Of course."

He smiles. "Love you."

"Love you back," I say as I watch his long, lean body walk out of the kitchen.

I grab the remainder of the burgers and wrapped salad, pick up the dressing and open the fridge, look for a place for everything on the shelf.

When I close the fridge door, I notice Mariah's note.

Trena Christie-MacEachern

Meet Linda tomorrow at
Calvin's for coffee – 12:30
Bring the dough

I freeze. I read the message over again and take it from the fridge and walk into the TV room to see Mariah.

Her feet are hanging over the arm of the sofa, her ear pressed to the phone. I tap her on the shoulder. She looks up.

"Mariah? Who's this?"

She shrugs. "Said her name was Linda something."

"Sullivan?" I gasp.

"Yeah, that's it. Although it didn't really sound like a girl, Mom."

I nod, then let her go back to her conversation.

Linda Sullivan. I reread the message, in Mariah's scrawl. Coffee at 12:30.

I crumple the paper, stuff it in my pocket. Linda Sullivan was the code name I had for Charlie when my parents wouldn't let me talk to him on the phone.

~

I haven't had coffee at Calvin's in years. I didn't even think it was still open. It was a little Mom and Pop shop, opened before the big coffee houses took over. We used to come here when we were younger, trying to act like the gang from *Friends*. Everyone did. That was one of the reasons why it was so popular.

The menu was primarily coffee and tea, hot chocolate, a few cold beverages, muffins, toast.

Now it's a small grill. Sandwiches and soups, everything to go. No one took anything to go back in the day. We just hung out with real cups, drinking regular coffee. Now it's plastics and Styrofoam, bottled water and juices.

I park out in back, away from the cafe altogether. Even though this place is out of the way, I don't want to be seen here. I don't even want to go in. There will be lunch patrons and what if I know some of them? I don't need someone asking why I'm here, or whom I'm with.

My watch says 12:20. I feel a breeze and wish I had taken a sweater. The spring sun, although warm, is deceiving. You think it's nicer out than

Karma

it really is.

I shiver, pull my sleeve down my wrist as I walk to the main entrance. A man holds the door open for me as I approach. I cringe inside. He's as tall as Jimmy wearing a suit and tie. He's holding a coffee to go and is eating a muffin.

I nod at him and another man follows him out. The two walk up the street together.

On the outside, Calvin's hasn't really changed much so I'm instantly taken back. I think of all the memories we shared here. But gone are the couches and the oversized lounge chairs where we liked to sit and hang out. Now, in its stead, there are small, wooden chairs and tables. It's no longer cozy. It's cold. People don't have time to sit and relax.

There's a lunch rush and a lineup at the counter. Large standing refrigerators with glass doors are pushed against the wall, holding all the premade sandwiches and cold drinks. It starts by the door and it's pick, then pay at the counter.

A large chalkboard hangs over the back wall with today's specials: Tomato soup and grilled cheese sandwiches. $4.95. I opt for a small coffee. I don't need to be hanging around here.

Charlie isn't here yet. I look at my watch again: 12:25.

I pour my coffee into a takeaway cup and stand behind a woman in dress pants and a cardigan. She looks smart, I think. Her hair is pulled back in a bun. I can't guess how old she is and wonder what she does for a living. I often wonder what I would have become if I hadn't had a baby so early in life, and if I had finished my degree.

I put my bag on the counter and rummage through my purse. I pull out a five and, as the lady ahead pays for her tea and muffin, it is my turn at the cash register.

"Just a coffee? she asks blandly.

I nod and she places another Styrofoam cup in front of me.

"Two coffees," his smooth voice states.

Turning, I see Charlie grinning.

The cashier looks at Charlie, then back at me.

My hand is still holding the bill. The cashier takes it and hands me my change. There's a bowl for tips. Without thinking, I toss her all the coins. She doesn't even say thank you. And I don't know if I'm more pissed about that or for Charlie butting in line and getting me to buy his drink.

I pick up my purse, grab my coffee, as he does, and find seats as far as I can get us from everyone else.

"Thanks," he says, smiling. Obviously happy with himself.

Trena Christie-MacEachern

We sit down at a table for four. He sits opposite me.

He's as cool as ever. Wearing a tight-fitting tee that tells me he still works out. His short sleeves expose his biceps. He's wearing tailored denims and dark brown loafers.

He's not wearing a ring. But then again, neither am I. He looks smug.

"Linda Sullivan." The words blurt out of me like someone else had said them.

He smiles, that goofy, child-like grin. "I knew you'd remember. Pretty clever, eh?"

Isuddenly the walls feel like they are closing in. "I can't stay here," I snap, and bolt for the door.

He rushes ahead of me, holding both our coffees, and uses his back to open the door.

"After you, miss," he says calmly, attempting to hand me my coffee.

Keep walking, I tell myself. *It will be better outside. No eyes watching.*

I don't trust Charlie. There is probably someone in there that is keeping an eye on him. *On me!* A shiver runs through me and it isn't the wind this time.

"You cold?" he asks, concern in his voice.

I don't answer. I just keep walking around the block to where my car is parked. Then I stop when I see it. I don't want to sit in there either.

I start digging through my bag and find the envelope with the money. I take it out and try to hand it to him. But he is still holding my coffee and his so I stand awkwardly, wondering for a moment what to do with it.

I grab my coffee and stuff the envelope in his hand, start off again. "It's not all there," I say gruffly.

"Hold on, Karma," he says aloud. When I don't respond, he shouts, "Wait! Karma!"

By this time, he has jammed the envelope in his back jean pocket and has me by the arm, leading me away from my car and to the playground area. "Would you hold on? Jeesh, I want to talk to you. Don't be so spastic!"

I stop and glare at him. The f-ing nerve! No words form as I'm so angry at this very moment.

He glares back and then his head falls back and he laughs out loud. "I know that look. That pissed off look. Cat got your tongue when you're pissed, Karma. You haven't changed much."

I whack him on the shoulder. He smiles at me, like it's a sign of love.

"Smarten up, Charlie! I don't even want to be here. Jesus. Calling my house, talking to my daughter. Luring me here. Blackmailing me! You're a

Karma

fucken' asshole!" I'm red in the face at this point.

But my words don't faze Charlie. He just smirks, perfect teeth inside a smug face. "C'mere. Up here. Let's go sit up here."

He still has hold of my arm and I jerk it away from him. I don't know why I just didn't leave after I gave him the money. Probably because I don't have it all and I knew he would have to contact me again. I need to know what else is going to happen.

We walk up a small path to an overhanging elm. Its branches outstretch with large oblong leaves already offering shelter and shade from the early spring sun. We duck under the foliage and walk the muddy embankment to an opening in the fence that leads to a small park. Swings, slides, and sandboxes are there, along with a few benches and picnic tables where folks can sit to watch their little ones play.

I remembered when I used to take Paulie to these parks, in the hope he would take an afternoon nap after. We'd spend half the morning here. I'd pack some snacks and I'd often go with my neighbour who had her little ones. It was something I both dreaded yet looked forward to.

I take the picnic table nearest the oak. He sits opposite me. I take another sip of my coffee, watch a mother push her little girl in the swing. They are the only two here, not including Charlie and me.

"I couldn't get all the money," I say, not looking at him. My eyes are focused on the mother and her daughter. The little girl's blond hair whips in front of her face and then blows behind. She is laughing. I think of her tangles.

"Figured," he says. "Envelope is small."

"I want the pictures," I say coldly. "Whatever it is you have of me."

"You'll get them when I have the rest of the money."

"Charlie. You jack-ass. Read my lips. I can't get any more money! I have nearly eighteen hundred in that fucking envelope. I had to sell my own anniversary ring to make up that cash. I don't have that kind of money. Who do you think I am? And by the way, if we are in the throes of passion, how could you possibly take pictures of that? You only have two hands." My body's shaking I'm so pissed.

"Karma," he says my name softly. "Shhh. Relax."

"I won't fucken' relax," I bark. The mother looks over at me this time. She holds the swing to stop it, then places her daughter on the ground. They leave hand in hand, not looking back.

I didn't mean to curse so loud.

Charlie stares into my eyes. "Your ring?"

I look down at my bare hands. Touched where my wedding rings were supposed to be. There is nothing there to remind me that I'm married. Only in my heart.

"Charlie?" I stare into his eyes now. "Why are you doing this? To me. To Jimmy. It was a mistake. And you're making me pay for me. Literally! You son-of-a-bitch. What did I ever do to you?"

"I never wanted to hurt you." Charlie reaches for my hand.

"Bullshit!" I snap. "You hurt me back in high school. You're doing it all over again on a different level."

"I love you, Karma. I would never hurt you intentionally." He's studying me. His face is stone serious.

"Would you stop? You're making a mockery. My God, to what level would you stoop, Charlie? What is wrong with you?"

"I—I...just thought you would be easiest to target." He sounds sheepish now.

He bends his head down and stretches out his arms so they are in front of him. He holds his hands together, rotates his thumbs around each other.

"What in the hell does that mean?" I feel like flinging my hot coffee at him. But I can't.

I take another gulp, grimace, and burn the roof of my mouth. "Fuck!" I place it on the wooden table.

I no longer feel the cold, the chill. I'm beyond hot and push up my sleeves, pull my hair back in a ponytail and put on my sunglasses. "So, what? You're going to keep harassing me until I get the rest of it? Then what? I mean, I don't have it. You gonna show Jimmy the pictures? Ruin my kids lives too? Like you ruined everyone's."

Charlie clenches his teeth and his muscles in his forearms flex. I hit some kind of nerve.

"Listen," he says, calmly. I've never seen Charlie in any mood other than charming and happy. Occasionally serious when the mood required it. But today, I see another side of him. It isn't anger so much, as fear, I think.

"Calm yourself down," he says in a low whisper. "Do you want everyone to see us? To hear us? I'm trying to be discreet. You don't know the half of it. You never do. So, I'll explain it to you. Yes, I need the money. There are people looking for me because it is not 'my' money. I had a good little thing going, selling some...pharmaceuticals, if you will."

"Drugs, Charlie. They're drugs. You're nothing but a pusher."

"Shut up and listen." He raises up on his seat then lowers himself again. "I had a stash that I was holding on to for another guy. That's all. I

Karma

don't do the hard stuff. Just a few pills here and there. Good cash."

"Why don't you get a real job?" I snap.

"Let me finish," he huffs. He takes a breath and looks around, "Lotty was a regular." He put his hands up. "And, yes, I know what you may think. But I was honest to God trying to get her off of it. I was trying to help. Ask Allan. She was doing good. But she found my stash—the stuff I was hanging onto for another fellow. That's all I was doing, hanging on to it. I didn't plan on selling it. It's just not my thing, but I owed him a favour. And she friggen got a hold of it. Took it. All of it. Everything. And then she disappeared. I don't know what she was planning on doing with it, selling it, using it. I don't fuckin' know. But either way, she's dead because of it and I'm to blame. And that shit costs money and I don't fuckin' have it and they're looking for me and if they find me without the fuckin' money, I will be as dead as she is."

I looked at him. "You're full of shit."

"Karma! Okay, whatever. Don't believe me!"

"I don't! So why me? You think I have ten grand in a sock drawer? Like a stay-at-home mother of two makes a lot of money."

"I asked Jimmy. I know he has a decent job. Figured he put some away. He always did. He never spends money, the bastard. He's probably rolling in it and you don't even know it."

"You really have some nerve. And because Jimmy thought you were full of shit about some new company venture"—my hands do quotes around 'new company venture'—"you tried me? Tried to get at Jimmy that way?"

Charlie nods. "I didn't think you'd have to sell your ring," he says in a low tone. "I didn't think you'd have to sell anything. Just take out one of them RSP things."

I laugh out loud. "Just like that?"

Then it dawned on me. Everything. He set me up from the get-go. He took me to an imaginary house, got me drunk, slept with me. My eyes widen.

"You had this planned from the start, didn't you? You planned to seduce me right after Lotty died!"

I feel even more like an idiot. The tears start to come to the corners of my eyes. *How could I have been deceived like that?*

"Oh, Charlie," I say mournfully.

I let the tears fall now. I didn't care anymore. "I've been a fool. And I let you take advantage of me. I honestly thought there was a piece of you that still cared for me. You were my first boyfriend, the love of my life,

135

Trena Christie-MacEachern

and I held on to that for *so* long!"

I wipe my face with my hands. "But you just used me. I'm so disgusted with myself on so many levels." I can't finish what I have to say. "God, Charlie. Thanks. Thanks a lot."

I get up and start walking away.

He runs after me. "I didn't plan it. I told you before, I love you. I've always loved you. You were my first. too."

"Get away from me. This is over. Show Jimmy the pictures. I don't care. Just get out of my sight." I am breathless and weak.

"You need to hear this, Karma."

"No," I shout. I keep walking out of the park area, under the oak, down the small path to the parking lot.

He grabs my hand and spins me around. "You don't get it! You never got it."

"I don't want to hear."

"You were too good for me. I always knew that. I knew you needed more. I knew that day, sitting in the grassy field on our free, that you were going to go places and I wasn't. I knew I couldn't ever get a good job like Jimmy could. I didn't have the marks. I didn't have the smarts. I knew I would disappoint you in the long run. I needed someone who already had money. I would marry someone that would leave me with some cash and get some kind of living and then you and I would be together. That was my plan. All along. I was coming back for you."

"Shit, Charlie. You're full of it."

"Why do you think the marriage didn't last?"

"Because you were probably unfaithful and—"

"I kept calling your name when we were together. All the time. When I called her on the phone, I'd say your name. When we ate the supper she made, slept in our bed."

"So, you screwed two women. Classy, Charlie. Real classy."

"She wanted me on her arm. She used me, too. It just didn't end up the way I wanted it to. I didn't know Jimmy had a thing for you. I didn't know he was going to get you knocked up. I wanted you to have my babies. Be my wife!"

He is screaming at me. "God, you were and are the only woman I've ever loved. Ever will love. And I'm sorry I asked you for money. But you are my last resort. I wasn't going to tell you I had pictures, but it just came out. I was just going to plead and see if you could twist Jimmy's arm. I'd pay it back. That was my plan all along. Once I get these goons off my back. Jesus. I can't even go to my own house. Karma. This is seri-

Karma

ous. I'm scared. I'm fucking scared!"

"Whatever," I say. "A little too late. You put me through hell. I don't know what to think anymore. I don't believe anything you say and you've no one to back you up."

"Lotty would have backed me up."

"She's dead. For the love of God."

"That wasn't supposed to happen. We had a plan. She didn't stick to it. Allan's my last hope."

When we get to my car, he opens my door.

"Allan's fucken' sick, you moron. Leave him alone." I turn and face him. "He's been through enough."

"He's my last hope. If I can't get it from you. He's all I got left."

"Jesus, Charlie. I don't even know what to say."

Inside the car feels like one hundred degrees. I roll down my window and blot my face with a tissue.

Charlie sticks his head in. When he's this close to me, it feels like he paralyzes me.

In a low whisper, he says, "Karma. It's all the truth. Every bit of it. I have to go now. Take care, please."

He kisses me on the temple. "You and the gang are always what mattered to me. Always. Despite what you think."

Nervously, I fumble for my keys.

"I care about Jimmy, too," he says. "But I loved you first. Remember that. And I would never ever intentionally hurt you. I always had a plan."

I start up the car, put it in gear, pull away without saying a word. In my rear-view mirror, I see Charlie watching me, his demeanour, calm. He stuffs his hands into his front pockets, but then as I round the corner, he pulls his hand out and brings it to his mouth.

The bastard blows me a kiss.

13

Now

One Head Light is playing on the radio. It's a catchy tune so I turn up the volume. I turn it up loud. It's probably too loud but I need to drown out the sound of my thoughts.

I don't want to think about anything. Jimmy. The kids. Charlie. Charlie the asshole. Dad. Allan. Poor Allan. Mom. *God!*

I look at the time. It's only quarter to two. I still have an hour-ish but I know I don't want to go home. Not yet. And I don't want to go to Mom's. I can't face Jimmy. Or Allan.

Everything's a mess.

I think back to my and Charlie's conversation. *The liar! All he does is tell lies. He said I should ask Allan about whether or not he was trying to help Lotty. I couldn't possibly ask that of Allan now. Not yet. It would be too intrusive. And I can't get Jimmy to ask Allan.* Nope, I can't do that either. *Maybe I should call Trudy and get her feedback? But, if I phone Trudy, Suzanne will be there barking at me. I can't handle that either. My temples are throbbing.* A splitting headache is coming on.

The car ahead of me stops abruptly and I slam on the brakes. Although I'm probably following too close, I lay on the horn anyhow. It's all this pent-up rage. Frustration. *Fuck!*

The man in front of me rolls down his window and gives me the finger. I don't need this shit, not today.

When I see an opening, I blow past him. Only I don't get far. I'm in front of him at the next set of stop lights.

I'm not even sure where I'm going.

I check my reflection in the rear-view mirror. It looks like I haven't slept in days. There are dark circles and bags under my eyes. My face is dry and pale and my lips are chapped.

The light turns green and I step on the pedal, head north. I drive, just drive.

Karma

I take Exit 35 and drive for another thirty minutes 'til I reach Chesterbrook, the next town over. The driving calms me, especially on the four-lane. I'm breezing past everyone. I know I'm driving too fast but I need to clear my head.

Going home is not an option right now. Too many guilt-ridden memories there and my head is doing so many circles I feel like I'm on the tilt-a-whirl.

My stomach starts to rumble and I realize I haven't eaten since breakfast, and the coffee I had with Charlie won't cut it. There's a strip mall up ahead so I pull in. I'll pick something up at the grocery store here. There is also a small cafe, along with a pharmacy and an optometrist's office.

The pharmacy reminds me of something else I need to pick up but I'm trying to avoid. A pregnancy kit.

I hope I won't see anyone here I know, as I don't have the mindset for idle chit chat. With a heavy sigh, I grab my purse and head in.

The double automatic doors open and I step inside a store that is bright and lavish. The fragrance counter greets me first and I realize this is a place where I can kill a couple of hours easily. Perfumes and jewellery are showcased front and centre but I can't let myself get distracted. I've got to take care of my business first.

As I walk around the store I find what I'm here for. It's ironic they carry the women's menstrual pads and tampons beside the birth control section.

I grab the first box I see and stuff it under my arm. I try to look nonchalant and continue to browse. I tell myself, *This is no big deal I have a pregnancy kit under my arm*. It's such a vast difference from the last time.

I certainly didn't need to buy a kit when I was pregnant with Mariah. Not expecting it, number one, followed by the rudest morning sickness ever. It was as if my body was punishing me for being neglectful of birth control.

Paulie was a whole other story. Jimmy and I had tried for years and every month we'd be wildly disappointed. We often wondered if Mariah would be an only child. But, finally, our prayers were answered.

Now, here I am the third time out and elation would be the best way to describe a negative response.

It feels like I'm going to be sick. I can't fully fathom conceiving another baby, particularly Charlie's. Not now. Not like this. Not after how hard we tried for Paulie for so long. It took too much out of us.

Now, I wish I had a cart. This box I'm holding feels like a cancer. The sharp edges are digging into my armpit and elbow, and holding it clearly

Trena Christie-MacEachern

for even the cashier or anyone to see, will usually elicit one of two responses and neither I can handle. People don't want to hear the negative. It's supposed to be a wonderful thing and everyone is supposed to squeal and jump up and down and hug you and tell you they are just so excited for you. Right? But in those cases when you may be pregnant but not totally thrilled because it's a mistake, or unwanted, or it's not a good time, or is it his? Or something worse, did something happen to you?

"Can I help you with anything?" the saleslady asks, her dyed red hair all shoulder length and perfect. Perfect makeup, perfect lips, perfect smile. I'd like to tell her to piss off. Instead, I pretend I don't hear her, wander over to the hair care section. Walking mindlessly, picking up items, putting them down. Maybe she thinks I'm a shoplifter? She follows and asks me again. I smile sheepishly.

"No, thank you. I'm browsing."

"Would you like a basket?"

Yes, a basket. "Please." I try to sound upbeat.

She is wearing a navy uniform, pants and blouse, small heels. Small gold earrings in her ears. She has great posture. Very erect. Her finger nails are perfectly manicured. I wonder if she files her nails while waiting for customers to come in. She picks up a wire basket and hands it to me. She watches as I place the pregnancy kit inside. She looks at it and then eyes me again, says nothing. I put my purse over the box.

"You know?" she says to me. "You'd look nice with some ash highlights in your hair. I could help you pick out some colours. I'll just be over at the cosmetic counter if you need any more help."

She smiles again and stands by the glass counter, straightening up boxes of skin cream. I'm happy she's discreet.

Even though I have everything I came for, I find myself still walking about. The basket gives me purpose. I'm at the magazine rack now, flipping through the countless stacks of beautiful women. I wonder why some girls get all the luck: beauty, wealth, and fame.

My stomach does a gurgle and I realize it was the hunger that took me here. I throw in a bag of chips and a Kit Kat to munch on so I don't tear the head of anybody. Just as I turn to cash out, I eye a display case of lip glosses.

Back in the day, I would have killed for one of those roll-on tubes.

I pick up one for Mariah, throw it in the basket.

As I'm about to get in line to pay for my things, I hear my name. "Karm! Is that you? Karmalita Smallwood?"

I look up. A woman in a white smock is smiling and waving from be-

Karma

hind the counter.

I'm staring at her but nothing is ringing. It's like someone is talking but no one is there. Her hair is pulled back and she's wearing glasses.

I wave awkwardly, slowly. Still nothing. But I don't want to seem rude. "Sorry," I say.

She comes out from behind the counter. "It's been a few years," she says. "Come on. I didn't change that much, did I?"

I'm still looking at her. Everything is out of context. Me. Here. My current state of mind is not helping. Tired. Hungry.

She starts laughing. "You seriously don't recognize me.?" She doesn't say it in a mean way.

Then she takes off her glasses.

I gulp. It is the same, sweet smile. She's heavier, and her hair is darker. She's older, of course, but so am I. Vicki Meagher. Son of a bitch. Charlie's ex. Isn't this f-ing ironic. I cradle the basket like it's a newborn.

"My God. I'm sorry. I'm....Yes, Vicki. Wow. I didn't know you worked here. Holy. How have you... been?"

She laughs again. I don't remember her being this friendly.

"Right! I forgot! You studied to be a pharmacist. You and Trudy were in sciences together. And Lotty."

"You haven't changed a bit, Karm."

I suddenly feel more self-conscious. About what I'm wearing, my hair, my pale lips with no lipstick. I run a hand through my hair then remember I have it tied back and my sunglasses are sitting on top of my head. By mistake I flick them and they slide down. I grab them and throw them in the basket, hoping Vicki thinks that I meant to do that.

"Yeah, I followed in my dad's footsteps. This is his place. Well, ours now. I made some changes."

It's very impressive. It's great. You're doing great. It's one-stop shopping."

"That's the point." She laughs. How's everyone?" she asks with genuine interest and curiosity. *Strange.*

"Good. Well, some of them."

This is awkward. *Does she know? Did Charlie tell her? Did she look at my basket?*

I look down to see if she can tell what I have in it. Nope, only a big bag of chips and a magazine. It looks like I'm just shopping, and eating junk food.

"Allan's sick," I blurt.

She raises a hand to her mouth. Her eyes widen. "Oh, I'm sorry. I didn't

141

Trena Christie-MacEachern

know. I lost contact with everyone since—."

"Yeah."

The elephant in the room presents itself. "I'm not with Charlie anymore. I suppose you already know that."

"I'm sorry." I shift the basket to my other hand. "I just...heard."

"And sorry about Lotty," she says. "After the accident, we sort of...but she was lovely. So bright. It's awful how things turned out."

I nod. "I'm sorry, too."

We stare at each other for a few moments.

"Oh my gosh," she says. "All these apologies."

The basket is getting really heavy in my arm.

"I'm holding you up," I say,. "I'm, ah, just going to pay for this and—"

"I'm just going on break." She touches my arm. "Do you have a minute? I'd love to hear about Allan. Can we grab a coffee and catch up?"

I force a smile, wondering how I'm going to get out of this and get something into me more substantial than another coffee.

"Perfect," she says, taking my silence for consent. "I'll meet you out front after you pay for your items."

~

I'm not sure how I feel about sitting with Charlie's woman, ex, the girl who stole him away from me. Plus, the wedding that trumped my own nuptials and the last time I saw Lotty as the person I once knew.

I'm a disgraceful person. There's no way around it. Why am I here? With her? I should be running screaming into the hills, yet here I wait for Vicki to come and sit so I can fill her in about a person she barely kept in contact with, so I can pick her brain about my ex and the situation he is in or, at least, how he got there. *I'm pathetic.*

The cafe is bright and cheerful, small, but clean. She's at the counter ordering a toasted bagel and a small tea. She's getting me a latte. I've never had one before but she's paying. I grab a seat. A latte is the least she can do. I should have ordered a steak, if they had one here. I'm starving.

I'm drumming my fingers on the table waiting for her to sit down. She is picking up napkins. I get up to help her. Her bagel is held against her chest and she's carrying two cups in her hand.

She's smiling and looking confident. Like we are friends just getting together for a chat. It couldn't be any further from the truth.

"Here you go," she says almost too sweetly. "I got you a cookie, too. I

142

don't like eating alone."

She places a white-chocolate, macadamia-nut cookie in front of me. It's the size of a wagon wheel and my eyes light up.

"Thanks," I say, almost too excitedly.

"Don't mention it." She unwraps her bagel, all glistening with butter, and takes a bite. Opens the lid of her drink, blows on the tea while chewing. Her fingers are delicate and her nails short.

It seems strange to be looking at this girl I once knew. How I felt such venomous loathing for her. But now, I'm watching her eating a bagel like nothing has ever happened between us.

"You try the latte?"

I nod.

"The cookies are amazing." Her eyes gleam. "If you don't want it, I'll take it."

Then I feel possessive of the cookie. Something that is mine and she wants it back already. I snap a piece from the corner and stuff it in my mouth, letting the chocolate and dough melt. Mmm, it is so good. I pop in another piece and then take a drink.

"Holy shit that's good," I blurt.

She laughs.

"I know, right? I've had me a few of those."

I laugh. Looking at her, evidently, she has.

"You okay?" She stares at me. Her eyes look directly into mine, not even blinking. She takes another quick sip of her tea.

My eyes furrow and I feel like I'm making a face at her.

She laughs. "Do you find this just a bit awkward?"

"Yep," I say. I look down at my cookie, feeling nervous and stupid all of a sudden.

"I'm sorry," she says. "If you want to leave, you can just go. I don't want to keep you."

This gal certainly has her own voice, but I try to sound just as confidant, even though I feel like a heel, and my breathing is shallow. "No, God, no. I'm fine."

"You look nervous." She's on her second half of the bagel.

I wave my hand, "No, no. Just have to keep check of the time as I'll have to be home for the kids."

"Right. Me, too." She laughs. "Not kids, though. I'll have to get back to work."

She asks about Allan so I tell her about him, about his symptoms. She listens intently. We talk about Lotty too. She heard about her. Says she liked them both. Never imagined how their life went so south.

"So terrible, eh? Poor Allan. He doesn't deserve what happened to him. All that feels like ages ago."

Then I find the nerve to ask a few questions myself. "Did Charlie try and help Lotty? When she was sick?"

"Oh God, yeah. She was heading down a dark path. After the accident. But no one could help her. Only Lotty could help herself, yeah? Charlie even took her to Suzanne's uncle to do a cleanse. But even then I knew she wouldn't make it. That she'd never get clean."

"Really?"

She nods. "I'd never tell Allan that."

"Allan hoped she would just hit rock bottom and make her way back."

"I knew that much, but I did hope for them. Sometimes that's all we have. But she was hard-wired. You could see it in her eyes."

She crumbles up her napkin and sits back in her chair. "I didn't think you'd be so easy to talk to." She takes another sip of her tea.

"Pardon?" I ask.

Vicki smiles, exposing a dimple on one side of her cheek.

I try to remember her the way I knew her. But it was getting hard to distinguish between the temptress, the wife, and now this pleasant, albeit brazen, pharmacist sitting opposite me.

"Charlie always said you were a little crazy. I was kind of scared of you."

My mouth drops.

She throws her head back and laughs out loud. "He's full of shit, eh?"

"Yes!" I shout, choking on a piece of cookie. The tears come to my eyes as I swallow the crumb down. I take a slurp of latte, dab my eyes with my fingertips.

She nods.

I grab hold of the table on either side "I can't believe he said that."

"I don't think he wanted me to talk to you. Made up stuff to keep me away from you."

"Why?"

She shrugs. "Oh, I'm sure Charlie had his reasons."

I sit stunned, release my grip on the table.

Vicki turns her attention to a young woman entering the cafe. She has shiny, long, golden hair. Like Rapunzel. "You know, Charlie was a mystery. Never really knew anything about him."

She directs her attention back on me. She doesn't seem to care about anything. She seems very cool and calm, not giving a hoot about what

Karma

people think. An admirable trait.

"Is that why your marriage ended?" I ask brazenly.

She smiles broadly. "You don't know?"

I narrow my eyes. She looks out the window again, at the young woman heading to her car. I shift in my chair, move in closer, put my elbows on the table.

"I'm gay."

I sit back. I try to take it all in. "So, Charlie didn't know?"

She dies laughing. Mouth opens wide, head thrown back. Her shoulders are shaking.

"Yes, yes, he knew," she finally manages. "Oh my God, you're not crazy. You're a scream."

I laugh awkwardly. Not sure If I'm supposed to. "But, but," I want to ask her so many questions.

She reaches out and her warm, delicate fingers touch my hand. It isn't a sexual thing, but almost out of friendship.

"I wasn't interested in Charlie back in high school. I was interested in Suzanne."

I gasp.

"But Charlie sort of knew about it even though I didn't act on it then. He just had this intuition. You know Charlie? Friends with everyone. He was so charming. And we were just going to, you know? Hang out. My folks were against my lifestyle. I found that out pretty quick. I think they may have suspected early on and just wanted to make it clear that it was not going to happen in the Meagher household. I was young. Then Charlie called me. He needed a tutor. I obliged. I knew you were dating. He liked you. I knew that. But he kept running into me. Then he found out my dad was well-to-do and, and he went about and made an impression on him. And once Dad liked him, Dad really hoped I had this interest in this guy. Well, something sealed the deal for Charlie. Told Dad he was going into the sciences, sales, whatever."

Vicki rolls her eyes. "You know Charlie? Never worked a day in his life. If he could focus that talent somewhere," she seems exasperated, "he could be something. But then, I didn't know this at the time, he was taking his mom to different doctors' offices all over town, getting prescriptions and selling them. Making some side dough so every time we were together, he always had money. He never flashed it. Just made Dad know that he was working odd jobs, supporting his mom, taking me out, flashing that smile. And he said you were out of the picture by now. I mean, you were busy working and stuff so we didn't see a whole lot of you. I

Trena Christie-MacEachern

just knew then that I wanted to get the hell out of there and start my life, see people I really wanted to see and I did meet someone. Someone I really liked."

She shakes her head. "But once Charlie found out, he used it against me. The bastard blackmailed me. Told me the best thing for us to do is pretend we're in love. I could go on dating my girlfriend, he could get the fringe benefits, live off me. It sounded like a good gig. Thought he had a job. Or was taking classes. Or whatever. I just never really concerned myself with him you know? But Charlie was everywhere. It was like he was omniscient."

She checks her watch. "I think I need something stronger than this coffee."

"But you got married."

"Yep. Big charade. Tried to pull the wool over everyone's eyes. My parents especially."

"So, what happened to your perfect life?"

"Things were quiet and good for a while. 'Til I realized what he was doing. My dad owned the pharmacy. He would come over, hoping Dad could, you know? Help his mom with her pills. Dad caught on pretty quick and he would never do that. Against the law for one, against protocol, not honourable. Dad mentioned it to me. Not right away, of course. He was concerned. I kept an ear to the ground and started figuring out what Charlie was doing. But he had me. I stayed quiet for a while until I realized he wasn't going to stop there. He'd go after my dad and the pharmacy. So I finally came out. And when I did, threatened to expose Charlie, his plan backfired. Then he left. But I know he's still selling. That's his bread and butter."

"Why didn't you just report him? Call the cops and get him arrested?"

"I thought about that for the longest time. But, as you know, there is something about Charlie. He obviously had some sort of rotten upbringing. And I just couldn't do it. A part of me really cared about him. Am I pissed at what he did? Of course I am. But I was privy to it so I used him, too. But Charlie is a survivor and if he gets knocked down, he'll get back up. That's how he operates. But really, other than what I told you, I don't know a thing about him. Never seen a picture. Can count the times I saw his mother. She wasn't even at the wedding. Don't know about his childhood. Just your group that hung out. That's all."

"Really?" I think for a moment, wondering if I should ask Jimmy about it. I also want to tell her about what he told me at his fake house, but I realize I'd be opening a whole can of worms. And I don't know this girl,

146

Karma

even though she just shared a lot of personal information.

"Gosh," she says, "look at the time. I have to get back."

"Oh, right, right. Me too."

"Hey, it was nice. Finally getting to have a conversation with you. I'm sorry the way things turned out, but I think things are okay with you, aren't they? You still with Jimmy?" She's looking at my ringless fingers.

"Yes," I say. "Still with Jimmy."

"Well, Charlie always spoke highly of Jimmy and Allan. Even when he was drinking and we pretended to be a normal couple."

I smile.

"And, for what's it worth," she says, "not that you need to hear it you're married and all and that ship has sailed, but sometimes when we would be sleeping together, because we were sort of friends in a weird kind of way until things got weirder, he would call out your name in his sleep."

I sit in stunned silence.

"Okay, I really have to go." She reaches out again for my hand, as her gesture, I suppose, to apologize or say goodbye.

And as I sit silently watching her leave, I wonder what really brought me here? Of all places.

Then I catch a subtle, familiar fragrance. The same one she used to wear.

The scent disappears as quickly as it arrived and I smile when I think of her.

Lotty.

~

But if it was Lotty who led me to that pharmacy to get the lowdown on Charlie, was it her as well that caused me to crash my car?

I knew I hadn't been myself. Not since Lotty passed away. It was hard to shake what had happened to her. The whys. She had so much to live for. She made a wrong decision to grab the wheel on that night in July and it changed everything. It was like the demons were just waiting for her to slip up.

As her bones started to heal, the agony didn't leave. The prescriptions dried up. She shouldn't be needing pain killers anymore, the doctor's said. But she did. And they didn't seem to understand the gravity of her situation. She was hurting bad.

And when they wouldn't listen, she found her own alternatives, stronger, uglier, deadlier. Although I didn't think, like Vicki, that Lotty

147

Trena Christie-MacEachern

was bound to end up the way she did. We all hoped it was just a phase, a setback.

And all these things cross my mind at lighting speed when that burgundy car comes out of nowhere and slams into me.

Yes, I was not paying full attention. Yes, my mind was on other things as it had been the past while. Yes, my life flashed before my eyes: my kids, my parents, my husband, my friends, my life.

Then I see her.

She is smiling. Her mouth is moving but I can't make out the words. She is trying to tell me something so I reach forward.

Then there is commotion and chaos. But through all of it, calmly sitting nearby, is Lotty.

The smell of strong fumes knock me out and then I'm looking up into a light, like a small flashlight. Fingers press against my face, forcing my eyes open.

"Can you tell me your name? Do you know what day it is?"

I look around, try to, and moan.

"Owww!" Everything hurts. My nose and hand feel fat.

I focus and realize I'm in the ER in the hospital

"Easy does it. You were in an accident but you're going to be okay. Is there anyone we need to call?"

Great, I think. *F-ing great.*

Karma

14

Now

I look worse than I feel. Or I feel worse than I look. I can't figure out which. Either way, I look like a basket case hobbling out of the hospital.

I had called Mom to get me, and for her to tell Jimmy. I didn't want it to be a big deal. But it was, so they contacted Becky to pick up the kids after school because he didn't want me showing up and scaring the hell out of them, looking like I do.

I have a sling around my arm holding my shoulder in place, lots of cuts on my face and hands because of the broken glass; but it's my pride, really, that hurts most of all. I just don't know how I am going to explain myself out of this one, but at some point, I'll have to.

Mom didn't really say anything; she spoke with the doctors and got the update on my recovery, which she pretty much knew once she saw my chart and had a look at me. She just sat on the bed and asked me how I was feeling, stared into my eyes, looked at my gashes and bandages. She brushed the bangs out of my face.

"Okay, honey, let's get out of here."

And that was all she said. No questions asked, not, "What were you thinking? Didn't you see her coming? Why were you in Chesterbrook?" or, "Jimmy's going to have a fit." She knew all these questions would get answered eventually as she had been through similar circumstances in her own time.

She understands but, most of all, she knows I don't need someone harping on me. It only makes matters worse.

I did, however, break down and cry in her car for a brief moment. The aftershock of it, the post traumatic. Realizing, maybe, I could have died, or the fact that your brain finally catches up to you in present time, getting realigned with your physical self and then, damn, everything hurts like a frigger.

They gave me some pills for the pain which I have every intention of

Trena Christie-MacEachern

taking. Again, I think of Lotty. This was how it started for her. *Will I follow suit?*

Mom parks her car in the driveway, hops out of her side and comes to my door. I hear the flip-flop of her sandals on the pavement.

She wraps her arm around my back, careful not to touch my bad arm and shoulder. I am aware of her breath as she lifts me and the smell of her when she holds me. It's her mom-fragrance. Not perfume. She never wore that, not that I remember. It isn't her deodorant either, or hairspray. Everything she wears now is odourless. It's just a warm scent, like something earthy, but not like dirt. It's a clean smell. It's the smell of comfort and caring.

Back when I was a teenager and when she was dealing with her own demons, she smelled like stale booze and smoke. But not now. She smells like someone I love, and I would recognize that scent anywhere.

I try to lie my head against hers, to tell her how much she means to me, but I can't form the words. I don't want to start blubbering like an idiot. So instead, I take my good hand and place it on top of hers and hold it there.

I feel the warmth of her skin, the bones beneath her flesh. I want to thank her for coming to get me, for being there, for not asking all those questions even though I probably would have told her anyways, and just as I'm about to, the door jerks open.

Jimmy.

His eyes are wide and he looks disoriented. "Are you trying to kill me?" he shouts.

He has both hands in his hair, his eyes are wild, his face, pale. "Jesus Karm. Are you alright?"

"Yes," I say, almost too quickly. I don't deserve his attention, his concern.

He comes to my other side, the side that is hurt, tries to help me walk, only he is getting in my way. It's awkward, the three of us huddled together, hobbling to the door.

"Alright, alright! That's enough."

Mom backs off without any hesitation, understanding, no doubt, my annoyance. But Jimmy doesn't waver. He holds the small of my back, opening the door for me and I walk in under his arm. A giant trellis. Mom follows behind and then stands at the door,

"Karm, honey," she says in a very small voice. "If you want me to stay, I'll stay. Otherwise, I can pick up the kids or—"

"That's fine, Mom," I snap, feeling agitated. And then, turning towards

150

Karma

her I readjust my attitude. "Sorry, Mom. Thank you for everything today. I appreciate it. Really. I think we will be okay from here."

I look up at Jimmy and he nods, but tells her if she wants to stay, she is more than welcome to.

She shakes her head. "You have things covered here. I'm going to go check on Allan. I'll be there for an hour. Home after that. Okay?"

"Thanks, Mom." I wave her off and she retreats out the front door, closing it behind her.

"Where do you want to sit? In the living room, on the couch?"

"The couch is fine, Jimmy."

"Are you hungry? Can I get you anything to eat?"

"Nope," I say. Although, thinking about it, I haven't really eaten since breakfast.

"What about the kids?" I ask. "Are you going to pick them up?"

"Later," he says. "They're okay with Becky for now. She said she'll keep them as long as we need. I wasn't sure how long you'd be."

"I didn't need to stay. I'm fine. Really. Mom checked me over and so did the on-call doctor. I just have a few scrapes and things."

He gives me a funny look as he helps me take a seat on our sofa. Once I'm comfortable, he lifts my feet so I am fully stretched out.

"Need an extra pillow?"

"I'm fine, Jimmy."

"You don't look fine," he says matter-of-factly. "Why were you there anyhow? Across town?" He's eyeing me, waiting for me to blink, to stumble. To lie.

"Errands," I say casually. "You know? I think I am kind of hungry." I need to veer him off course. "I don't think I ate lunch, or had much for breakfast either."

My mind is racing. Adrenaline keeps the thought processes wired, not always in a good way. "Any cold cuts left in the fridge? A sandwich would hit the spot."

"Uh-huh. Just take a sec. I'll make it the way you like it. With mustard and mayo, cheddar, pickle on the side. I can run to the store for potato chips."

"Thank you, Jimmy. But the sandwich will be fine."

"Tea? You want tea with it?"

I nod. "Ouch!"

"What's wrong?"

He squats beside me, staring into my face, concern etched into him. He strokes my cheek, looks at my cuts, touches my head gently. "Does it hurt

151

here when I touch you?" he asks in barely a whisper.

And it did, hurt. Part of my head felt swollen. But I took his hand in mine and told him I was okay.

"It's just a few bumps and bruises, but the lady that slammed into me is worth the worry. The poor thing. Mom said the family had been worried about her driving so they were actually going to take away her license. She wanted to prove to them she was still okay to drive. She snuck off with the car. She wasn't hurt, thank God. Scared, mostly. She drove a big car, a Crown Vic, and when she hit into me, her fender barely dented. Mom said she couldn't stop crying when she saw me, though. I feel so bad for her."

"Feel bad for her? She shouldn't have been driving at all."

"I know, Jimmy, but she's old."

"Look at you. Jesus, Karm, you could have got killed. And all I could think of was Allan. That I was going to lose you like Allan lost Lotty. She played over and over in my mind."

"Funny, I thought about her, too." I paused, "And, Jimmy? What did you tell the kids?"

"I said you had to take the car to the garage and I would be running over to get you."

I nod—"Ow"—and touch my head. "The doctor gave me some pain killers. I think I need one now."

"These things make me nervous." He looks at the prescription bottle on the coffee table, picks it up, reads the name: Tylenol with Codeine Tylenol number three.

I reach for it. "I know, Jimmy. But I'll be okay. Save the worry talk." I grimace as I'm starting to feel the effects of the accident. Everything is beginning to ache and throb. My muscles just realized I had them in a state of agitation for the past number of hours.

He takes out two pills and walks to the kitchen to get me a glass of water. I place the pills on my tongue and gag when I taste the bitterness of them. I drink a big gulp of water, forcing them down.

Jimmy goes back into the kitchen and starts preparing my sandwich. I can't see him as I'm facing the wrong way, so I stand up and turn myself around, planting myself in the arm chair, waiting for him to bring over the footstool.

I'm physically drained. That little bit of moving just did me in.

Jimmy comes out with my food. Never before did I see him whip something together so quick, along with a hot cup of tea, quick version, putting the bag in to steep. He rolls the footstool over and sits opposite

Karma

me, hands me my sandwich. He made one for himself, too, and places his plate on his lap.

I take a bite. My teeth sink into the soft bread, cold ham, crisp lettuce. "Mmmmm," is all that comes out of me. I didn't realize how hungry I was.

I wolf down the sandwich so fast. He's still on his half while I start on my tea. "You know," I say, "you might think I'm crazy but..." I stop. He *will* think I'm crazy.

"What?"

"Oh, forget it." I blush. I dance my fingers on the plate, picking up the bread crumbs and a piece of cheese that fell out of my sandwich.

"What?" he asks again. "Tell me."

I take a drink of tea, letting the heat slide down my throat. "When I was in the car, you know, before the paramedics came?"

"Yeah." Jimmy keeps eating but holds my gaze.

"Lotty was there. She was with me."

He stops eating.

"What do you mean, with you? She's dead."

I swallow. I feel funny for saying it. "She was there. With me. Seated in the passenger seat, looking at me. I knew I was okay then. That everything was going to be okay." Even saying it out loud makes me shiver, like something divine had happened. A miracle of some kind.

"The officer told mom it could have been serious. If the lady had been driving faster. If my back wasn't turned. I tried to reach for her. To t-touch her."

Jimmy's eyes widen. He takes a drink from his cup. He's staring, taking it all in.

"Well," he says, running his tongue under his lip, "you did hit your head. I suppose you could have had some hallucination or something."

"It wasn't a hallucination," I protest. "She was real. She was there. I felt her. She was warm. It was...warm. I can't explain it. It was calming. She calmed me. I know it sounds crazy. It is crazy." I look down, embarrassed I told him. I should have kept it for myself.

He comes over to me, bends down and kisses me ever so gently on the top of my head, reaches for my plate on my lap and pads off to the kitchen.

"I know you miss her. We all do."

"You don't believe me?" I holler.

He turns back and his face lights up. "Whatever it was, Karm. Lotty, or a hallucination, or whatever, I'm just glad you're okay."

He winks and I exhale.

Trena Christie-MacEachern

All the other stuff can wait until tomorrow. But I silently acknowledge it's the second time today Lotty got me out of a pickle.

~

The rose lies withered, its head bowed at a disturbing angle, as if repentant, yet the Baby's Breath looks as fresh as the day it arrived. Delicate buds of white wisps stand proud and tall.

This was my favourite flower when I was a teenager. I wanted to wear it in my hair at prom, in my bouquet on my wedding day, when I fantasized about that when I was younger. It reminded me of love, eternity, happiness.

But seeing the drooping flower, I wonder if it's making a mockery of my current existence? Part of me dying with this eternal secret, meanwhile, the exterior of myself, still looking like I have it all together. The façade. The nice home, the great husband, the happy children.

How many times did I want to throw out the bastard flower? Along with the enclosed note that took away my breath.

To Karm from Linda S.
Hope you're feeling better
xo

Charlie's code name. He knew I had been hurt. Heard from whom? But I will never ask Jimmy if Charlie ever spoke to him, or inquired about me. And I will never tell Jimmy where the bastard flower came from. So, I'm stuck with its mockery.

If I throw it away, he'll become all the more suspicious.

I was surprised when it arrived. Who could have thought of me?

I was touched when Mariah came in with it after the doorbell rang. It sounded like something out of the movies. "Ooh, Mom. A special delivery for you," she squealed.

The two of us laughed while we pulled off the plastic bag to get a proper look. To see who had been so thoughtful.

But my reaction went from surprise and elation to shock, trying to keep my face in check when I read the note. And when Mariah read the card over my shoulder and asked, "Who's that again?" and lying—*my friend whom I go walking with*—I felt so ashamed, so remorseful, I wanted to cry.

And now that it's survived without me slamming it against the wall, or shoving it down the garbage disposal, Mariah tells me she'd like to keep the vase in her room, hoping, that dreamy look that came over her face, for when someone sends her flowers someday. I wanted to gag.

The vase is held tight in my hand, and I still want to smash it to smithereens and drag Charlie's bare feet across the shards, I take a breath and pause. *I could simply tell Mariah that it broke?*

I drum my fingers on the table, wondering what I should do. The dead rose signifies what is left between Charlie and me, death of a relationship —death of what could have been. I hadn't thought about him like that for years, and then, God, whatever happened that night that made him believe he could still be in my life. And finally, death of the love Jimmy and I share, if word gets out before I figure out how to tell him.

I feel the strain behind my eyes and between my shoulder blades. I lift the vase to throw it in the trash. My foot is on the lever, the silver lid is opened wide, awaiting.

I hesitate.

Something inside is preventing me from tossing it. I see Mariah's face and the disappointment she will feel.

I sigh and pick out the dead rose, which crumbles in my hand, the stem still rigid and thorny. I pull out some of the wilted leaves, leaving the Baby's Breath in the vase, and walk into Mariah's room, deciding where to put it.

I'm proud of myself. Mariah will cherish it. *And Charlie, well he probably just sent it to be thoughtful*, I tell myself. A simple caring gesture. He's happy I didn't get really hurt.

I place the vase down on her nightstand. My hand hovers, fingers formed in the shape of a C.

But as quickly as I want to believe the positive, my thoughts start thinking the opposite. Maybe he didn't send it as a thoughtful gesture at all. Maybe it's a reminder that I still owe him a shit ton of money.

That son-of-a-bitch. I stop in my tracks.

But I'll never really understand Charlie's actions because he's MIA, according to Allan. He's hiding because he owes that money. How the hell did he get money for a flower if he owes so much and, and...?

Quite simply, the flower is a reminder of what I did to Jimmy. To my family.

I grab the vase off her bureau and toss in the garbage can after all.

~

Trena Christie-MacEachern

The car will be in the shop for a couple of weeks. They didn't write it off completely, as we initially thought they would. I'm happy the damage wasn't too bad, and the insurance company didn't give us too much grief.

After the call with the insurance company, I take a sip of my coffee and flinch. Jimmy didn't put in sugar. He drinks his black.

I open the cupboard and take out the sugar dish. It's still one of my favourite gifts. Even more so now.

Lotty had made it in pottery class and gave it to me on my twenty-fifth birthday, the time Jimmy hosted a surprise party. The box was all wrapped in white tissue with an oversized royal-blue bow on top.

At first, I thought it was jewellery from Jimmy. That's what the box reminded me of as there was no card with it. I still remember everyone looking at me, smiling, oohing and ahhing, before I even opened it, trying to guess its insides, imagining what it could be.

Lotty didn't even say it was from her until I opened it and held it up. The pottery felt smooth in my hands, and it was my favourite shade of blue. She included a small silver spoon to go with it.

"That's from me and Al," she cooed. "Our names are on the bottom."

She came through the crowd to examine it with me. "I know how you like your coffee," she said, her voice demure and delicate. "And I know how you love this colour."

When I hugged her, she kissed me on the cheek. I remember thinking how special that was, her peck. She never really showed anyone any kind of affection. Only to Allan.

But on that night she did, and I remember her soft lips on my face. And for some reason, that's what I remembered most of that evening.

But staring at this simple sugar bowl even though I look at it every day, makes me melancholy. But why now? Why today? Did the accident open a portal for me and Lotty to reconnect? Is she trying to tell me something?

I feel her presence when I remove the lid and spoon the white crystals into my mug. How the last while she has been on my mind. Is she here with me right now so I won't be alone when I tell Jimmy my dark secret? Because she was alone those last days? Maybe she's here to let me know that it's going to be okay? Because every time I think of her, it's always been a happy, sweet memory. Nothing tragic or awful, not the way she lived the last couple of years. Certainly not the way she died.

"I'm here, Lotty," I whisper, "I'm listening."

I stand motionless, waiting for a sign but the only sound is the ticking of the wall clock.

Karma

Now that my coffee tastes as it should, I place the sugar bowl back in the cupboard.

~

The rain wakes me early. It's coming down in torrents, pinging off the window and eaves.

Jimmy is already up. He gets up between five-thirty and six so he can read the paper and then run. His movements woke me as he was trying to locate his running rain jacket. I tried going back to sleep but I flip and flop and realize there's no point being restless in bed. I get up and tiptoe past the kids' rooms. They still have another hour or so.

I grab my mug and head back to the chair in the living room, my spot, where I can stretch my legs and enjoy my morning cup of joe without any disturbances. With Jimmy just heading out for his run and the kids still in bed, I can just sit and think or read the paper or my magazine.

But I keep thinking of Lotty. Her presence is here somehow, even as I stare out the window, watching the rain coming down. I shift my sore arm. I'm actually not doing a whole lot of relaxing at all.

I wish things could go back to the way they were. When it was just the four of us. How happy we were...And I was content being a stay-at-home mom and wife, preparing dinner and doing errands, whipping up pancakes on weekends, watching movies.

Why can't I go back there? Is she forcing me to re-examine my life? Is that why Charlie and I happened? Am I truly not happy?

"But I am," I say out loud, as if the spirits are listening.

"You all right?" he asks, coming into the living room in his running gear. "The face on you. And you haven't sat still since you got up." His hands are on his hips, his ball cap low over his eyes.

"It's pouring out," I state, as if he can't tell the weather. "And cold."

"A little rain can't hurt you. And I'm not going to be gone long, I'm already behind schedule."

"That because you made me coffee?"

He smiles, knowing that's exactly why, but he won't admit it.

"You forgot the sugar again." I look up at him, smile sweetly. "But it's good now."

"I've been leaving it out," he states, "because it causes inflammation." He bends down close to me, runs his fingers through my hair. I grab his fingers, hold them tight,

"I'll want to talk to you after, okay?" My heart beats fast in my chest.

Trena Christie-MacEachern

"Yeah? About what? The sugar?" He laughs then.

And there it is: the opening, the words, me, Charlie, the night of the funeral. *Say it, Karmalita! Say the words.* My thoughts are spinning so fast and my heart is pounding, I feel weak and sweaty.

"I—"

"How about after my run?" He looks down at his watch. "I've gotta go or I won't get this in."

"Oh, of course." I wave him off. "Sure. Sure. You go. Sorry to keep you."

He winks at me and then goes to the door. I get up and brush back the curtain, watch him as he takes giant strides down the driveway, the brim of his baseball hat sheltering what it can from the driving rain. He turns left, looks down at his watch again, then breaks into a run. In a second, he's gone.

I stare out the window still watching, even though there's nothing to see. No one else on the road this hour. I let go of the curtain so it falls back in place, realizing I'm trembling.

Back in my chair, I'm too nervous to even hold my coffee. Instead of having a peaceful, carefree morning, I'm sitting on my hands, breathing deeply, trying to get the nerves to go away.

15

Now

Jimmy.
I slept with Charlie.
Jimmy, I think I slept with Charlie.
I awoke naked in his bed.
Well, the bed really wasn't his, nor the house, for that matter.
I confronted him about the money. He's sort of blackmailing me.
Says he has pictures of us.
The two of us, me and him. Not you and me.
He wants ten grand. I managed to get a couple thousand to-
gether.
I sold some things from the basement.
And my ring. I'm sorry, I sold my ring that you gave me. The an-
niversary ring on our ten years together. But I don't have any more
money to give him.
Can you spot me?

I know I can't ask for the money, even though I spin the words and the story over and over in my mind, practising how I'm going to say them.

Staring at myself in the bathroom mirror, I realize the toll this is taking. I look old. I feel it. I see it. There are dark circles under my eyes. Lines have formed around my mouth and chin. I don't recall having these before all this happened.

My hair looks lacklustre too, like I've been out in a sandstorm. It's dry, and colourless. Maybe I need hi-lights? A facial?

My eyes aren't even bright. They're dull, like the light went out of them—dull hazel, no hint of green. More like the colour of dried mud, useless soil that can't grow anything.

I put my hand on my stomach, wondering if anything is growing in there. I've lost track of my period. When was I supposed to start? I've

Trena Christie-MacEachern

been on and off the pill so much, forgetting to take it when I should.

I didn't want any more surprises after Mariah. Everything had to be planned. I silently curse myself.

But somehow, I don't yet believe I'm pregnant. Yet I feel all of the symptoms. Besides being extremely tired, worn out, and forlorn, my emotions are all over the map. I'm terrified, ashamed, angry, sad, and haven't had a proper sleep or a proper meal in lord knows how long. So, who knows?

I study my body in the mirror and all the bruising I had incurred from the accident. Scratches and scrapes are healing. Some have turned pink and scabby.

After I readjust my robe and tighten the belt, I turn on the water to wash my face. I put my hair up in an elastic, bend low over the sink and continue practising the words for Jimmy—the hows, the whys of what happened. Hoping when I say it out loud, it will sound honest and not contrived.

"Who you talking to?" He asks as he raps on the door

"Eyack!" His voice startles me. My nervous reaction causes me to blast the water on full force instead of shutting it off. I grab the towel off the counter.

"You alright in there?"

Jimmy opens the door just slightly, pokes his head in, looks around. "I thought Mariah was with you. You're chatting away to yourself."

I blush scarlet.

"Can I come in?" he asks.

"Hold on a minute. There's water everywhere."

He steps in and closes the door behind him. "Doesn't matter," he says.

It's like the sprinkler system went off in the bathroom. I look up and Jimmy is standing before me drenched to the bone. Everything is dripping.

"Oh, a little water won't hurt anyone."

He looks silly and uncomfortable and his clothes are pasted to him.

I stand up and reach for his ball cap, flip it off. The only part that is dry is the top of his head, the round patch around the crown where monks shave. He looks hilarious.

Then he shakes himself like a dog and I'm laughing, as I tell him to stop it.

"I'll have to wipe everything down again," I tell him, and I feel at ease and relaxed for a moment, having let my guard down.

He must sense it because he comes closer, opens my robe. His soaking-wet clothes are cold against my skin and I squeal softly, playfully, "Stop. Stop," I protest.

Jimmy has his arms around my back, holding me.

"I love to hear your laugh," he says breathlessly. And then his lips meet mine and he kisses me full on, big open-mouth, slow kisses. The kind that make your toes curl and you know exactly what he wants and what's going to happen next.

He pushes me back against the counter, his hand slips inside my robe, slides over me. He lifts me onto the vanity with such ease, like I weigh no more than a pillow and, as much as I want him, I feel like I can't until I tell him the truth about what has happened.

I stop kissing him but his soft lips trail down my neck, around my collar bone.

"Jimmy."

"Mmm hmmm."

"I. I have to tell you something." His mouth is making its way down my chest.

"Now? Tell me later," he murmurs.

"Jimmy!" I say, a little more agitated, a little more forcefully. But he doesn't listen. In frustration, I place both my hands on his shoulders and push him away so he stops and looks me in the eyes.

"What's so urgent it can't wait ten minutes?"

"Ha-ha," I say sarcastically, nervously. Then I find I'm small again, scared. He is so close, so unbearably close and I know that everything I will say will hurt him. I can't look at him. I don't want to see his face when he hears the words.

"Well?"

"It's...just that," I pause. I take a deep breath, close my eyes. I'm waiting for my inner strength to kick in.

"Maaa?" Paulie is outside the door.

"Yes, sweetie."

"I don't feel so g—" Followed by a wet cough, which isn't a cough.

Our eyes lock for a split second, then bulge. Jimmy, in record time, flings open the door, two hands Paulie by the waist, hauls him inward while a trail of vomit spews from his mouth, splatting on the door and the shower stall before Jimmy gets him in position over the toilet.

~

Poor Paulie. It breaks my heart to see him so sick. And because I was so

Trena Christie-MacEachern

absorbed with Paulie, I nearly forgot about Mariah and getting her up for school. She did pretty good, though. She made her own breakfast and prepared her lunch.

Jimmy was super late as he's picking up his friend, Tom, today. It's because he's going to get the car after work and Tom will drive it home.

I just waved him off, crouched down on the floor with a bucket of hot, sudsy water and a rag, mopping up Paulie's vomit that managed to reach almost everything at or near the washroom. It was like he was in *The Exorcist*.

He's lying on the couch with his eyes closed tight, mouth open, his small arm covering half his face. His cheeks are aglow and there is a sheen on his skin.

His forehead is burning hot so I place a bucket beside him on the floor, instructing him if he feels the urge to throw up, to do it there.

I'm not sure if he understands me. He nods anyhow, and his eyes close again.

I rinse cold cloths and place them on his forehead, hoping they will cool him off. We already tried the liquid Tylenol, which didn't stay down long. It came up quicker than Mariah's volcano experiment.

Popsicles are next on the sick check list. I have them hidden in the freezer for times like this. I'll give them to Paulie when he wakes. Although I don't want him to have sugar, I don't want him to dehydrate either, and water is too heavy on his belly right now.

Between finishing the washroom clean-up, to rushing back to him when I hear him gag, to holding the bucket for him to vomit, I'm running around like the chicken with her head cut off.

It's constant and I'm getting nothing done. So, I position myself in the chair opposite him and stay put for a while. Finally, he drifts off and sleeps. It's a good sign. I study his eyes and hope he is dreaming.

After a few moments, I recheck his washcloth, which has warmed. I remove it so I can run it under cool water again when the phone rings.

I'm debating if I should answer it but figure it might be Jimmy. Glancing at the clock, he's probably wondering how the morning is going. I run to it. I don't want the sound to wake Paulie.

"Hello?"

"You sound beat."

Dad. I don't often hear from my father anymore. Once he moved on, I only see him sporadically. I feel he left both me and Mom, in a sense, even though he didn't. I know he tried in his marriage, but with Mom's condi-

Karma

tion, and his needs, for lack of a better word, they proved to be incompatible. That's what Mom said. Although sometimes I didn't believe her. I think she said that just to make me feel better, or maybe herself.

"Hey, Dad." I'm trying to sound cheerful, happy to hear from him.

"What's up, Karm?"

"I've been cleaning up Paulie's vomit all morning." When was the last time Dad saw Paulie?

"Oh, the poor fellow. Flu?"

"Yeah, I guess so. He woke up this morning and just started throwing up. He has a fever and is laying on the living room couch right now." I veer in Paulie's direction. "He's sleeping, anyhow. I was just getting him some cold cloths for his forehead."

"Your mother used to do that for you when you were sick."

"Yeah, she told me."

"And flat Ginger Ale, and popsicles, I believe. Orange. I think you liked those."

I chuckle.

"But you didn't get sick a lot, really. A few colds here and there."

"Um, I should check on Paulie. He's pretty warm. He's not keeping his Tylenol down yet. I'll have to try again."

"Oh, yeah, of course."

"Hey Dad? Did you call for a reason? Something up?"

"No, not really. Called to chat, I guess." He pauses. "But I wanted to tell you too that I had to take a wheelchair and a portable oxygen tank to Allan's apartment. Your mother asked if I could lend a hand. He's not well, eh?"

"No. He's not. I imagine Allan took a fit seeing the wheelchair." Mom. Always trying to help out.

"Yeah, anyways, that fella you used to date, Charlie something-or-other, was there with Allan."

"Oh yeah, really?" Feigning disinterest.

"Well, it was none of my business, but one, why didn't this Charlie guy help out with the wheelchair? Not that I mind. And two, looked like they were into something. They had all these papers. Looked like financials or accounts or something. I didn't want to be nosy. But Charlie looked, I don't know....I never really liked the guy. Suspicious."

"You never liked him because I was dating him." Why am I sticking up for Charlie?

"No, more than that. It was like he was up to something. I don't know, can't put my finger on it. He stashed the papers away, threw a magazine

Trena Christie-MacEachern

or something on top of them. I just stayed for a bit. Said my hellos. I like Allan. He helped your mother a lot. I have a lot of respect for him. Anyhow, after I saw him, I thought of you. And just thought I should give a quick call. But again, it's none of my business. I was just worried for Allan. I know he's a good friend of you and Jimmy."

"Okay, Dad, thanks for calling. I appreciate it." I switch the phone to my other ear and, even though I need to get off, Dad starts asking more questions.

"Hey? Maybe we can get together some time?"

"Who?"

"Me and you, or me and Jimmy and you and the kids?" he blurts.

"Sure."

"We could do a barbecue. We can host it here. Or, if that's too hard, maybe your house?"

"Yeah, okay," cutting him off. "I have to go, Dad. Thanks for calling."

"Okay, sweetheart. Bye bye. Love y—"

Even before he finished his sentiments, I hang up the phone.

I shouldn't have been abrupt. I didn't really mean to. Paulie is sick. He's my first priority.

I go back to the washroom and rinse the washcloth under cool water, ringing it out 'til its damp. Paulie, is now stretched flat on his belly, his head turned at an awkward angle. The sheet kicked onto the floor, half covering the bucket.

I fold the cloth and place it on his forehead, tucking the other end under him. I brush his cheek with my knuckles. He flinches so I step away, sit back in the chair.

Dad's conversation about Charlie and Allan comes back to me. I know Dad never liked Charlie. He found him in my bedroom. A line was crossed that day. I could only imagine how Jimmy would feel if he found someone with Mariah in her room. The thought makes me uncomfortable. But Mariah would never do that...take a boy home to her room.

She and I are as opposite as night and day in that regard. We had different upbringings, for starters. I was pretty much on my own by the time I hit junior high. No wonder I made some poor choices. Although I never considered having Mariah a poor choice. She was, and is, the best thing that ever happened to Jimmy and me. She brought us together, which I'll always be grateful. She was the tie that bound us.

And if I didn't get pregnant with Mariah, what would have happened to Jimmy and me? I can't imagine my life without him, and then, without Jimmy, we wouldn't have had Paulie.

Karma

My thoughts now drift to Allan. He stood as Charlie's best man, and then Lotty got hurt that night. Is that the price ones pays for having a relationship with Charlie? Does he leave a trail of destruction wherever he goes? Then, gosh, after learning from Vicki about their fake wedding, maybe Lotty's death could have been averted altogether?

I chew my nails and tell myself not to go down that road. The should haves, could haves, would haves. All the wishing in the world won't bring Lotty back or make Allan any less sick.

Just strange for Dad to pick up on Charlie acting odd at Allan's. What's going on there? Charlie hasn't bothered me for any more money. Not since my accident. But he did say that he might ask Allan for help.

Charlie did seem scared. Maybe that's what Dad was picking up on. Yet, I can't see Allan giving Charlie anything. Not after what he did to Lotty—getting her hooked on those drugs.

"Maaaa?" Paulie groans. "I'm thirsty."

He is sitting up on the sofa, staring off, his eyes still glassy, his cheeks still rosy.

"Hold on, Paulie. I'm going to get you a Popsicle. What kind do you want?"

I open the freezer, pull out a pink and an orange. I'm about to break the pink in half when I hear him say, "Orange."

I smile, replacing the pink frozen treat in the freezer.

~

The rest of the day is a blur, from cleaning up after Paulie, to trying to make him food he would eat. Jimmy checked in once and said he'd be home on time. Asked if he needed to bring anything from the store.

I go about my day as normally as I can, given my horrible secret and now I have a sick boy to take care of.

There's a small roasting chicken in the fridge and I decide homemade soup is the best remedy. There's something wonderful about the aroma of stewing chicken. It leaves a satisfying homey scent throughout the house.

As I chop the remainder of the vegetables, I think of all the times I cherished with my kids, all the fun things we did over the years. Today, for some reason, is making me nostalgic. Maybe it's the soup.

When I was really young, all I wanted to be was a mom, a stay-at-home-mom. You couldn't drag me into an office back then if you tried. I didn't want my kids to be raised by others. No, I didn't want that. I

165

Trena Christie-MacEachern

wanted their lives to be different than mine because both my parents worked. They were never home. In one sense, my pregnancy with Mariah seems like fate. But maybe I'd have to go back farther. If not for Charlie, then I wouldn't have hooked up with Jimmy.

Now that both kids are in school, my life is really just an endless game of household chores, chauffeuring and fill-in-the-blanks until everyone is home again. Gone are the days of playing make-believe and finger-painting, afternoon picnics, and playgroups. My days are empty and unfulfilled and I don't think I realized how much of a void they filled, until now.

But the thought of having another baby is totally out of the question. I loved my time with my kids, and we did say we would try for a third, but it's almost too late to go back.

So here I am, chopping vegetables, trying to figure out my career goals. Do I go back to school? Finish my degree and become...what, now? I never really had those plans laid out even when I was in college. It was like the world knew I wasn't ready so I became a mother instead. Fate.

Hmph. *Some theory.*

While the chicken cools, I check on Paulie. He's sitting in the TV room now. He's still wearing his pyjamas, and is on top of the brown, fuzzy blanket, two Popsicle sticks are stuck to the coffee table and a half-empty glass of Ginger Ale is beside him. His hair is tousled and he looks so small and fragile and pale.

I don't disturb him. I stand in the hallway instead, observing. He's watching cartoons. He hasn't seen any of these shows for a year.

He glances over at me for a minute. His mouth looks swollen, his lips tinged orange from the popsicles. I smile at him. But he doesn't really see me; he's still in that flu trance.

Padding back to the kitchen, I make him toast just the way he likes it. I place the four triangles on a plate beside his knee on the sofa.

He looks up at me with those soft, sweet eyes, and down at the shapes. He lifts one with his small hand and takes a nibble. He barely chews it.

I'm on guard, waiting to see if the crumbs he manages to get in will stay down. I take a seat beside him, run my fingers through his hair. He stops, holds the piece in his hand, staring at Batman, wondering whether the Joker is going to try and foil him again. He doesn't.

Paulie takes another nibble, places the toasted bread back on his plate and lies down.

I stroke his cheek and face. I wonder what life would be like if I didn't have him. If I didn't go this route with Jimmy.

I can't even fathom the thought. The children are my life now. I live

Karma

and breathe for them and I feel myself getting agitated because all of this is my fault. My stupid idiotic fault. My life as I know it can be changed in a heartbeat.

What if? What if I am pregnant? And whose is it? Yet, I can't go there either because it pains me to think of myself with Charlie and what I have done to Jimmy.

My hand is still resting on Paulie's warm body and I say a little prayer right there. I promise myself I won't let whatever happens destroy me. Destroy my family. Amen.

With nervous energy I get up and keep going, back to the kitchen and at least finishing dinner. The dinner for my family.

Staying busy helps occupy my day. And what a long day it has been.

At long last, Mariah gets home. She is doing her homework at the table when Jimmy comes in, seeming kind of smug, with a cat-ate-the-canary look. He hollers to me, tells me Tom is outside.

I see Tom and my car. It looks as good as new. Mariah stands at the doorway, munching on one of Paulie's crackers, not knowing what all the fuss is about. She didn't see the damage, so the car looks much the same to her.

Tom and I have a quick chat, and I run my hand over the smooth, metal hood, thinking back to the day of the accident. You can't see a dent anywhere. It looks brand new. I don't bother to open the door, just peer inside. Everything is clean and spotless.

"Looks great."

"I'll be half an hour," Jimmy says as he nods toward Tom.

"I have homemade soup, Tom, if you'd like to come in for a bowl before you leave."

It's not often we see Tom anymore. He worked with Jimmy for the past number of years and I can count the times he's been here. I'd sometimes see him at the annual Christmas party. And Jimmy went to his place for an occasional beer. Once, he and Tom ran in a race.

He's a nice guy, quiet. Slim, like Jimmy, but not as tall. He was married for a few years and then his wife just up and left him. I felt bad for him, because it appeared she left for no reason. Her departure, we found out later, was because she just had enough of the quiet, unassuming, practical, no-drama marriage. She wanted some excitement.

Go figure.

I really hoped Tom would've come in, but he declines gracefully, politely, and waves me off before getting in the passenger side of Jimmy's car.

Darn.

By the time Jimmy strolls in the second time, Paulie has had a few spoonfuls of his soup and seems to be recovering from his morning of throwing up. He's still a bit pale and still in his pyjamas, but at least he's back playing and talking to himself like he normally does.

Jimmy checks in on him before he gets out of his dress pants, then he checks in on Mariah. He seems different in a way. Happy? Happier? I shouldn't be concerned. Being happy is a good thing.

"Hey. You seem like you had a great day. Are you ready for soup?"

"Ready for anything," he says, his lips turned up making him look impish.

He grabs a bowl and hands it to me. I scoop the hot liquid into it, making sure he got lots of veggies and pieces of chicken. He has this smug I-know-something-you-don't-know grin pasted on his face.

"Okay." I chuckle. "All good, Jimmy?"

"If you say so."

My brows furrow, wondering what the hell is up. My mind starts wondering. Maybe he got a promotion?

"Something happen at work?" I ask inquisitively, placing the bowl in front of him. He sprinkles pepper on his soup then blows on it. The steam rises up in front of his face.

"No, but I learned something today," he says. He's grinning full on now.

I watch him take a mouthful, then that face when you realize what you're eating is too hot. His mouth is chewing and blowing as he tries swallowing.

"You have something to tell me?" He asks, turning serious.

I look down at the table. My breathing slows to almost an immediate halt. *Do I have something to tell him?*

Who was he talking to? Tom? Does Tom know Charlie? Charlie hadn't bothered with me for a while, but maybe he got hold of Tom who had to tell Jimmy? My mind is racing like a NASCAR.

And I can feel the thump thump thump deep within my chest. My eyes scan everywhere but him. I cover my face.

Jimmy's voice breaks my silence. "Karm!"

I meet his gaze.

"You want to tell me something?"

My eyes are wide, my mouth is dry. *Holy fuck. Holy fuck. Is this it? Is this how it's going to come out? By somebody else telling my husband what the hell I was doing...*

In barely a whisper, I say, "I can explain."

Karma

Jimmy keeps eating his soup like he is starving. And I'm waiting to tell him something but I'm completely tongue-tied. Even practising saying out loud what had happened didn't make a lot of sense because, in every sense of the word, nothing makes sense.

"Is that why you blew me off this morning?"

Beads of sweat pool in my armpits. I know the tears are at the starting gate.

"Jimmy. I, I. I don't..." I can't say it.

"Jimmy. I'm sorry." The tears come flooding hard and fast. "I'm so sorry. I'm sorry. Please forgive me."

"Heyyyyy?" Jimmy places everything down and comes towards me. "What's the matter? Why are you crying?"

"Because you know. I don't know who told you? Was it Ch—?"

He's hugging me now, squeezing me. "It's okay. I found the bag in the car. God, Karm, I'm happy. Aren't you? It's happy tears?"

He looks down at me, his hands are holding my face.

"What? What bag?" I'm completely puzzled.

He dashes to the hallway and brings back the bag from Vicki's pharmacy.

The bag.

The day of the accident. Where I had purchased a few treats for the kids, the lip gloss for Mariah and a pregnancy kit.

He holds it up and shakes it like there's a special surprise inside. Then he pulls it out.

My mouth drops open, realizing he has found it, that he might think I'm pregnant before I know I'm pregnant. And, to make matters worse, I still don't know if I am, or whose kid it is. *Fuck Fuck Fuck.*

I grab the box from him and throw it back in the bag.

"Whoa!" he says raising his arms in the air. "Not the reaction I was expecting."

Now I'm pissed. I didn't plan on him finding that. I need to desperately get my shit together.

"You're not...happy?"

"It's not that, Jimmy," I snap. "I just don't know yet."

"Know that you are, or how you feel about it."

"Both!" I take the bag and put it high in the cupboard and slam the door so I won't think about it, like putting it there will make the whole thing disappear.

"Jeesh, sorry. Thought you were happy. Thought—maybe, we would have a third. We did talk about it."

Trena Christie-MacEachern

"I know, Jimmy. We did. We did." I sigh. "Just not, now."

"Well, if not now, when? Paulie is five. Mariah is almost a teenager. We don't want too many years between the kids."

I rest my elbow on the table and my head on my fist. "I know!"

"Well, I'm sorry if I ruined your surprise. If it was supposed to be a surprise."

I can see the disappointment on Jimmy's face. He really wants another baby. Mariah was the surprise he wasn't ready for, Paulie took forever, and now he wants one just to round out the family. Be a big, happy family, that's what he always wanted.

I just can't see myself mass-producing, plus, now that Paulie's older, I can't see myself going through all of it again. Jimmy's working most of the time and I'd be stuck home. I thought it was time for me to get out in the world and become something, be something. Not that being a mom isn't special. It is. But when I think of my own mother, it was her career that helped sustain her after I left and her marriage broke down. What will I have to help me go on if...?

"Jimmy, I think I want to go back to school and finish my degree." Diversion. Best tactic. I didn't think I was ready for me to say that either, but...

"Ohhh!" That was not what Jimmy was prepared to hear, either. His brows furrow. "I didn't know that's what you really wanted. It's the first I've heard of it."

He glances back up where I stashed the kit and then quickly looks away. He's disappointed in a sense. "But don't get me wrong," he stammers. "If you want to go back to school, I'll totally support you. The kids are in school now and..." he rests one hand on his thigh and the other on the table and I know he's telling me all this because he really would support me, but his tone is sad and his eyes don't really meet mine. His version of our lives is for us to have a house full of kids and me staying home to look after them.

"Are you not happy?" he finally asks, looking fully at me.

"Jimmy! Yes! Yes, I am. I just need something else in my life."

"And a baby wouldn't do that?"

I roll my eyes. "Jimmy!" I shout.

He smirks. He's teasing me now. "I'm sorry. Just a thought..."

I sigh. Hypothetically, nothing is ruled out yet.

He gets up and walks toward me again, wraps his arms around me, rests his head on top of mine. I can feel his warmth around me. He kisses me lightly on the head.

Karma

"Maybe we could become foster parents. Or adopt?"

I sigh again. This man won't let up.

I hold him close. I know I will have to tell Jimmy about that night. Although the thought of telling him will be like sticking a knife in his back and I'd much rather die a thousand deaths than to have to tell the man I love that I cheated.

He deserves to hear the truth. With tears in my eyes, and a heavy sob in my throat I breathe out, "Jimmy, I'm so sorry. I have something else I need to tell you. I can't put it off any longer."

His body tenses with mine.

"And you're not going to like it."

Trena Christie-MacEachern

16

Now

It's been two days since I last saw Jimmy.

I can't believe I told him, yet I couldn't go on with the lie. It wasn't fair to him. It wasn't fair to us.

Yet, as I lie in our bed, in the room we share, with no sign of him, I can't believe he has left me. Left us.

But why would I think otherwise?

To see his face when I told him, when he finally put two and two together of the why I was no longer sleeping with him because I felt dirty and ashamed, and then, the pregnancy kit stashed in a plastic bag stored in the high cupboard—it all made sense to him and his world crashed down upon him.

He didn't cry. He just looked at me with those big, beautiful eyes. I felt his grip slacken when the words came out. It was like I socked him in the stomach then pissed on him for good measure.

He didn't say anything. He had no words. He was just hurt and that broke me more than anything.

Charlie. That name. That person. That man has been in my shadow since the day I first moved here. Charlie was everywhere then, like a sandstorm, and even now, as I try to move on with my life after everything, he is still haunting me. Haunting us.

Why can't I let him go? Why is he still a part of my life? What am I doing that keeps him here?

Because of Charlie, I am hurt and hurting all over again yet on a different level.

I tried to tell Jimmy in the most delicate way possible what had happened, why it happened. That I was drunk and sad about Lotty, that I was vulnerable, hurting, and he wasn't there when I needed him to process what had happened. But it's still my fault, even though I don't fully recall all the details. Perhaps I'm simply blocking everything as a way to

Karma

safeguard myself.

But as I finally shared the information, as I watched it pass from my lips to his ear and then to his brain, and I witnessed the sadness wash over him; recalling his downcast look and then his rejection of me, in his touch and look, how he pushed me away with his fingertips and stood at arms-length, staring at the floor and then the cupboard, while he processed what I had said to him. Only then had I wept.

And as I wept, I tried to explain. I told him repeatedly I was sorry but it didn't matter. My words no longer mattered. I tried to hug him but he pushed me away. And although I wanted to keep it a secret, the crazies made me blurt it out because that's how much I love him. That's how much he means to me. And I would do anything for him and us and our family even when he walked away.

Even though I kept repeating those three words, I watched as he went to our bedroom and put some of his things in a bag and I knew then he was leaving and yet, I still couldn't believe it...even though I knew he had every right. Every God-damn-right-in-the-world, and I told him he could hit me and say anything, the nastiest, meanest stuff he had thought all the years we'd been together and I'd take it because that's what I deserved.

But he remained quiet and aloof, like I had taken everything from him, including his words, and then he went to each of the kids' rooms and whispered in their ear a sweet something, kissed each of them on the cheek or the top of the head, walked down the stairs and out the door to his car, without looking at me for an instant.

He didn't even hesitate. He just sat in the car and turned on the ignition and put the car in gear and pulled away. Like he was going to get milk or start his day going to work.

And he just left, while I stood in the door, tears streaming down my face, my voice harsh, holding a balled-up, soggy tissue squished in my hand, staring at him, imploring him with my thoughts and eyes to come back. But my words no longer came out either. I had said everything. Told him everything that I should have told him weeks ago.

Why am I such an idiot? Scumbag? Whore? Why did I let this happen? Why did I let Jimmy go?

Yet my legs and body would not even move from the step, from behind the screen door. Somewhere deep inside, I told myself to remain where I was and not to chase after him because it would only make matters worse.

That's what I told myself, and when Tom called the next morning and

173

Trena Christie-MacEachern

wondered where he was and why he didn't pick him up, I just played stupid and told him he must have forgot and went back into our room and lay on his side of the bed, smelling his scent on the sheets and wondering if he had left me for good.

That was two days ago. I have no idea where he went or what he is doing. But I lie in our bed and stare into space and pretend to the kids that he is away working and they are okay because Paulie is too young and Mariah is at the age where she has her own stuff going on and is too busy to realize that we are fighting because all the time Jimmy and I were together, we never fought.

We never had big blow-out arguments because we never had anything to argue about, and he never believed in fighting. Until now. If that's what this is.

My eyes are sore and puffy. I have red dots all over my face and a chafed nose.

I thought telling him would make it all better. That the spilling of the beans would calm my nerves and let the healing begin. Instead, I opened the flood gates to endless possibilities of insanities and terms and innuendos and outcomes. I am making myself crazier. If I could call someone to help me, I would, but I can't do that. I can't possibly tell anyone what has happened because:

1. I'd be letting them in on my indiscretions and I don't know how Jimmy would feel about that. It's high time I put his feelings first, and,
2. Everyone has enough shit going on I can't possibly add to their mountain, and,
3. I deserve every bit of this plus more, but it friggen' hurts so Goddamn much I can't breathe; and finally,
4. I deserve it. I deserve to suffer.

Then my mind settles on the person who helped me end up here. Charlie.

Fucken' Charlie. I hate him. I hated him since the day I met him. I hated when we broke up and how he made me feel. I hated him for an eternity and yet he's still meddling in my life.

Fucken' Charlie.

My face is taut with a maniacal expression that probably parallels the Joker from Batman. If the kids could see me now, they'd have nightmares for the rest of their lives.

Karma

On my bureau, are framed prints of Jimmy and me on our vacation, and of the kids, and, ironically, a group shot of all of us back in college when I started dating Jimmy and Lotty was still alive and before the accident. Charlie is in it with Vicki.

I want to throw that picture, biff it across the room and let it smash into smithereens. I stare at it and at the smug, fake smile on that asshole of a person.

I could kill that son-of-a-bitch on what he did to me. Made me do. Taking advantage of me when I was vulnerable. So much like him to want something that isn't his.

Charlie. The cause of all this shit. I'll have to find him.

And so, my focus on hurting has turned around.

I'm going to find that sorry ass and hurt him like he hurt me.

I feel a sudden surge of adrenaline.

That man doesn't know what's coming.

Time to stop being the victim. I sit up, and set out a plan.

~

Getting the kids off to school is my first priority. Paulie, is going to a friend's house afterwards and Mariah has soccer practice. The two kids are looked after. Check.

Except now, I don't really know where to start. Glancing down at the list I made on a note pad seems ridiculous. I was never much of a planner —more of an impulsive, jump-first-ask-questions-later-sort-of-girl.

How many times have I tried picking up the phone to call Jimmy at work the last few days. If he's actually at work. Yet, I simply can't bring myself to dial the number. Humiliating myself again isn't a priority here. I have done enough of that.

Sometimes, I wish I could find a small hole, and crawl inside it. Let the ground cover me and all my thoughts of everything I have done, and let them be forgotten. Then I could crawl out again and begin anew. Like the tulips and crocuses that pop up every year in springtime.

My hands quiver as I reach for my coffee cup, contemplating those thoughts. I had one too many already this morning. Filling my gut with caffeine instead of a proper meal has soured my stomach.

I finally make the decision to eat first. The phone rings and I refuse to answer it. It's probably a survey or a telemarketer as I'm sure as hell it isn't Jimmy. It hasn't rung since he left.

Even Mom hasn't called. I figured she knows. Somehow, she knows

Trena Christie-MacEachern

and is leaving me alone. Mom dealt with enough shit herself to know when things went awry. She has a sixth sense that way.

I can hear her voice now: "When you know you've done wrong, you don't need people to be telling you."

The phone quits and starts again. I'm not sure if I'm ready to talk to Mom yet so I will the phone to stop ringing. *Go away. Stop.*

When I glance at the clock and realize it's only nine forty-five, a thought crosses my mind. What if it's the school calling? Only then do I rush to get it.

As soon as I pick up the receiver, the call disconnects. I wait a few minutes and check our messages. Nothing.

Just as I turn around, the phone starts up again.

This time, I catch it on the first ring. "Hello?"

"Finally," he breathes. "What took you so long to answer?"

It's Charlie. Fucken' Charlie. "Where exactly are you, Charlie?" I bark. "I have a bone to pick with you." I can tell he's smiling on the other end. He doesn't even flinch when I set into a litany of insults.

"You done, sunshine?" He's as calm and cool as an evening, summer breeze. He's not irritated at all, taking it all in as if I'm hollering at someone else.

Nothing I say or do seems to faze him. I want to tear out his eyes. Pull his hair. Instead, I bang my fist on the table, and throw my magazines across the floor.

"What is it you want from me, now? My soul? Is that it?"

"Calm down, girl. It's all good."

"Well, nothing is good here! You son-of-a-bitch." My voice is trembling and I'm trying to keep it together.

"Karma," he says quietly. "Just breathe. Breathe for me, honey. Take it easy. Big breaths. In and out."

Without even realizing it, I'm leaning on the kitchen sink, bent over at the waist, doing exactly as instructed. My eyes are closed and I'm taking deep cleansing breaths. I think of nothing else but the air going in and out of my lungs before I remember why I am doing this and whom I'm doing it for.

"There. Better now, Karma?" he asks. "Listen. Everything's good. Okay?"

"No, Charlie. Everything is not good." It feels like my heart is going to rupture. Jimmy is gone because of this asshole. Because of what we did.

Water pools at the back of my eyes and I will the God-damn tears to go back to hell. I'm not going to cry anymore. Especially for Charlie to hear.

176

Karma

So I think bad thoughts. Remaining in an angry state will help keep me from breaking down.

"Jimmy knows," I state loudly.

There's silence at the other end, but only for a moment.

"Jimmy knows what, Karma? Knows what, exactly?"

"You son-of-a-bitch." I can't help myself. I'm seething. "You know God-damn what."

"No, I don't, Karma. Do you want me to come over and we can talk about this in person?"

"No!" I scream. I'm thinking everyone and their dog in my neighbourhood can hear me.

"What does he know? That I asked you for money? Is that it? Because I already asked him for it, so he knows that much."

"No, you shit. About us. Us! The two of us." I simply can't say it any better than that.

And then I hear him. He's laughing. Not just a chuckle but a full-on, someone told him the best joke, guffaw. I can picture his eyes squinting and his head thrown back, or forward, his lips turned up at the corners and that delirious, crazy laugh he has when he finds something deeply funny.

I'm totally insulted. "Charlie. What in the hell?"

"I'm sorr—" he laughs some more.

When squeals and yelps start to come out of him, I hang up. I slam down the receiver so hard I think maybe I broke it. *What's so God-damn funny.*

In my angered state, I want to pull the phone cord out of the wall. I want to smash the plates and the glasses out of the cupboards and throw them on the floor, just like they do on television. I want to kick and scream and knock over the table. I want to do it all.

The phone starts to ring again. It rings and rings and rings. I let it ring until it stops. I don't want to talk to Charlie. I don't want to hear what he thinks is so fucking funny. I need to figure out what the hell to do.

Where is Jimmy and what's to become of us? Are we really over? Is having a baby with him just a way to keep us together?

Is that all I am, all I'm good for? To have Jimmy's children? And what if this is Charlie's baby? What then? Do I keep it?

All these thoughts are making me crazy. Insane. I need to get out of here and clear my head.

But *why do I continually sabotage myself? Is that how I was raised? Mom punished herself so I must, too? Is that it?*

177

Charlie is calling again. Now he won't leave me alone. He knows that he's got me back in his web and I'm stuck inside it.

The phone's annoying chime reverberates in the room. I cover my ears with my palms. I want it to stop. To go away. I should have just left, run out the front door and gone for a walk, a drive. Anything.

But instead, I answer it and bark defensively, "If you have something to say. Say it! Or stop fucking calling here!"

There is a brief silence on the other end, followed by my mother's voice. "Karm? What's the matter? You okay?"

"S-sorry Mom. Thought you were"—my mind scans for an answer —"telemarketers. What's up?" I say quickly, hoping I sound sincere. "I'm heading out. I have an appointment," I lie, changing the subject so she wouldn't keep me on the line.

But she doesn't hear my excuse at all. She has other things on her mind, more concerning than me.

"Karm. It's Allan. You better come."

Karma

17

Now

I don't want to see Allan right now. Of course, I want to know he's doing as well as he can, but he's in good hands with Mom, the nursemaid and primary caretaker. She would make sure of it.

Not wanting to see him makes me sound cold. But that's how I feel at the moment. Cold and ugly because that's what Charlie David has done to me. Any chance of happiness I had, either with him, or without him, he has ruined.

He was *the one*, I had thought, all those years back, but he took that away from me, too. It's a wonder I have any love left in my heart at all.

And now, all I want to do is hunt him down, and—do what? Slap him? Berate him? Run over him with my car? If one could live out their fantasies even for the briefest of moments...

But, Charlie, no doubt, would survive somehow and then I would get charged and go to jail and never see the light of day again.

My foot presses down on the accelerator as my thoughts spin around and around. I know I'm out of control. My knuckles are white and bulging on the steering wheel and I'm chewing gum like my life depends on it.

The car ahead taps its brake lights for me to get off its tail and I slow my speed and give them some space. For extra measure, I turn on the mellow channel on the car radio, the easy-listening station.

The 'Piña Colada' song is playing, and I click it off because that, too, reminds me of Charlie.

I'm not in any shape to see Allan or Mom. I have cried for the past two days. My eyes are so sunken and deep into their sockets they would probably think I look like a castaway. I've no makeup on, I haven't washed my hair, and I'm wearing my old sweatpants because I can sleep in them and wear them during the day.

I pray Mom is too busy with Allan to notice me.

Trena Christie-MacEachern

The fact she hasn't even called the last couple of days, makes me think Allan really isn't good. And! Maybe Jimmy isn't absent at all? Maybe he's been staying with Allan. Staying by his bedside to give Mom a break. Now I'll simply look like the uncaring loser showing up in slob clothes.

Angry-anxious thoughts pick up momentum as I pull into the parking lot behind Allan and Lotty's. Gazing in the rear view, I run my fingers through my hair, and try to make myself look presentable. Decent. I sweep my locks into a loose bun, tuck in the stray strands, and rummage through my purse for some lipstick, and breath mints.

When did I last brush my teeth? Pressing my palm to my nose I blow into it and try smelling myself. One last check in the car mirror, I realize I look as bad as I thought I did—worse—and, to be on the safe side, pop in two mints.

As I get out of the car, I think about all the times Jimmy and I came to this apartment. 2079 Phyllis Street. We helped Allan and Lotty move in. It was only supposed to be for a few years. Rent was low here. They were saving for their dream home. They wanted a three-bedroom bungalow with a finished basement and large backyard. They wanted to have a couple of kids. Lotty used to joke "twins" because it ran in her family.

Either way, a bedroom for both, and she loved the colour yellow, so when they moved in here, although the walls were already painted rental-space-beige, Lotty went out and bought the brightest in-your-face-sunny-egg-yolk yellow, and painted the living room and kitchen in that hue.

That was six years ago. And when I see that colour now, it actually makes me sad instead of happy because Lotty is gone, and Allan is sick.

Whenever I think of her, I, take a deep breath and remember how she was. Quiet but happy. Sunny lemon happy.

The outside of Allan's building is in need of some major TLC. The building looks shabby, almost rundown. Bricks are missing from the outdoor balconies, making me wonder how safe they actually are. When you enter the foyer, the carpets are worn and they smell of stale cigarettes and lord knows what else. The scent bowls you over. I'm holding my nose as I press Allan's room number and wait for a moment 'til I hear Mom's voice over the intercom.

"That you, Karm?"

"Yes, Mom."

Then the, aaaaaaaaaaaa, harsh sound of the door buzzer to let me in. It sounds oddly like it has smoker's cough, too.

If I had more energy, I'd run the six flights, but that's not happening today.

The elevator closes and the numbers go up without any stops. When the doors slide open, and I step into the hallway on Allan's floor, the wind goes out of me.

Charlie is coming from Allan's apartment. but I can see someone has already got the better of him.

He looks at me with a lopsided smile, a fat lip, and a blackened eye that's already turning Christmas red and green. All my dialogue, antics, and boxing moves have left me. Disappeared like a magician's trick, in a puff of smoke.

But Charlie doesn't stick around to see if I find my tongue. He points to his face with his index finger and says, "Took one for the team."

He walks into the open elevator, it pings, the doors close and he, like my plans to challenge him or beat him up, has gone.

I'm frozen in place, wondering if I should chase after him. Maybe catch him on the main floor if my legs will move. *I have to say something! I can't let him get away.*

The elevator has stopped on fourth. Without hesitation, I run toward the stairwell, only to be met head-on by my mother, who's holding a basket of laundry.

"Jesus, Karm. Watch where you're going."

"Sorry, Mom, I'll be right back. There's something I—"

"Karmalita!" she snaps. "You're not going anywhere! I am in need of some help here."

Then she whispers, "Our friend is very sick, and we will stay and help make him comfortable 'til his stubborn ass will allow us to take him to the hospital."

"But, Mom. I-I'll just be a—"

Mom shoves the basket into my stomach, places both hands on my shoulders, and steers me into Allan's apartment. "What's the matter with you, anyway? You look as bad as your husband. You two fighting?"

"You saw Jimmy?"

Mom does a quick scan on my face, hair and overall attire. "Jesus Murphy, Karmalita. What's with you? Looks like you haven't slept or even bathed in the last couple of days. And Jimmy's got bumps and bruises. You look like you've been crying, and Charlie has a fat lip. I hope it's not a ménage-à-trois or something more serious."

"*Mom!*"

"Hit a nerve, did I? We'll talk about this later. Now, get in there and see Allan, and fold those clothes."

Trena Christie-MacEachern

She is bothered which makes her snippy. "And Allan's too stubborn for his own good."

I'm scared to walk in, scared of what I'll see. But Mom has everything in tip-top shape: soup bubbling on the stove, biscuits cooled on a rack on the counter, some sort of make-shift brew-ha-ha in the blender.

"What's that?" I ask in disgust.

"Oh, don't be a prude. It's only fruit and wheat germ, prune juice. Well, a lot of prune juice. Allan's in a bad way. From the pills, you know? Now, fold those sheets and I'll get you a bowl of soup. You haven't eaten in days either. I can tell from your hair."

A sigh escapes my lips. I can't get anything past her. She's a mother and a nurse. She has it all covered.

There are two full sets of sheets and pillow cases freshly washed because, Mom tells me, Allan is doing a lot of sweating. I finish with the sheets and tiptoe to his bedroom, push the door open.

Mom has the blinds down and a blanket over them to keep the sun out. It's such a stark contrast to the rest of the house: the bright, vivid yellow, and the darkened room where he sleeps.

I see him. His physique under the covers resembles a teenager's as he's lost so much weight. He's curled in a fetal position, with his face almost buried under the sheets. He has a glass of water beside his nightstand with a straw sticking out of it, and pill bottles arranged neatly there. Mom has magazines and a small TV set up against the other wall, his radio, a book or two, and, of course, the picture of him and Lotty at Charlie and Victoria's wedding.

It was taken before the accident. They looked so happy and handsome in their bridal attire. Seeing that picture causes a lump in my throat and I have to stifle a sob.

And poor Allan needs his sleep. I step back, place the sheets on the vacant chair outside his room, lean against the wall with my hands behind my back and take a minute. Breathe.

Mom places a bowl of her soup on the table and gestures for me to sit. She's also buttering me a biscuit. The soup is chicken and rice with some small, cut-up vegetables: carrot, celery, turnip. I blow on it before inhaling it. *God, I'm hungrier than I thought.*

"You get that into you and you'll feel better." she states.

I nod, and I'm suddenly brought back, feeling more like a teenager, sitting at the supper table after school.

When I'm finished eating, Mom whisks the bowl from in front of me, plunges it into the sink of sudsy water before turning it upside down to

Karma

dry on the wire rack. She remains quiet and I watch her as she tidies. Obviously, she, too, has other things on her mind. She wipes the table down.

"It's good of you to do this," I say, as she busies herself around the kitchen, Allan's kitchen.

She empties the water in the sink and narrows her gaze on me for a second. "I don't do this because I'm looking for appreciation. You, Karm, of all people, should know this.".

"Of course, I know, Mom. That's not what I meant." She's still snippy.

"Allan has been a friend to me. Helped me out of dark places, if you recall."

"Very well, actually."

"Exactly. Even after I got sober, because of him, he gave me a sense of purpose. I knew I needed to help people. People like me. Sometimes we turn down paths we had never intended. I never planned on becoming an alcoholic. My God! I thought I was happily married. I had you."

Where is this coming from? I smile meekly at her, but she continues.

"I tried to have more but that wasn't in the plan and I guess I couldn't admit it. Your father and I couldn't..."

Instinctively, I place my hand on my stomach, wondering if I am.

I think Mom and Dad's marriage went south because they couldn't have any more children, and my marriage might because I may be having another.

Mom's eyebrows raise and she takes a seat beside me. She stares at me hard, searching my face before saying anything.

"Karm, I know you're going through something right now. I see it in your face. Jimmy was here the other night and he wasn't himself, either. Charlie was here, too. Although I didn't see it, I believe the two of them got into it. Whatever it's about. Which is probably you. And I don't need to know."

She looks down at the table and puts her hands up, fingers spread. "I don't need to hear it. Whatever it is will sort itself out. And whatever will be will be."

My mouth is open, shocked at her ability to see things I tried hiding and nod slowly. Thankful again Mom is leaving it at that. Thankful I don't have to get into it with her because the whole thing is ludicrous and insane. "Jimmy was here?"

"Yes. He and Charlie and Clyde. They take turns staying over with Allan. I'm here all day and I need my sleep, too. But I will stay if Allan gets worse."

"How much worse?" I ask, glancing at Allan's door.

Trena Christie-MacEachern

"He's dying, Karm. And, sadly, he wants to."

"Can't he get treatment? Something?"

Mom shakes her head. "It's up to him. I'm doing what I can for him now. He has his pain medication and he's eating a little. I try to make something that he likes, but he doesn't have much of an appetite. As long as we get something into him, and he sleeps..."

Mom reaches for my hand and gives it a squeeze. Her eyes mist but she leaves it at that.

Allan calls out, half groan, half suppressed yell.

Mom tells me to wait here 'til she checks him out. I get up and walk behind her, to see my friend but she stops me. "Leave us for a minute. I'll check if he needs anything."

I look at her, puzzled.

She whispers, "He may have to go the washroom and he may be embarrassed if you saw him not looking his best. He may want to brush his teeth, wash up."

"Ohhh." My cheeks redden. "Of course. Sorry."

I sit back down at the table and Mom goes into his room, like she owns the place.

"Hello Allan," she coos. "How did you sleep?"

I hear some grunts and the two of them talking. "Someone's here to see you when you're ready. Okay?"

The bed squeaks, there is ruffling of sheets and blankets, Mom opening the blinds, thrusting up the window. "Let's get some fresh air in here."

And then him, relieving himself in the bedpan.

After a few minutes, Mom comes out with it, walking briskly to the bathroom, emptying its contents into the toilet. She rinses the bedpan, washes her hands, gathers up some toiletries, and then she goes back to him with a bowl of water. She doesn't bother to look at me, just keeps on her duties as nurse.

She disappears into his room again, talking to him all the while. Sometimes it sounds like arguing, but I know it's just Mom's nursing attitude. I recall that voice of hers so well, especially when I was sick and wasn't doing exactly as I was told.

Allan makes his way to the washroom and I move to the couch, not really sure what I should be doing. Al doesn't even really acknowledge me, just shuffles to the washroom as best he can. He turns on the fan, which blocks out the sound, and I watch Mom as she enters and leaves his bedroom. She comes out with a pile of sheets and towels and walks in with the ones I had just folded.

Karma

She's humming all the time, like someone who enjoys their job. Not simply cleaning up after a cancer patient, but the purpose behind it. Making someone as comfortable as they can brings meaning into your life. I remember Mom saying that one time.

"Do you need some help?" I offer, feeling a sense of loss as she walks into the kitchen and fills up a bucket with Pine Sol.

"Nope," she says, and continues her business, dragging the mop out of the broom closet.

I begin to wonder why I'm here at all. I'm sitting on the couch after getting fed, and watching someone else do the chores. Mom even did the dishes.

The smell of fresh comes from Allan's room as Mom scours the floor. The mop clangs as it enters the bucket, thuds as it hits the bed frame. She's rinsing and squeezing the liquid out of the mop and I wait for my cue when to enter or when to give a hand.

Allan's still in the washroom, and I wonder if he's okay in there? *Should I check on him? Does he need anything?*

I suppress my offering, as nothing would be worse than bombarding someone with attention when they don't want it. Especially in the washroom.

Restless, I turn on the TV and flip through the stations: the news, *The Price Is Right*, a soap opera, *Scooby-Doo*. I loved that show as a kid and, in some sense, felt our group was like that gang of friends, all hanging out and doing their thing. Thelma, the brainy one, was Trudy. Scooby was definitely Suzanne, and I laugh out loud, almost uncontrollably.

I hear a chuckle from the bathroom. "What's so funny?" Allan asks, as he comes out. He has slicked back his hair. It's nice to hear his voice, his laughter, even though it isn't the hardy belly-laugh I remember. His voice is weak and strained.

My eyes light up when I see him, then my smirk disappears. "Oh, just making comparisons."

Allan makes his way to the couch, sinks in beside me, and puts his feet up on the coffee table.

"You want to eat something, Al?" Mom bellows from his room, multitasking.

"No, Cathy. I'm okay for now, thanks."

He looks at me with tired eyes. "Your mom is something else."

He leans into me, bumps me with his shoulder. That's when he takes me all in, scans my face and attire.

"Jesus, Karm. You look like shit. Maybe your mom should stay with

Trena Christie-MacEachern

you."

"You're one to talk," I say, humouring him.

Allan looks the worse for wear. His hair is thin and greasy, he's swimming in his clothes, his face is pale, he has bags under his eyes, and there is a strange smell emitting from him, although it is masked by toothpaste and the cologne he must have just doused on himself.

"I've got cancer. What's your excuse?"

I laugh out loud.

Allan laughs, too, and his eyes squint. He touches my knee with the back of his hand. "Good to see you, Karm. Glad you came by. But honestly, you do look like crap. What's going on?"

Sighing, and avoiding the question, I focus back on *Scooby Doo and Friends*. "I think Thelma could have been Trudy in real life. What do you think?"

He chuckles. "Yep, maybe."

Then I look at him straight on. "Didn't we call ourselves the lunch bunch, after the *Breakfast Club* movie?"

"Heyyy, ya. I think we did."

"Who came up with that?"

"Jeesh, Karm, I dunno. You, maybe?"

He makes a silly face. I swat him playfully. We seem to be dancing around the elephant in the room, talking about no nonsense stuff, gibberish, before I finally ask,

"Seriously, Allan. How are you?" My face is serious now. But I can tell Allan really doesn't want to get into it.

He waves his hand around his face like he's trying to swat a fly. "I could really use a smoke."

"What?" I can't believe what I just heard. The stuff that made him sick in the first place and that's what he wants most of all.

"Karm, just because I'm dying doesn't mean I'm not craving. I still smoke. Just not around your mom so much because it's...I don't know, disrespectful, her in the health care profession and all. But she knows I do when the guys are here. If I'm really craving, I'll just have one in my room."

"Really?" I ask, sounding naïve.

"It's okay, Karm. Really. Don't look all scared. Relax. It's not going to do me any more harm at this point." He smiles a sad smile.

I stroke his hand. It's cool, and thin. His skin even feels different. "God, Allan, I'm so sorry you're going through all of this."

I want to wrap my arms around him and tell him it's going to be alright. I want to hug the cancer right out of him, but I can't. I can't lie and I can't even hold him tight. He's so feeble.

Instead, I lean against him and let my warm touch envelop him. "You're like a brother to me. I hope you know that."

Allan nods. He's always known, I think, especially, since he and Mom got so close.

Mom comes out of the room, snapping off her rubber gloves. She has another load of wash and is going to take it to the laundry room.

"We're out of milk," she says. "I'll run to the store and get some. Anybody need anything?"

"Something to go with tea," I say.

"All right. Be back shortly."

She throws her purse on top of the laundry basket, takes Allan's keys off the hook and out she goes, closing the door behind her.

Allan and I sit in silence for a moment or two. He looks so small, like he's wearing his father's button-down plaid shirt as dress up. His sweatpants are knotted around his waist and he curls up. He rests his head against the arm of the couch and he has his feet on my lap.

I throw the blanket that was on the back of the sofa over him and he tucks it under his chin and closes his eyes for a moment.

"You tired?" I ask.

"Hmmm. But I can't really sleep. I'll just rest my eyes here for a moment, if you don't mind. I don't like being in that room. I slept mostly on the couch after Lotty died."

I didn't say anything. What could I say? I watch him, rub his bony foot through his sock. We remain that way for several minutes, 'til I see his eyes flutter open.

"You scared, Allan?"

His sleepy eyes study me. He looks at me a long time before answering. He's thinking of his answer. Thinking whatever he provides will impact me positively or negatively.

"It's okay if you are. I am." I squeeze his big toe. "I think everyone is. Jimmy, Mom, Charlie, Clyde. We are all dealing with this, your sickness, as best we can."

"I'm sorry I'm putting you guys through all this." His face is grim.

"No, no, you're not, Allan. You're not doing anything to us."

He closes his eyes again, goes quiet. "I'd prefer to talk about something more interesting. You, for example. What's going on with you and Jimmy? And Charlie?"

"Argh! This is supposed to be about you, Allan! Not me. And not Jimmy

Trena Christie-MacEachern

or Charlie, either. We are having a bit of a disagreement, is all. We'll work it out."

I look away from him, wondering if he heard me and Mom talking before. Wondering if he can read my moods, like Jimmy.

"They are my brothers, you know. No one means as much to me as they do. You do, too, of course, and your mom, and Lotty. But as far as brothers, they have been there for me more than you'll ever know. And when I go through this next phase of my life, they will be here, too."

He touches his chest. I know the three of them have been buddies since little kids. He wipes at his eye and sniffs, which gets me all misty.

"But it's going to be all right," he says.

"Allan, I want you to get treatment. I want you to go to the hospital and get the help you need. Mom is good and all, but she can't do everything."

Allan shakes his head. "I have it all worked out, Karm."

"What do you mean? Are you going to get some radiation? Chemotherapy? It should help some, buy you some time. Heck, maybe it will cure you all together?"

I think of a lung transplant and suddenly, feel jubilant. Why hasn't anyone thought of it before? Maybe there *is* hope. It might be just a glimmer, but it's better than nothing.

Just then, Mom walks in holding a brown paper bag in her hands. It crinkles when she sets it on the counter.

"I got cookies and pastries. What's your pick? Allan? Will you have some tea, or some of the shake I made earlier? You can have it warm or cold."

Allan sits upright, the blanket falls off his lap. "What kind of cookies, Mom?" he jokes.

"The kind you like." And she winks at me.

~

It's a straight line, not a cross. The cross would mean I'm pregnant. The line means I'm not.

I leave it in the washroom, busying myself around the kitchen while I wait for the timer to go off the second time. I walk back into the bathroom ten minutes later, study it again, thoroughly this time, making sure the line stays a line. Not even a faint cross. A wonderful, perfect, horizontal line.

Cupping my hand to my forehead, I inhale, feeling both relief and dis-

Karma

appointment, and flinch. How can I even possibly be disappointed? But for Jimmy, I am. If it were his. God, I still don't have a clue if it could have been his or not.

Time to toss everything out and hide the evidence. I spill the urine down the toilet; the rest of the stuff I cram in a bag, knot it and hide it inside the main garbage, throwing other trash on top: left-over supper from the day before, a salad-dressing bottle that was near empty, our last phone bill.

As I head toward the kitchen. I suddenly have this crazy-nervous energy. I should shower, put on something presentable. Not wear my old, baggy sweatpants, my mope clothes. I have to be done with it. I need to snap out of it.

Allan told me in so many words that Jimmy would be coming home tonight. Obviously, they had talked. Allan talks with everyone, helps everyone out, even though everyone goes there to see Allan, to help *him*. I think the reverse happens. Allan actually helps us. He listens without interrupting, gives advice only when asked, cares, understands, doesn't judge. He had similar conversations with Charlie, and me, and Mom, and Jimmy. It's his gift.

Allan is like some sort of magnet, some kind of disposal unit where people just drop off their shit and he absorbs it. Absolves you, making you feel better about yourself and your situation. Maybe that's why he's so sick. His body can't take the poison anymore. He's been doing it all his life.

I turn on the water faucet and let it run until it's good and warm, almost hot, and toss my slob clothes in the laundry bin. They still smell like Allan's apartment, which gives me the willies. I don't know what it is specifically. Maybe the mixture of pills and sickness? Mom's cleaning products? Maybe it's the scent of death.

My flesh turns into a sea of goosebumps and I try to rid my brain of that thought. Thankfully, the water feels nice, the perfect temperature to wash away my troubles—even if it's temporary.

As I'm washing my arms and chest, I take a good look at myself.

I knew I was thin, running like a crazy woman before Lotty disappeared, and thinking I could keep up with Jimmy—that was my initial goal. I needed something we could both do together and I had thought that was it, exercising, trying to stay connected. Then I ran just for something to do, aerobics to pass the time, the gym to add versatility.

Was I eating then? All of it seems a blur, a million years away.

And then Lotty happened. The stress of learning what she had been

189

Trena Christie-MacEachern

going through, and then her disappearance. Everyone searching. It was desperate times.

Allan had looked for her for days before he called the police. Before he contacted us. He didn't think it would be that bad. Nobody did. That sort of thing doesn't happen.

Then, worst of all, her unexpected death, the insurmountable sadness and the grief from that, and Allan's illness, which he also tried to keep secret. Lord, it's a wonder we were not all in the hospital, dealing with exhaustion.

I want to cry, to let it all out, every bit of it. Actually, screaming would be better. Or smashing things. I want all this insanity to be over.

But instead, I'm standing under running water and somehow it helps to break the negative thought processes and soothes my jumbled nerves.

After I finish showering and hop out, steam fills the room and fogs the mirror.

As I dry my hair, I'm trying to decide what to wear.

Should I get dressed-dressed to show Jimmy I'm doing okay? But I don't want to look needy or desperate.

I opt for my v-neck sweater and jeans. Minimalism. Clean, presentable, practicable. *Frig, I'm making myself stressed just by deciding what to wear.*

But spending time with Allan puts everything in perspective. The way he is makes me think about everything. The importance of family and friendships. How much turmoil have we put ourselves in while Allan is slowly slipping away? We don't know how much time we have left with him, or how much any of us have, for that matter. Like Lotty. How were we to know she'd pass so young? Or Daniel Timmons, the kid Mom ran over.

I hear them before I see them. The noise. Paulie is kicking at the door like he does. It's a habit now, but when he was little and couldn't reach the handle, he'd kick at the door for us to let him in.

He comes in first, flipping off his shoes and dropping his school bag. Mariah is talking to her father about her practice.

"Mmmm," she says as she rounds into the kitchen. "Something smells good."

The brownies are already cooked and cooling on the counter. She gives me that wide, toothy smile—her skin glowing from her after-school activity. Her hair is tied back off her face in a thick ponytail. "Mom! You're awesome."

Sheepishly, I return her smile, when I see Jimmy standing behind her.

190

Karma

The two of us are feeling at odds with each other, using Mariah as a shield.

Jimmy has one hand on his daughter's shoulder, looks at me as I look at him, saying nothing.

This catches Mariah's attention. She laughs, stares back at me and then up at her father. "What's going on?"

"Nothing," I say casually.

"Go get changed before supper, Mariah," Jimmy says in a dull, flat tone. He looks as scruffy as I did before I cleaned up. He turns his back, says casually, "I'm going to take a shower."

With nothing to say, I continue with supper. Even though I know the recipe for rice by heart, I have to read it over and over.

~

It has been three full days that Jimmy has been home. Yet the silence and discomfort between us continue to bloom like an ugly mould: toxic and black. Neither of us knows what to say or how to begin. He can't even look at me, or only briefly, and I can see the hurt, or the hate, or both, in him. He often turns away from me, focuses his attention on Paulie or Mariah.

I feel so left out, not being able to chat, having to pretend; to sit and smile with a fake grin plastered on my face, then begin the supper wash-up, even though it was always Jimmy and I who did that process together. But I do it without hesitation, pretending I'm scouring away the scum and dirt between us. Yet, as the days march on, we seem to be drifting farther apart.

When Mariah asked why I was so aloof, I'd tell her my thoughts were on Allan and she'd nod like she understood. She'd wrap her arms around me or lay her head against my chest, and stroke my hair or pat my shoulders before going in search of the television—or the phone, especially, as most her pals would be calling her after dinner.

With Mariah occupied, hearing her laughter, chatting away to her friend about the upcoming dance and Paulie in the TV room, zoned out watching the crazy *Animaniacs*, Jimmy beside him staring like he, too, is some sort of robot, I finally find the nerve to talk to him. I lean in and stammer,

"J-Jimmy, do you think we could...talk?"

My belly is doing backflips and my hands are sweaty. I had thought in my mind one hundred ways to approach this man, from writing a letter

191

Trena Christie-MacEachern

and leaving it on his side of the bed to full-out yelling and pointing fingers just to get his attention. Instead, I decide to go the calm, practical approach. Standing at his side, not altering my tone at all so Paulie doesn't get suspicious there is something going on, or, rather, *not* going on between us. As far as I know, both kids are in the dark about their father, and my indiscretions, and our current state of affairs; that we haven't spoken to each other in a week.

Jimmy doesn't respond, just sits like a rag doll, his arm on the back of the sofa, one leg extended on the cushion, the other long leg jutting out on the floor. His expression doesn't change.

Paulie is sitting on his knees, has one sock off, the other foot stuffed into the cushion, and he's leaning on the opposite side of the couch. He's mesmerized as the cartoon characters jump around the screen.

"Jimmy," I say a little louder. "Did you hear me? Can we ta—?"

He blinks and darts his eyes in my direction briefly before he lets out a heavy sigh etched with fire. "Nothing to talk about," he says.

I freeze to the spot. Tethered like an anchor. My cheeks are burning and tears begin to force their way to the corners of my eyes. Never before has Jimmy ever treated me with so much contempt. I can feel it in every ounce of my being. He's hurting. And I just don't know how to fix it.

"Jimmy," I say again, a little more breathless. You can hear the emotion in my voice. "If we could just talk..." *Clear the air, like the way thunder does in the summertime when the humidity is too high. Yes, there will be lightening too, crashes and bangs, maybe even rain, but then the skies clear. I certainly didn't expect for us to be hunky-dory all at once, but if we make a start...*

We always talked and cleared things out. But today, it isn't happening. *Is it ever going to?*

But he doesn't look at me, even though I'm standing right in his space.

The minutes pass and I'm still tethered to the spot. It feels like I'm playing an invisible game of chess with Jimmy, waiting for his next move, or mine. His words keep running over and over in my mind like a bad play.

Finally, he reaches forward and taps Paulie on the shoulder. For a moment, Paulie, too, sits stone-faced and rigid, entranced by his program 'til his father calls his name.

"Paul. Want to get a treat at the store?"

In a blink, Paulie's up, grabs his sock, turns off the television and hollers to his sister, "Mariah! We're going to the store!" As loud as his little voice can holler.

Karma

Mariah opens her door, her hand covering the phone, "Can I go to Laura's for a second? I have to take over my pink shirt."

Jimmy nods. Meanwhile, Paulie's getting his sneakers on and is out the door, slamming it behind him.

"Laura. Awesome. Dad's taking me. I'll be there in five minutes. Hold on, Dad. I just have to get my shirt."

Jimmy's standing at the door, waiting for Mariah, who then dashes out wearing her flats and has her shirt bunched in her hand. She rushes past me.

I watch them in the hallway that leads to the front door. Mariah turns back and looks at me, "Mom. You coming?"

And just as I'm about to open my mouth, Jimmy speaks,

"No! Mom can't come." He says it so definitively. So ice cold.

Mariah doesn't question it. She's out the door and then Jimmy's eyes meet mine. They are dark and brooding.

"Just so you know. This is how it feels to be selfish, Karm."

He turns his back and walks out.

18

Now

I knew it was childish, stupid, hateful. Even before I took myself there. But there was nothing left for me to do. Jimmy is home, but not home. We are playing games. He won't talk. The two of us wandering around our house like ghosts, passing through rooms like we don't really exist, feeling cold and hollow.

I can't stand it anymore. I made a mistake, yet Jimmy won't even allow me to explain. He shut me off and turned away. I've never seen him so angry, so hurt. The scorn in his face and his eyes, the tone of his voice when he said those last words to me, "this is how it feels to be selfish."

But the more I think about it, how does he have the gall to say such a thing? Doesn't he remember what we were all going through during that terrible time? How many days did we look for Lotty? Searching endlessly. Trying to keep some kind of normalcy at home with the kids, but feeling a deep sense of dread in our guts when we went out night after night exploring those awful places: dives, drug hangouts, and cheap motels, hoping, praying that we would find where Lotty had ended up. Scared out of our wits that something would happen to us, that we'd be the ones caught in the crossfire and wouldn't come home ourselves. Didn't Jimmy get that?

While he went to work in his tailored pants and shiny shoes, the rest of his friends were hunting, scouring every nook and cranny. Going back to the same wretched places again, handing out posters, and stapling pictures of Lotty around town and in bars just in case someone would have seen her. Jimmy was oblivious to it all, wanting the police to do their job, or for Allan to hire a detective.

Most of the gang and I had been together a number of nights on the look-out, going out after supper or after the kids went to bed. I even arranged daycare for the mornings just in case I didn't make it back in time. Those were hard fucking days and I'm sure I went through some kind of

Karma

post traumatic, seeing what I saw and not being prepared for it and then the shock of Lotty being found, but not how we wanted to find her.

God! I caught my breath at the memory and snorted, what I call a grief spasm, and stuff a few of my things in an overnight bag: my pj's, a change of clothes, my toothbrush.

Leaving my house is the only solution. I can't take the silence and the anguish anymore. If Jimmy wants to torment me, he'll have to do it without me. I never planned anything. I didn't even want to go to the funeral, especially the reception at The Bullhorn by myself. I begged Jimmy to come with me. Even for just an hour. It was his best friend's girl, after all. He knew Allan since he was a little kid. All of his old buddies would be there. Everyone, that is, except Lotty.

He broke the group up and by not being there that night spoke volumes. Everyone noticed, but nobody said anything because that was the kind of people they were.

Whatever happened to Charlie and me that night had nothing to do with Charlie and me. We were over years ago. He knew that. I knew that. But there was something with the way the evening went, and Allan so anguished, his grief so uncontrollable, and the stories he shared with everyone: his hopes and dreams and losses and eventual heartbreak, plus, too much booze.

Yes, I can't drink and probably shouldn't have had any more than a glass, two at the most, and cheap house wine at that. And does anything really count, because I have no memory after walking into Charlie's pretend house and him dumping that awful story on me.

At first, I thought what had happened to Charlie and me was just collateral damage. Plainly and simply. The way one says they are not hungry yet when you put down a bowl of chips, they take a few without even giving much thought that they are putting it into their mouths.

But not anymore. I was a target. An easy one. Charlie took advantage because he knows me so well. But whose fault is that? Mine? All of it? Doesn't Charlie shoulder any of it?

But Jimmy doesn't see it. I would never intentionally hurt that man, nor do I think, deep down, Charlie would, either. The two of them shared something unspoken, make that the three of them: Allan, Charlie, and Jimmy. They were like brothers.

They didn't step on anyone's toes, never raised their voices, never stole anyone's girl, intentionally. Even Jimmy said he never pursued me until he knew for certain that Charlie and I were finished. He even asked Charlie, called him on the phone. Oblivious me.

195

Trena Christie-MacEachern

But now I know Jimmy has fallen out of love with me. He can say I hurt him, that I cheated, whatever, but he won't let go of the anger and he won't talk to me and I can't live like that.

He knows he is being intentionally hurtful to make a point. I'm the scapegoat. I'm the sacrificial lamb. And he knows that, too.

So, I pack. I'm getting the hell out of Dodge, as they say. Jimmy can mind the kids and get them off to school and do all the answering of questions and the picking up of kids for after-school programs. I'm going to do exactly as he said I would.

Selfish will be my middle name.

~

The bar hasn't changed much. Got dirtier, dingier, or maybe one just notices these things more as one gets older.

I'm at my old hangout spot, The Bullhorn. Except this time, I don't have to sneak to the back. I sit up front by the bar, on the high stools, where everything has almost remained the same since I was a teenager. Sure, they may have changed the colour of the walls and added new posters, but even some of the staff have remained.

Half-pint Harry is sitting in his usual spot. At a low table at the far end of the counter, ashtray in front of him, shot glass and beer bottle. I often wondered if he knew the nickname had been attached to him.

But of course, some drunk twenty-something on spring break or summer vacation would parade up to him, yell his name at the end of the night. He'd do a salute, or a cheers and smile with his stained-coloured, broken tooth, and yellowed fingers.

As I sit here, I wonder about him. How many years has he been coming? Is he here every day? Does he have a home? A family?

I fight the urge to ask as it's pretty much just him and me here. I could strike up a conversation. A couple just left, having had a coke and a beer with their hot hamburger sandwiches and fries. I forgot, too, how good the food can be. Especially after you haven't eaten all day, or are hungover from partying the night before.

I'm already on my second glass, feeling tipsy. Vicki is to meet me but she's still nowhere in sight.

But, like clockwork, once nine o'clock hits on a Thursday, the crowd starts spilling in. Underage kids, like us back in the day, arrive. This place turns the other cheek so it can pay the bills.

The college kids are here too since their classes are over. The regulars,

196

Karma

like Harry, just come to drink and sometimes to socialize, and folks like me come to get the hell out of the house and, with luck, get someone to wonder where you are.

I sip at my second glass of The Bullhorn's house white, Chardonnay at its finest. Not that I know much about wine but this is going down a bit too easy, and secondly, my bartender, Tim, keeps refilling my glass up a little extra. He's giving me a little more bang for my buck, which I appreciate, so I give him a bit more of a tip than I probably should. Jimmy is good for it.

With my back to the room, I didn't really notice how much the bar is filling up. I turn and see Eric. He's laughing. At first, I think he's laughing at me because I'm sitting here alone. However, he doesn't notice that's it's me. I'm simply another customer to him.

The cash box is sitting open on a small, square table and the rubber stamp is lying beside it for the paying patrons coming in. Didn't seem that long ago that some other old dude was taking our money; now it's us that are old.

"Eric!" I holler jovially, waving. But with the music and the buzz of everyone coming in, he doesn't hear me.

I hop off my stool, grab my glass, and saunter over to him. I had even managed to get a little dressed-up to come. Not dressed-dressed, but good-fitting jeans, my low cowboy boots that go with everything, and a white, button-down, dress-shirt tucked in with my big, shiny, belt buckle. My hair is long, longer than I usually wear it, and I added my big hoop earrings and my decorative leather watch. I opted not to wear my wedding ring. I left it at home on the bureau in my bedroom.

I tap Eric on the shoulder and he turns.

"Hey, handsome."

"Heyyyy angel."

He pulls me into a tight bear hug. He smells good and is still noticeably very handsome. He pushes me back and does the look over. This always made me cringe, getting ogled by Eric, but tonight, I don't exactly mind.

He scans the crowd. "You and Jimmy have a big night out? Your anniversary or something?"

I don't say anything, just punch him in the shoulder.

He's distracted for a moment as the door opens and three busty girls walk in with nothing on but a lot of makeup and little to leave the imagination. Eric swallows a smile. It's as if he was told he could have all three and they are all legal.

Trena Christie-MacEachern

"IDs, ladies."

They giggle, which is a big give-away, but, sure enough, wallets are opened, money is handed over, arms are stamped, and there's a "thank you, Eric," by the last gal in a breathy, seductive way.

My mouth is hanging open, and I blink a little too many times, which Eric notices. He laughs and grabs me by the shoulder and pulls me close to him, hip to hip. "Where's Jimmy?"

"Ahh," I stammer, take another drink of wine, "girl's night," I lie. "But they didn't show yet,"

"So, you're just hanging out?"

I nod.

"That's cool. That's cool."

Eric looks pretty well exactly the same as in his high school days. Golden hair, blue eyes, high, chiselled cheek bones, slim build but muscled in the right places: the abs, the biceps. He's put on a few pounds, which only makes him look better, filling out that once-lean, almost lanky physique. I could see from the girls who walked in that they'd take him in a heartbeat.

Eric is still a playboy and hasn't settled down. He can obviously still get away dating the younger girls given how he still looks, but that life-style won't last forever. Can't.

"You still with Lucille?" I inquire. Trying to see if we have any common ground.

A few more people arrive, ones who don't need any ID: two couples older than me. He shakes his head and they pass over their money.

As he is stamping, he says, "Nah, we broke up."

"Oh, I'm sorry. I liked her."

He shrugs, chews his gum, nods. His eyes drift off for a moment as if he's thinking of her still.

"God, you guys were together like a long time?" I take another gulp of my wine.

"Yeah. A year. Year and a half." He rests his back side against the small wall that separates the main door from the bar itself, his hands behind him. I can see that he really cared for her, but yet, he wouldn't or couldn't admit it.

"Maybe you'll get back together?"

He shrugs again and changes the subject. "Who you with tonight?"

"Well, no one so far," I say with a laugh.

"You can hang with me 'til they come"—I nod—"so it doesn't look like you've been stood up, or maybe you're here to do a pick up?" He winks at

Karma

me and beams that broad smile.

Eric isn't like Jimmy or Allan. He'd take the girl if she was free, attached, married or otherwise. But I have no interest in Eric. He's cute and was part of our gang when we were teens, but that's the extent that we have in common.

My hand goes to my mouth. Would Eric try to pick me up? I'm more of his age than his last girlfriend. Lucille was at least ten years younger. "Pick up?"

He laughs. "Just kidding. I know you're not like that. But there are a lot that are. People that you think are home-grown family people will show up here and leave with someone else. Sometimes they put on a front for me. So and so needs a lift or he's had too much to drink. But I know the difference. There are cabs, you know. I see it all here. The expression on their faces if they see someone they haven't seen in a long time, to that look when—"

"Yeah, I get it. I get it." I raise my hand to discourage any more of this topic. It is, after all, hitting a little too close to home.

The door swings open and in walks Victoria. She is sensibly dressed, wearing cream-coloured, casual pants, sweater and flats. Her hair is cropped short. She sees Eric.

"Well, isn't this a throwback?" She places her purse on the table, roots into her wallet and hands Eric her cover fee.

Eric's eyes are wide, knowing that we are two of Charlie's exes. He chuckles without saying anything.

"What, Eric?" Victoria asks briskly.

He shakes his head. "Nothing."

Victoria eyes me skeptically. "Of all the places you wanted to meet. It's here? Sorry I'm late, by the way. Had a few things I had to do. And you kind of called last minute."

I take another sip of my wine, realizing it's all gone and loop arms with Victoria. "Glad you could come, Vic." Not that I ever called her that, but it seemed to suit her presently. "Let's go get a drink."

I salute Tim to come over and he takes Victoria's order, white wine like me.

"I can count the times I came in here," she says, scouring the crowd with her eyes.

"Really? God, we came here all the time."

"I know. I always wanted to come with you guys but I was never part of the crowd. Feels kind of funny being here now. I wondered what all the hoopla was about."

Trena Christie-MacEachern

"Just young kids partying."

"Yep." She looks at me. "So, why'd you call? Don't get me wrong, I'm glad you did, but we were never friends, really. The only thing we had in common, sort of, was—"

"Charlie."

"Exactly."

We both laugh and Tim brings us each a full glass of wine.

"On the house," he says. "Compliments of Eric."

We swing our heads over in Eric's direction and raise our glasses to him. "Thanks Eric," we shout.

Then I holler, "Come join us when your finished there."

Victoria looks at me quizzically, one eye raised higher than the other. "You know he's a piranha in the dating world." She glances in his direction.

"Nah," I say, swiping my hand in midair. "I mean, I know he dated a lot, but he wouldn't go near me." I hope. "He and Jimmy are friends."

Victoria raises her eyebrow again. "He hit on me when he knew Charlie and I were dating. And again, after we broke up."

She takes a small sip of her wine and makes a face. "I should have ordered a beer. This stuff is repulsive." She takes another small sip. "I have to work in the morning."

"He hit on you?" I lean forward across the table so I'm just inches from her face.

She nods. "He thought he could change me."

I throw my head back in full belly laugh and Victoria laughs along with me.

"He's cute but not very bright," she says.

I'm wiping my eyes with the tips of my fingers when Tim saunters over with two more wines.

"Did you order this?" I ask Victoria as I look up at Tim. She shakes her head.

"From those two fellas." Tim twists his head over his left shoulder.

Victoria and I look in his direction and see two young men, I'm guessing college, saluting us with their beer glasses and smiling broadly.

Tim places the glasses in front of us and says, "Go easy on them, ladies." And winks at me.

Now it's Victoria's time to laugh.

"I wish it were two women," she says, "but I'll take it. Doesn't matter what sex thinks you're pretty."

"Cheers to that." We clink glasses. I'm thinking this is my fourth glass

200

Karma

of wine.

After a couple of songs play, I see them making their move. "Uh oh," I say in mid slurp. "They're coming over."

Victoria groans and makes a face before she glances over her shoulder at them.

"Hello, ladies," says the taller one. He's not bad-looking. I'm thinking twenty-threeish, a bit of the Don Johnson look with the three o'clock shadow, sandy-coloured hair, a bit too many buttons open on his shirt for my liking.

The other chap is quieter: dark hair, broad shoulders, super-dark skin, like he's outside a lot without a shirt.

"Can we join you?"

Victoria looks at me like she's waiting for me to reply. After all, I'm the one who's married.

But my feet are twitching and the music is good so I say, "I think we should dance first."

Before tall guy can answer, I'm standing up. His name is Callum, but for the life of I can't hear and can't pronounce it so I keep calling him Colin for the first ten minutes. The tanned guy, Pete, stays sitting with Victoria. She doesn't want to dance because she just arrived. I tell her to try and catch up. I'm already three drinks ahead of her.

Rhythm was a Dancer is playing and the dance floor isn't packed, but it's good enough for me. Brazen, I lead Callum to the centre of the floor under the red and blue flashes of light.

Moving and shaking and thinking I can dance Michael Jackson or Paula Abdul under the table. God, I have beat when I have booze. I'm smiling and Callum is smiling at me. He's looking around, nodding at a few people in the crowd. A couple of girls start dancing with us, and when that song winds down, Billy Idol's *Rebel Yell* comes on. I don't remember the last time I danced.

And Callum, being the good sport, and because I'm making us thirsty, skirts to our table and brings down our drinks. I'm drinking and dancing, arm up in the air, shouting and singing. I'm waving Victoria to come down because this is so much fun and why didn't I do this before? Earlier? With friends? Just going out and dancing?

I bump Callum with my hip and keep bumping his thigh, his knee, 'til my butt is inches off the floor and he is laughing at me.

"Whoa!" he screams in my ear. "You got the moves."

This of course gives me more confidence, so I'm twirling and bumping.

Trena Christie-MacEachern

Victoria and Pete join us now while Tom Cochrane's *Life is a Highway* comes on. Everyone is on the floor and everyone is screaming to the chorus.

"I love this tune," I scream to everyone and slug back the rest of my wine and place my empty glass on the small stage that houses some of the speakers and DJ equipment.

Everyone is bumping into one another. Some blonde girl's long hair brushes my face and I'm smiling like someone just told me the best joke, that I won a million dollars, that everything that could go right, goes right.

I'm just so damn happy right now and my smile says it all. I don't want this feeling to end. This magical, drunk, fun-filled, dance night to ever be over. If I can just keep dancing and feeling the music and the sound of the guitar and the beat of the music, I'll die a happy woman.

Callum smiles at me, and I smile back. He stretches out his arm and places his palm on my cheek. The tips of his fingers slide back to hold and stroke the back of my neck under my hair line.

It feels good.

He does the same with the other hand, cupping my face, and then he brings me toward him, his mouth on top of mine.

I shake my head and pull back. "Nnnn na na na nah."

I wag my index finger at him while I move my head away. It still feels like I'm doing some exotic dance. I'm wild at him but I can't communicate effectively what I'm trying to say.

Victoria sees my expression and body language, grabs my arm, and pulls me away and then stands full front and centre while shouting at Callum. She is in his face like super commando, chastising the insubordinate marine at boot camp. I'm waiting for him to drop to the floor and do fifty push-ups.

This causes a ruckus. The crowd congeals. Eric and a bouncer from the back make their way into the mix.

The crowd is revved up shouting, "Fight! Fight! Fight!" They think the bouncer and Callum will go at it.

I'm trying to get out of the soup. It's hot and sticky. My mind is racing, as is my heart, and I still have Victoria's hand.

People are pushing us and each other, screaming, pointing fingers. The room is deafening.

Ace of Base comes on, 'All that she wants is another baby, another baby'.

God! I roll my eyes. "Do I need to hear that?" I scream in Victoria's ear.

202

Karma

Everything hits me at once. The sounds, the room, the heat, the air. I'm woozy, and now know I'm officially one hundred percent drunk.

I notice the other glass of wine I had at my table is in my hand, empty as well. I don't recall going back to the table, nor drinking it.

"What happened out there?" Victoria screams at me.

"Jimmy wants another baby," I snigger, singing to the song. "But I don't." I stagger and slur. My legs buckle.

"Jesus, Karm. Sit down."

"Nope," I laugh. "I better stand."

Callum and Pete are standing beside us now. Callum is trying to grab my hand. Victoria keeps swatting it away.

"Back off!" she barks. "She's married! And I'm gay."

They look at her and then each other. Callum takes my left hand, the one that's holding the empty wine glass.

"You're lying. She's not wearing a ring."

I look down at my hand and notice I'm not.

"Let's relax. We'll buy you another drink. C'mon. Don't be like that. We just want to have fun is all. C'mon."

Callum moves like a stealth toward me, wrapping his arm around my waist.

Pete is looking down at the floor, telling Callum to leave me alone and saying, "Let's go." He's pulling at Callum's shirt a little bit but it seems Callum likes a challenge.

College boys. For some reason, I decide to keep with the show.

Slurring, I tell him, "This is the story. Honest God's." I bow my head and put my hand on my heart. "Vic is my friend." I reach over, muckle onto her neck and then kiss her square on the lips.

Victoria's eyes widen and she laughs. I laugh, too.

"She and I both da-dated the same guy. 'Cept she mar-ried him and and, I was just in l-love with him." I sigh and hiccough. "We should get another drink. You can buy us another, another drink."

"You've had enough, Karm," Vic interrupts. She looks at the guys. "She's loaded. Can't drink for a hill of beans."

"How you guys doing?" Eric taps me on the shoulder. He is now standing beside us, hands on his hips, checking out Callum and Pete. "Everything okay here, ladies?"

"This your husband?" Callum asks me.

My eyelids are getting heavy but I'm still talking and smiling. I reach

Trena Christie-MacEachern

for Eric. "Nope!" I shake my head. "But this handsome man is my husband's friend and"—I point to Victoria, "—her ex's friend, and her husband and my ex are friends. Did I say that right?" I laugh. "But now Vic's gay but you're still her friend."

I look up at Eric, smiling, happy. "Right Eric? You're still Vic's friend, right?"

I curl right up to Eric, put my arms around his body and rest my head against his chest, like he's a pillow and I'm going to bed. He lets me stay right there, stroking my back, holding my arm in place.

There's a lot of murmuring then, noise, sounds I can't make out. I'm not sure how long I'm standing here, because I keep my eyes closed and the movement of Eric's body and his warmth and strong beat of his heart is like being adrift on a calm ocean aboard a raft. I just didn't want to let go. I let my hand drift down his back, feeling his belt loop and stick in a thumb, clinging onto him.

I drank too much. I know it and say it to whomever is with us, even though my eyes are closed.

Things get kind of confusing then. I'm scared to open my lids in case I get dizzy. Scared for Eric to move in case I get sick. I want to stay in this cocoon, whatever it is, and I sway like seaweed whenever Eric moves.

He and Victoria are bantering.

"Is she going home with you?"

"God, no. I'll probably never be able to lift her into the house. Or wake her up."

They laugh and my body vibrates against Eric's chest.

"Maybe I should call Jimmy?"

"Jesus, no. It's after midnight."

"More like one."

"Really? Frig. I have to work in the morning. No. You can't call Jimmy. You'll probably wake up the house. Or worse, scare the shit out of them, thinking something's happened. Bad phone calls come at night."

"Well, who, then?"

"Why don't you take her home? You know where she lives. And you can carry her."

"Yeah, all right."

Then there is murmuring again. Eric says he has to put me down, that I have to sit while he finishes up but I can't let go.

"No no no, Eric."

I'm being lifted. The room is swaying. I know I need to lie perfectly still, keep my eyes closed and wait for everything to stop spinning and

Karma

for the world to be upright again.

I no longer hear Victoria. Her voice disappears with the buzzing in my ears and the noise of the crowd. Everything gets quieter and dark. I must in the back room? In the office? On a sofa?

I'm thankful for the quiet. I nod off and know I'm officially MIA.

Trena Christie-MacEachern

19

Now

Waking up, I adjust my eyes to the light. I have no idea what time it is. My tongue is stuck to the roof of my mouth. My head is pounding and I am one hundred degrees.

As I try to lift my head, it feels like it weighs twenty pounds more than it should. I have to pee and so badly that if I don't go, I'm going to wet myself right here on the spot.

Ugh. I'm too afraid to move.

My arm hurts and once I pull it out from the covers, I see an angry red line from my elbow to my wrist, then notice I'm wearing a white t-shirt and it isn't mine but I still have on my bra, but no pants or socks.

I lift my head, plunk my legs on the floor and look around. I'm in someone's bedroom I don't recognize. On someone's bed!

I strain to listen for any sounds, to try and hear if anyone is outside the door, for footsteps or noises, a radio? Nothing.

What day is it? Saturday or Friday? The alarm clock says 1:11 on it, but I'm not sure if it is morning or night. I have no idea how long I slept, how I got here, wherever here is, and what happened after clinging to Eric at The Bullhorn.

Cupping my hand to my mouth I let out a belch, wondering if anything else is going to come behind it.

A glass of water is on the night stand and a couple of Tylenol. Before I do anything, I take the two pills. My throat feels raw, like I'd been smoking or puking, but I have no recollection of doing either.

I have a flashback of eating a hot dog. Or was it a sausage with sauerkraut? My body gets icky with the thought.

It was outside at some parking lot, a vendor? But where? I see myself holding the bun and topping the dog/sausage with everything around the vendor's station—fake bacon bits, ketchup, mustard, onions.

Then I feel a gag coming on.

Karma

As I try and stand up, I'm feeling more eighty than thirty. My shoulders are hunched, my back is stooped, and I'm wondering if my legs will make it to the washroom.

I tiptoe to the door. There are clothes hanging on the bureau. On the floor, there is a basket that is half full of dirty laundry. There are no pictures in the room and the blinds are drawn.

At this point, I don't care that I have barely anything on. I creak open the door and stand motionless. My bladder is convulsing. I curl one leg over the other with hopes everything won't empty down my leg. My eyes feel thick, sealed with last night's makeup, sleep, and scum.

A door is directly across from where I'm standing. It is brighter out in the hallway, and I see the bathroom and charge into it, manoeuvre my ass over the toilet seat, squat and aaaaaaaahhh. Instant relief. I imagine how a camel feels after travelling the desert.

This isn't how the night, rather the morning, was supposed to pan out. I had no intention of wanting to disappear from my family, yet what did I expect to happen? The night before, I did toss a few items in an overnight bag but fully expected to land at my mothers, or Allan's, or even Victoria's.

Maybe this is Victoria's? Maybe I did end up going home with her?

Yet, this place doesn't seem like something Victoria would call home. It's not artfully decorated, nor is it neat. It looks more like a bachelor's pad. It has no character, no colour. Just a place to eat and sleep.

Is Jimmy wondering about me? Is he worried? Should I call him and let him know? But then again, we aren't talking, so...and I'm sure me being absent is a welcome sign until we get things sorted.

How are we going to get this sorted? I can't take back the past, nor can I change anything that has happened. If Jimmy can't get over it? Well...?

I sigh and check out my desperate appearance in the bathroom mirror. With smudged mascara, my hair flat on one side and sticking up on the other, I look like a washed-up circus clown, an out-of-work circus clown.

I run my fingers through my hair, wishing I had a comb, or at least a tooth brush.

I'm rummaging through drawers and find some hand cream and—surprise surprise!—a new toothbrush still in its package.

First, I smear cream on my face in a thick glob to remove my old makeup. I let the water run warm and take the end of the towel, wet it, and run the cloth over my face, removing the foundation, the eye makeup, and last night's snack.

Then I start brushing my teeth. It feels good to remove the fur and bad taste.

Then I pause. My blood starts to churn with bad thoughts.

Maybe Eric called Jimmy and he didn't want me and...My mouth falls open, followed by a froth of toothpaste.

Did I sleep with Eric?

No! Not a chance in hell. Eric wouldn't do that. He'd want the girl active.

But this *is* Eric's place. He left me a glass of water and some pills. He knew I was loaded last night. Thoughtful Eric.

Feeling a small sense of relief, I know I need to get dressed and out of this apartment. I click off the light and make my way slowly out of the washroom.

"Hello?" I holler, but the empty space and bodyless couch tell me I'm alone. I scan the room. There's a mismatched sofa and love seat, TV, coffee table, blinds. No plants. No pictures. It looks like someone has just moved in. Either that or it belongs to someone who just moved away from home and is getting started in the world.

I proceed to the kitchen to check things out, to see if there is any food, maybe get another drink. A sign is posted to the fridge with a magnet stating "popsicles" in what looks like Jimmy's print.

Was I simply too hammered for him to take me home and so he left me here?

Sure enough, when I open the freezer, orange and pink frozen treats stare back at me. These must be meant for me.

Jimmy knows I can't drink, shouldn't drink, and how I feel the next day. Although he wouldn't have known I was heading out to drink. Whatever.

I give up trying to do some investigative journalism, and grab a package. It's orange. I break it in two and stick one half in my mouth.

I eat two more popsicles, and manage to keep another glass of water down. My stomach makes funny gurgling sounds and, I'm getting the willies being here alone.

Will Eric think I'm looking for something more than a bed to crash if I'm here when he gets back from wherever?

No sense trying to find out. I gather my meagre things, get dressed, and walk out. The door clicks behind me. I turn the handle to double check it's locked, hoping I didn't leave anything behind.

Although I'm not exactly sure where I am, the golden arches ahead and a wafting scent of grease and meat give me a sense of direction. Eat first, find car later.

Karma

~

With sustenance in my body, I feel better than I deserve and wonder why I ever take a drink. As I gobble down my fries, I watch the teens hanging out, the tired moms and single dads eating with their kids. It makes me sad. I wonder if my kids are eating out somewhere, too.

Like the man I'm watching in the dark-blue t-shirt. He has a day's growth on his face, and he's making faces at his three-year-old and giving the baby in the highchair pieces of his bun. I can't take my eyes off them. As haggard as he looks, and the dirty faces of the wee ones, also make me lonesome. I feel an emptiness. When you watch someone else's life, it looks grand even though it may not be.

"Mama!" the baby squeals and I look up to see a very pregnant woman waddling over to their table, all full-faced and glowing, looking a bit tired but smiling nonetheless. She catches me staring and looks uncomfortable. Her eyes shift from me to her doting husband.

I'm beginning to stand out when I want to be incognito. I gather up my wrappers, pack up my tray and take my leave before sucking back the last of my drink.

For a split second I'm riffling through my purse in search of my keys to the car, and then I realize that I didn't drive here. I left it parked at The Bullhorn.

Nothing screams too much to drink like picking your car up the next day at a bar. I hope I don't run into Eric.

Once I cross the intersection, I realize I'm not far from The Bullhorn and the walking is doing me good. Thankfully, I didn't wear a dress and heels. Of course, I'd rather be curled up on the sofa with a soft-serve, watching a mindless TV show, than having to pick up my car right now, however, my memory is opening up as I walk.

It comes in dribs and drabs. I hope I can put most of it, if not all, together later, like pieces of a giant jigsaw puzzle.

I remember eating a hot dog and laughing. It felt like I hadn't eaten for days when I stuffed that in my face.

But who was with me? I don't recall it being Victoria. Maybe it was Eric?

There was a whole bunch of bodies standing around, eating, smoking, talking. I think there was even a fight of some kind but someone broke it up.

"Get out of here!" someone hollered. A man's voice. Deep and gravelly.

Trena Christie-MacEachern

He said it with authority.

But I wasn't interested in the ruckus. I was interested in what I was eating and the person I was with.

We walked a bit and I had to go to the restroom. But there were no washrooms in site. So, I went behind a building. The building was brick and it was surrounded by a chain link fence which was open in a spot. That's where I went in to squat and when I did that, the metal dug into my arm and scraped it.

I remember the pain and let out a squeal.

"What's wrong?" he asked me. "Are you okay? Did you hurt yourself?"

~

I'm outside The Bullhorn now. The walk from McDonald's took me no time.

I spot my car, and it's not the only one in the parking lot. Workers and patrons are here, cleaning or preparing or drinking or eating. The bar that never closes.

The place looks pretty worn down. The sign itself—black letters on white Plexiglas, outlined in red and green borders—is faded. There's a hole below the word 'horn', like someone put a rock through it. Its large hip roof needs shingles and the exterior, although white, needs a fresh coat of paint.

We always thought this was a classy, grown-up place when we were kids. They had framed out the windows and planted window boxes back in the day, but even that has aged and now looks lack-lustre.

The flowers never lasted in the boxes. Boys would take turns trying to pee into them to the whoop of the crowds. They would have contests to see who could actually reach. This was often the after-hours entertainment, much to the dismay of the owner or staff or anyone who worked at the bar. Anyone other than the dumb misfit friends of the drunk and disorderly.

After a while, they just put in plastic flowers and greenery, but they would either get stolen, or yellow from the sun, or fade, making the facade look like a waste bin.

Nevertheless, it was a place that the public retreated to faithfully every Thursday to Saturday in great droves, and through the week, too, for their afternoon pint or evening meal. There was something that made you feel at home here, youthful, nostalgic, that no one could give up.

"Hey! That you, Karm?"

Karma

I turn around to see Eric closing the door of his car, walking towards me. It's mid-afternoon and I feel suddenly uncomfortable seeing him, but there's nowhere I can run now. I have to face him.

I raise my hand, wishing I had sunglasses on to at least hide my sunken, hungover eyes and face.

"Hiiii, Eric," I say, embarrassed, cupping my palm to act as a sun visor. Squinting, smiling.

He comes towards me, not looking as handsome as last night but, again, I probably look like shit, too.

He saunters up to me, gives me a light squeeze, smiles down. "How you feeling today?"

I laugh. "Better than I should. Thanks for last night. For, ah, looking after me."

"No worries, no worries." He's smiling, looking relaxed. "Glad you had a good time."

"Yeah. Well. If I can remember any of it."

He chuckles. "You could never drink, Karm."

I look down at the ground, studying my shoes, I kick a rock away from me. Then feel stupid for doing it.

He looks at his watch, "Well I better go, doll. Great seeing you again." He points his finger at me like he's shooting a gun, grins and turns on his heel.

"Eric!" I shout after him. "Um, was it your place I stayed at last night?" My voice is a bit high-pitched. My face flushes hot too and the food that I just ate seems to be making a churning in my gut that wasn't there before. "I kind of remember eating a hot dog, but that's all."

Eric runs his fingers through his hair and looks at me, brows furrowed, then smiles broadly. "Oh, shit, Karm. Really?" I bite the inside of my cheek.

"I put you in the office so you could sleep. You were pretty out of it. When I went to check on you, you were gone. I thought you just sobered up and left. So no, I haven't a clue." He laughs again. "But you got home, I see. And safely."

"Yeah," I laugh, my face still hot. "Uh. Th-thanks, Eric."

By this point, all I want to do is get the hell out of here. Go home, take a shower. See the kids. And Jimmy, too.

So, where did I stay? And who took me there? And why was I all alone this morning?

I take the keys out of my bag and stick them into the lock but they

211

Trena Christie-MacEachern

won't budge. I take the other one and stick that one in the lock too. Nothing. In frustration, I accidentally drop the keys on the ground and see them sprawled out on the asphalt.

Three keys are on the key chain, with a key tag in small, rectangular script: Property of Charlie David.

20

Then

She had a great, heaving bosom, and when I was small, I used to poke her in the chest with my two index fingers, pretending they were spiders making a web over her. 'The Itsy Bitsy Spider," I'd' sing. My small fingers would disappear into her flesh. She felt like bread dough, soft and spongy.

She'd laugh and do the same to me, except her fingers were strong and thick. Her nails as hard as concrete. Her idea of gentle poking felt like I was being ramrodded with the edge of a sharp stick.

"Owww, Grandma! That hurts."

"Oh, sorry dear, I was just playing. I was tickling you! Come, then. Sit on my lap and we'll read a story."

Grandma's lap was like sitting on the edge of a sofa with no arms. You could only sit for a few minutes before it felt like you were slipping off. The best way for us to read was on a bed or a recliner so I would be tipped back, resting my head against her neck, her breasts and soft belly acting as warm pillows on which I could lie.

She smelled like baby powder and lavender. Later, I learned the lavender she used was a perfume. It wasn't the real lavender at all, only imitation. The baby powder was used under her rolls of flesh to stop the chafing of her skin. Nevertheless, I loved the way she smelled. It made me content and sleepy and I felt safe and loved.

"What story should we read today?" She thumbed through the books she had on her bookshelf. They were either nursery rhymes or fairy tales. Today's selection was *Cinderella*. Something she had read before, but at the age of five, magic and fairy godmothers, along with a beautiful dress, were right up my alley.

I'd listen intently when she'd change her voice, mimicking the cross and hated step-mother, the ditsy step-sisters, the squeaks of the mice, or the way she deepened her voice to sound like the handsome prince.

Trena Christie-MacEachern

Grandma always asked if I had any boyfriends, and when I shook my head, she'd laugh. Her rouged cheeks looked like wrinkled apples, her teeth protruding under her twisted smile, but her eyes sparkled.

Sometimes, I'd lie and tell her, "Yes, there is a boy who...pulled my hair, took my pencil, butted in line at school."

She always told me that it was their way of saying 'I like you', which often confused me. *Why would someone do something mean if they liked you?*

Gran sometimes told me other stories. Stories not from a book. She told me about a handsome prince who worked in the coal mines who would come to see her after school, or at the shore on warm, spring evenings. She said she had a pretty dress just like the one Cinderella wore. Maybe not as glamorous, with sparkles and fine jewels in her hair, but she said it was a pretty cotton, with a ribbon around her waist.

She said that the prince's name was Joseph, but all his friends called him Joe. Little Joe, because he wasn't as tall as all the other boys his age, but just tall enough for her.

Grandma said she didn't mind that he wasn't tall because he was polite and kind and he was made just for her. She'd stare off, focusing her gaze into the distance as she recalled the memory, or at the picture she still had in her living room of the two of them.

She said he had a nice suit, too, and when they got married, they lived just like the prince and the princess in the book. They were happy and had two children, my dad and his sister, who is my aunt.

But stories don't always have a happily-ever-after, she used to say. "We don't always live in fairy tale land."

One day in the spring, there was an explosion at the mine and her husband, my grandpa, didn't come home. Grandma used to cry a little bit when she told me this part but she doesn't anymore. She said she hurt a long time because she loved Little Joe so much and she missed him so.

She told me when I get big, not to pick just one prince, but maybe two, or even three because if one leaves, or dies...She'd look at me with those big, round eyes, as blue as the sky and as full as the moon. "What are you going to do then? You don't want to be alone like me, do you?"

Her stiff, hard hands opened, palms up on her lap, her narrow shoulders shrugged like she was waiting for the answer herself. Then she'd hand me one of her homemade cookies she had made fresh that morning.

And if I dropped a crumb or two over her, that was okay. Grandma's house was full of crumbs and wrappers.

Karma

~

Now

I run like I'm being chased. Even though I probably shouldn't, having just ate that friggen' burger and fries and milkshake, but my brain is on fire.

How the hell did I end up with Charlie's keys? Was it his place I had just slept in? Oh! My! God!

There is no other answer but to go back there.

I'm disoriented. Of course, I didn't pay particular attention to the streets when I first left the building. It brought to mind the time I parked at the Eaton's mall and got too distracted with long lists of what to pick up: hair gel, mascara, not black-black but black-brown, the Herbal Essence shampoo that smells like orange blossoms, not cherries, because that one smells like vomit.

Mariah gave strict instructions like I was her personal assistant, not her mom, while she was curling her hair. She was trying out a new style for the dance she and her friends would be attending. And after the groceries, and the lists for Mariah's things, the extra pair of sneakers I had to purchase because Paulie lost his again (I actually think he's giving them away, or possibly selling them), so I had tossed two pairs in the wagon that day just in case, which was so much for me to carry.

And of course, it was a Thursday, Seniors' Day, so every white-haired antique was out shopping, or browsing, or dining, and the parking lot was fuller than usual, and the truck I thought I parked beside was no longer there and I wondered around like a simpleton for an eternity, frantic, thinking someone stole my car. I was about to call Jimmy and tell him the awful news when I suddenly realized I went out through the wrong doors. Tension eased out of me when I finally found the elusive car parked right beside the silver pick-up under the letter G, where I had left it. Even my fingers thanked me. I had gripped the bags so tight my hands began to cramp.

I'm trying to tell my brain to calm down but it's racing. I'm charging through the parking lot like a crazy person, retracing my steps.

I go past the McDonald's three times before realizing I had left from the rear entrance, and when I see the narrow path connected to the street behind, I slow.

Finally, voila, the three apartment buildings stand side by side.

But which building? The only thing that was on my mind when I left was getting something in my stomach.

This situation does nothing for my ego. No memory for directions, no stomach for drinking, and no brain for thinking. There appears to be

Trena Christie-MacEachern

some deficit on my part that keeps luring me to an ex-boyfriend. No wonder Jimmy is furious. I would be too.

With a deep inhale, I force my brain to focus. Think, think, think. Nothing. Blank.

Squeezing my fingers into a tight fist, I take my chances and my frustration with door number one.

It's a heavy, steel-framed and glass door, and I can barely open it. It instantly slams shut behind me.

First problem, no tenant list. Just a buzzer. You type in the room number and the person in the apartment answers from a telecom. This is hopeless.

F.

I begin strumming my fingers on the wall, hoping some flashback or memory will come to me. If someone would at least come down and I could ask? Or if I could at least get inside and knock on a few doors?

Then I remember. *You've got the stupid keys, Karm. In your pocket. Charlie's keys.*

Of course. If this is his place, they should open the main door.

I dig them out of my purse. There are three of them. All gold, all similar but a few teeth are different in each of them. The third key is the smallest, probably for a mail box.

The first key won't do anything. It's a dud. Key number two slides in the lock but won't turn.

"Damn it."

I'm not sure what I'm trying to prove. Just because I have a set of keys does not mean anything. These could have been in my purse since the last time and, personally, this wandering around double-checking where I slept last night,..rather, woke this morning, doesn't prove anything either. I should simply make my way home, take a shower and relax.

Even though I think these thoughts, I'm now walking toward identical apartment complex number two, and I recognize a large potted fern in a brass planter in the corridor by the elevator.

I scan the names on the wall by the apartment buzzer, and see the name A. David. Charlie's middle name is Anthony. The air goes out of me. Sickened, I toss the keys and leave.

~

There is a knock on the door and I'm reluctant to answer it, wanting to wallow, which is my way of dealing with myself. I'm not talking with anyone, digesting internally the hows and the whys of my situation.

But now the doorbell chimes. I finally get up and walk down the hall, move Paulie's book bag out of the way, wondering why he didn't bother to answer the door, forgetting he's in the basement, digging out old photos for a school project.

Two young girls, maybe eleven or twelve speak in unison, "Would you like to buy some cookies?" One is a Girl Guide, the other a Brownie, looking smart in their uniforms.

I study their banners with all their various badges sewn onto them. I wanted to join when I was younger, so I could meet new friends and get out of the house and away from the disaster of my mother.

"Come on in," I say. "Let me check my purse."

They stand patiently in the porch while I ask them questions: What grades are you in? Do you like Girl Guides and Brownies? Do you have many more houses to sell to? Where will you go this year for summer camp?

The older one has her hand on the knob. "Thank you very much but we really should get going."

"Oh sorry." I laugh, the money still in my hand. "Yes, of course. You're not here to visit." My face flushes. I'm embarrassed by keeping the girls because I didn't want to go back to my thoughts. I pay them and send them on their entrepreneurial way.

As I watch them leave, I think about my own friends. I don't see Suzanne and Trudy near enough and haven't even talked to them lately. They call, of course. Trudy always invites me to visit her, which I can't seem to fit in my schedule. Then sends postcards as a teaser from whatever fascinating part of the world she is visiting. She's a lucky girl.

And I haven't really attempted making new friends since Lotty got sick.

Suddenly, I feel a pang of emptiness, like something is universally missing from my life. Like I jumped on the roller coaster without thinking what direction it was heading, whether I'd like it or not, realizing too late I don't really like motion or thrills.

Am I really that kind of person? A shark that swims around looking for vulnerable victims? Taking what I want and spitting out the rest? Is Charlie my equal and that's why we're still crossing paths?

None of it makes sense but all of it rings true. There's no explanation for me getting together with Charlie, nor showing up at his room. That's the reason Jimmy and I are at odds right now. Is it my way of wanting to be punished? Drinking and sabotaging my relationship?

I'm mindlessly eating yet another Girl Guide cookie. There's only one row left in the box and my stomach feels acidic from all that sugar and nothing else. I put the box away so the kids can have at least one for dessert.

The phone rings and after a few minutes, Mariah hollers.

"Maaaa! It's Grandma. She wants to talk to you."

I pick up the kitchen extension, hearing the end of Mom's and Mariah's conversation.

"Grandma loves you, baby girl. Don't be going crazy over all those boys at school. Most of them are not worth it."

"Grannnn." I can practically see Mariah's eyes roll around in her head from here.

"Hi, Mom."

"Right, Karm? Most of the boys are trouble. Look at all you've been through."

"Not now, Mom."

"You have something to tell me, Mom?" Mariah asks, cracking her gum. The sound is grating on my last nerve.

"Mariah, hang up the phone."

"But Mom—"

"Now, Mariah."

Grunt. "Okay!"

The phone clicks.

This is not the conversation I want to be having right now. At all. Ever!

"Mom. I don't think you should be telling Mariah stuff. Especially about me. You weren't even there for a lot of it." I can't believe I just blurted that out. I really am from a different orbit.

There's silence on the other end and I wonder how she is going to handle it. Will she be the cross-talking take-it-back or else combatant? Or be melancholy, like she was during her drinking days? I brace for it.

"Sorry, Karm, You're right! Not my business to say. But you know how girls are around boys when they reach puberty. We saw it at the hospital all the time. Young things like Mariah, pregnant, or worse, with venereal diseases because the boys they liked showed them some interest."

"Okay, Mom. Is that why you called?" I know I'm not in the best mood, still trying to fix the issue I had created, or to figure out if it is even fixable.

"No. I'm calling to ask a favour. Sorry I'm so late in asking but I've been busy at the centre and I took a few shifts down at the hospital. I'm wondering if someone can stay with Allan tonight? I put a call in to both

Karma

Charlie and Jimmy, but I haven't heard back from either of them. I'm sure one of you can offer your assistance?"

Mom's questions are more like statements. She naturally assumes we can oblige. It's Allan, after all. Before I even respond, she's reminding me A) he's our best friend, is dying, refusing medical help, and B) we have to do all we can to help him.

"God, Mom. Yes, I'll do it." *Spare me the lecture.*

I frown. At least Allan will be happy to spend time with me.

"And, Karm, it might be good to tell the kids soon. Before things get really bad. Okay? I'll leave that up to your discretion."

My discretion.

Interesting choice of word. My discretion always seems to get me into trouble.

~

I'm not sure what I'm supposed to do next. I'm home. But it doesn't appear that anyone missed me. Especially Jimmy. He's still avoiding me. Probably because I left my wedding ring at home when I went out. He backed out of the driveway as soon he got home from work. As soon as he saw me.

It certainly wasn't my intention to stay out all night with...and now he's probably thinking the worst scenario.

Did Eric tell him? Or Victoria? Or maybe Charlie took another picture and showed him. It would be something the bugger would do.

To occupy my time, I tidy up the kitchen. It seems no one does anything when I'm not here. There's a stack of plates and bowls on the counter. Glasses in the sink. I rinse them under the water and put them in the dishwasher and wipe down the counter.

There isn't much in the fridge. Groceries haven't been on my mind lately. There's a frozen package of hamburger so I take it out to thaw.

I'll whip up a pot of spaghetti. All Jimmy has to do is get the pasta.

~

The sauce is ready and I'm sitting at the table, waiting, wondering if Jimmy is going to show up before I have to leave again. The clock says 6:15 and I have to get there before seven. But I know the drill. And I don't want an argument. I tell the kids I'm leaving and they can have bread with their sauce instead of noodles. I grab the car keys.

Trena Christie-MacEachern

As I'm heading out the door, I realize I don't want to be here when Jimmy gets back. I don't need that look, or that attitude, either. I decide it's best if I spend the nights with Allan for the next while, to give Jimmy the space he needs. For as long as he needs it. Life is too precious for anyone to stay angry.

21

Now

Gripping the steering wheel, I sit and look up at Allan's window, and my breath quickens. Here I am whining about life with Jimmy and there Allan is, dying, and in pain, and not complaining at all. We all need lessons in gratitude. Myself especially. No doubt all these feelings and anxieties are compounded from sheer lack of sleep the last few days. Drinking doesn't help either.

My watch says it's time to go, yet I hesitate. The curtains open and I see Mom peering out but she doesn't see me.

It's time.

There's no way around it, and no time to lollygag. I open the driver's side door and put my feet on the ground.

I hope Allan won't be asking about what's been happening, about any of it. He knows I can't lie and doesn't need to be wasting his energy on my kind of foolishness.

When I walk into the apartment, it smells off, like something rotting backed by Pine Sol, that musty-lemon scent.

Mom is in Allan's room and they are laughing. It seems so long since I heard that sound, it sounds almost foreign.

"That you, Karm?" my mother asks.

"Yeah, just me."

"It's Karm, Al. Come on in. We're in here."

When I walk in his bedroom, my eyebrows raise. His room is all aglow in light. The curtains are drawn and there are mini lights wrapped around Lotty's Ficus tree. Candles are lit and shimmery fabric is draped over the standing lamp which is poised in the corner.

"What's happened here?" I ask.

Mom grins wide. "Isn't it marvellous?"

Allan is sitting upright although his face is pale and there are dark shadows under his eyes. "Cool, eh?"

Trena Christie-MacEachern

"Oh, you missed all the fun, Karm," my mother says. "When the kids were here, they wanted to put on a play for Allan so we sort of decorated."

She looks around the room, then back at him, holds his hand. "It was great. Wasn't it, Allan?"

My heart skips a beat. "My kids?"

"Of course, your kids. Who else? Why didn't you come, by the way?"

I swallow and clear my throat. "Um, I was—"

"Doesn't matter," Allan winks at me with glassy eyes.

I notice his skin, particularly on his hands and arms, is bluish in patches.

He lifts his hand to me. I take it and give it a squeeze. It's cold. "I'm so happy to see you. So glad you're here."

He yawns then and I mimic him. Mom doesn't say anything for a few minutes. Just watches me watch Allan.

"You look...good, Allan. You're sitting up. That's good."

I look at Mom. She bows her head and turns it just so that I know it isn't.

"Are you calling me handsome?" Al laughs and then we all do.

Mom pushes herself off the bed, tucks the blankets around Allan's legs, and pulls up the side bar.

A plastic bag is attached to the bed, pooling with dark liquid. I try not to stare as I don't want to embarrass Allan.

He notices me anyway and turns up both his palms. "Ah, it's no big deal."

"That's right, Al."

"Although I'd still rather sleep on the couch."

"Well with this bed, you can raise the back so you're sitting up comfortably, and it's easier to get you in and out of this one."

Mom finagled and got him a hospital bed. She has people in high places whom she can count on in times like these.

"It was good of you to get this, Mom."

"It wasn't me, honey. It was Charlie."

"Charlie? How did he—?"

"I didn't ask. Probably better not to know," she whispers.

She looks at Al. "Okay, then. I'll be off. Karm? You have my number if anything changes. Al, anything else you need before I go?"

"God, Cathy, I think you've done enough."

"Nonsense. You're good for the soul."

Then she is on her way. She doesn't do the huggy thing or get all

222

Karma

misty-eyed. No. That is not my mother. She is fearless, powerful, especially when she needs to be. Her way of showing she cares was raising the arm on the bed so he wouldn't fall out.

She grabs her purse and turns her back to us. We hear the pad of her shoes as she walks down the hallway.

"So." I smile, not knowing exactly what to say.

"So," he says.

"I'm sorry I missed the other night. I really am. I would have loved to see the play."

He squeezes my hand. "It's okay. I figured you and Jimmy had a—"

"Yeah, we did. He's so angry, Allan. And I've been stupid."

"Don't be so hard on yourself. You aren't the only one to blame."

I bite my lip and feel the tears coming but I don't want to do this now. I shake it off.

"Stop it, okay? It was Jimmy, too, and Charlie. Everyone plays a part. Christ, maybe it was me, too."

"Oh, for Pete's sake, Allan. Why would you think that? You had nothing to do with it."

"I did, sort of. We are all to blame. We sort of created the beast."

"What are you talking about?"

"First thing first."

"Okay." Nodding, confused.

"You see those papers over there?"

"Yeah?"

"Would you drop them off at O'Brien & Lewin, down on North?"

"Who are they?"

"Ed O'Brien is my solicitor."

My eyes narrow.

"Not for you to worry about. Will you do it?"

"Of course, I'll drop them off, first thing in the morning."

"Nope. Tonight."

"Tonight?."

"Promise me."

"Yes, I promise. But what's the urgency?"

"Karm, if you can't tell, I'm dying here." His voice is raspy.

"If you went to the hospital and got help, maybe the tumour would shrink and—"

He grabs my hand again, holds it tight. His cold fingers on mine. He stares at me without talking. His breathing is deep and rattly but he smirks at me, holding my gaze. I'm entranced by him.

Trena Christie-MacEachern

"It's important it gets there tonight, and it's what I want. Okay?"

I nod without interrupting and he brings my fingers to his parched lips.

~

We watch an episode of *Melrose Place*, followed by *Roseanne*. Al doesn't say much.

I eat Mom's leftovers for supper. Bologna and beans. She figured the beans would be a nutritious alternative to the shakes, yet Al isn't in the mood to eat anything.

"Al?"

"Hmmm."

"Are you scared? I mean, of what comes next?"

"No more than you are."

I look into his eyes. They are hopeful and serene, not an ounce of fear in them that I can see. He looks tired, though. Sleep lays stuck to the corners of his lashes and I have a sudden urge to wash his face. A simple gesture.

What else can I do for him? Offer him? He's probably more in tune with life than I am. Ever was.

"I miss Lotty something terrible," he says in a sad tone. "But knowing I'll be with her soon, makes all this easier."

I feel a lump in my throat. My God, how much he loved her. After everything she did. I know she was sick, addicted that is, and did God knows what and left him umpteen times and he worried. God, how he worried. 'Til it made him sick. I think that's what happened to him. His body kept fighting for him but it was too much. It just gave way.

"If Lotty survived, would you be going to the hospital? I mean, to help yourself? To try different treatments?"

Al lies back. I put the TV on mute. It's mostly background noise, anyway.

He shrugs. "I dunno. It would be something Lotty and I would have to talk about together. If she could handle it. If it wouldn't be too much for her. Would I want to put her through all that? The chemo and radiation, hair loss? This way"—he runs his hand through his locks—"I still got mine." He winks.

"You devil." He can still make me laugh.

He pauses and I know he is thinking. He wants to tell me something.

"What?" I ask.

Karma

"I told the others last night, and been telling everyone, but I think you're the last."

"What?"

"Now, now, none of that." He takes my hands in his again. "They all know that, when things get bad, and they will, I have an exit plan."

"An exit plan? You mean—?"

"You know exactly what I mean."

My mouth drops open and a hush falls over the room.

"Karm, you understand? Tell me you understand?"

I nod even though I don't, just because he needs me to.

"Wh-when?"

"I can't tell you that. We've all been saying our goodbyes in our own ways, right?"

"Oh God, Allan, I don't think I can do this. Losing Lotty was enough. I can't stand to lose you, too."

For a few minutes, I crumple on top of myself. He allows me this. But I know I can't keep crying. Lord knows how much time we have left. I can't be wasting it with tears.

Sniffing, I twist my head in search of a tissue.

"Sorry," I say, as I blow my nose. "I'm so sorry. It's not fair."

I hop off the bed and walk out to the kitchen to catch my breath. That's when I notice Mom, and probably the rest of the gang, had been up to.

A number of things are wrapped up and put aside. Lots of Lotty's dishes and special things. She liked collecting pottery. Mom had a box with Lotty's name. I'm sure it will be given to her siblings and parents. Boxes of stuff on top of the table, too, but I can't bear to see what's inside.

The papers Allan wants me to drop off must be his Last Will and Testament. Whatever he has, all his worldly possessions, will be calculated for their worth and separated and divided, or given to whomever, Jimmy, me, Mom, Eric, Charlie. Charlie could use all of it, given his very empty apartment, or hideout, or whatever it was.

Mom left instructions for Allan's medications, what and when to take, but all I want to do is go into a ball and cry. I can't think of anything else. And this is harder than I thought, staying with Allan at this stage of his illness.

I no longer feel strong enough to stay with him alone. I wish Jimmy was here, or even Suzanne. They'd be better at this than I am.

I'm standing in the kitchen wanting to kill time but not knowing what to do. The apartment is as neat as a pin. Neater than I've ever seen it, be-

Trena Christie-MacEachern

cause Mom is chief in charge here. She doesn't like idle time. So, there's nothing to even clean.

Allan isn't eating anything so I can't very well whip us up a tray of muffins. It's too late to start packing stuff and I wouldn't know what to pack, anyway.

Instead, I'll go back to Allan's room and sit with him but as I peer in, he has already drifted off. His head has lolled to one side, mouth open, little sounds emitting from his throat.

He looks uncomfortable. His face tells me so. It isn't the peaceful slumber you see in children. He looks like he's in pain, and a lot of it; masking it for me but it shows up in his dreams.

~

An hour later he blinks awake and I greet him with a smile.

"You slept. I'm glad. Can I get you anything?"

"A sip of water."

"Okay."

I pass him the cup with the straw and hold it for him. He takes the minutest drink.

"How 'bout a candy?"

"Yep." Mom keeps a dish filled. He likes to suck on them after his naps.

"I didn't think you'd still be here. What time is it?"

"It's not late. Allan. It's not even ten."

"Charlie's supposed to be coming by."

"He is?" My eyes widen in surprise. "Why? It's my turn." I clear my throat.

"Karm. You'll have to go when he comes? Okay?"

"He doesn't need to, Al. I'm here."

"Karm. Please. It's what I want."

"Alright, sure. If that's what you want."

"Thank you, Karm." He pauses for a minute. "You and Jimmy alright?"

I take a deep breath. I'm not sure I want to get into this with Allan but... "Jimmy's not talking to me right now."

"At all?"

"Nope." I draw pretend letters on his sheets.

"He'll come 'round."

I purse my lips.

"Charlie doesn't have any pictures," Allan says, matter-of-factly.

I jolt. "He doesn't?"

Karma

"He has group shots of us, which he showed me, but nothing that would get your knickers in a knot."

"He said he did!" I bark.

Then I pause, think back. Charlie told me I would be easy. That son-of-a-bitch. "Why would he lead me on like that? Does he really hate me that much?" My initial reaction of relief has switched to feeling pissed.

"I have it all looked after. Okay?"

"What do you have looked after?"

"Charlie."

"What do you mean?"

"Those papers I'm getting you to deliver. I'm giving everything to Charlie, on one condition."

"Why, Allan? What's the condition? He doesn't deserve anything. God, the crap he's put everyone through. He's—"

Allan touches my arm. "It's okay. Lotty got him into it."

"He got Lotty into it," I spit.

"He was trying to help. He didn't know she'd get addicted."

"And you believe him?"

"With every inch of my soul."

"But Allan, he's lied to me! To you...taking you to that house that wasn't his. Lied to Victoria. Her parents. I can go on."

"You're hurt because you still love him."

"I do not," I pipe, furious he said such a thing. "I love Jimmy."

"Karm, Karm. I'm not denying that. Of course, you love Jimmy. But you still love Charlie. A part of you always will. Probably because he was your first, like Lotty was mine and you are Jimmy's."

I think over his words as he speaks. "Charlie has done things...things that have significantly impacted my life. I can't even begin to tell you."

"Like killing his father." I know I sound sarcastic.

"No, Karm. He killed *my* father."

"What?" It's then I see the truth. It's in his eyes. A secret he kept for so long. "Who else knows?"

"Well, now that you do, you, Jimmy, me, and Charlie."

My palm flies to my open mouth. "But he told me it was his father."

"Yeah, who knows why with Charlie, but it slipped out. But no. it was mine and I don't believe there was any way out of it. Dad was in a state that night. I usually took it, the beatings, but that time," Allan makes a whistle that sounds like a bomb dropping, "he was off his rocker. It wasn't just the booze he was on either. We were scared. He had me cornered in the basement with that look in his eyes. I'll never forget it.

Trena Christie-MacEachern

It's like there was nothing there. They were cold. Dead. And poor Jimmy. he was paralyzed. He never saw anything like that. You know his family?"

I nod.

"They'd never raise their voice if you burned down the kitchen. Charlie, well, he was used to it. In and out of foster, saw a lot, use to protecting himself. When my dad starting beating on me, Charlie went for the bat. We had been playing with it earlier, zipping rocks with it. He didn't falter, not for a minute. I saw him grab it. He hit my dad in the back of the legs first, just to distract him so we could get out. But that only made him angrier. He chased us up the stairs. Charlie was screaming and I could barely see. My eyes were already swollen. But Charlie turned around and I heard it. The ping, the crunch. I knew it was bad. Then the thump thump of Dad falling down the stairs. Nobody did anything. Just stood there, waiting. You couldn't even hear us breathe. Then Charlie ran down to check, and asking if I was okay. We still didn't know then for sure, if... Charlie grabbed me and Jimmy and we ran. Jesus, we ran out of my house. We ran all the way to Jimmy's. Hid in his room. He was so honest and reliable, you know? Even with his mother. Anything he said, she believed. But he lied that night, told her we were doing homework. Working on a project. I never did homework. But we stayed there, so quiet-like. I slept for most of it. I think she forgot we were even there. He just brought in food. We stayed there 'til Sunday night. School was the next day, and then I stayed with Charlie for a few days, called in sick. His mom wasn't in good shape then, but he didn't say anything because if he did, he was back in the system again."

"Ohhh," is all I can say.

"Charlie saved my life. I knew he did, and Jimmy's, too. Jimmy was a sitting duck there. He was scared shit-less. If Charlie didn't do what he did...Jimmy wouldn't be here either. I think we all suffered something from that night. But Jimmy, man, he didn't speak for a long time after that."

"So then what happened? What about your face? What about your Dad? Did they find out?"

He shook his head. "Dad had been on a rampage for a few days before, smashing things at the bar where he hung out, at our house. When he didn't show up on Saturday night, one of his drinking buddies stopped in, sometime Sunday, and found him. Thought Dad got into a fight somewhere, or we got broken into. People he may have pissed off. They investigated, but not really. Nobody liked Dad, especially the cops. He was an asshole."

Karma

"Oh, Allan, I'm sorry. I never knew."

"That's the sort of people Jimmy and Charlie are. Die-hards. They'd carry that shit to the grave."

I'm speechless, processing.

"Lotty took Charlie's stuff and he needs to pay them back. He's been trying, but you saw they weren't happy with the shortfall."

"I thought Jimmy did that."

"God no." Allan sniggers. "Jimmy wouldn't swat a fly."

He starts to cough. His whole body shakes. His torso rattles and barks. I wait for him to catch his breath. His coughing goes on for an eternity.

"Jesus, Allan. You okay?"

He arches over like he's going to vomit. "Water, meds." He extends his hand.

He takes a sip, just enough to wash the pill down. All I can do is watch.

Then, barely a breath in, before his body does it all over again. coughing and wheezing. His face is pained as he struggles for air, holding his chest, waiting for it to end. Is it ever going to end.

I think I should call Mom.

It's like he knows what I'm thinking. He karate chops his hand in the air over and over.

Finally, the fit subsides. The energy is zapped out of him. He lies silent and I watch his chest heave in and out. I count the minutes. I realize every second he's suffering.

He passes out and I stay with him, standing silently, scared to make a sound. I'm not sure how long I'm watching, waiting. How much longer must this man suffer. Clasping my hands, I say a silent prayer. Asking for help. Asking for guidance. Please someone.

Then the door clicks open, and my mouth drops, as I remember the Aesop adage *Be careful what you wish for.*

Trena Christie-MacEachern

22

Now

Charlie saunters in with a swagger, with a small bag draped over his shoulder. He looks like shit, if I can say so myself. I eye him from the bedroom, crane my neck, then tuck myself back in, focus on Allan.

He walks in and stands beside me, staring at our best friend. He hangs onto the side rail, 'til Allan's eyes flutter open. The coughing starts again. My arm remains outstretched with the meagre offer of water. Charlie doesn't acknowledge me. "How you doing, mate?" he asks Allan. "You going to make it?"

I whack Charlie on the shoulder.

Al shakes his head and sits back. His head sinks into the feather pillow. Al lies still with his eyes closed, water dripping down his cheeks.

I grab a tissue and dab at his face.

"Want something stronger than that?" Charlie asks, as Allan takes a drink of the water.

"Be nice."

Charlie rummages through his bag and brings forth a bottle of whisky. Jameson Irish.

"Get a couple of shot glasses, will you?" he says to me.

"I think everything's packed," I whisper.

Well, something, then." Charlie unscrews the cap.

I search the cupboards. There are a few dishes stacked beside the sink, probably so Mom can eat with Allan. There are plastic cups tucked in the corner. I bring three of those.

"Here." I offer the cups, but the boys are drinking straight from the bottle.

Charlie drags over a bar stool and sits perched on it. His face is black and blue and swollen. His lip is cut, his hand smashed, and two of his fingers are wrapped in cheesecloth.

"You should throw some of that on your face," I say as I toss the cups

Karma

at him.

He smirks at me, winks. Nothing I say fazes him, it seems.

"You're looking better than the last time I saw you, I see."

My face burns so I redirect my attention to Allan, who doesn't appear to be listening.

Charlie pours me a drink and I take it, suck it back in one gulp. It burns my throat but I feel like I needed it. Hair of the dog, they say. My eyes water and I stick out my tongue.

"It's not a shooter, you hag." Charlie laughs, "You sip it."

My face flushes again. "Jesus, Charlie. Insult for insult, eh?"

"I didn't mean it like that."

He leans in and bumps me with his shoulder. "'Member the time we all did shooters grad year? Spring break? It was a night. One of my best times, if I can recall."

"We were young," I say.

Al smiles in a sad way. "I told Lotty that night that we would be together forever."

Our smiles fade.

Charlie sips his whisky, holds the cup to his lips for a few seconds. "You're really not doing too good, are you man?"

Allan doesn't answer right away. We stand in silence watching our friend suffer and wither away from cancer and heartbreak.

What I wouldn't give to take away his suffering, his pain. My eyes well up again and I run from the room. I don't know where to go. I certainly don't want Allan to hear me.

I feel stupid and foolish, even though I shouldn't feel this way at all. I want to be strong for Allan, for me, too, and especially for Charlie. I don't want him to see me cry.

From the living room, I can hear the two of them chattering low. I take a seat on the sofa where Allan and Lotty often sat side by side, watching television together. I rub the sofa with my hand, feeling the worn fabric.

This doesn't look like Lotty and Allan's home anymore, not the cheery apartment two people once lived in, happy despite the cheesy-coloured walls. It feels empty now, like a hospice: cold, nondescript, generic, flat.

This isn't going to do. There's no need for me to be here. Charlie is here. I need to get far and away from him. I wipe my eyes and stand up, grab my coat.

"Guys. I'm going to leave. I'll just take this now, okay, Al?"

He nods slightly.

"Okay, Have a good night. Don't drink too much. You'll feel like shit to-

Trena Christie-MacEachern

morrow."

"You know what that's all about." Charlie winks at me again.

"Ha ha," I say sarcastically.

Allan reaches up his hand. "Come here, give me a hug."

I walk over and lay a kiss on his cheek and settle into his shoulder. He puts his arm on my back and kisses me on the top of my head. Like a brother. He smells sour, acidic.

"Love you, Karm. Thank you for being so good to me. For being my friend, and Lotty's, too."

"Of course, Allan." I stand back staring at him, assessing. "Same," I squeeze his hand. "I'll see you tomorrow. Okay?"

I nod my goodbye to Charlie.

"I'll follow you out."

"No, no, that's okay."

But he follows me anyway. He opens the door, closes it after us, and we stand in the hallway, his hand still on the knob. His look makes me uncomfortable. He looks sore, for starters, but also like a stranger. I don't recognize this person anymore.

I must have made a face because he says, "Don't feel sorry for me."

"Jeesh. I don't." Even though I do. He always has me feeling on edge.

"You want to make sure you have Allan all for yourself? Talk about these papers?" I shake the folder in the air. "Go ahead. I won't bother you. His meds are on the counter, by the way. Mom left what time he's sup‑posed to take his next—"

Charlie touches my arm. I pull away.

"Don't touch me."

"Karma. Please. Don't be like this."

"Like what?" I snap.

"Angry."

"I'm not angry!"

He smiles then, sort of. His lips turn up at the corners.

The old Charlie did that all the time. It was one of the things I loved...really liked about him then. That look always told me everything was going to be alright. I inhale and feel myself calming.

He sticks his hand in his pocket and pulls out his keys. "Go back to my place after you deliver that."

My eyes widen. "Indeed, I won't."

He shakes his head. "It's not what you think. It's the only place where I can talk to you. Alone. To explain."

"Explain what? Your lying? Why you preyed on me? Why I'm such a

Karma

fool?"

Charlie raises his finger to his lips. "Lower your voice. We don't want to upset him. He needs peace. He needs to know everything is going to be alright."

"With who? With you? Us?"

"Everyone. It's all he's ever wanted."

I inhale again, furrow my brows, cross my arms. I'm tired. Exhausted. I still feel hungover. I didn't eat right all day. My husband isn't talking to me, my ex won't leave me alone and my friend is dying.

"Please?" he asks.

He stretches out his hand and dangles the key over my arms. I refuse to budge.

He grabs my hand and stuffs the key into my palm. The metal bites into my flesh.

"Just for a little while. Please. It's important. I won't be here that long. Eric is coming to stay the night. Then you can go home."

"What if I don't?" I say, "how will you get into your apartment? I threw away your other key."

"Don't worry about me," he says, confidence in his voice." You know I'll figure something out."

~

I'm back at Charlie's barren apartment. I did what he asked. Why? Because I'm a fucking idiot? Stupid, can't think for myself.

I did what Allan asked, too. I dropped the envelope off at the solicitors.

Of course, it was closed. It's Friday night. It didn't make any sense but I didn't argue with Allan about it. Maybe he made plans with Ed whatever. Maybe someone was going into the office in the morning, waiting, especially for this? Who knows.

I strum my fingers on the makeshift coffee table. There's no TV, just a mattress on the floor in the single bedroom. Not even a curtain on the window, just a sheet. Jimmy's dorm room looked like a better set up than this catastrophe he calls an apartment.

There isn't even any food in the refrigerator. There's a kettle on the counter with a dirty mug and a jar of instant coffee. Who lives like this?

I think I should call Jimmy and let him know that I'm here, but I stop myself. Why ask for more punishment?

I look at my watch for the umpteenth time. It's late and I'm exhausted. My lids get heavy with the waiting.

Trena Christie-MacEachern

At two, I hear him. I had left on all the lights, but somehow, I managed to doze off on the small sofa. This must have been where he slept when I stayed here the night before.

He creeps towards me holding two cups and a small brown paper bag. He sets the drinks down.

"Here," he says. "I brought you tea."

"Tea? At this hour?"

I sit up feeling sore. Like I had just fallen down a flight of stairs or exercised too heavily.

My ear throbs. It's asleep. Lying at an odd angle on a hard surface for any length of time will do it.

Stretching out I yawn, and flex my feet and toes.

He pulls two sugar donuts out of the bag. Places mine on a napkin he retrieves from his pocket. He picks up his drink, takes off the lid, smells it.

"Cheers," he says.

"What are we cheering for?"

"Friendship, I guess."

I nod slowly, wiping sleep from the corners of my eyes, spit from my cheek.

We sit in silence, drinking our beverages, nibbling on our donuts, feeling awkward.

"How did I end up here the other night?"

"You called me."

"I did not."

"You did. You called me from The Bullhorn. Told me you were fighting with Jimmy. And you were sideways. I could hear it in your voice. Figured you should eat to save your head in the morning. You know you could never drink. I had to carry you."

Jesus. "You mean here?"

"Yep."

I'm mortified. Ashamed. God, how this man controls me still. How I let him.

I sit in silence, eating. The night ticks away.

After a bit, I break the quiet. "Why did Eric come so late? I thought you were going to stay with Allan tonight?"

He stares ahead, then turns and looks at me. I notice his eyes are red and wrinkly. Like he has been crying.

"You okay?" I ask. "Something...happen?"

Charlie goes into full-on bawling. His shoulders shake and he bows his

Karma

head, splatters his drink all over the floor.

I take his coffee from him, and he places both of his hands over his face, covering himself.

"Charlie! What in the hell? What happened?" My voice raises an octave.

Then at the realization, I start crying too. Between sobs, I ask, "Is it Allan? Charlie? Is Allan...?"

Charlie nods and cries, sobbing, snorting. The whole couch is vibrating.

When he stops, he takes a deep breath and stands up, wipes his palms on his jeans. Walks to the window, stares out at the sky.

"Yeah, he's gone."

But then he turns to me, his face staunch and serious. "Now don't go and tell Jimmy yet. It isn't what Allan wanted. Okay? It's all planned. Eric will arrive in the morning. He'll make the calls then."

"Planned?"

"Listen to me." His hands are shaking.

Through sobs, I listen.

"Nod that you understand me? Okay, Karm? Leave it be until morning. It's what Allan wanted. Okay? And no sense waking everybody in the middle of the night. There have been enough sleepless nights."

I nod.

"And I'm only going to tell you this once. Okay?" He sounds angry now.

I feel drunk. Disengaged I'm sleep deprived and emotional and here I am sipping on caffeine and sugar in the middle of the night only to be told the worst news.

I stuff my hands in pockets looking for a tissue. When I don't find one, I wipe my nose with my sleeve.

"For God sake, Charlie. What is it?" I ask gruffly.

"Allan told me exactly what he wanted. How he wanted to..." The tears are at the threshold of his lids again, but he wipes them away. His voice cracks. "He wanted simplicity. He wrote it all down. Okay? He wanted to be with Lotty. That's all he ever wanted. Me and Jimmy were at odds about that. About the how. That's why he was so angry with me."

"That wasn't the only reason he is at odds with you."

He points a finger at me, yelling. "I didn't sleep with you. Okay? I know I led you to believe that, but I needed the money and I'm sorry I used you that way. It was never my intention to hurt you, despite what you might think."

"So, you just stripped my clothes off and we cuddled naked in the

235

Trena Christie-MacEachern

bed?"

"Pretty much, Karma, and yes, I probably would have slept with you if you were able-bodied. But you passed out. I couldn't very well have sex with a comatose woman, could I?"

I gasp. "But you would have?"

"But I didn't. And don't think I'm all to blame, either. You can blame yourself. You were a willing party, if I recall."

I slap him then. Hard, on the side he's still swollen from his last fight.

He goes down holding his cheek, groaning like a wounded animal.

I didn't mean to hit him so hard, although I do believe he does deserve it.

"I'll never understand you, Charlie David. Never. Not as long as I live. You said you loved me yet you never did. You treated me like a dog. Oh my God, what you did to me. You hurt me beyond words."

Charlie is hunched over, opening and closing his jaw, his hand to his cheek. I see the agony in his face.

"Why did you want me to come here, anyway? So, you can remind me what a lousy wife I am, a terrible girlfriend, an awful mother? Does that make you feel better? I'm such a sucker."

"I needed you out of the way."

I glare at him, grab my coat. Barge towards the door. I can't take another second of any of this. I'm no longer sad. I'm furious.

"Wait! Wait, Karma."

If my eyes were daggers, I would have killed him with my stare.

"I'm leaving for good. I needed to tell you in person. You'll never hear from me again. Okay? I'll disappear. I'll start over. I've got the money now to pay those leeches back and I'll return your money that you loaned me."

"Keep it," I snap.

"Seriously. I know you're angry, and you have every right, but you'll understand, soon. I'm sorry. I was always sorry. I just wanted to tell you the truth about the night at Lotty's wake. And I just wanted to see you again before I go. I love you, Karma. I always did. You were just too good for me and I knew I'd never be enough for you. I was just a screw up. I wanted better things for you. I always wanted you to be happy. You and Jimmy won't have to worry about me anymore."

Then he runs to me and hugs me tight, kisses me on the side of the head before ushering me out the door and locking it behind me.

~

Karma

My head feels like a helium balloon. Swollen, floating, disengaged from my body. I'm in and out of it. With lack of sleep and Allan's passing, I just don't know what to do with myself.

Jimmy is no better.

The kids are quiet around us, like they sense when to be good. Mariah makes us tea. She's such a caring soul.

She even put a load of clothes in the washer. I'll have to remember to tell her not to put the jeans and the towels in at the same time.

I'm on the couch, flicking through the channels, waiting for Mom. She said she'll come over after they take Allan's body. She doesn't want to leave him alone.

I couldn't bear to be there when they take him out. That was his home.

I feel sick and cry again, thinking of them taking him out.

A hand touches me on my shoulder. It's Jimmy. His eyes are raw.

He has come around a bit, although still stand-offish, hands me another cup of tea. I don't want it but Mariah made it, wanting to make us feel better.

"She put some lemon and honey in this batch." he whispers, "And eight bags in one pot."

It makes me laugh and I almost spill my tea on myself. I don't why I find it so funny. She's trying, the dear, and we must commend her for it.

I take a sip, stick out my tongue. Boiled tea. Strong and sweet.

"How much honey?"

"Couple of tablespoons."

"Jeesh, Jimmy. This will put hair on my chest. Maybe you should drink it."

I offer it to him. He puts his hands out.

"I already had two. She sat and watched me drink them."

I start laughing again. Then, immediately, the tears fall.

"I'm sorry. I'm just so...sad."

Jimmy sits beside me, puts my tea on the table and hugs me and I hug him back. He holds me hard and close and I feel his strong body against mine. His long angular arms wrap around me, and I take in his familiar musk scent. He hasn't shaved and his whiskers prickle my skin.

"I miss you," he whispers.

"I miss you too," I say, tears still rolling down my cheeks. I've cried so much my face hurts.

I pull away. "I'm sorry, Jimmy. Will you forgive me?"

He doesn't move, remains close. I can feel his heat radiating from his body. I'm sure if I close my eyes, I could fall asleep right here, beside him,

Trena Christie-MacEachern

in safe and comforting arms.

This is love. Real true love.

I rest my head against his chest and shoulder and we remain like that without saying anything for several minutes. He takes my hand in his and I let him.

"Mom's coming over."

Jimmy nods.

We sit silently for a while together, then Jimmy asks, "Karm? Cathy said he was fine yesterday when she was with him. What happened? I thought we had more time."

"He was good when Mom was there. Was it for show? I don't know. You know how Mom kept on him to try"

I pick at my fingers. "All those smoothies and home remedies. Maybe he was worse off than we thought? He had a few bad coughing fits after I arrived. It was terrible. I was so scared."

"Allan wanted doctor-assisted suicide."

"He mentioned an exit plan."

"I know. I couldn't go along with it. Charlie was all for it, though. But getting one is expensive. And I wasn't bankrolling for that."

I twist my head and look up at him. "Was that why you and Charlie were fighting? Was that the reason he wanted the money from you?"

"One of the reasons."

My hand goes to my mouth. "Jesus, that man."

"Who knows what goes on in that brain of his? I don't understand what makes him tick."

Mom comes in the house then, all business and questions. "Who moved him?" Her hands are planted firmly on her hips, mouth set in a straight line. "Did you?" She focuses her gaze on me.

I shake my head.

"No, you couldn't. You'd be too weak and you'd drag his catheter all over the floor."

"What are you talking about, Cathy?"

"Allan. Eric found him on the couch this morning. I know he didn't walk there by himself. Someone help you move him?"

"Well, Charlie came by."

Mom and Jimmy share a collective sigh while Mom curls forward, puts her hands over her face.

"He told me he was leaving. He said...I thought he left two days ago."

"Who was leaving? Charlie?"

"That means..." Mom and Jimmy look at each other again.

Karma

"What?" I ask, almost hyperventilating. "What? It means what?"

Jimmy stands up. "Fuck!" He strides down the hallway and slams the bedroom door.

I'm dumbfounded. "What, Mom?"

"Allan didn't pass on his own. Charlie probably gave him something to help him along."

"You mean—?"

Mom looks like she's in agony. "Bastard. I should have known. Charlie was the only one for it. But not any of the others."

"But wasn't he dying, Mom?"

"Yes, but that wasn't the way to go. Injection. He died like Lotty."

Mom is quiet for a moment, whispers. "That's what he wanted. Jesus. That's what he meant."

"Oh my God!"

"I know."

We sit in silence, taking in this new information. Charlie David. What the fuck?

"Well, there's nothing we can do now, is there? He's gone. At peace, I hope."

Mom looks up. Not that she's a holy person, but she does bless herself. "Come here now, Karmalita. I need a hug. I'm going to miss my friend very much."

She says it so casually. Yet when I hug her, she finally weeps.

Trena Christie-MacEachern

23

Now

Allan is cremated, according to his wishes. His Will.

He left everything he had to Charlie. We weren't surprised and Charlie remained absent, like he said he would. It felt strange in one way for him to be absent, yet we weren't really a gang anymore.

Allan is gone, as is Lotty. And, of course, now so is Charlie.

Eric is here, however, and Clyde and Jimmy. Trudy and Suzanne. We can't believe we are meeting like this again. What's left of us. Another wake, another burial. Seems surreal.

"It's called life," Mom says. She's sitting with us at The Bullhorn. She isn't having a drink, just a tea, and we all sit in silence and barely speak.

Trudy is beside me, holding my hand. We have chatted a bit about the goings-on, so she's up to speed with everything I have been going through.

"I wish I lived closer so we could hang out and I could be there for you." She smiles, her big eyes sparkling. She hasn't changed much since that first day I met her.

I squeeze her hand.

"In the summer, I'm taking someone home I want you to meet."

"You met someone?"

She nods and chuckles.

"I think he's the one. We've been talking—"

"Thank God you finally told her," Suzanne barks. "Trudy's getting married, everybody."

Trudy smiles bashfully. "I didn't get to tell Karm yet. You just blurted it."

"Ha. Sorry. Well, everyone knows now."

Cheers replace the gang's sullen silence. Everyone pushes their chairs back and take turns giving her hugs.

Even before I get one in, Eric hollers to Suzanne from across the table.

240

Karma

"What's he like, Suz? Up to your snuff?"

"Yeah," she cracks. "I like him. Good head. Good to Tru—all that matters." She winks at Trudy and Trudy smiles broadly.

It's finally my turn to hug her, and then I take my seat beside her again.

"So," she says, "I want your help with the wedding and would like you to stand with me. Maybe you can come out and spend a week with us and we can do the girl things we missed out on for yours?"

My lips start to quiver and she leans in, rubs her hand over my back in a circular fashion.

"Oh, Trudy. That means so much."

"Well, you mean so much to me. I hope you know that."

The waiter comes to our table to check our drinks and bring us our food. We sit and eat and drink and tell stories. We start by offering our memories of ourselves when we all first started hanging out.

I don't think I ever laughed as hard as I do that afternoon. I feel so connected. It's like Allan and Lotty were there in spirit, watching us, making sure that we were all okay.

"How did you guys ever get together as a group, anyway?" Mom asks. "Were you always such good friends?"

***

We look around at each other. We don't really know. It's mentioned how Eric and Clyde hung out sometimes. And Allan and Lotty, of course.

Then Suzanne pipes, "Karm. I think it was you."

"Huh?"

"When you showed up in senior year. Remember? It was just me and Tru. And then it was all of us somehow, right?"

We look around the table. It's mentioned how everyone knew one another, how the whole graduating class wanted to befriend Eric because of his dad's bar. The group chuckles loudly and clinks glasses. That Clyde and Suzanne were cousins, and Jimmy and Charlie had hung out with Allan. But Allan was the glue between us all. There is a collective murmur, everyone agreeing.

Then Suzanne pipes, "But it was just me and Tru, then you came, Karm. And that first time here. Remember how chicken-shit you were?" Everyone laughs. "You just sat your ass down at the first available table, where all these nuts were sitting."

I feel my face flush. "So I bought them a round."

"Then we lost her," Trudy chimes in, and everyone laughs harder. "So all of us went looking for you."

Trena Christie-MacEachern

Mom has her head cocked sideways, half-laughing. "Really, Karm. I thought you were such a quiet girl." Her smile reaches her eyes.

"Pretty innocent when you think of it. Everyone was just having fun." Jimmy says.

"But you didn't even stay that night," I blurt.

"No, but I took you home." Jimmy grins at me from across the table.

"Well then, I guess you two were meant to be," Mom says, and she touches my hand with hers.

A warmth radiates from my body then. The idea that maybe I was responsible, or had a small part in forming our group,overwhelms me. I feel myself smiling broadly. All my life I wanted kinship and friendship, to belong, and here it was, right in front of me, all the time.

"How'd you end up here, anyway, Karm?" Eric asks.

I look toward Mom.

"I don't care. Tell them. If it wasn't for him, for my wrongdoing, and what happened to that boy, Daniel, we wouldn't have moved here. I would have kept drinking. I'd still be in a loveless marriage. No offence, Karm. We are better friends than husband and wife."

I nod.

"And I met Allan, who helped me tremendously. And God knows what would have happened to you, either, Karm. But you found your niche here with this group. You're all special. All of you. Thank you for welcoming me into your family. This family of friends. Aren't we blessed?" Mom lifts her teacup.

We all nod in unison, and raise our drinks in the air.

"Oh, I almost forgot," Mom says. She rummages in her bag and pulls out two packages. She hands me one.

I don't recognize the handwriting, but take it and tear open the package. As I'm pulling out the contents, Mom continues talking to the group.

Inside my package is an envelope. Inside that is a cashier's cheque for eighteen hundred, and a small, clear plastic, sealed bag with my anniversary ring, the one I pawned.

I gasp and look around. No one is looking at me, not even Jimmy. They are studying the other item Mom is passing out. I slip on my ring.

I have a note, too.

> Karm,
> As promised. What I owe you. Have a great life. I will miss you and love you forever.
> You were always the one.

Karma

C.

"...not sure when it was taken. But Allan wanted me to make copies and give one to each of you. Karm, I'll keep yours since Jimmy will have one. Is that okay?"

"Course, Mom." I nod.

A silence falls over the table. It's a picture of all of us. The last group shot, taken our senior year before we all disbanded. I remember it well. It was taken here. At The Bullhorn.

The group of us. All so young, life just starting. Eric, Jimmy, Charlie, me, Trudy, Suzanne, Allan, and Lotty, perched on his lap like a cat.

All of this because of that boy.

I sometimes wonder about his family. As does Mom, I'm sure. It was good we left that neighbourhood. Spirits haunted us there.

Trena Christie-MacEachern

Karma

Epilogue

Before then

Daniel felt light—lighter than air. Like an enormous boulder had been removed, lifted from his chest.

Tonight was the night.

It was decided.

He decided.

It was eleven forty-eight on a Tuesday, the first week of June. It wasn't a normal school night. Exams were in the next couple of days. Today had been a study break.

He peddled hard at the crossroads of Smith and Carnel Streets and then coasted all the way down Logger. He had twelve minutes left. Twelve whole minutes. His wind breaker flapped hard in the breeze.

Traffic was sporadic on this sullen, wet evening. He looked up, hoping to see the stars. The calendar told him it would be a full moon in a week's time, but not tonight, the night of all nights. Tonight was overcast with rain. *It fits the mood*, he thought.

The temperatures stayed cool into this last month of spring, but it didn't matter. Last time they had this kind of a cool, wet spring was a dozen or so years ago, according to Don Galesby, the local TV meteorologist.

His parents watched him every evening after the six o'clock news, after supper. After the chores, the dishes washed, leftover food put in the fridge, counters wiped, salt and pepper put away.

Small talk: How was school? How was work?

No one really listening.

Asking for the sake of asking.

Talking for the sake of talking.

He felt like he was on a hamster wheel, everything going in the same direction with no purpose. The mundane, the boring, the obscure. He wasn't himself anymore.

Trena Christie-MacEachern

Things had kind of skyrocketed in the last several months, taking off in all directions away from him. He felt he had no more control over his life, any more than he could control the weather.

He laughed.

Rain spattered down on him. It wasn't heavy yet, but already he was soaked to the core.

A car horn blared as it passed him, telling him what he already knew. That he was being reckless, weaving in and out around street lights, playing chicken.

He was mad. He knew it. Tears streamed down his face at one moment, he screamed at the air the next. But the day had come.

He was off to Killiam's Ledge. The thirty-foot-high trestle all the kids jump off in the summer. Or slip, if they aren't careful. It was nicknamed Killer's Ledge.

Two teens lost their lives there fifteen years ago, doing the same thing others had done safely hundreds of times before. One had slipped and hit his head, and another hit the rocks before the water.

Then others went there when they felt they had nothing else to lose, or gain. Depending on the way you looked at it.

Daniel felt elated.

Finally.

The pain he had felt for years but couldn't explain: the self-loathing and hatred, his gut kept telling him what to do but he didn't listen at first. All of it, all of his troubles were going to be gone and he smirked. The first real upward turn of his lips in months. Years.

He was super, supreme, cool Daniel Timmons on the outside; smart, helpful, a great athlete, prospects, so many prospects. He had a girlfriend, would be off to college in the fall, academic achievements, scholarships... everything looked great on the outside.

The inside was a different story.

People didn't understand. They didn't want to hear, to listen. "You're a lucky shit, Daniel Timmons. You got it all and you're still whining like a pussy."

"Go to hell," he wanted to reply.

He couldn't do any of it anymore. Face anyone anymore. He was nothing, a nobody and there was no point to anything. Get up, go to school, change classes, go to practice, go home, eat, make small talk, do homework, go to bed. Do it all over again. And again. And again.

Daniel screamed louder this time, letting the air and the rain enter his parched throat.

Karma

He biked around at night, after his parents thought he had gone to an early bed.

"Aren't you smart, Daniel? Going to your room, finishing your work, and then getting a good night's sleep."

When did he last have a good night's rest? Even they didn't see any change in him, his loss of appetite, loss of weight, missing practices, making up excuses. They thought everything was hunky dory and they all turned a blind eye.

"Try harder," were their replies.

Star Athlete Daniel Timmons Receives Prestigious Scholarship.

They thought he was above everything, that nothing would happen to him, could happen. He was on the top. Was always on the top.

Daniel screamed again.

But he'll show them. He had planned this for months. When the timing was right. Before the shit hit the fan, before everyone finally found out he was a loser and a good-for-nothing.

He even wrote it in a letter to his parents. Written in his own neat handwriting in blue ballpoint. He bought a stamp at the post office a week ago, and finished the letter last night. He tucked it into the secret compartment in his small knapsack and he would mail it tonight.

His family would get it in a day's time. Maybe two. He would be gone by then. Then they would all understand why. Why he couldn't go on.

He deserved it and they deserved to be rid of him. They'd be happier. He wrote that, too. "You won't miss me. How do you miss scum?" He liked that part.

His legs weren't even tired. He just cycled and cycled. He was waiting for midnight. The witching hour. The minute before his eighteenth birthday. He couldn't stand to see another day.

The cars whooshed past him on his way to the post office. He'd slip the envelope in the slot and then cycle away to Killiam's Ledge like he planned. He held the letter in his fingers.

He turned a hard left, a horn blared, and something hard, harder than concrete, struck the left side of his body and he instantly became airborne, his body flying in an unnatural state, the letter disappearing into the night.

He slammed onto the pavement and rolled and skidded before he finally lay still.

His eyes fluttered. He tasted something sweet and wet in his mouth.

Trena Christie-MacEachern

He closed his eyes for a moment, and then he was gone.

The End

Karma

Trena Christie-MacEachern

Acknowledgements

> "Tell me, what is it you plan to do
> with your one wild and precious life?"
> — Mary Oliver

I wish to extend my deepest gratitude to Brenda Thompson, founder of Moose House Publications, for believing in my work and giving my story a home. To Andrew Wetmore for your editing prowess, and your emails, often humorous, always helpful.

To the Shean Poets & Writers - I feel so lucky to be part of this amazing group whose writing I admire and whose friendships I cherish.

A special thank-you to my friends Harolyn Grant and Marie MacNeil for your help with the final proofing.

To my long-time allies—my bffs, my sisters—Debbie Green, Wanda Chandler and Cindy Northen Fraser.

When I wrote one of the last scenes, with Karm surrounded by her longtime friends at the bar, I thought of all the special women in my life who have sat with me at my table. From cousins to classmates, college pals and co-workers, and the closeness of neighbours, you have all helped me in the creation of this book. With love and thanks.

Finally, I am grateful to my parents, and most especially to my husband and our three children, whom I love more than words can say.

Trena Christie-MacEachern

About the author

Trena Christie-MacEachern's debut novel, *The Light of Day,* was short-listed for Readers' Choice with the Dartmouth Book Awards in 2024. Her short stories have appeared in Canadian literary magazines and anthologies.

She lives in Unama'ki, Cape Breton, in the village of Judique, with her husband, Glen, and their border collie, Lucy.

Milton Keynes UK
Ingram Content Group UK Ltd.
UKHW021458011224
451693UK00013B/1280